Not Quite
What It Seems

ALSO BY MARI WALKER

Never As Good As the First Time

NOT QUITE WHAT IT SEEMS

Mari Walker

St. Martin's Griffin ☙ New York

This is a work of fiction. All of the characters, organizations, and events portrayed in this novel are either products of the author's imagination or are used fictitiously.

NOT QUITE WHAT IT SEEMS. Copyright © 2010 by Mari Walker. All rights reserved. Printed in the United States of America. For information, address St. Martin's Press, 175 Fifth Avenue, New York, N.Y. 10010.

www.stmartins.com

Library of Congress Cataloging-in-Publication Data

Walker, Mari.
    Not quite what it seems / Mari Walker. — 1st ed.
        p. cm.
    ISBN 978-0-312-37541-6
    1. African American dancers—Fiction.   2. African Americans—Fiction.
3. Man-woman relationships—Fiction.   I. Title.
    PS3623.A35955N67 2010
    813'.6—dc22

                                                        2009040016

First Edition: April 2010

10 9 8 7 6 5 4 3 2 1

Dedicated to my daughter, Dawnesa Walker. Life is only what we make it. . . .

ACKNOWLEDGMENTS

First of all, I want to thank God for blessing me with a gift, and allowing me to share it with all of you.

Thanks to my children, Dawnesa, RJ, and Kevin, for always loving me. (I know y'all do, even when you don't show it! Smile.)

To my family and friends who always support me; I am not going to try to name you all this time, because the last time I left out a few of you. Having said that, I do have to thank a few special people by name:

My author friends: E. Lynn Harris—thank you so much for putting my first book up on your Web site and for allowing me to talk about myself and my book at your signing for *Just Too Good to Be True!* in Dayton. You were a wonderful person, and I am eternally grateful for your kindness. Rest in peace.

Joylynn Jossell—thank you for just being the gracious, funny, sharing person you are!

Monica Anderson—thank you for the wonderful words of wisdom you dropped on me when I was going through a rough patch!

To Joey Pinkney, thank you for your friendship and your insight and honesty. You always give authors truthful, unbiased reviews, no matter what!

To Royale Watkins, TRFL! Go Mixtape Comedy! Gotham NY! Terry Belcher, for the long talks and delicious home-cooked meals. To Adonna, Ebony, and Courtney. Connie Turrin, for telling everyone at the State about me and my books! (How many did you buy? Ha ha!) Cindy F., Tracey B., Joan Woodburn, Denise, Ray, Chara, and all of my coworkers at the Ohio Department of Health.

Thanks to my marvelous editor, Monique Patterson, for all she has taught me about writing a novel, and for helping my stories be the best they can be! Thanks to her assistant, Holly Blanck, for all your input on this novel. Thank you to my agents: Elaine Koster, for giving me a chance, and Stephanie Lehmann, for all of your hard work and enthusiasm over my work.

Thanks to all of the book clubs, online and off, for supporting me and my books! To all of the booksellers who buy and stock my books!

Thanks to all my FaceBook friends for your love, encouraging words, and support.

And to each and every single one of my readers, who spend their hard-earned dollars on my works, even in these rough times. I appreciate you all! Remember, when times are the most rough, bend, but don't break! Your destiny awaits you regardless.

Not Quite What It Seems

PROLOGUE

It's a funny thing how the body sometimes knows what's really going on before the mind does. Like how my body was screaming: *Let him go you fool! He's hurting us bad! My head hurts. Why are you still holding on? Let go before he kills us!* But my mind was telling me the opposite: *It's OK. Just keep clenching those teeth and hold on. That's it, feel the flesh splitting beneath the strength of your teeth? Taste that salty coppery mix of his blood? You got him now. Don't let go. Ignore the pounding of his fists against your skull, ignore the black fuzziness that is trying to cloud your thinking. Clench harder. Harder. HARDER.*

The mind is a powerful thing, because I found myself agreeing with mine. I clenched my teeth together even tighter, feeling his flesh pop like an overdone hot dog between my lips. It was his fault. Fool shouldn'ta tried to make me do something I didn't want to. Shoulda just let me go when he had the chance. Then he wouldn't be squealing like a little bitch right about now. He was saying something to me. No, he was yelling something that my mind didn't want me to hear, because it was making his voice sound like the parents in those Charlie Brown cartoons. You know, "whah whah whah whah," like a horn sounding off instead of words.

Uh-oh. Body starting to overcome the mind now. *Pain!* It was shooting from my head to my toes and back to my head again. The throbbing heat from the blows his fist had rained down on the side, top, and front of my head was explosive. He must have been feeling the pain my teeth were inflicting upon him, too, because the blows were coming more slowly. Just in time, too. My thoughts were growing fuzzy. I could barely hold my teeth together around his tense, bitter flesh. He was really wailing now. He roared and must have gotten his second wind because he brought his fist down on top of my head again with a blow so hard, my teeth finally met, and I felt his flesh tear off in my mouth. I fell back on the floor and heard him let out another massive roar. I spat and his flesh flew out of my mouth and onto the floor as a black curtain began to close over the room. The last thing I saw was him toppling over, his hands covering the hole on his body that had not existed seconds ago. Blood flowed between his fingers.

"Bitch! You bitch, you bitch . . . I'ma fuck you up!" was the last thing I heard before the black curtain finally fell.

1

The throbbing, pounding bass line vibrated against the highly polished wooden planks that formed the stage floor and created a synergy that sent a tingling through the soles of her feet and penetrated her to the very core. It ignited a fire inside that caused her limbs to move almost independently, propelling her forward into the intricate movements that made up the dance she was performing. She always came alive when she danced. Her passion and love of the art overtook her and filled every inch of her being with unspeakable joy. She knew with everything she had that this was what she was born to do.

The music pushed Jadyn forward. Here we go. She had selected Aaliyah's "Try Again" as her audition piece.

> *"It's been a long time*
> *We shouldn't have left you*
> *Without a dope beat to step to . . . step to . . .*

Spin and step kick and leap . . . leap twirl fling out arms strut to the front like a homeboy strut strut punch the air punch punch kick! Hip shake hip shake roll the stomach. Spin on toes leap drop down. Snap the head down and rest.

A thought broke through her subconscious, threatening to break her concentration on the dance. *You have to tell him it's over. You have to tell him tonight.*

Sheer will alone caused the thought to retreat to the far corner of her mind as she pulled out the next dance move.

Drop to the floor on her bottom, bring her legs up and spin like a street dancer, bounce back to her feet, two back bends into walkovers, tip toe tip toe tour jeté.

The pesky little voice found its way back into her thoughts. *Tell him. Tell him you're leaving him. Tell him it's over.*

She pushed the thought away again and focused.

Snap kick twirl twirl snap kick twirl twirl.

Jump leap splits touch your toes in the air. Repeat. Feet touch the stage crouch snap head down end of song.

That was the end of Jadyn's audition. She felt fantastic, and knew she had nailed every step. Every move of the choreographed piece had been precision perfect. She felt the slick wetness of perspiration against her taut muscles.

Slowly rising to her feet, the judges had her full attention as she pushed an errant sweat-soaked lock of hair out of her eyes. A stage hand flung her a clean white towel, which she caught with one hand as she moved toward the front of the stage, mopping her damp brow, breathing hard.

The judges whispered to each other from their center seats in the third row from the front.

It was the woman judge who broke the silence. She peeked up over the top of her glasses as she addressed Jadyn.

"That was unbelievable. You really move well. How long have you been dancing?"

"Since I was five. Really even before that. My mother said that I would sit on the floor and move my arms and legs to music even before I could walk." She grinned at the end of her sentence, but the judges didn't return the gesture.

Removing her glasses and chewing on one end briefly, the female judge eyed Jadyn before slipping the glasses back in place.

"Well, you have talent for sure. But then, so do a lot of young women. Tell me, why should we select you and not one of them?"

Jadyn had not anticipated this question. She stared at the woman, whose skin was the color of peanut butter. Her fine hair, cropped closely to her scalp, was unruly and refused to follow the pattern of the precision cut, with tufts jutting straight out. But it only served to make her more beautiful.

Jadyn cleared her throat. "The reason to choose me is because I'm good. I know I'm good. Now, the others, they may be good, too, but you see, I'm also determined. I have patience, and I plan to persevere until I make dancing my career. I have no illusions about this business. I know it's gonna take a lot of hard work. But I'm not afraid of hard work and I know how to listen to advice from people in the business who know more than I do."

"That will be all, miss." The white male judge to the left of her spoke. "Look, we aren't going to prolong this. We'd like to see you back tomorrow to see how well, and how quickly, you can pick up the group choreography."

Jadyn's heart started pounding and, before it soared up to the ceiling, a big grin spread itself across her face.

"You mean, I got the part?"

"No, we mean we're giving you a callback. You've got one more hurdle before we can offer you a part. Be here at ten o'clock sharp tomorrow morning. Here is the music for the group choreography. We want you to listen and get a feel for it," he said, holding up a CD.

A callback! That was almost just as good. Jadyn trotted down the stage steps and took the CD from the judge's hand.

"Thank you! Thank you all. I'll be here, believe that. Thank you again."

She leapt in the air as she ran off the stage and into the dressing room.

Once she was dressed again in her pink Baby Phat sweatsuit, Jadyn swung the bag that held her dance clothes over her shoulder and bounced out the side door. She sprinted down the short alley and burst onto the sidewalk, still unable to contain the joy she felt at actually getting a callback. She nearly knocked down an old man who was shuffling by, pushing a rusted, squeaky grocery cart. She steadied him with one hand, still holding on to her bag with the other.

"Sorry, sir. Are you OK?" she asked before moving past him.

"Watch where you walkin', dammit!" the old man cursed her, swatting his free hand in her direction.

"OK, I said I was sorry!" she threw over her shoulder, glancing back at him briefly before turning her face back toward the street just in time to see that her bus was pulling away from the curb.

She ran up and pounded on the glass door, running alongside.

"Hey! Hey! Hold up!"

But the bus driver pretended she didn't see her and roared off down the street leaving Jadyn standing in a cloud of black exhaust.

"You bitch!" Jadyn couldn't help yelling after her. But then she shrugged it off. She wasn't going to let a missed bus ruin her day. She wasn't going to let that old ass bastard ruin her day, either. Unh-unh. Not gonna happen. She'd walk the eight blocks to the lot where she'd had to park the car, because all of the other lots had been full. She didn't mind. Today, she could fly!

The audition for STOMP had gone well. She could remember her aunt Denise taking her when she was five to see the production of Annie, the musical about the orphan who had been adopted by a millionaire bachelor. She had fallen in love with the idea of becoming a dancer onstage the moment she'd seen the production. Especially the scene with the song "It's the Hard Knock Life." The kids her age singing and dancing was a whole new thing for her. She had told her aunt who then had paid for Jadyn to take dance lessons ever since. The hours of practice at Ms. Deborah Rashad's dance studio all these years had really paid off. She had to call Ms. Rashad, who had been her instructor and mentor from the very first lesson at Felicia Allen Dance Studio, named for Ms. Rashad's mother, who had founded it. Jadyn had to thank her for pushing her so hard. She hadn't always understood why she seemed to single her out for more work and more studio time, almost from the first day Jadyn had landed in her studio.

"Jadyn, you seem to have a natural talent," she had said with a smile as she pulled her aside one day. "Have your mother come to practice with you next week. I would like to discuss the direction she wants us to take in developing your skill in the dance."

"Yes, Ms. Rashad," she had told her, a little unenthusiastically. Yes, Jadyn liked to dance, but extra studio time? Between homework and dancing, she didn't see when she would have time to play Nintendo with her cousin Nite. But she had been obedient anyway and told her mother what Ms. Rashad had said. Her mother, her aunt Denise, and Ms. Rashad worked out a plan that gave Jadyn three extra hours of studio time per week. As the years went on, by the time Jadyn was fifteen, she practically lived at the studio. She could practice whenever she wanted in exchange for teaching some of the younger students. Ms. Rashad had offered her a job there more than once, but even though Jadyn had grown to love Ms. Rashad, she didn't want to be tied down, or feel obligated to stay when the opportunity came for her to travel.

She thought about calling her right then and there, but decided the news was too good not to deliver in person. She would stop by the studio later.

If she got the part in *STOMP*, she would be doing a ten-city tour, from New York to L.A.! Suddenly, a frown wrinkled her brow. The thought of leaving brought back the thoughts that she had squashed earlier. She had to tell Taji that they were no longer a couple. She was planning on breaking up with him even if she didn't get the part.

She was tired of all the drama. Tired of Taji all but ignoring her, always studying some book or working late. At least, he told her he was working late. She had her doubts at times.

Not to mention the fact that he couldn't satisfy her in bed. Well, to be fair he could sometimes, maybe even most of the time, when he wasn't distracted by his homework and working on the plans for his grandfather's business. He could rock the boat, the man in it, too. It was just that sometimes he would ram himself inside her before she was ready. And he would do it so hard that she would cry out. To make matters worse, he mistook her genuine pain and anguish during lovemaking for passion, and pounded her even harder. She thought about the last time he'd made love to her. One of her friends had told her that there was no such thing as a man being too big.

"Girl, you got to know how to work it. Don't let them big-dick brothas intimidate you. Look, get into a position where you can control the movements, like on top. That way you control how deep he can go. You know what I'm sayin'?"

So Jadyn had tried that. And it had worked at first, but then Taji had gotten all excited, grabbing her thighs and pulling her down hard at the same time he pushed himself up.

"Oh!" she had squealed.

"Yeah, baby, you like that? Hunh?" He held her there wriggling his hips around.

"Oh, that's good baby . . . You runnin', give it to me . . . ," he moaned as she held tightly to his hands.

Her friend had been right about one thing though, she could control things to a large degree in that position. So she had leaned forward and grasped his hands, entwining her fingers in his so that he couldn't grab her thighs again, and raised her hips, gyrating them in a way that was comfortable to her.

She would have to remember to thank her friend for the advice, though it didn't work all the time. Taji would still get carried away. And if she told him it hurt, he would say:

"I know, baby, I know, it hurts so good, don't it?"

And on and on it would go until he had finally come.

Even when she tried to talk to him about how he was too big when they weren't in bed, he would grin and take it as a compliment, never taking her seriously.

She shook her head against the memory as she rounded the curve a block away from her car. Her watch told her it was 9:30 A.M., only a half hour before she had to be at work. She had to hurry or she would be late.

She turned the lock on the champagne-colored Toyota RAV4 that Taji had given her for her birthday and climbed inside. His parents hadn't been too happy with that gift, reminding Taji that she was not his wife and he shouldn't be spending that kind of money on someone he might not be spending his life with. But Taji had insisted that if it was his money, he should be able to spend it as he saw fit. She smiled at the memory. He didn't care that his parents thought she was a gold digger—which she wasn't. Yes, she had accepted the car, she needed transportation. But they didn't know how many gifts she had turned down, like the credit cards he had tried to give her, for example. She didn't want him to feel like she was taking advantage of him. Nor did she want to get so dependent on the things he was giving her that they would weigh her down if she felt like leaving. As she did now.

To be truthful, she had to admit that being with Taji wasn't *all* bad. He did spoil her to death and she didn't lack for anything, for sure. He had even put the title of the car in her name so she would know that the car was truly a gift. He looked damn good, he could make her head spin when he kissed her. She guessed the problem was that he was spoiled because things had come so easily for him that he felt he didn't have to work at anything. Not even lovemaking.

Pulling into the mall parking lot where she worked, she glanced at her watch and saw that she only had six minutes to get inside. She had to hustle!

2

___

She loved her job at Saks. Though it didn't pay much—twelve dollars per hour—she got a generous 40 percent discount on everything in the store except evening wear.

Jadyn worked all morning waiting on women who were looking for that next special outfit to wear to that next special event. Working in the new Polaris Fashion Place Mall that was only a year old made Jadyn feel good. And working at Saks Fifth Avenue, a genuine New York boutique for the rich and famous, was the best thing to happen to her in a while. She was amazed at the young men who had been hired to walk around the store, carrying glasses filled three-quarters of the way with Champagne, offering it to the wealthy women who perused the racks. There was also a live pianist playing soothing music in a nearby corner of the main room. Jadyn liked to think it was "music to shop 'til you drop by." She smiled as she walked out of the back room carrying an armload of dresses that one of their regular customers, Mrs. Lichty, had preordered online.

She had very expensive tastes, though in Jadyn's opinion, she would never be able to do the dresses justice, with her skinny arms and legs and pancake butt. She never understood anorexic white women and why they thought "thin" was better. She guessed thin was OK, but some of them, like Mrs. Lichty, went beyond thin to skin and bones!

Jadyn could actually see her bones sticking out as she stood in the dressing room in her bra and panties waiting to try on her selections. She could swear she could count each one of the woman's ribs. Her thin lips were pressed together, and you could see that she had tried to make them look bigger by using the lipstick to draw over the edge of her top lip. If she'd used a liner pencil to define a new lip line, she might have gotten away with it, but as it was, her lips reminded Jadyn of a kindergartener who had colored outside the lines.

The only things that were pretty about her were her jade-green eyes and thick chocolate-brown hair. It was cut into a slick bob that was tapered in the back and fell in layers, with a side part that made her bangs slant across her forehead dramatically.

"Are you going to stand there staring or am I going to get to try on my things?"

Janice Lichty placed a hand on her bony hip and glared at Jadyn. She better be glad that Jadyn was in a good mood, because job or no job, she didn't tolerate disrespect from anyone. So instead of telling this bird of a woman to stick it, she just smiled her best smile and gave her what she wanted.

"So sorry, Mrs. Lichty! My, have you lost more weight? You're looking so thin, I don't know if these size twos you picked out will fit!"

Mrs. Lichty's whole attitude and demeanor seemed to brighten. "You think so, dear?" She turned from side to side peering at her reflection in the mirror and sucking in her nonexistent tummy.

Jadyn continued to schmooze. "Yes, I do. Here," she said carefully placing the dresses on hooks inside the dressing room, "you go ahead and try these on, even though I'm sure they will look great on someone as slender as you, I am going to see if we have them in a smaller size. I'll be right back."

"You are such a big help, Jay. I wouldn't come here if it weren't for you. Hurry back, dear, you must tell me about the color and fit!"

Jadyn backed out of the room still smiling. "Be right back, I promise," she said and as she drew the door shut, she grimaced. Simple heifer. Funny how a smile and a lie could change an old squeezed-out lemon into a lemon pie.

"Jadyn, I'm gonna need you to work the register today; Selena just called in late again. I swear, I'm going to fire that girl. If she goes out partying, she better get herself home in time to get her ass up and come to work!"

Jadyn turned to face her boss. Caroline Kennedi Van Horn looked nothing like her namesake. She was pale and freckled with orange-red hair. Her eyes were a washed-out blue, even though she wore piercing blue contacts most of the time to hide them. Jadyn guessed she was pretty enough, in her own way; tall and lanky at five ten or five eleven, some might even consider her model material. Caroline's mother had loved the late President Kennedy and his family so much that she had named her children for his. Caroline's older brother was named John Fitzgerald Kennedy Van Horn. Jadyn had never heard of anything so dumb. It sounded like the woman was obsessed.

"I know, Caroline, this is not good. I just told Mrs. Lichty that I would find her a smaller size."

Caroline gave her a knowing look before sighing and leaning in close to whisper, "If that woman loses another ounce, she is going to blow away like a kite with the next gust of wind that whizzes by."

Jadyn giggled, though the crack was corny as hell. "You know? But anyway, what are we going to do with her?"

"I'll take care of Ms. Vogue, you go ahead and open up the register and work the front."

"OK, but I hope Selena makes it in today, because remember, I'm supposed to get off at one o'clock today. You know I got dance class and I need all the practicing I can get before the callback in the morning." Jadyn didn't like the look that her boss gave her before she hurried off to help Mrs. Lichty.

"Yes, for your sake I hope she does, too."

Caroline must have done a good job with Mrs. Lichty, because she came up to the register with her arms full of merchandise.

"Mrs. Lichty, I'm glad you liked the Christian Dior outfit I picked out for you. It really does look like it was tailored just for you."

"I know, Jadyn. Thank you so much for your help. You have such good taste and you always have such a good eye for what looks good on me. Caroline should give you a raise if you ask me, for doing what you do so well!"

Jadyn grinned and she and Caroline exchanged looks. Caroline was standing in front of the plate-glass window at the front of the store that was directly in front of the register. Jadyn's smile froze before beginning to slide from her face. She stared at the man who had suddenly appeared outside the window. He was pretending to look at some items on display in the showcase, but Jadyn knew his real purpose. He wanted to make sure that she had seen him. It was Ian, her stepfather. Although Jadyn's mother, Samai, had divorced him years before, he always seemed to cross paths with Jadyn all over town. The most creepy thing about it was he never spoke to her, or barely even acknowledged that she was there. But Jadyn knew that he knew what an impact his being in her view would have on her. Although she wanted to look away and pretend he wasn't there, she was transfixed. She watched him linger at the front window, watched him as he slowly raised his head and looked her in the face, boldly, before allowing a hint of a grin to play at the corners of his mouth. Then he was gone.

"Jadyn, are you all right?" Mrs. Lichty asked.

Her question snapped Jadyn out of the trance.

"Oh, I'm sorry. You were saying?"

"I was saying you don't look so good all of a sudden. Are you ill?"

"No, no, Mrs. Lichty, I'm fine. Really. I guess I just need to quit skipping breakfast. I'll grab somethin' from the candy machine as soon as I'm done with you here."

Mrs. Lichty watched her suspiciously and glanced over her shoulder before looking back at Jadyn.

"For a second there, it looked like you'd seen a ghost or something. You really should try to eat well, you being a dancer and all. Breakfast is the most important meal of the day you know."

"You're right, and I'm gonna start being better about that. You know I've got another audition tomorrow?" Jadyn tried to lighten up the air between them.

"Really? Who for?"

"It's this traveling dance company for *STOMP* I auditioned for earlier this morning, and I got a callback," Jadyn said as she pulled a plastic suit bag from the rack for Mrs. Lichty's clothing.

"Well, best of luck to you, Jadyn. You certainly are beautiful and talented enough to light up the stage, be it Broadway, or elsewhere."

She reached her hand toward Jadyn as she handed the plastic-encased garments to her.

"Thank you, Mrs. Lichty. Have a wonderful day!"

As Mrs. Lichty walked toward the exit, she threw over her shoulder, "Thank you, Jadyn, you do the same."

After Ms. Lichty left, Jadyn's cheery façade faded away as quickly as steam rising from a teakettle. Making excuses to Caroline, she rushed into the restroom. No sooner had she opened the door to one of the stalls, she leaned over the toilet, vomiting violently. She straightened and put her hands to her cheeks, trying to calm down.

Her mother had divorced Ian six years earlier. How had he found out where she worked? Was she tripping? Of course. It was just one of those things, him being out there in front of the window that way. She walked over to the sink and washed her hands. Staring at her reflection in the mirror, distant voices worked their way into her thoughts.

It's not that bad, is it?

Jadyn turned and pulled several paper towels from the dispenser and stuck them under the cold water. Squeezing out the excess water, she patted the towels against her face.

Nobody will believe you if you tell, Ian's voice whispered from her past.

She threw the towels into the trash as pushed the thoughts away. Not now. She couldn't deal with this now. Not here at work. She needed to talk to KeMari Reynolds, her therapist. Jadyn had never imagined telling anyone what had happened to her all those years ago. But one night, she had been watching an HBO special on women who had been raped and how they denied the truth of what had happened to them so completely that reality became skewed and they no longer accepted the rape as something that had actually happened to them. It was that night that Jadyn had recalled all the things that Ian had done to her as a child and had called the 800 number flashing on the screen. KeMari had answered her call. She listened to the flood of emotions and pain that had poured from Jadyn's lips almost involuntarily that night. Once she had started, she couldn't have stopped if she'd wanted to. KeMari had listened and then convinced Jadyn to come to her office to see her. She had been so kind to her from the very start, even telling Jadyn that she would see her pro bono, when she told her she couldn't afford to pay for counseling sessions. That had been two years ago. Jadyn had been talking to her ever since.

She would help in sorting out the tangle of emotions Jadyn felt any time she thought of the past life she had lived with her mother and Ian. The one who had sneaked into her room at night and raped her, almost from the time he had moved in with them. She squeezed her eyes closed against the memories, fighting hard to stop the hot tears of shame and misery falling from her eyes. And the question. Always the question that overtook her mind, body, and soul. *Why?* What had she done to cause him to do all those nasty things to her as she lay helpless and alone in her bed?

Walking back to the stall, she unraveled a long stream of toilet paper and dabbed away the tears before blowing her nose. *Get a grip on yourself, girl,* she told herself as she squared her shoulders and threw the crumpled tissue into the toilet bowl. *You better than this. You can handle this shit. You know not to let it get you down.* Composing herself and making lies become her truth, she stepped out of the stall and strode out of the bathroom. She had to get back to work before Caroline came looking for her.

When she walked back out onto the sales floor, she saw that Selena had made it to work after all. Good, now Caroline couldn't object to her leaving early as they had planned before Selena had called. Now she hoped she could make her escape without having to leave Caroline shorthanded. She needed to speak to KeMari as soon as possible.

As Jadyn walked into KeMari Reynolds's office, her stomach was a tangle of knots and she had the urge to run away. She had to force herself to walk up to the window and sign in to see her therapist, and then to walk over and sit in a chair instead of running back out to her car and peeling out of the parking lot.

Two things made her stay: She wanted to talk about Ian and she wanted to feel better about seeing him. She wanted to feel better about her past and KeMari was the only one who she felt comfortable talking to about it.

KeMari was the same height as Jadyn, but was built differently. At thirty-two, she was twelve years Jadyn's senior. Her hair was cut short and she wore it flat against her little baseball-shaped head. She had almond-shaped eyes, big full lips, and a warm, welcoming smile when they had first met. KeMari had no children, but had shared with Jadyn that she wanted a child very badly. The fact that she was childless surprised Jadyn somewhat, because she was kind of thick around the middle, like a woman who had had at least one child, though the rest of her was kind of petite.

"Hi Jadyn, come on in," KeMari called to her as she stood in the open office door. Though she had barely sat down, Jadyn was relieved that KeMari had come out so quickly before her fears could get the best of her.

She stood and walked briskly into her office. KeMari closed the door behind them.

The atmosphere in the office was soothing, with muted green walls and a leafy green fern hanging from the ceiling in one corner, beside the downy soft tan suede sofa, on which Jadyn sat. The only light in the room came from the small shaded lamp that sat on one corner of her desk. A faint, fragrant aroma filled the air. Jadyn inhaled deeply as she allowed herself to settle back in the comfortable cushions.

"Ahhhhh, cucumber melon . . . one of my most favorite scents," she said, closing her eyes. She could feel the tension slowly leaving her body. As she opened her eyes again, her gaze fell upon a picture that hung in the center of the wall facing her.

It was a picture of a young woman perched on a chair on a roomy veranda. She was wearing a flowing white and pale pink floral summer dress, draped in a sheer wrap that left her shoulders bare. Her feet were propped up on the banister that ran the length of the wrap-around porch, with white columns rising up on either side of her. From the lighting in the picture, it appeared to be sunrise and you could almost smell the swamp grass growing just beyond the porch along with the scent of magnolia blossoms that framed the porch. The girl gazed at something far away and her expression seemed so serene, that you wished you could step into the picture and share the beautifully painted scenery. It only served to make Jadyn feel more comfortable.

"Well, Jadyn, you seemed pretty upset when you called. What's up?" KeMari spoke and interrupted her reverie.

Her voice and the way she spoke was so natural and unaffected. It was one of the things that Jadyn liked about her from the very beginning.

"You know what, KeMari? I was just sitting here thinking how wonderful it would be to step into that picture up there on the wall and just chill for a while, you know? Just get away from it all!"

KeMari glanced up at the painting. "Yes, I know what you mean, if only getting away from our problems that way were possible. We'd drive all the travel agencies and airlines out of business, wouldn't we?"

Jadyn looked over at KeMari and smiled. But the smile quickly melted away as she ducked her head down and frowned.

"Why do I keep running into him? And why does seeing him make me fall apart like I do?" Jadyn began to wring her hands as she spoke. "I wish he would just disappear . . ."

KeMari scribbled something on the tablet that she kept for her sessions with Jadyn. "You wish he would disappear. Is that really all you feel when you see him?"

Jadyn hopped up from the couch.

"No! No, that ain't all I feel! Did I say that was all I felt?" Her eyes flashed in anger as she turned her back to KeMari and strolled over to the window.

KeMari didn't react, she just kept writing.

"I hate him so much. I wish I could take my fists and beat the shit out of him for what he did to me! Why would a grown man get pleasure out of having sex with a child? A child that is supposed to be like your daughter? And how could my mother have been dumb enough to marry a sick, twisted-ass bastard like him? Sometimes I feel like kicking her ass, too!"

Jadyn continued to wring her hands as she paced the floor between the sofa and the window.

"Why me? What did I do for him to want to do those things to me? What did I say to make him think I wanted him to sneak into my room every night and touch me the way he did . . . make me touch him . . . ooooooooooh. Why? Why?"

Jadyn stopped in front of the sofa and plopped down on it, holding her face in her hands.

KeMari spoke. "It's fine to express the anger that you have inside over the way you were treated by your stepfather. It's even OK for now for you to get those feelings of resentment over your mother's bad choices out in the open."

Jadyn felt her standing next to her, trying to press a tissue into her hands. But Jadyn wasn't crying. She was trying to hide her face because of all of the shame she felt.

"It's all right, Jadyn. You're safe here." KeMari's voice was soothing.

Jadyn removed her hands from her face and took the tissue from her therapist's hand. She was surprised to feel a lone tear making a hot trail down her face. She wiped it away impatiently, but more followed.

She watched KeMari walk back to her desk and take a seat.

"Crying is a natural response to the hurt and anger you feel about what was stolen from you. Don't be ashamed to let it out. Holding in the tears and frustration only makes it worse."

The tears were coming in a steady stream now. KeMari picked up the box of tissues and reached across the desk with them.

Jadyn pulled more tissues from the box and continued to dab at the tears.

"Jadyn, the reason that you feel the way that you do is you haven't forgiven Ian for what he did to you."

"Forgive him?" Jadyn's voice began to rise. "What do you mean forgive him? You mean I'm supposed to just act like what he's done to me is all right? That he can just get away with treating me like trash! Never! I will never forgive him. And how could you expect such a thing?" she said angrily smacking her open palm down on the arm of the sofa.

Jadyn stared at her with all the disbelief and horror she felt spewing from her eyes. She watched KeMari once again rise from her desk and walk over to her, this time taking a seat next to her.

Jadyn broke down and leaned into KeMari's shoulder as she

cried. "I don't understand. How can you expect me to let that bastard get away with what he did to me? How can you expect me to act like nothing happened?"

KeMari stroked Jadyn's shoulder as she poured out her frustration. Jadyn watched through red-rimmed eyes as KeMari stood, walked over to the water cooler, and filled a cup. She carried the cup and handed it to Jadyn, glancing down at her watch just as someone knocked on her door.

"Yes?" she called.

The chubby, dark-skinned receptionist poked her head around the door.

"Sorry, Ms. Reynolds, but you wanted me to tell you when your next appointment arrived."

"Yes, Dee, thank you. Could you please offer them some coffee or something else to drink and let them know that I'm running about ten minutes over?"

"Of course, Ms. Reynolds," she answered politely as she closed the door.

Stepping behind the desk, she closed the notebook she had been writing on and slid it into her desk before walking around to perch on the side of the desk nearest Jadyn.

"I guess I should be going, then." Jadyn began to rise, but KeMari held up her hand and waved her back down.

"Jadyn, I want you to understand that forgiving someone for a wrong they have done you is not the same as saying what they did to you is OK. It doesn't mean that at all. It isn't letting that person off the hook for their deeds. It's letting you off the hook. It's allowing you to take back the power from them. It's about you saying, I will no longer allow you to affect me with the things you did to me when I was a helpless child. You're saying I will no longer allow you to hold me captive in my past, so that I can't move into my future."

Jadyn glanced up. "Don't you see? He still gets away with what he's done to me. With ruining my life!"

KeMari sighed.

"No, Jadyn. Not at all. It may appear that he is getting away with what he's done. But is he really?" Rising from the desk, she reached her hand out to Jadyn who stood as well. Draping an arm over Jadyn's shoulder, they began walking toward the door. "We can't really know how this man sleeps at night, or whether or not he is tormented by the cruel things he's done to you, and no doubt others. And in the end, we all must stand before God who will ultimately judge all of us."

Jadyn turned her head and looked into KeMari's face after her last comment. She had never thought about things quite that way before. It was a new thought that Ian might not be skating through life despite his evil acts. She pondered this as KeMari gave her shoulder a gentle squeeze before she continued.

"I'm sorry we don't have more time to spend together today, Jadyn. But please, think about what I've told you today about forgiveness. Open your heart to the possibilities that forgiveness will open for you. I want to help you work through this. Please see Dee on your way out and make an appointment so that we can explore this further," she said pleasantly.

Jadyn turned toward her.

"Thank you, KeMari, I will."

3

The closer she got to the car, the more she began to dread going home. She thought about going over to her cousin Nite's house for a while. She actually reached into her pocket and pulled out her cell, flipped it open, and began to punch in the phone number, but then flipped it closed again. She knew she had to go home and deal with the situation with Taji. Avoiding it was only going to prolong the problem.

It wasn't just about the lovemaking; she had goals and dreams that Taji didn't respect or encourage. She wanted to make it in the dance world. She wanted to be a star. And not just some damn video hoochie, either. Jadyn refused to be just the typical video vixen, dressed in some skimpy swimsuit, shaking her almost naked ass in front of the camera, suggesting sex with the rapper of the moment. She remembered how disgusted she had been when she had seen Nelly's "Tip Drill" video, where he had swiped a credit card between the butt cheeks of one of the video hos. Wait a minute—she backed up her thoughts. She had to keep that in proper perspective. Just because the girl in the video was misled about how her two minutes of fame was making black women look to the world, that didn't make her a ho. But that card swiping thing did suggest that her ass was for sale, whether she realized it or not.

Nah, Jadyn wasn't trying to end up like that. She wanted to dance on Broadway and every other legitimate stage, and on the big screen, too, if the opportunity presented itself. Taji didn't understand that. His goals didn't match hers. He wanted to get married and get her pregnant. He wanted a son. He wanted her to have that son and stay home and take care of that son. Taji was on his way to becoming an electrical engineer and taking over the family construction business that his grandfather and his great-uncles had started forty years earlier. He had plans to take it to another level; he was going to turn it into an architectural firm.

"Baby, you know my family has money," he would say to her. "You not gonna have to lift a finger. All you gon' have to do is have our children, keep your hair and nails done, and keep that body tight. I'll take care of everything else. I want to do it like that. I'm gon' give you anything and everything you could ever dream of," Taji had told her.

"That's your dream, Taj, what about mine? I want to dance. That's my dream. I might want to get married someday. But not now. I can't have children and get my dance career on, too. Can't you understand that?"

"Why, Jay? Why do you need that? You and me gon' have money out the ass. There's no need for you to chase that dream, when you could just live like a queen. My queen."

That was the argument they always had. No matter what they started out talking about, lately it always came down to arguing about that. All the fussing and fighting was wearing on her and stressing her out. She knew it was bad when it could invade her zone. The zone she went into when she danced. Usually nothing could touch her when she was there, caught up in the rhythm and movement that drove her, sometimes into a frenzy, and worked her into the release that came when the song ended.

So when thoughts of Taji and breaking up with him had invaded her territory and threatened to interrupt her performance, she knew their problems were troubling her too much. It was time for her to go.

She pulled up to the entrance of the gated community where she and Taji had lived for nearly a year. She punched in the code that would allow her entrance to the tree-lined streets, with sprawling ranch-style condos and two- and three-story homes. The houses looked like mansions compared to the neighborhood where Jadyn had grown up. Taji's rich grandfather paid the mortgage each month on the luxury condo that the two of them shared. He had paid for all of the furnishings inside, as well.

She remembered the things that Taji had told her about his grandfather. That he had worked hard at the family business all his life to make sure that it grew and flourished. But more than that, Tanaka Hietkikko had been a shrewd investor who seemed to possess extraordinary skill when it came to figuring out the exact moment to buy stock and when to sell it to maximize his investments. This had resulted in him tripling, even quadrupling, his net worth. He had also made sure to save his money in interest-bearing savings and checking accounts, so that even when his money was just sitting in an account, it was earning money for him.

In exchange for the generosity and graciousness he was constantly extending toward his heir apparent, he insisted that his only grandchild go to work each day to learn the family business he would someday inherit. The grandfather was very pleased with his brilliant young grandson who at twenty-one had already earned his bachelor's degree in science and engineering from The Ohio State University and was now working on his master's. The grandfather showered his approval upon him every chance he got.

There was a big problem, though: Taji's grandfather was kind of old-fashioned about marriage. Mr. Hietkikko wasn't happy about his grandson's living arrangements with Jadyn. He wanted his only grandson to settle down and have a great-grandson for him. He was always threatening to cut Taji off if he didn't either get married to Jadyn or stop living with her.

But Taji was headstrong with a mind of his own. He didn't back down from his grandfather's threats. He had only been to Japan once, when he was very little and he was totally American in his views, determined to do things his way. It was only recently that he had begun making trips to Japan on a fairly regular basis, maybe once or twice a month, for a week or so each time. His grandfather had thought that it would be good for him to become familiar with operations there and also to show his face around the office so that management and staff could become familiar with him. Taji was someone who could command the respect of others. He was sharp, with an intellectual prowess that belied his young age. The grandfather was so proud of his grandson's demonstrated leadership abilities that he could somehow never find it in his heart to carry out his threats.

Jadyn wondered if there was something wrong with her mind that she could entertain the thought of leaving Taji with all that he had going for him. Good looks, personality, his eloquent speaking ability, the charismatic way that he held his colleagues' attention, no matter the subject. Whether it was how the college football associations should change the manner in which teams are selected to play for the national championship, or the inner workings of the political landscape and how it impacted everyday citizens, when he spoke, people definitely listened. Not to mention he would be the head of one of the most successful financial empires in the world once his grandfather retired and handed the reins over to him.

While having a lot of money would no doubt be very nice, the fact of the matter was, Jadyn had never really cared much about material things. The thing that made her happiest was dancing and being onstage. That had been one reason Taji had been attracted to her in the first place. The fact that she hadn't been moved by all that he possessed, like a lot of girls were.

It wasn't that Jadyn didn't appreciate the finer things in life— she did. She just wasn't the type of female who let those things be the motivating factor when she chose a man. If they had, she would have hooked up with one of the many ballers that she had come in contact with growing up. For Jadyn, making her mark in the dance world was the driving force inside her, and she wasn't about to let a man dazzle her with a little bling and take her off course.

Taji had been different for her, too. He hadn't even acted like he'd come from such a wealthy family when she first met him at a campus frat party that Nite's boyfriend, Justice, had invited them to. He hadn't told her about his money until after they'd been dating for over a month.

Jadyn couldn't help but smile as she thought back over how things had been the night she and Taji had first met.

Nite and Justice had tricked her really. She hadn't been seeing anyone at the time. She'd been too busy concentrating on going to dance classes, auditions, and working. There really wasn't time to meet, much less date anyone. But Nite didn't see how a woman could survive without a man in her life at least some of the time.

"Girl, now you know as well as I do that you just *gots* to get a whiff of some male hormones every once in a while," Nite had told her one day when she had dropped in on her uninvited, as she usually did. She had wrapped an arm around Jadyn's shoulders and pulled her close, gazing into her eyes playfully and whispering, "That is unless you gay. You ain't gay, are you?"

Jadyn had pushed her cousin away and laughed. "Girl, please! If I was don't you think you woulda been the first person to know?"

Nite opened her eyes wide in shock, grinning at the same time. "Oh no I wouldn't be. Whoever you was getting busy with would know first, wouldn't they?"

Jadyn laughed out loud. "You are a fool, you know that?"

Nite leaned her shoulder against the wall, still smiling.

"Hey, I'm just keepin' it real. I ain't got nothin' against some-body doin' what they do, just not over this way."

So Nite had taken it upon herself to try to hook Jadyn up with one of Justice's friends and had invited her to a party on campus. When it was almost time for Nite and Justice to pick her up for the party, she was tempted to call and tell Nite she wasn't going. But she wasn't particularly tired, having had the day off both from work and dance practice, and since it was Friday night and she didn't have anything else to do, she decided to go.

It had been a hot summer night, so she had dressed in white leather shorts with a matching white leather halter that featured bronze stitching and trim. On her feet she wore bronze three-inch sandals that buckled around her ankles. She finished her look with bronze earrings, bracelets, and a white and bronze choker. She also wanted a fresh-faced look, so she applied only a little blush, lip gloss, and eyeliner.

The blare of a car horn sounded, just as she was pushing the lip gloss brush back into the tube. Taking one last look in the mirror and fluffing her hair, she switched off the bathroom light, grabbed her purse, and headed out the door.

When Nite saw her, she leaped out of the car and gave her a hug.

"Hey cuz, you look so good! I love that hot pants outfit!" she said.

Jadyn gave Nite's outfit the once-over. She wore a pair of Daisy Dukes with a powder-blue tank, a wooden necklace, bracelet, and earring set that featured blue gemstones embedded in them, and ecru strappy sandals that laced up her calves. Her wrapped hairdo framed her face beautifully and tied her look together. She was stunning.

"Girl, *we* look good! You know you are wearin' those Daisy Dukes!" Jadyn said.

"I know, we are gon' be killin' them at the party," Nite told her cousin as she climbed back into the truck. Justice frowned as he spoke.

"You gon' be killin' who?" he asked with one eyebrow raised.

"Oh, stop, baby. You know the only man I'm worried about killin' is you!" Nite reached up and grabbed the seatbelt, pulled it toward her, and twisted slightly in her seat. She clicked it into the slot as she ducked her head so that her hair fell around her face like a blanket, shielding it from his view. She made a face at Justice's question and at the same time gave Jadyn a conspiratorial wink. Jadyn pressed her lips together so she wouldn't laugh.

The party was a dud and so was the man that Nite had thought would be a good match for her. Oh, he was OK looking. Well, he was tall anyway. At least Nite had gotten that part right, otherwise she had missed on everything else.

"Jadyn," Justice came up to her after he had tracked down his friend and brought him over, "this is Caine Walters. Caine, Jadyn Collins."

"So nice to make your luscious acquaintance, Ms. Jadyn. May I have the pleasure of escorting you onto the dance floor, your fineness?"

Luscious acquaintance? Your fine-ness? Oh my damn. Was he serious? Jadyn gave him a half smile as he took her hand and walked her out onto the floor.

"You know you rockin' that leather outfit. You got all the women up in the place lookin' at us. Of course you know they are eatin' their hearts out wishin' it was them in my arms and not you. You know the women practically be scratchin' each others' eyes out trynna be the next one to be with me." He had the nerve to look at her as if he expected her to respond to his blather. OK, to be polite, she guessed she could give him something. So she looked up at him and said, "Really?"

"So you know what I do? After I go up and select one of them, I say to the rest of them, 'Don't be disappointed, ladies, just take a number and stand in line'!" Then he proceeded to crack up laughing.

Did he really think that what he had just told her was funny? Jadyn managed a weak smile.

He was a good dancer, she had to give him that. But that was about it. A slow song came on and he wrapped his arms around her and said, "Feel those guns? I pumps iron every single day." He even flexed a little. "Rock hard baby, rock hard. And that ain't the only part of me that gets a workout, and you best believe it's solid as a rock, too. And when I hit 'em with the rock, the ladies be gettin' addicted. I gotta send 'em to rehab to get 'em up off me!"

She could sum up her date in three words: pretentious, self-delusional, and boring. He kept going on about how good women thought he was and how he had to constantly break some woman's heart because she was slain by his good looks and blah, blah, blah, blah! She caught Nite looking in their direction and gave her an evil look and mouthed, "I'ma kill you!" Nite had looked surprised and mouthed "What?" before shrugging her shoulders with a little smile and taking a sip of her drink. Jadyn rolled her eyes and turned her gaze back to her date. He had noticed nothing because his back was to Nite, as he rambled on incessantly about everything that made him great.

After the slow song, Jadyn excused herself saying she needed to take a restroom break.

"Hurry back now, you don't want one of these other ladies to steal me away while you gone, now would you?"

Yes! Please feel free to torture somebody else.

"Be right back," she said, a fake smile plastered on her face.

She walked toward the restroom, but then noticed the balcony and darted out onto it, hoping he hadn't seen her. She needed a breath of fresh air. She knew she should've followed her first mind and not come to this party at all. Now she would be stuck with this fool for the rest of the evening.

When she was certain he hadn't followed her, she strolled over to the railing, leaned on her elbows, and drank in the evening sky. It was cloudless, making the stars sprinkled across the blanket of dark blue look like ice crystals twinkling in the moonlight. Inhaling the night air, she exhaled loudly as she lowered her gaze and took in the downtown skyline, which though rather drab during the day, seemed transformed from the tenth-floor balcony with the stunning midnight sky as a backdrop.

"Fabulous," she whispered.

"The view is pretty fabulous from where I stand, too."

The male voice startled her and she spun on her heels toward it, hoping the voice didn't belong to Caine Walters.

Her eyes fell upon the most tasty treat they had feasted upon in a while. An extra-chocolaty delight.

"I wasn't trynna scare you. Would you mind if I join you?"

Damn! His voice is silky smooth.

Jadyn had flushed and tried to decide if she should tell this man she had a date, or trade Mr. Fantasizer for Mr. Fantastic. He saved her the trouble.

"I've been watchin' you since you first hit the door. After a while, I could see you wasn't really feelin' dude. And when you made a break like the place was burnin' down, I knew fa' sho'." He was grinning as he moved to Jadyn's side.

Jadyn had smiled and looked up at him as she spoke.

"Was it that obvious? I wasn't trynna be rude, but between you and me? That nigga could make himself feel better than I ever could. He was steady strokin' his own ego—and I do mean nonstop!"

Dude chuckled and sounded sexy as hell as he extended his hand.

"I'm Taji. Taji Hietkikko." He had looked directly into her eyes as he spoke and it was like the sun had suddenly risen at midnight and was beaming its rays directly down upon her.

"Jadyn Collins," she said, extending her hand, as well. He enveloped her hand in his, bent at the waist while lifting her hand to his soft, warm lips, pressing them against her skin. At that moment, the girl group Total's voices floated into the air singing "Can't you see, our love was meant to be, you were made for me . . ." He took hold of her other hand, a crooked little smile slipping across his handsome face.

"Come on, that's my song. Gotta get my dance on now," he said, trying to pull her back into the room.

Jadyn resisted.

"Oh no, I'm not going back in there. Mr. think-he-all-that-but-ain't-none-of-that might try to tie me up."

"Oh yeah," he said, taking her in his arms and pulling her against him, holding her hand close to his chest. "Then we gon' have to dance right here then."

Jadyn didn't resist this time, instead let her body sway right along with his movements. And he smelled good, too!

"'Oh baby, can't you see what you do to me? Our love was meant to be' . . . ," he sung along with Total. "Come on, baby, sing it with me." Jadyn grinned up at him. He was irresistible. She joined in with him. "'I wanna be alone togethaaa, somewhere just you and me, ohoooh ohoooh!'"

They laughed. But as their laughter slowly faded, he gazed into her eyes so intensely that to Jadyn everyone seemed to fade away and there was no one else on the planet but the two of them. It was as if their souls had stepped out of their fleshly confines, embraced, and instantly become one. The feeling seemed to hold them both captive, and neither of them could break eye contact.

"You want to go someplace where we can talk?"

Part of Jadyn wanted to say no, she didn't know this man from Adam. But the bigger part of her suddenly never wanted to leave his side. And that part controlled her mouth as she whispered, "OK, but I have to let my cousin know I'm leavin'," still staring into his eyes.

"That's cool," he said as he offered her his arm. Jadyn took hold and they walked back into the room.

Nite had insisted that Taji give her his driver's license number before they left. Jadyn was impressed that he hadn't hesitated at her cousin's request, but had whipped out his wallet and read her the numbers as she scribbled them down on a scrap of paper.

"Yeah and don't try to have my cousin out all night, either. I'd hate to have to send the law after yo' ass," Nite had said, her face one big frown.

"Don't worry, I'ma treat your cousin like the diamond she is," he told Nite, giving her a wink.

They had gone to a late-night campus coffee shop. He ordered lattes for both of them, and she sipped hers slowly as he talked. He told her he was in school studying engineering, and about his grandfather wanting him to take over the family business. She told him about her love of dance, and the dream of one day being a professional dancer; to dance in stage productions and be in popular demand.

He had listened so attentively and at one point had held her hand, sending shivers through her body. They had clicked right from the beginning and the hours passed like minutes as they talked about anything and everything.

By the time he had taken her home, the connection seemed even stronger. He had gotten out of the car, opened her door, and held her hand as she stepped from the car. They continued to hold hands as they strolled to her front door.

"Well, here we are," she said, and found that she really did not want him to leave, but was afraid of what she might do if she asked him to stay.

"Yeah, here we are," he said and fixed her with that gaze again, making her get a feeling that heated her body from top to bottom. Then he began leaning down toward her and her body actually trembled in anticipation of their first kiss. He must have noticed because he wrapped his arms around her.

"Cold?" he had whispered.

"No," she had said. *Just the opposite.*

He placed his finger under her chin and tipped her head up as he brought his lips down on hers. It was the sweetest, most gentle kiss, and it made her weak in the knees. When he released her lips, her head was actually spinning. He spoke first and his words echoed her thoughts.

"I better let you go before I get us both into trouble." He smiled. She melted. *No, don't go.*

"OK," was all she could manage as she turned to unlock her door. As she pushed it open, he took hold of her arm and pulled her back, giving her the sweetest hug, and kissed her on her forehead.

"I'll call you," he had said.

"OK, good night," she had said.

"Good night."

Once she was inside her apartment, she had leaned back against the door, both frustrated yet relieved he was gone.

The old memories made Jadyn smile. She couldn't help wishing that she and Taji could somehow recapture the magic they had enjoyed when their relationship was new.

4

As she pulled into the driveway and turned off the engine, the memory of how they met was cut short and faded away when she noticed that Taji was already home. She had hoped that he had been working late, as usual. Instead, his jet-black BMW was parked in the driveway in front of her. That meant that he was in for the night, because he would always park on the curb if he arrived home first and was planning on going out again.

Tell him. She opened the car door before reaching back and grabbing the bag from the backseat. Stepping onto the pavement she closed the door firmly. *Tonight is the night.* Walking up the four steps that lead to the front door, she played and replayed in her head the words she would say to end the life she now knew and trade it for a new one. Thinking again about how it had once been between them, she wondered how things had changed so much. How had they lost what had once been so strong?

As she turned the lock and pushed open the door, her jaw dropped at what she saw.

Their favorite song, Prince's "Diamonds and Pearls" was playing softly in the background. There was every kind of rose in creation, in every color, but mostly red, lining a path that led from the doorway to the dining room table. Big bouquets of them decorated the table. More bouquets were placed around the dining room and it was all so beautiful. It was as if the room had suddenly been transformed into a garden. Roses filled every corner, except one. That one corner was stacked high with boxes of all sizes, gift wrapped with pretty orange and red paper. Orange, her favorite color.

And then there was Taji.

Despite their problems, the one thing Taji Hietkikko was, was handsome. His Japanese–African American ancestry blended into a fine specimen of a man, there was no denying that. His coal black hair was almost straight, but had little dips and slight waves through it. His skin was the color of cocoa, and the straight masculine nose with the slightest flare at the nostrils bespoke his African American heritage, while his slightly slanted, almond shaped eyes proclaimed the Japanese blood that flowed through his veins. He stood six-two and if you couldn't count them, all you had to do was touch him and you could feel the six-pack ripple through his shirt. That's how tight he was. The hair on his chest, like the hair on his head, was soft and lay flat against his chest and ran down to his navel in silken waves.

And he took her breath away.

Looking at him standing there in a black knit crewneck sweater and black Dickies, she knew that the physical attraction was still as strong and undeniable as it had been that first night they'd met, despite the problems that had developed in the bedroom.

"Happy anniversary, baby." The words, a tender, mellow tenor, melted over her in a wave. She could see the love in his eyes as he gazed at her so intensely. She almost wanted not to feel the way she did. She almost wanted to stay with him. Almost.

It was their one-year anniversary. Whoopie. She had been so caught up making sure her audition was tight, and with the pending break up with Taji, that it had totally slipped her mind.

It figured that she would forget the anniversary of their meeting now that the relationship was at its end. But the fact that *he* had remembered, now that was the surprise. What was she going to do now? She couldn't break his heart tonight could she? Not after he had gone to all of this trouble to celebrate the one-year anniversary of the day they'd met. She covered all of her frustration with a smile as she rushed into his embrace.

Tears clouded her eyes as she swallowed the hard lump that suddenly rose in her throat, burying her misery in his chest.

"Thank you, baby," she said hoping that she sounded happier than she felt.

"My baby," she heard him say tenderly, "always gettin' all emotional just because I show her some love." He stroked her back as he held her.

Once again, he had absolutely misunderstood what she was feeling. OK, now she knew she couldn't carry on the farce. She had to tell him how she felt.

"Taj, we need to talk. I need to tell you what's goin' on in my head. . . ."

"Baby, I definitely want to hear all about your day," he said, gently pushing her away from him. "But first, I want you to eat some of this good anniversary dinner I have ordered especially for you before it gets cold." He ushered her over to a chair and pulled it out for her. She had no choice but to sit. He took a seat across from her.

Jadyn tried again.

"Look, I really appreciate you going through all this trouble for me. The roses are beautiful, everything is so beautiful, but I—"

"Nothin' is too good for my baby, right? It ain't really what I wanted to do. I wanted to carry you out of town to some exotic place, but you know learning the business is kickin' my ass right now. You know, all the changes we going through up there."

He stood and popped the cork on the Champagne bottle before pouring the liquid bubbles into the fluted glasses. He set one of the glasses in front of her. "But enough about my day and yours . . ."

Enough about her day? She hadn't told him jack yet.

"Let's just enjoy the evening. I don't wanna spoil this special day with shoptalk." Lifting his glass, he glanced at her glass and then into her eyes, indicating that she should follow his lead. Reluctantly, she reached for her glass and lifted it in his direction.

"To us, and a whole lot more anniversary celebrations like this one," he said, gazing at her as he made the toast.

The glasses made a tiny *chirp* as they clinked together as only fine crystal could. Taji swallowed his Champagne in one gulp as she took a tiny sip of hers.

"Baby, I know that I haven't had a lot of time to spend with you lately. Studying every spare moment and working at learning the family business. But believe me when I tell you, it's all for you. For us. For our future. You know that, right?"

Jadyn hesitated. She did understand that Taji had taken on a lot, but that didn't change the fact that their relationship had suffered. And it seemed as if he wasn't really interested in her dancing anymore. She struggled to find the words to convey to him all that she was feeling.

"Yes, I understand, but . . ."

"Good!" he exclaimed, ignoring her "but." "Now, I don't know about you, but I'm ready to get my grub on!" Taji slapped his hands together and rubbed the palms back and forth before reaching for the chafing dishes.

Jadyn managed a half smile and reached for a dish. Removing the cover and setting it to the side, she was pleased to discover it held glazed scallops, her favorite. At least he got it right when it came to picking out the foods she liked.

Taji continued to speak but his voice faded into the background as Jadyn wondered how she could make him listen to her. She pushed the food around on her plate, managing to eat very little despite the fact that it was prepared precisely the way she liked it.

He *would* have to make this harder than it needed to be. It just made it more plain to her that he didn't really know her at all. Or even care to. Like that night she had awakened from one of her many nightmares again. She hadn't been asleep, really. She had tried to will sleep to come, but it was no use. She was just too afraid. Afraid that she was going to have that damn dream again. The dream where she was murdered.

The man was always standing in the shadows, huge, dark, and threatening. He always came at her in darkness, but with a bright white light at his back. Then the light would go out and all she could see was the black form moving in the shadows. *Oh no! ohnoohno . . .* The whispering, that was what scared her the most. He was whispering as he came closer. She was so afraid that she put the pillow over her head so she couldn't hear him.

All of a sudden he was right on top of her, aiming the Magnum right between her eyes, the cold black steel touching her. Whispering . . . always whispering. She wanted to scream, as his fingers began to squeeze the trigger. He stared at her with dark white eyes and she froze. She could feel the paralyzing terror as he spoke to her. *"Say your prayers, bitch. Nighty night. I'ma kill you and your mama. And you better not tell."*

And then he shot her.

Jadyn stared down at her plate, unable to disconnect from the shadows of her past.

"Jay! Come on babe, are you listening to me?" Taji's voice pulled her back to the present. His voice was stern, but she could tell he was struggling to keep it soft, too. It instantly snatched her back to reality.

"I'm sorry, baby. I can't seem to keep my mind off the audition."

"I was tellin' you how good you look tonight."

Typical of him to not even ask about her audition. It was all good though. After tonight what he did or didn't notice about her would no longer be a problem.

5

Looking down at herself she noticed that she still had on the pink Baby Phat sweatsuit and not a lick of makeup. He hadn't even given her a chance to shower and change.

"So you think I look good, hunh? I got on the same clothes I wore to the audition and to work." She intentionally brought up the audition again, for no other reason than she wanted to. She knew it wouldn't get a reaction out of him.

"Yes, I think so. You know you always look good to me. You not one of those high-maintenance bitches that gotta pile on the makeup and dress all up in Versace to look good. You got that natural fineness goin' on. You that one yo' ass look better than some women's faces!"

Jadyn had to laugh. He could be funny sometimes. It never ceased to amaze her how he could turn into such a homeboy type when he was at home with her or around some of his friends, but then could speak with such precise English when he was around his family, or when he spoke with someone from the office. Taji laughed, too.

Her throat suddenly felt dry so she picked up her glass of Champagne and took another sip. This time something hard bumped against her lip. She looked into the glass and saw something sparkle. Then her eyes focused on the ring as it registered in her mind exactly what she was looking at.

It was a white gold band holding the biggest diamond she had ever seen. It was humongous!

She delicately picked the ring out of the glass with her pointer finger and thumb. As she held it in front of her, dripping Champagne, she lifted her eyes and gazed into Taji's face. He was beaming from ear to ear.

Taji pushed back his chair and patted his lap. "C'mere, baby." He made his baby browns soft and sexy. If only the rest of him could live up to the promise in his eyes.

Should she go to him? Or should she end the pretense and tell him what was on her mind? He had been planning all evening to ask her to be his wife and she had been planning all evening to break up with him. What should she do now?

If she went to him, it would be on. He would start kissing and feeling her up and they would end up in the bedroom. The last place in the world she wanted to be tonight.

"I can't do this anymore, Taj." She rose to her feet.

Taji looked puzzled. "What? What do you mean, you can't do this?"

He leaned forward in his chair, his face becoming a mask of concern.

Jadyn made a sweeping motion with her arm. "Any of this, Taj. I mean all of this." She placed the ring in the middle of the table. "It's what I been trynna tell you since I got here. I don't want to hurt you, but . . ."

"Then don't." Taji got to his feet and walked around the table until he stood face-to-face with her.

"Not tonight. Don't spoil this, baby, please."

He took hold of her arms and tried to kiss her but she broke away.

"I tried not to, but it's a lie. I'm not feelin' this. It's beautiful. It's the most beautiful ring I have ever seen anywhere in my life. The flowers are beautiful, the food is delicious, the music is perfect, but not for me."

"Jay, I—"

"No, Taji . . . let me finish. I can't . . . we can't go on like this. You and me are on two different levels. You don't understand me and I know I can't get to you. You're here in the room with me but you don't hear me. You never hear me. How can you even think about asking me to be your wife?"

"How can you say that? You have everything any woman would want and more. There is nothin' I don't give you. That car you driving, I bought that shit! That Baby Phat on your back . . . the fuckin' Gucci on your feet. That's me, too!"

Taji's voice was rising. He was getting angry the way he always did when he was hurt and frustrated.

"I'm sorry, Taji, but you just made my point. I'm trynna tell you how I feel and you want to talk about what you bought me! Just like earlier, when I told you my mind was on the audition. What could be the most important fuckin' audition of my life and do you even ask me how it went? Hell no! You just start talking about how good I look!"

"Audition? You ain't said shit about no damn audition!"

"I did. See there, that's what I'm talkin' about. I been tellin' you about my audition for weeks now. Been spending hours in the basement practicing. Tell me you didn't notice that, Taji!"

"Why should I notice somethin' different about you practicing dance moves in the basement, hunh? You *always* practicing dance in the basement."

"So what? You just were so focused on what you want to say and do that you can't hear me! You never hear me. The audition is all I've been talking about to everybody. On the phone, here at the house, every chance I get. But it just wasn't important enough to you, that's all! That's why you didn't hear me! You never hear me."

They stared at each other. Taji flexed his jaw and she could see the muscle tighten as he ground his back teeth together. Jadyn brushed the errant lock of hair out of her eyes that just never seemed to stay in place, and folded her arms in front of her. This is the kind of shit she was sick and tired of. She wasn't trying to waste any more time on this dumb shit. She could be miserable by her damn self!

It was Taji who gave in first. He walked over to her side of the table and picked up the ring. He took the gold velvet box that had held it from his pocket and put it back inside. "You're right, baby, maybe I did jump the gun with this." He walked over to the mantel above the fireplace and set the ring on top, and then walked back to Jadyn, pulling her close, though she resisted.

"No, Taj . . ."

"Come on, baby . . . Come on . . . you right. Let's just pretend I never showed you the ring. Let's start over." He wrapped his arms around her, enveloping her in his embrace. The smell of him filled her nostrils. The spicy, clean scent of Armani overtook her, mixed with the natural clean smell of the Coast soap that he always showered with, and the faint manly sweat of him. It was intoxicating. Though a part of her knew she shouldn't, she stopped resisting and allowed Taji to engulf her and pull her against his wide, well-chiseled chest. She rested her head there, hearing his voice rumble in his chest as he spoke.

"I know, baby, that you think that I don't hear what you sayin' half the time. I know you think that I don't care about the things you care about. But you wrong. You dead wrong. I'm always listening with my heart even when you might be thinking I'm deaf. I've heard your heart, I have, lovely. I've paid attention to each and every thing you've said."

He stepped back a little, reached down and tucked his finger under her chin so that she had to look up at him. His eyes, his intense deep brown, almost black eyes, captured her attention. They smoldered with something unknown that made that hot feeling flush her entire body. Like when you took a drink on the rocks with no chaser, and the liquid ignited your body with a fire of its own. But Taji was the brew that set her blood boiling when he gazed into her eyes as he did now. She was truly amazed that no matter how angry she got with him, he could still have such a strong affect on her senses. She felt her knees turn to jelly.

"I can show you better than I can tell you how well I've been listening." He kissed her deeply, beginning the intimate tongue dance that Jadyn loved. She felt her resistance melt away and she returned Taji's kisses with a passion of her own. He slipped his hand under her jacket and gently palmed and squeezed her breast through the fabric of her bra, rubbing his thumb back and forth over her nipple at the same time. He bent slightly and lightly kissed the tips of her ears, exhaling and allowing the air from his lungs to tickle the spot he had just made wet.

"Can I show you, baby? Hmmm? Come on, baby . . ." He continued to plant little wet kisses along her ear and down the side of her neck.

"Taji, I . . ." She was feeling the intense need to tell him that it was over melting away like butter on a hot stove. She knew that she shouldn't give in to him, but it was so hard not to when he smelled so damn good, and his body was so freakin' tight! She could feel the muscles rippling in his stomach as he moved his upper body to plant kisses lower . . . down the nape of her neck. He nuzzled her there.

"You what, love? Tell me . . ."

"Oh, baby . . . don't . . . I can't think when you . . . do . . . that."

"Think about what. . . . Hmm?" Taji whispered. "What you need to think about, hunh? Tell me . . ."

He moved his hands over her breasts, grasping and releasing them. Massaging them in the most tantalizing fashion, making her nipples strain against the cloth. Pressing his hips against her, she could feel him growing rigid and unbending. He was molding her lips with his, sucking lightly on her bottom lip and capturing her tongue, drawing it deep inside his warm mouth.

As their tongues danced and darted in, out, and around one another's, he began sinking slowly to the deep plush carpet, taking her with him.

Suddenly, she wanted to hold him in her hands, to feel his hardness and stroke him. But as she reached for his zipper, he moaned and brushed her hand away. Easily capturing both her hands in one of his, he raised her arms above her head.

"Mmm-mmmmh. I want you to relax, baby. This is all about you tonight, anniversary girl. I need to show you how good I listened, remember?"

He began unzipping her jacket with his teeth. Still holding both her hands with one hand, he used the other to remove her jacket and then her bra.

He bared her breasts and moaned deep in his throat as he

lowered his head and captured her hardened nipple with his lips. Allowing his tongue to flick over it, suckling at the same time.

It was Jadyn's turn to moan. She tried to move away from him, but he held firmly to her hands and continued to kiss first one nipple, then the other. Slipping his hand inside her pants, he let his fingers roam free, stroking her intimate parts. Allowing one finger entry and playing there for a time. Jadyn pressed herself against his hand, hushed sounds escaping her lips.

Pushing her pants and panties down past her hips, he returned to her nipples, worrying them with his lips and tongue, licking the tips of her breasts like a child with an ice cream cone. Since he still held her hands captive, she could only wriggle and kick her legs to rid herself of the sweatpants that were bunched around her thighs.

Finally releasing her hands, Taji slid down her body until his head was on her belly, his tongue circling her belly button. He continued sliding downward moving his lips and tongue everywhere. Opening her legs wide and placing her thighs on his shoulders, he slid his lips close to her opening, allowing nothing to touch her skin except his hot breath. She squirmed and took hold of his head with both her hands, trying to guide his lips close enough to make contact, but he resisted, still allowing his breath to tease her, as he reached up and gently squeezed her breasts and his thumb stroked her nipple causing her to shudder.

"Oh, baby, please . . ."

"Please, what?"

"Please . . ."

"What do you want, love?" Taji managed to ask while blowing puffs of hot air on her. Jadyn looked down and saw him reach into his pocket with his free hand and pull out what appeared to be a cough drop or something. The hot feelings racked her body as she watched him bringing it up and popping it into his mouth.

"What are you doing? What is that?" She couldn't help but ask.

"You don't worry about what I'm doin'. You just lay back and enjoy the ride to ecstasy."

Jadyn's mind was reeling. Never had Taji made her feel like this. Confusion clouded her thoughts. Why now? Why had he suddenly turned into Mr. Super Lover after she had made up her mind that she was about to leave?

Her thoughts were cut short as Taji took his fingers and spread her apart as he extended his tongue toward her sweet tender flesh, making contact. The warmness of his tongue and a new coolness on top of it brought feelings so intense that she had to flex her toes and point them toward the ceiling as she sucked air between her teeth in a hiss. The surprising sensations caused her to instinctively try to bring her legs together, but Taji was too quick for her and moved her thighs apart with one swift move. Simultaneously pushing his lips and tongue forward and connecting with the pearl, allowing his tongue to bathe it and his lips to plant wet kisses, alternating between the two.

Jadyn was stunned, but only for a moment. She pressed herself against the warm coolness of his mouth and wiggled her hips with the motion.

"Oh, yesssssss . . . oh yesssssss . . . that is so good!"

Taji withdrew from her and she whimpered, needing him to continue.

"You still think I don't listen to you, I don't ever hear what you say to me?" The desire was evident in the soft throaty tenor as he spoke.

"No, baby, wait . . ." She reached for him, trying to hold him there, feeling the sudden lost contact to the nth degree. She saw that Taji, needing to get naked, was peeling off his clothing as fast as he could.

"What's the matter, baby?"

Before she could answer he laid on his back and pulled her toward him.

Oh no. Fun time is over already, Jadyn thought. *Here's where the ramming starts . . .*

But Taji pulled her onto his chest and with both hands tugged her buttocks toward his face, nudging her legs open. And again he was there, bathing her intimate parts with his tongue, kissing her over and over and over again.

Jadyn was on fire with the sensations that he was giving her, as he used his hands to guide her hips to match the motion of his tongue, and it was driving her out of her mind!

Baby baby baby pleeeeease!

She felt little tremors begin up and down her thighs. He must have felt them, too, because he quickened the tongue strokes, wiggling it up and down and back and forth.

Taji moaned loudly and pushed his hips up into the emptiness before he turned sideways. Shifting her slightly, they took the classic position so that she could give him as much pleasure as he was giving her. Jadyn immediately positioned herself so that her legs were open and her intimate parts were close to his mouth, and her lips were kissing his lower parts. He groaned loudly before kissing her there. She moaned into him, giving him a buzz as she pulled him into her mouth, sliding her lips and tongue down the length of him and back up again. It became a challenge: Who could give more pleasure than they were receiving? She massaged and sucked him, increasing the pressure until she could feel his orgasm bubbling inside of him. He must not have been ready for that, because he forced her up off of him and pulled her forward until she was sitting on his face. The smell of her seemed to excite him even more and he opened his eyes and watched her. "Oh . . . baby . . . oh Taj, please baby, ohhhh baby . . . don't . . . don't stop!"

He obliged her by licking her up and down, back and forth as she rode on top of him.

"Taj, right there . . . right . . . there . . ." Jadyn's body began to twitch and jerk. She moaned loudly as her first orgasm begin to overtake her.

He was making her feel so wonderful, she wanted him to stop and not to stop all at the same time. But even as he pleasured her, those little niggling thoughts returned. Why now? Damn, why couldn't he have made love to her like this before she'd decided to leave him? Oh Lord, but he was doing it well tonight! There was no denying that. Could she still leave? She no longer dreaded the moment when he would penetrate her. Now she wanted, no *needed* him inside her, in the worst way. Shifting her hips slightly, she pushed at Taji's shoulders trying to let him know she was ready. Taji seemed reluctant to leave her succulent flesh.

Positioning himself behind her, he pulled her hips back and began slowly penetrating, inching in, then slowly pulling back, each time only giving her a little more. She couldn't understand what she was feeling. She wanted all of him and was shocked at the thought. She tried pushing her hips back to capture more of him, but he held on to her waist, maintaining control.

He was making her frantic and what she once dreaded she now craved more than anything. Just when she thought she would die of the pleasure torture he was giving her, he pushed himself inside her at that very moment, driving himself deep within her silken folds.

Jadyn squealed once again, surprised not only by the intense pleasure but also at the complete absence of pain. He unleashed a loud,
deep moan as he stroked her slow and steady, and she felt no pain
at all. Only the exquisite sensations that left her feeling senseless.
Totally under control of the spell that such utter bliss had cast
upon her, she was afraid she was going to lose her power of speech
and be reduced to a stuttering, babbling fool! But she didn't care
right at this moment. She was going to enjoy every second of this
night and everything Taji had for her. She banished the negative
thoughts.

To hell with everything else tonight!

"Baby, baby, you feel so good. You so soft . . . so warm . . . ,"
he moaned as he pulled back and pushed himself in again, penetrating deeper with each thrust, pumping his hips faster and
faster.

"Oh yes, baby, give it to me, baby! Yes! It's good, it's . . . it's . . .
I can't . . . I can't take . . . I can't take it!" she cried out.

"Yes, you can, baby, yes you can. Come on . . . Let's go! You still
wanna leave me? Hunh? Stay with me baby . . . I . . . can't hold it . . .
I'm gone . . . baby . . . Are you gon' stay with me, baby? Hunh?"

"*Yes!* Yes! Oh baby, I won't leave you . . . I can't . . . I won't, I
won't!"

Taji moaned and thrust himself deep and hard one last time,
and their bodies jerked and twisted as they soared together, each
triggering the other's climax. Jadyn fell forward and collapsed on
the carpet, taking Taji with her. He quickly rolled onto his side,
holding her tightly so as not to break their connection. They lay
like that for a moment, panting loudly, catching their breath. He
brushed her hair away from her neck with his free hand and gently
kissed the back of her neck. "I love you, Jay. You know that, baby?"
he whispered in her ear.

Jadyn worked her hips back against him, smiling. "Yes, baby, I love you, too," she said sleepily.

She could feel him growing firm inside her again. Tonight, it was as if he was insatiable. She just didn't know if she'd be able to keep up with him. But they were both about to find out.

6

It was well past midnight when she and Taji had finally made it to bed. She woke abruptly an hour later, flinging the blankets back, and reaching over to flick on the fan that she kept by her bed for times like this. For times when she had The Dream.

The Dream always made her feel hot and suffocated, she couldn't breathe and she was afraid. So even though the temperature had dipped into the low forties outside, she turned the switch to high. As the blades began their swift circle dance, she welcomed the cool breeze that blew the stale air around in their room and made it seem fresh. She stuck her face right next to the plastic screen that separated the twirling blades from her face until she finally could breathe. Her heart slowed and she realized that she wasn't any place but in her own bedroom.

Taji stirred beside her and grumbled, "Damn, baby, you got that fan on again?" He grabbed the blankets and comforter and pulled them over his head, mumbling all the while. "You and them damn nightmares! You need to take your ass to see a shrink so I can get some sleep!"

But tonight the nightmare had seemed so *real*. She had actually *heard* the voice. She had heard him speaking to her and the voice seemed so familiar that recognition had almost put a face to the nightmare. Almost, but not quite. And the harder she pushed her brain toward the familiar, the farther away the face drifted. So when Taji said what he did, her reaction shocked her. She began to cry, to really weep. Her chest heaving and sounds of pain and hurt wrenching from some unknown place deep within.

Taji threw the covers back and sat up. "What's wrong with you now, hunh?" he said, switching on the lamp beside the bed. "Can't a brotha get some peace in his own house? Damn!"

Jadyn couldn't speak, she just stared at him with the pain and misery she felt overflowing and unstoppable. Ordinarily, Jadyn would have slapped the taste out of his mouth and given him a good cussing out for being so insensitive before jumping out of the bed and going to sleep on the couch. This time, she couldn't react to Taji's insults because she felt that she was coming apart at the seams.

Taji looked at her, finally reaching over and pulling Jadyn into his arms.

"Come on, c'mere baby. Shhhh . . . don't cry, it's all right. Whatever it is . . . it's OK. Shhh . . . Shh . . . Taji's here, baby. I'm sorry I hollaed at you . . . I'm just tired, that's all."

Jadyn couldn't stop the tears as the words came, her voice broken from the pain of the memories.

"Taji, this time I-I heard a voice and . . . and . . . I recognized the voice, I think . . . and he . . . he told me . . . he told me that he would *kill* my mom and my grandma . . . he said I better not tell, and he wanted to hurt me . . . And I was so scared. I was so scared Taj because he was in my room . . . and I felt helpless . . . I felt . . . so . . . *damn helpless* . . ."

"Baby, who? Who tried to hurt you?" He held Jadyn tightly, whispering in her ear.

It was hard for her to speak, her voice choking on the emotions she felt. "I don't know. I can't think, I'm so confused. Sometimes it's Quin, the man who shot my mother. Sometimes it's my stepfather Ian. I'm so tired of pretending, Taji. So tired . . ." She dissolved into tears and weeping, as she curled her body even more tightly against Taji's chest.

"It's OK, baby. Look here, whatever happened it wasn't your fault. Do you hear me? It wasn't your fault!" he said holding her head against his chest and stroking her hair, trying to comfort her. Suddenly, just like that, Jadyn began to grow cold in his arms and the tears stopped as she began to push him away and roll out of his lap. But Taji tried to hold on.

"No, no, no. *No!* Jadyn. Come here, baby, it's OK, you can talk to me. Please . . ."

But she jerked away and stared at him.

"I *know* it's not my fault. I was just a kid, I wasn't the one who gave my mother drugs and got her all strung out! Much less cause that maniac to come after us!"

Jadyn stormed into the bathroom and slammed the door behind her.

The ringing phone woke Jadyn from a troubled sleep.

"Hello?"

"Jadyn? This is Hiroshi Hietkikko. How are you doing?"

It was Taji's dad.

"Hi Mr. Hietkikko," Jadyn said, at the same time wondering what had prompted him to call. Taji's dad was nice and everything, but he wasn't the type of person who called often. He was always conscious of his rule not to interfere in his children's lives. She rolled over and let her hand slide along Taji's side of the bed. It was cold and empty. Rubbing the sleep from her eyes, she stole a glance at the alarm clock on the nightstand: 8:00 A.M. He must have left for school already. She hoped Taji wasn't hurt! But, no. She doubted that Mr. Hietkikko would be sounding all nice and calm like that if he was.

"Taji isn't here right now . . ."

"I was hoping to catch him before he left. Well, he is probably already in class, so I won't call his cell. I know you're wondering why I'm calling, so I'll get straight to the point. Taji's grandparents are flying in from Japan this weekend and his mother and I are throwing a barbecue in their honor. The entire family will be attending. His mother's sister, Sherry and her husband, my sister Toki is bringing her husband and the twins, and a few of our close friends will be there. And of course you are welcome to come along, too." Mr. Hietkikko had paused between the "friends will be there" and the "of course you are welcome" managing to make inviting Jadyn sound like an afterthought before he continued.

He had never made his disapproval of her and Taji's living arrangements a secret. She wasn't even sure that he approved of Taji choosing her as his girlfriend. Taji had told her about his father's strict Japanese upbringing and how angry his grandfather had been when his father had chosen to marry an African American instead of a Japanese girl. Taji had explained that he didn't think that his grandfather was racist or anything, just that his grandfather hated the fact that interracial marriage was still frowned upon in Japanese culture. He didn't want his family ostracized and his only son to bear the burden that an interracial marriage would bring. Jadyn didn't see the difference between that and being racist, but she hadn't told Taji that. What would have been the point? It wouldn't change his grandfather's feelings on the subject.

"Sorry about the short notice, Jadyn, but I wasn't sure that I was going to be able to arrange for my parents to come until just a little while ago. You know how it is, getting older people to travel so far and everything. I don't know if you and my son have made other plans for Saturday, so I hope you don't mind this change of plan," he said.

Mind? Was he joking? She couldn't help wondering why he was suddenly worried about how she felt about anything. The only thing she knew for sure was that she wasn't feeling no cookout at his house. She thought about telling Mr. Hietkikko what she was thinking, but she was trying to remain respectful for Taji's sake.

"No, Mr. Hietkikko, that's fine. I understand. What time should we be there?"

"Everyone should be arriving around four o'clock. Please tell that son of mine that four doesn't mean four fifteen or four thirty."

"OK, I'll make sure we're on time." *At least, I'll make sure he gets the message.* Jadyn thought.

"Oh and Jadyn?"

"Yes, Mr. Hietkikko?"

"My father is still very . . . traditional. I hope you will respect that fact and try not to be so . . . so . . . pro American women, if you know what I mean? My father wants a great-grandson very much. He has this idea that Taji should settle down, get married, and get on with the business of making a family." Mr. Hietkikko paused and cleared his throat, before he went on. "What I mean to say is, he doesn't agree with the American way of living to-gether without . . . without a . . . formal commitment . . . and . . . well . . ."

Jadyn could tell that Mr. Hietkikko had taken the conversation in a direction that was making him uncomfortable. She decided to be more gracious than he and let him off the hook.

"I totally get it, Mr. Hietkikko," she lied without missing a beat.

"I have no plans of trying to upset your father unnecessarily. Don't worry."

Mr. Hietkikko cleared his throat again before speaking.

"Thank you, Jadyn. I look forward to seeing you on Saturday, then."

Yeah right.

"OK, thank you. Goodbye, Mr. Hietkikko."

7

The doorbell rang and Jadyn threw on her robe as she padded down the steps to answer the door.

"Who is it?" she called while peering through the peephole. She saw that it was her cousin Nite at the same moment Nite yelled, "Open the damn door, who else but me gon' ring your doorbell this damn early?"

Jadyn flung the door open and as she walked away said, "How in the hell would I know who you is? You could be some kin'a ax murderer or some shit. You know serial killers always getting people either real early in the morning or real late at night!" She strolled into the kitchen, paused, and glanced back at her cousin. Nite walked in, closing and locking the door behind her.

"Leave it to you to bring up some o' dumb shit like somebody gettin' killed by a maniac." Nite turned around and pulled back the curtain on the living room window to sneak a peek outside before following Jadyn into the kitchen.

Jadyn smiled at her cousin's actions. Nite was more like a sister than a cousin. At five-seven, Nite was a full four inches taller than Jadyn with a flawless ebony complexion and a body to match, with her small waist and high, round behind. When she walked down the street, she had many a man hanging out of car windows almost wrecking their cars trying to get a better look at her big butt. Her permed hair was thick and heavy and fell to her shoulders, trimmed in layers that framed her heart-shaped face. Nite was always trying to tame her thick eyebrows with tweezers, but usually ended up paying her hair stylist an extra five dollars to shape them with a single-edged razor. They accented her round eyes perfectly. Jadyn had always teased her about her straight, almost pointed nose, telling her that her mom had taken her to a plastic surgeon to get a "white girl" nose job like La Toya Jackson's. In reality, Nite's grandmother on her mother's side was white, and that's whose nose she had gotten. It was that same grandmother who had given her the name LaNite, not only because she had been born at midnight, but also because her grandmother thought she was such a lovely baby, she lit up the night.

Jadyn and Nite had been partners in crime since they could walk, since the two of them had been born only a few months apart. Nite had been born first. The first memory Jadyn had of her cousin was when they were about three or four years old. Jadyn had pulled a vase from a table and sent it crashing to the floor. Her mother had been scolding her when Nite ran over and wrapped her arms around Jadyn and held her tight, kissing her on the cheek.

"Did you hurt y'self? It's OK, baby," she had said in her little toddler voice, her face scrunched up with concern.

Jadyn had returned the gesture, hugging Nite and holding on to her just as hard, with tears running down her cheeks.

Then Nite had turned to her aunt Samai and said as strongly as a three-year-old could, shaking her head and sounding angry: "Jay not broke that. Lee' her 'lone dammit!"

Their mothers had looked at them and laughed. Aunt Celia, Uncle Earl's ex-wife, and Jadyn's mother Samai had been very close back then, and had spent much of their free time together. Jadyn and Nite had become inseparable, sleeping over at one another's homes so often that it was hard to tell who lived where.

"What you got to eat? I need some nourishment. How 'bout cookin' up some bacon, eggs, and some wheat toast for a sister?"

Jadyn gave Nite a cold look before she rolled her eyes and playfully flipped the bird at her cousin.

"You know where the refrigerator and stove are, tramp, so why don't you make yourself useful and play the chef role, while I get dressed?" Jadyn wasn't worried about Nite being insulted by her calling her that name or even by the rude gesture. They traded insults all the time and had done so since they were teenagers. It wasn't malicious, it was just playing around to them. Her cousin was the only one who would understand and not get upset, and she felt the same way about Nite.

Nite sighed. "Don't you know how to treat a guest in your home, troll?" she asked as she rose from her chair and walked over to the fridge, opening the door wide and shuffling through the contents.

"Yes, I most certainly do know how to treat a guest. And if you're around when one comes to visit, you'll find out!" Jadyn said trying to sound serious, but barely able to hold back the smile that was trying to break forth and ruin her fake attitude.

Nite straightened up and locked eyes with her cousin, curling her lips up at one corner in a smirk before they both burst into laughter.

"OK, I'ma let you get that one off. That was a good one," Nite said between chuckles.

Nite stopped laughing and narrowed her eyes as she took a closer look at her cousin. "Hold up. Is that a damn *glow* I see radiating from your face?"

Jadyn smiled a goofy smile and batted her eyelashes.

"Oh hell no! Taji finally gave you that shit, didn't he? All the complainin' your ass been doin' about how he don't know how to work it and he laid it on that ass, didn't he?"

"Cousin! I can't explain it, but last night. Whoo-weeee! Yes. He. DID! My, my, my! That man had me climbing the fuckin' walls!" she said gleefully.

"Unh-hunh? And how do you think he just all of a sudden learned how to turn from Clark Kent to Superman?"

"Girl, I do not know, nor do I care right about now. You see what I'm sayin'?" Jadyn held her mouth open and gave Nite a wink.

"I know that's real, girl!" Nite said, as they both laughed and high-fived each other.

"Look, I was just about to jump in the shower and get dressed, so act like you at home like you always do and I'll be back in a flash," Jadyn said as she moved up the stairs.

8

In the shower her conversation with Nite about Taji's newly acquired lovemaking techniques came back to her. She had dismissed her cousin's questions, but on the real, Jadyn had been asking herself the exact same thing. As she grabbed the bar of soap and began lathering her washcloth, the questions filled her mind once again. How had Taji learned all those tricks he had put on her? Had he been watching the porn network while she was away from home? Had he been renting X-rated videos and doing research on how to please your woman in bed? Vigorously, yet gently rubbing the now soapy washcloth over her skin, she recalled how Taji would consume volume upon volume of books that contained information on the particular subject he was researching. Now that did sound like something he would do. He loved doing research when it came to getting good grades in school and updating plans to take the family business to the next level. She had seen him poring over books and business plans 'til the wee hours of the morning and sometimes even into the next day.

But would he be so businesslike about his approach to lovemaking? Yeah, he definitely could be.

She stood under the very warm water spewing from the shower

head, rinsing the soap from her body. Picking up her favorite body oil, she squeezed a generous amount into her palm and began slathering it over her wet skin. She loved the way the fruity, flowery fragrance tickled her senses and how her skin drank it all in. It was her signature scent and it would stay with her all day. Taji loved it and always inhaled deeply whenever he was close to her.

Maybe he was seeing someone else on the sly and maybe she was teaching him the ABCs of giving a woman multiple orgasms and having her climb the walls type shit. Jadyn thought about all of the long hours he was away from home supposedly working or at school. He definitely had the free time to creep on her if he wanted to. And he was so damn fine, she knew that he would have not one problem recruiting willing sex playmates. No, that couldn't be it, either. He wouldn't be creepin' on her and thinking about marrying her at the same time. It just made no sense. And after the way he had loved her down, she was wondering if she had done the right thing turning down his proposal. She could definitely do a lot worse in a husband. Maybe that's why he had proposed though, to throw her off the fact that he was freakin' somebody else. Men could be sneaky and dirty like that. Marry one woman and have a freak on the side.

Stepping under the warm spray, she rinsed the excess oil from her skin. Anyway, she wasn't the jealous type. She figured if it was in a man to cheat on his woman, no amount of worrying and acting all crazy was going to make him quit. She didn't understand how some women would follow their men when they left home, or set up traps to try to catch them cheating. After all of that, most of the time the man either kept right on cheating or left her ass for the other woman anyway. So she just put herself through all of the stress and nonsense for nothing.

No, Jadyn wasn't trying to lose any sleep over that shit. If she wasn't strong enough to keep her man at home, let the bitch have him, if there was a bitch. She wasn't going to go through changes worrying about this imaginary shit. It was what it was.

Stepping from the shower, she grabbed a fluffy tan towel from the stand she kept next to the tub, and began patting her skin dry, before applying shea butter. By the time she had gotten dressed in a pair of jeans and a baby T-shirt, Nite had whipped up breakfast for both of them.

"So what brings you by so early?" Jadyn forked up some scrambled eggs and took a bite of toast.

Nite chomped into a slice of crisp bacon and washed it down with a sip of steaming hot coffee before she spoke.

"I don't know, cuz. Just need to talk to my ace." Nite's voice became somber as she spoke. "You know me and Justice ain't been feelin' each other at all lately. Me and him went by Dad's house to chill 'cause that girlfriend of his cooked up some dinner plans for the four of us. I don't know why that bitch don't know by now that me and her ain't got nothin' to say to each other, other than hi and 'bye. She steady be trynna do that bonding shit when the heffa should know I ain't never gon' have no love for no skank that broke my mom's heart. Just 'cause Dad all in love with her ass don't mean I am." Jadyn's mom and Nite's dad, Earl, were brother and sister.

"I know she be trippin' when I go by Uncle Earl's. She get all up in my face and shit talkin' 'bout, 'You so pretty, your hair look so good' and all that kin'a bull! She need to quit tryin' so damn hard," said Jadyn.

"You feel me? Anyway. Me and Justice go over there, right? And Dad start talkin' 'bout he ain't gon' give me no more money 'til I get my shit together and git my ass back in school, right?"

"No, he didn't girl! What do he mean, git your shit together? You already a phlebotomist drawing blood up at the hospital and everything. People be makin' fuckin' careers out of that shit, so what he talkin' that go back to school shit for?" Jadyn was proud of her cousin's accomplishments and couldn't understand her uncle's suggestion that Nite go back to school.

"OK? That's the same thing I'm wondering. So I'm not trynna have Justice all up in mine, right?" Nite took another sip from her mug before she went on. "So I tells Dad can we discuss this later on instead of during our romantic foursome. He gon' start gettin' all loud and shit. Talkin' 'bout I'm being disrespectful and don't fuckin' tell him what the fuck to speak on in his own house!"

"Whaaat? Unh-unh!" Jadyn knew her uncle Earl had a temper that could flare up with not even a moment's notice. She had witnessed him going off on someone a time or two.

"Yeah, girl! But that ain't it! Listen up! Justice ass gon' chime the fuck in and say, Mr. Davis, I been trynna get Nite to go on back to nursing school for months now. She do me the same way! Start tellin' me to mind my business, or worry about gettin' my ownself back in school."

Jadyn let her fork fall into her plate as her eyes grew wide, showing disbelief at what Justice had done. "WHAAAAAAAAAAT! No he did not! I know you checked his ass behind that dumb shit!"

Nite frowned and cocked her head to the side. "Checked him? Girl I straight cu-locked on his ass. I let him know what time it is. Then *Dad* gon' side with his ass like they old buddies or some shit. And tell me I need to calm the fuck down and listen to someone who's trynna help me make my situation better and shit." Nite polished off the last of her eggs and toast, and continued speaking with her mouth full. "Girl, I told them both to kiss my ass and got my coat and left!"

"I know you ain't tell Uncle Earl to kiss your ass!" Jadyn raised her eyebrows dramatically and made a face as she spoke. She knew her uncle would never tolerate disrespect from anyone, much less his own child.

Nite rolled her eyes and curled up one corner of her mouth again before she answered. "OK, I didn't tell him that out loud, but I sure said it in my head as I was leavin'!"

Jadyn laughed out loud. "Unh-hunh. That's what I thought. 'Cause I know Uncle Earl wouldn'ta let you get that off. In front of people, too? No way!"

Nite started laughing, too, as she pushed her empty plate away and cleared the space in front of her. "I know! He would've smacked the shit out of me! And I woulda started cryin' and shit. Trynna apologize before he really went off on me!"

Nite pulled a quarter bag of weed out of her purse along with some papers to roll a joint.

"That's what I'm talkin' 'bout! I'll be right back," Jadyn said as she rose from the table. "I need to get some incense. You know Taji don't smoke and I don't want to hear his mouth when he gets home."

Nite didn't say anything. Jadyn retrieved the incense and hurriedly took her seat at the table. Nite finished rolling the joint and brought it to her lips to lick the flap shut before pressing it with her fingers. Placing the joint between her lips she flicked the flame on the lighter and took a few hits before blowing a little smoke in Jadyn's direction.

"Pass that right on over here!" Jadyn told her cousin as she rose slightly from her seat and reached across the table. Placing the joint between her lips, she inhaled deeply before handing it back to Nite. She was glad now that Nite had come by so early. She needed to get her buzz on. It would help calm her nerves before she left for her callback.

"You and Justice and me and Taji. What the fuck is goin' on? Maybe something is trynna tell us we need a change."

Nite passed the joint back to her and said, "I hope you get that role, cuz. Maybe that would be just what our asses need. A change of scene."

"Yeah, that is exactly what I was thinking before Taji broke my shit down last night. My head is all fucked up behind that shit. It's like I don't know what to do about me and him now." The thought briefly crossed her mind to tell her cousin about the ring, but she decided not to.

She passed the joint back to her cousin. "It's like I need a man's perspective on this. One who could explain it all to me. It's times like this that I wish my dad was in my life."

"I don't know about all that. I got my dad around me and I'm still confused as hell about the shit men do. And Dad be gettin' on my last nerve most of the time."

Jadyn thought about what her cousin had said earlier. Even though her uncle Earl and Nite did seem to get into arguments a lot, she couldn't remember a time when Nite had really needed him that he hadn't come through for her. She was always calling him for money when she was short. And he had come to her rescue on more than one occasion when she ran out of gas or needed a flat tire changed. Nite's father had also attended every special event that occurred in Nite's life. She remembered Nite's high school graduation party, when he had put together a slide show with clips from her childhood. Jadyn would never forget the look of pride in her uncle's eyes as he watched Nite walk across the stage and later on, each time he looked at her at the party. Never had Jadyn missed her father more than on that night.

"Yeah, you might be right about that. But it still couldn't hurt, right? Before last night, I thought Taji never listened to me. But he damn sure heard me about the lovemaking, didn't he? It's confusing as hell because I was ready to leave his ass."

"Yeah, men are stupid like that. For some reason they want us to think they don't hear us. Don't ask me why. But let's not forget the fact that your man is paid! Talk about picture me rollin'! A woman would be a fool to walk away from a man that is paid and is superfine, too, without a damn good reason. And I hate to tell you this, cuz, but from what you told me it don't sound like you got one," Nite said before taking another hit off the joint.

Jadyn didn't care what Nite said, she was still feeling the absence of a strong man in her life that she could bounce her feelings off of. One who would care about her and what she was feeling and give her loving counsel and a strong shoulder to cry on if she needed to.

Jadyn thought she would share with her cousin her thoughts about finding her real dad. She didn't want to tell her about the reoccurring nightmares she had about being murdered. She was still trying to understand how she felt about all those memories herself.

"I just wish that I had my real dad around. I been thinkin' about trynna find him," she said all at once.

Nite inhaled deeply and choked back the smoke as she spoke. "Oh yeah? What made you think that after all these years?"

Jadyn suddenly wanted to tell Nite about everything. About Ian raping her and him showing up at her job, the nightmares. But she played it off. She didn't know how her cousin would take it. She didn't want Nite to look at her differently. She might not understand why the nightmares scared her so bad. She might even think she was crazy.

"I don't know. I guess listening to you talk about how you and Uncle Earl be acting toward each other."

Nite stared at her incredulously. "What? The way we always at each other's throats?"

"Yes, in spite of that. It may be true that y'all be at each other, but I can feel the love he has for you and you for him." Jadyn held up her hand to keep Nite from commenting. "Don't even start, Nite. You know y'all love each other. I miss that. I want to know a father's love."

"What about Ian? You known him and been around him since you was five years old. Wasn't he like a father to you?"

Nite's last comment made Jadyn angry. "Hell no! He ain't never been like a father to me! Don't you never say that shit to me ever again!" Jadyn stood to her feet but Nite grabbed her arm before she could walk away. Jadyn jerked her arm free, but stayed where she was.

"Daaaaaaag! I'm sorry, Jay! What did I say? What's the matter?"

Jadyn slumped back down in her chair and held her face in her hands, again wanting to spill her guts to her cousin, but afraid of what it might do to their relationship.

"Nothin'. It ain't nothing, cuz," she said lifting her head and running her fingers through her thick hair. "Pass me the joint."

9

Jadyn brushed her teeth, changed into her dance leotard, and pulled a clean pair of jeans over them. She didn't want to walk into the audition smelling like weed.

Once she arrived at the studio, she was surprised to find that there was only one other girl there. She had assumed that there would be a whole group for the callback. The three judges were now one. The man who had given her the CD at the end of the audition.

"OK ladies," he began. "This is it. It is down to the two of you, so you need to dance today as if your lives depended on the outcome of your performance. And in a way it does. One of you will walk away with the role of a lifetime and one of you will . . . well . . . you get the picture, I'm sure. Madoline, you're up first."

A tall, thin white girl, dressed in a black leotard and white leg warmers tiptoed to the stage entrance. Her blond, wavy hair was pulled back from her face in a tight ponytail. Her boobs were tiny, almost nonexistent, and Jadyn was surprised to see that her butt, though small, was round and curved away from the arch of her back, instead of almost blending into her back, the way a lot of white girls' butts did. She guessed her butt had gotten that way from all the squats dancers had to do. Jadyn thought the black leotard made her appear a bit washed out, but she was pretty enough.

Glad she has to go first, Jadyn thought. *Gives me a chance to see what she got.* She hadn't noticed this girl when she had auditioned, so she must have been at one of the other cattle calls.

Someone she couldn't see cued up the music and the girl leapt onto the stage. She did a leap split in the air that was so high, she looked like she was flying. And her split was perfection, wide and almost flat, her back almost at a perfect ninety-degree angle as she spread her arms and touched her toes. When she landed she did a series of precise little relevés and passés across the stage before twirling in perfect tour jetés, grand and petite, followed by pirouettes. Oh, she was good. Better than good.

Jadyn turned away. No need in adding pressure to her nerves. She unbuttoned her jeans and stripped them off. So what, the girl was good, she told herself. She was better. Closing her eyes, she took deep breaths in . . . and out . . . in through her nose . . . out through her mouth. She followed that with stretches, first her legs then her arms, doing a few jumps straight up in the air and landing lightly on her feet. She was unstoppable . . . the best . . . she would do her. Forget everything else.

"Jadyn Collins! You're up!" The judge called her onto the stage. "Are you ready?" he asked her.

Jadyn's heart pounded.

"Yes," she answered firmly.

As the first bars of the music blasted from the speakers Jadyn began in the classic position: feet at an angle, arms out in front of her in a circle. The music started and began to infiltrate her pores as she moved, slowly stretching one arm out in front of her, bringing one leg up off the floor and stretching it out behind her. Bringing her back leg up higher at the same time stretching her head toward the floor until suddenly she was perfectly balanced on one leg. She had perfect control. As the music rose to a crescendo she broke out of the pose and exploded into a series of leaps across the stage. She was the music and the music was her as she moved. Bending, twirling, bouncing across the stage. She felt weightless, the confidence showing in her face and she changed her expressions to match her movements. All too soon the music was at an end as she did her trademark move: a handless cartwheel into a perfect split. End of the routine.

"Bravo! Perfection! Jadyn, you were born to be a star!" the judge said before he caught himself. He had gotten caught up in the magic that was Jadyn's dance. He regained his composure as he glanced over at Madoline, who had her arms folded in front of her and looked as if she were about to burst into tears.

"Both of you gave incredible performances. You are both very talented young ladies indeed. Well, I'm going to tell you. This is a very difficult decision, one that I'm going to have to talk over with the other judges."

Jadyn frowned. "With all due respect, sir, you said that we would know today who got the part."

"Yes, yes, I know. But I'm afraid that isn't possible. As I said, I must discuss certain things with the other judges. One of us will call you before the end of next week with our decision."

Madoline picked up her bag and almost ran out the door.

Jadyn turned and began to walk offstage.

"Jadyn," the judge called.

"Yes?" She turned back to face him.

"I just want to make sure we have the right number for you. 555-735-9595?"

"Yes, that's it."

"OK then. Thank you." The judge walked out of the auditorium without another word or backward glance. Jadyn couldn't wipe the smile from her face as she changed into her street clothes.

10

When Saturday morning rolled around, Jadyn had decided to go to the cookout with Taji after all. If she was going to give their relationship another try, she may as well begin with being more sensitive to his needs, too. Besides, if they were going to stay together she would have to meet the rest of his family sooner or later. Might as well make it sooner.

She dressed in pale yellow jeans and a long-sleeved white cotton tee that had narrow, pale yellow stripes running the length of it. It had six tiny buttons at the neck and a drawstring at the bottom, that accentuated her small waist when the pulled the ends of it together. On her feet were white leather sandals that had toe loops trimmed in gold around the big toe. The white leather strap that held her foot in place was also trimmed in gold.

Her stylist at the salon had straw-set her hair, so that she now sported a head full of tight, springy curls. She loved the way they bounced every time she moved her head. Although she had dreaded the three hours she had to sit under the dryer to set the curls, the results had made it all totally worth it. She was glad that her stylist, Dyla Brown, was not the type who stacked appointments, so that she had three or even four women scheduled to have their hair done at the exact same time. She had left beauty salons for good more times than she could count because their stylists had this same scheduling problem. So when her cousin had recommended Dyla to her, that had been one of the first questions she had put to her.

"No, Jadyn, I don't stack appointments because I want to give each of my clients the time they deserve without rushing through the process. I want to make each visit a relaxing, enjoyable experience because I know that if my clients are happy we're all happy."

"Well, Dyla, I hope you're being totally up front with me, because I am so sick and tired of going to get my hair done at eight o'clock in the morning and not leaving the shop until four or five o'clock in the evening."

No one wanted to spend an entire day for a process that should take no more than two or three hours, depending on what you were getting and how long and thick your hair was.

"Oh, I feel you Jadyn. I wouldn't appreciate having to spend my day like that and so I'm not going to put my clients through it, either. I believe in mutual respect. I respect my clients' time and I expect them to respect mine as well, by coming in on time. If you're running late, all I ask is that you give me a call and that you not be more than fifteen minutes late. As long as we respect each other, we will get along fine."

"I can respect that," Jadyn had said and she meant it. She could totally see her point of view and she agreed with it wholeheartedly. That conversation had taken place six months ago and she had been going to Dyla ever since. Their relationship had grown and developed until they were more friends than just stylist and client.

So when she had told her that she wanted a special style for the cookout that would hold up through the smoke, heat, and humidity of the outdoors, Dyla had known just what she would need.

"If I were you, I would do a spiral curl. I set it on really thin rollers, almost the size of straws, and sit you under the dryer. The curls are very pretty and durable and hold up really well under the conditions you've described."

By this time, Jadyn trusted her judgment and went ahead with her suggestion. She loved the style so much that she had tipped her ten bucks.

She had actually been so pleased with the way her curls had turned out, that she had gone and gotten a manicure and pedicure, convincing herself at the time it was because it was the end of May and she had to get her feet sandal-ready for the summer. Later on she had to admit that she was really just going all out to make a good impression on Taji's family. She'd always used Vaseline on her feet, and always had socks or something covering them at all times, even when she was just walking around at home, so she never got the heavy calluses on the heels and soles of her feet like a lot of other women did. She admired her glossy, neatly polished toes and the smooth skin on her feet that gleamed as she slid the sandals on.

She finished her look with round, medium-sized gold hoops that Taji had bought her for Christmas, and a matching gold bracelet. She didn't put on much makeup, just some eyeliner and lipstick. It didn't make sense to her to put on anything else for a picnic. She really didn't need more than that anyway.

She smiled as she saw Taji's reflection in the mirror as he walked up behind her and draped his arms around her waist, nuzzling the nape of her neck.

"Mmmmmmm. Your hair smells good. And your outfit looks so cute on you."

Jadyn's smile became a grin as she gazed at his reflection while she spoke.

"You don't look too bad yourself."

He was dressed in a gold long-sleeved tee, blue jeans, and white Jordan's with gold trim. Around his neck was a fine gold chain that held a single charm, inscribed, *Taji and Jadyn Forever*. He had wanted to get a tattoo, but that was the one concession that he had made to his grandfather. He had promised not to get any tattoos. His grandfather thought they represented a man's inability to grow up, and that any man who wore a tattoo was refusing to leave the childhood game of scribbling on your skin when no one was watching. Either that or you were marking yourself as a thug.

Jadyn thought they were perfectly coordinated. She turned toward him, planning to give him a quick peck on the lips, but when she began to move past him, he grabbed her and pulled her back, kissing her more deeply.

"You need to quit 'cause you know you can't even handle this," she teased, and before the other night she would have meant it.

"Oh think so, hunh? Well, I ain't got no problem practicing until I *can* handle it," he told her, playing with the buttons on her blouse and pressing himself against her.

"Quit playin'," she said as she playfully smacked his hand away. An image of him naked and between her legs flashed before her eyes at the same instant. She wouldn't mind him practicing on her some more, either.

"Baby, go on downstairs and load the baked beans in the trunk so we can get out of here," she said turning him around and giving him a little push toward the stairs. "You know you don't even want to piss your dad off by being late."

"You got that right," he said walking down the steps.

"Grab some bottled water out of the fridge, too, will you? I'm thirsty."

"I only got two hands, girl. How am I gon' carry a pan of beans and some bottled water, too?" He made his voice loud so that it carried back upstairs.

Jadyn caught up with him in the kitchen. She opened the refrigerator and bent down to pick up the pan of beans before straightening up and passing the casserole dish to him. Then she reached back inside and pulled out two bottles of water in case he was thirsty, too.

Grabbing the keys to the BMW off the counter, she pressed the remote to unlock the door as she followed him out to the garage. When she pressed the remote again the trunk popped open and he bent over to set the dish inside. She secured it under the mesh grocery netting to prevent it from sliding around.

She handed him the keys and they climbed inside the car.

Jadyn was quiet as Taji slid a CD into the player. Ginuwine's voice filled the car singing "So Anxious."

Suddenly unsure of how she would be received by his family in general, and his grandparents in particular, her stomach began to twist itself into knots and she grew pensive. What if they didn't like her? What if she didn't like them?

"What's on your mind?" He slid his hand over and rubbed her thigh.

She opened a bottle of water and handed it to him while she thought about how she was going to answer. She watched him take a long swallow before letting the bottle drop into the cup holder under the CD player. She saw him glance her way before he spoke. "Thank you, but you didn't answer my question."

"I don't know. I was just thinking about your grandparents."

She opened the second bottle of water and took a sip.

"What about them?"

"Well, what if they don't like me? I remember you telling me that your grandfather didn't speak to your dad for years for marrying your mom just because she was black. How do you know he's not still prejudiced against black people?"

He glanced over at her again. "I never said that he was prejudiced. It wasn't that. He just didn't want my dad to have to deal with other people's prejudices. He didn't even want to have to deal with any of that. He wanted dad to marry a Japanese girl and just, you know, have a simple life."

Jadyn turned toward him. "See, to me that's still being prejudiced. But let me say that I think there is a difference between being prejudiced and being a racist. I think we all are prejudiced to a degree. It's only when it goes to the extreme when you hate someone based solely on the color of their skin that simple prejudices turn into racism."

"Yeah, I guess you got a point. But he can't still be prejudiced if he ever was, because I'm half black, and he loves me."

Jadyn straightened in her seat. "True."

"It really doesn't matter anyway. What is there about you not to like?" He squeezed her knee gently before taking her hand and entwining his fingers with hers. He then brought her hand to his lips and kissed it.

He could be so unintentionally sweet. In all honesty, he was sweet most of the time, even if he did have a quick temper. Actually, she had a temper, too. In fact, hers might be a little worse than his. She did go off on him sometimes. She knew that part of him was just trying to change the direction of the conversation, but what he had said was still sweet though.

"Now, just because you think I'm perfect doesn't mean everybody else in the family is going to."

He sneaked another peek at her before putting his eyes back on the road.

"Ain't nobody said you was perfect, punk. But you'll do in a rush," he said, smiling.

"What?" Jadyn turned in her seat again.

"Calm down, shortie. You know I'm just playin' with you," he said, still smiling and giving her a wink.

"I know you better be. 'Cause if you can't see that I'm perfect then you need to turn this car around and take me right on back home," she teased, getting into a joking mood right along with him.

"You trippin'," he told her as he brought her hand up and kissed it again. "Look, just chill. Be cool, be you, let it go, and have fun. You'll be fine."

"Let's hope," Jadyn said, still unable to quell her nerves.

11

Even though they were not late, most of the guests were already at the cookout when they arrived. The smoky-sweet aroma of the meat barbecuing on the grill and music filled the air.

"Dang, your people believe in getting things started early, don't they?"

"It's all good," he said, removing the dish from the trunk.

Taji's parents' house was huge. If she thought some of the homes in their neighborhood looked like mansions, then this had to be up there with a palace. The first things that caught her eye were the two long winding driveways that wrapped around the house and backed up to a four-car garage. They were filled with expensive cars. There was a Mercedes 350, a few Corvettes, Lexuses, Saabs, and Mazda Miatas. There was a Chrysler 300 and Cadillac trucks, among others. Jadyn recognized the Mercedes 350 as Taji's mom's car. She had seen it parked in front of the condo enough times.

"Come on, baby."

"OK, I'm coming."

As she stepped out of the car, she took in the solarium that ran the entire parameter of the backyard. It was beautiful, filled with big leafy plants and it looked so peaceful. Jadyn knew that she would have to check that out before she left. It seemed to be calling to her for some reason.

As they moved toward the house, Taji's mom spotted them and began walking their way.

"Hey, you two! You both look so cute!" Taji bent slightly so that his mother could plant a kiss on his cheek. She gave him a careful hug so that she wouldn't make him spill the beans. She kissed Jadyn on the cheek next and hugged her, as well.

Taji's mom was tall, small-boned, and had pretty, smooth, dark brown skin. She wore a two-piece jean outfit that Jadyn was sure was made by some designer that she had never heard of. It was beautifully cut, navy blue jean capris trimmed in brown leather, and had a matching jean and leather trimmed shell and jacket. On her feet were navy-blue jean sandals that were trimmed in the same leather. Her hair was a blunt-cut bob that was parted down the middle and fell just below her ears.

"Oh good, you brought the baked beans! Taji just take them into the kitchen over there and set them on any empty space you can find. I swear, your father has been cooking all night. You know we rarely cook anymore and when he gets the opportunity, I just don't think he knows how to draw boundaries on how much food to prepare. I tell you, I don't know what in the world we are going to do with all this food!"

Personally, Jadyn didn't see why getting rid of the food would be a problem. It looked as if there were at least a hundred people milling around on the lawn. She guessed that word of mouth must have brought out many more relatives and friends than his father had first anticipated when he had spoken to her on the phone.

"Well, Mom, there are plenty of homeless people who would love to have all the leftovers you could stand to give them," Taji said.

Taji's mother didn't skip a beat although Jadyn was a little surprised. She had never heard Taji express any type of concern toward the homeless. Then again, they never really discussed things like that, either.

"Now that's a really good idea, son. I'll be sure to mention your idea to your father. And your grandfather, too. I'm certain they will both be so proud of you for thinking about the less fortunate."

As they moved toward the patio that led into the kitchen, Taji's mom saw more guests arriving.

"Oh, there are Doctor and Mrs. Hutchinson. I'll catch up with the two of you in a little bit." She began walking toward her new guests.

Taji's dad was standing at the grill wearing an apron and talking to his sister, Toki, when he spotted the two of them and waved them over.

"Hold up, Dad. Let me put these away and we'll be right there!" Taji raised the casserole dish slightly as he spoke and then disappeared into the kitchen. Jadyn was walking so close to him that she ran into his back when he stopped short, searching for a place to set the casserole dish.

"Girl, why is you walkin' all up on me like that? My family got you shook? Now they can't be that bad."

"Now how would I know that? Outside of your mom and dad the only other member of your family that I have met is your Aunt Toki. Now it seems like I'm gonna meet all ten generations at once."

Taji set the dish on top of the microwave, the only space that he could find that wasn't otherwise occupied by a covered dish. He turned to face Jadyn.

"Look, baby, relax," he said, drawing her close to him.

"Man, that's what I'm trynna do." She let her head rest against his chest. "I really don't even know why I keep trippin' so hard like this. You know I don't usually have a problem meeting people and mixing it up with them. I mean, how could I have a problem and go to all of these auditions the way I do? How could I let this get me all upset, when my life is about meeting strangers and getting them to like me and my dancing? I don't understand it."

"I know this, and you know this, so like I said before, just chill and be yourself."

Taji held her tighter and she felt a lot of the tension begin to drain from her body.

"I know you're right, baby. But just stick close to me tonight, Ok? Or at least until I meet the rest of the fam and see what's what. OK?"

Taji began to rock her gently from side to side.

"Don't worry. I got you, love. But just tell me one thing?"

He loosened his hold and she leaned back and gazed into his eyes.

"What's that?"

"Does this mean you gon' follow me into the bathroom and hold my dick while I pee?" he asked, his expression a mix of amusement and concern. A smile played at his lips.

"Boy, be quiet you old nasty thang!" she said, pulling on his arms, trying to break out of the arm lock he had her in. She was struggling not to laugh at his crass but humorous remark. "You ain't funny."

"I'm just sayin' though, a brother can't even take a step without you shadowin' him, so I must know how far you willin' to take it." He was laughing now and so was she.

"No, let me go. You trippin'," she told him, still trying to break free from his arms. He had her around the waist now.

"OK, stop. I'm sorry. I was jokin'. Come on now, I said I'm sorry. You know I was just playin' with you."

As they tussled playfully, an elderly Asian gentleman strolled into the kitchen. The two of them froze momentarily before Taji regained his composure, releasing Jadyn and standing up straight. The gentleman stared at them stoically.

"Grandfather." Taji took a couple of steps toward him but stopped short. He brought his legs together and placed his arms at his sides, bowing his head and his upper body slighty. "It is an honor to see you again, sir."

Jadyn didn't know what to think. She just stood there and watched.

The gentleman stepped forward and embraced his grandson. Jadyn was amazed at how much the two of them looked alike. Taji looked more like his grandfather than he did his dad. He was almost as tall as Taji, had the same build, though he appeared to be softer in the places where Taji's muscles rippled. But that was to be expected. They had the same eyes and hair, except that the grandfather's eyes embued a deep wisdom and strength, and his full head of hair was totally white.

"I am the one who is honored and so happy to see you, Grandson." He released Taji and assumed the same stance that he had moments before and slightly bowed his head and upper body.

"Now will you stop trying to impress me with all of this old-fashioned crap that I'm certain your father instructed you to do. You and I have never stood on ceremony. We have never been traditional in the ways that we have related to one another. But thank you for humoring an old man."

Taji's face broke into a grin.

"That's why I love you so much, Grandfather," he said. "You never have a problem keeping it real with me."

"Yes, my child. But let's keep that between the two of us." He moved closer to Taji and lowered his voice a few notches, but not so low that Jadyn couldn't hear him.

"I enjoy seeing your father sweat."

Jadyn and Taji laughed out loud.

Taji's grandfather moved over to Jadyn.

He took her hand and raised it to his lips and kissed the back of it. Just as Taji had done when they had met for the first time.

"So you are the one that my grandson has chosen to give me many strong great-grandsons."

Jadyn was caught off guard by his remark momentarily, but decided he must be teasing her.

"Well, sir, Taji and I haven't really discussed having children, yet. You see, I'm a dancer. I hope one day to dance in the theater. If Taji and I ever do have kids, it won't be for quite a while."

She smiled, but his grandfather looked puzzled.

Taji stepped to her side and put his arm around her waist.

"Grandfather, I would like you to meet Jadyn Collins. Jadyn, my grandfather, Tanaka Hietkikko."

"Yes, I'm delighted to meet you Jadyn." Then he turned to Taji. "I'm a little confused. Your father told me that you had become settled and had chosen a young woman for your wife."

Taji's father stepped through the patio door before the grandfather had finished speaking, drowning out the last part of his sentence.

"So here you are, Father. I was wondering what was keeping our guests of honor. Where is Mother? Isn't she with you?"

Taji's grandfather turned toward his son. "She was still a bit tired after our long flight. She sends her apologies, but she is not up to attending a big party tonight. She has gone to bed. She said she will get something to eat a little later. Taji was just introducing me to the lovely Jadyn."

"Yes, well, Father, everyone is waiting for you. They are starved but we can't begin eating without you. Come," he said, taking his father by the elbow and guiding him out to the patio.

"Taji, check on Mother and then come on out and join us," he said before closing the patio door. Jadyn could have sworn he gave her an evil look right before the door slid shut. What was that all about?

"Taji, did your grandfather just say what I thought he said?"

Taji took her hand and began leading her toward the steps.

"To me it sounded like he thought you and me were married. And I could've sworn he called me your wife."

"Nah, you're just hearin' things. I didn't hear nothing like that." He started up the steps taking her with him.

"You're gon' love my grandmother. She is so adorable."

12

As they walked up the stairs, Jadyn couldn't help but admire the layout of the house. The winding staircase was freestanding and you could see the living room on the other side of it—if it was the living room. It could be the den for all she knew, but whatever it was, it was lovely. Done in deep rich chocolates, tans, and bright orange accents. The glimpses she caught of his parents' home as they walked upward was nothing short of breathtaking. And a glimpse is exactly what it was, as fast as Taji was moving.

"Slow down, Taji. We're not running from a fire or anything."

"Sorry, baby. I didn't think I was walking that fast."

By that time they were already at the top of the stairs and on their way down the hallway that led to one of the guest bedrooms. She was sure that a house this size had to have more than one.

Taji stopped at the second door that they came to and rapped his knuckles against the door as he called softly.

"Grandmother?"

There was no answer so he knocked again.

"Grandmother?"

They were both surprised when the door opened and his grandmother stood in the doorway.

She stood all of about five feet, if that, with very delicate features. She was petite, with her dark, shiny hair pulled back and secured in a tight bun at the nape of her neck, only a few strands of gray running throughout. Despite her small stature, she seemed to command respect. She wore a black pantsuit, trimmed in red and gold piping around the belled jacket cuffs and the hem of her pants. Her face was clear and unlined and seemed to defy both age and gravity. Her countenance lit up when she saw her grandson. She was a fine woman, with a voice just as soft as the rest of her appeared to be. She opened her arms and Taji somehow folded his six-foot-two frame into her welcoming embrace.

"My little Taji. It is so wonderful to see your face again."

Taji hugged her back. "I'm happy to see you, too, Grandmother, but Grandfather said that you were tired and taking a nap."

"You know your grandfather. He has always been overprotective of me. He insisted that I rest, so I laid my head on the pillow to humor him. Then I got up and got dressed after he was gone."

Taji laughed as he straightened and took Jadyn's hand. "Grandmother, I want you to meet Jadyn. Jadyn, my grandmother, Mai Ling Hietkikko."

Taji's grandmother took one of Jadyn's hands into hers and squeezed it gently. Jadyn smiled.

"So we meet at last. It's so good to finally meet you. I have heard many wonderful things about you from Taji and from his parents. Taji's grandfather and I anxiously await the birth of our first great-grandchild."

Jadyn once again found herself at a loss for words, the smile on her face slowly fading away. She glanced at Taji and back at his grandmother.

"It's so nice to meet you, too, Mrs. Hietkikko," she finally said.

"Please, 'Mrs. Hietkikko' is much too formal a title for a member of the family. I would be honored if you would call me Grandmother."

"But Mrs. Hietkik—"

"Jadyn, now you are going to hurt Grandmother's feelings. She said you could call her Grandmother."

"OK, Grandmother," she said, but Taji was going to have a lot of explaining to do once they were by themselves.

"Grandmother, you look so beautiful, and I swear you and Jadyn could almost pass for sisters," Taji said.

"Oh stop it. Jadyn, don't you pay one bit of attention to my grandson. He likes to joke around a lot."

Jadyn smiled. "He does think he's funny sometimes. But he's absolutely right this time. You do look so young and you're beautiful, too."

His grandmother waved her hand at both of them. "You both need glasses, I'm afraid."

Taji took his grandmother's arm. "Come on, Grandmother, everyone is waiting for you."

13

The rest of the afternoon was pretty uneventful, with Taji introducing her to his uncles, aunts, cousins, and friends. Though his father only had one sister, his mother had a rather large family. They all received her very well and Jadyn couldn't understand why she had been so nervous on the way over.

Some of the men decided they wanted to play a game of pickup basketball and Taji was more than happy to oblige them. His old basketball hoop was still attached to the front of one of the garages, so he told the men where to find it. He trotted over to Jadyn to let her know where he would be and to find out how she was doing.

"I'm good, baby," she told him. "Go ahead and play basketball with your cousins. I've been dying to check out the solarium over by the pool."

"Good idea. I'm sure you'll love it in there. It used to be my favorite place to just get away from everything or just to chill," he said.

"Hey man, you gon' play ball or stand over there droolin' over your woman all night? Ya little henpecked sucka!" One of the men called over to him good-naturedly, and the others cracked up laughing.

"See ya later, baby," he said giving her a quick peck on the lips before he turned away.

"Aw, shut your face, Langston, you just mad 'cause don't no woman want to be bothered with your ugly, buck-toothed ass!" Taji yelled back as he trotted toward the group of men.

Jadyn strolled out to the pool. The atrium once again took her breath away.

There was a small, Japanese-inspired wooden footbridge that formed an arch and crossed over the shallow edge of the pool. It ended in a rock-covered path that led to the door of the solarium.

As she entered, she was not disappointed in the least. The highly polished hardwood floor ran from one end of the solarium to the other and was so shiny, it resembled a basketball court. For a moment, she wished that she had worn socks so that she could kick off her shoes and slide across the glossy surface.

A burgundy sofa ensemble was positioned in the room to give a spectacular view of the pool, the house, and the magnificent landscaped grounds and gardens. There was a stereo system in one corner that drew her attention, so she ambled over to check it out.

Not only was there a tall wooden column built into the wall holding more CDs than she could count, but there was also a rack that held LP records. She guessed that those were for his parents to listen to as they relaxed and enjoyed the view, because she doubted that anyone from her generation played records anymore. Then again, maybe they were heirlooms and were displayed just for decoration.

As she flipped through the CDs one song in particular captured her intention. It was Aaliyah's "More Than a Woman." She had thought about using this song for her audition piece for STOMP but had elected to go with "Try Again" instead. Not that she was sorry since it had won her a callback, but she had liked the way she had choreographed "More Than a Woman," too. She pressed the ON button for the CD player. Removing the CD from its case, she pushed it inside the player.

The music blasted out of the speakers and she put her hand up to her mouth and searched for the volume control. Perhaps his parents had put on music and intentionally left the volume up to entertain as they lounged by the pool. She checked the position of the volume button before turning it down a few notches. She would make sure that she put the volume back where she had found it.

She thought to let the music play as she continued to explore the perfect little hideaway. But as the first bars of the song filled the air, she found herself wanting to dance. Glancing around the room, she saw there was more than enough space to accommodate her. She carefully pushed one of the lounge chairs back, giving her the perfect space to dance.

Slipping off her sandals, she tiptoed over to the stereo and started the music over, and quickly moved back to her little improvised dance floor.

She closed her eyes and let the music infiltrate her soul and as Aaliyah's voice began to fill the room, she started to move. The floor felt every bit as good as she imagined, even though she was gliding instead of sliding across its glasslike surface. She bounced and stepped across the floor, her body remembering the moves when her mind didn't. She allowed herself to be swept away by the music, not looking up until the song ended.

She heard clapping and turned to face the glass front of the solarium, surprised that a small crowd had formed alongside the pool. Taji's mother and father, his aunt Toki, his grandmother and grandfather, and a few assorted relatives and friends had all been watching her. Toki crossed the bridge and entered the solarium. She walked over to Jadyn giving her a hug.

"That was absolutely amazing, Jadyn! Taji told us that you danced, but we had no idea that you were this talented."

Jadyn blushed.

"We would all love it if you would dance for us again, this time with the music loud enough for us to hear."

"Toki, I love dancing, I do, but I'm not really dressed to give a real performance."

"Well, you seemed to be moving fine just a few moments ago. Please, Jadyn. Father and Mother really loved what you did. They want to see more, too."

Jadyn didn't know what to think. She hadn't thought anyone had been watching before. When had they all come to the poolside anyway? When she'd walked over, they had all been out in the grilling area.

"What brought you all out to the pool?"

"We heard the music come on and go back off again, so we came to tell whoever was out here to turn the music back on. To be perfectly honest with you, I was the one who saw you dancing and went to get the others."

Jadyn thought it over. She really couldn't say no to Taji's grandmother and grandfather. This was their day, after all. She did have one of her practice outfits out in the trunk of the car. Taji had wanted to wash her car the other day, so she had taken the BMW that day.

"OK, I'll do it. But first I need to change."

"Change? What will you change into?"

"I have something in the car. I'll be right back."

By the time she had gotten her things from the car and walked back, it seemed as if everyone had gathered around the pool to watch her.

As she reentered the solarium, she noticed that someone had moved the furniture into the adjoining room so that she had more space. She dashed into the bathroom to change. When she emerged, she had decided to do the audition piece for them. She set the CD player to "Try Again" and turned the volume dial to the setting that it had been on when she had first entered. Doing a few warm-up exercises to loosen her limbs for the leaps and spins that she was going to do, before hitting the PLAY button, she looked out and saw that Taji and the rest of the young men he had been playing basketball with had joined them.

Remembering that Toki had told her that she couldn't hear the music before, she hit PLAY and stuck her head out the door.

"Is the volume OK? Can you guys hear it?"

She heard a chorus of "Yes" and "Yeah" and "That's good."

Walking back inside, she restarted the music. As the song began she once again let the music take her there. She danced as if she were in front of the judges, executing every dance move precision perfect. But this time she was free to let go and have fun! She danced furiously, kicking, twisting, and spinning, leaping, twirling, and bouncing. She worked her way through the music as it became a part of her and she a part of it. She moved around the floor, thoroughly enjoying herself until the last bar ended and the dance was over.

Everyone broke into applause and Taji, his mom, Toki, and a few others came inside.

Taji's mother spoke first.

"Jadyn that was out of this world! Taji, why didn't you tell us that she was such an amazing dancer?"

Before he could answer, Toki broke in: "You are nothing short of stunning when you dance, Jadyn. We all think so. What are you doing with all this talent?"

By this time, Taji's grandparents had made their way inside.

"Well, I did have an audition for a part with a major traveling dance troupe. I got a callback, too. If I aced that, I probably will be touring with them for an entire year."

The look on Toki's face changed immediately. Taji's father looked away, staring out the windows. She heard a few whispers travel among them.

Jadyn was puzzled. They had all been so excited about her dancing moments before. Why were they acting like she had dropped a bomb on them?

"What's wrong?" she asked.

Grandfather Hietkikko stepped forward.

"This is most disturbing. How can you leave your husband and travel around the country when you are expecting our first great-grandchild?"

Taji took her by the arm and spun her around to face him.

"What do you mean you'll be on tour for a year? Just when did you decide all of this?"

"Wait a minute. What did your grandfather just say? Did he call you my husband? What great-grandchild? What is goin' on here?"

Jadyn looked from him, to his mom, to his Aunt Toki, to his dad—who was looking daggers at her again—to everyone else in the room, and then back to Taji.

He looked as angry as she had ever seen him, his eyes dark and stormy.

"You let me deal with my father and grandfather. I asked you a question. You mean you decided to leave town, and never once thought you needed to discuss that with me first?" He brought his face close to hers and folded his arms across his chest.

She had forgotten that she hadn't told him about the touring part yet. She hadn't felt the need to because the night he had made her climb the walls was the night she had planned to break it off with him. And even though she had decided not to leave him, the subject of her audition just never came up between them again. At least not until now.

Before she could answer him, his father called his name. He stared at her, the fire leaving his eyes and being replaced by ice cold. He turned and left her standing where she was, silently staring at his retreating back.

Taji, his father, and grandfather were out by the pool talking, and from the look of things, it wasn't a very pleasant conversation. Taji's dad was waving his arms around and frowning and Taji looked mad as hell. His grandfather's face remained stoic, yet she could see that he was upset. She sat inside the solarium, observing it all, though she couldn't hear what they were saying to one another.

Taji's aunt and mother had moved the rest of the guests back into the area where all the food was, to give them privacy. Toki had tried to get her to come with them, but she hadn't felt like it. All she really wanted to do was go home.

Jadyn saw Taji throw his hands up in the air and walk away, leaving the other two men standing there. Taji's grandfather moved closer to his son and stood nose-to-nose with him. The tension was obvious between them.

Taji opened the door to the solarium.

"Let's go," was all he said, without really looking at her. She didn't feel like arguing right then, so she just walked by him as he held the door for her. As they walked over the footbridge to the other side of the pool, she heard the grandfather raise his voice, and glanced in that direction. He was saying something in Japanese before turning abruptly and leaving his son standing alone.

14

The drive home was quiet and didn't get any better as they entered the house. Taji threw his keys on the counter and went straight upstairs, taking two steps at a time.

Jadyn walked into the living room and clicked on the television. Not that she really wanted to watch TV, but she didn't feel like dealing with the drama right at the moment. It was just a momentary diversion. In her head she kept hearing Taji's grandfather calling Taji her husband and saying she was carrying his first great-grandchild. She figured from all of the arguing between the three of them that it had been Taji's dad who had lied to the grandfather.

She wanted to call Nite to discuss all that had transpired this evening and to get her perspective, but didn't think it would be wise to discuss things when Taji was obviously still upset. She heard the shower come on and again considered giving Nite a quick call but nixed the idea as she turned the TV off and headed upstairs.

Playing and replaying different scenarios in her head about what she would say to him when he emerged from the shower, she entered the bedroom and immediately went to her dresser where she pulled out her pj's, laying them out on the bed. Returning to the dresser, she opened up the top drawer and removed a shower bonnet to help preserve her curls as long as possible. She closed the door and began removing her earrings along with the other jewelry she wore.

Opening her jewelry box, she carefully replaced the items inside, hanging the necklace on one of the many tiny hooks especially designed to hold them along with the bracelet, earrings, and rings.

Next, she took off her jeans and T-shirt, carefully rehanging them in her closet, before removing her bra and panties and throwing them into a lingerie bag. As she stood naked in front of the closet, Taji opened the door, dressed only in pajama bottoms, and walked into the bedroom. He glanced briefly over in her direction before sitting on the bed, stuffing two pillows behind his back, picking up the remote, and flicking on the TV.

Jadyn threw on a robe, not bothering to close it, picked up her pj's off the bed, and padded barefoot into the bathroom, closing the door behind her. She showered quickly, and gave herself her nightly facial, before returning to the bedroom.

Taji had turned off the TV as well as the light on his side of the bed and was pretending he was asleep. She knew he was pretending, because he could never fall asleep that quickly when he was upset. She sat on her side of the bed, spreading a fresh clean towel on top of the sheet first, and began applying body cream to her legs and thighs.

"So do you want to talk about it, or what?" she asked, trying to keep the frustration from her voice.

She spoke to Taji's back as she continued applying the cream to her arms and elbows, and he refused to turn her way.

"No," he said tightly.

"Why not? You know you not going to be able to sleep unless you get things off your chest."

"I said no and don't forget to put some lotion on that ashy butt of yours," he said, still not budging.

Screwing the lid back on the body cream, she let his last remark go. Ordinarily, it would have been funny, but right now she wasn't sure if he was trying to be funny or if he was just trying to get on her nerves. Folding the towel and laying it atop her nightstand, she pulled her nightshirt over her head, turned out her light, and climbed into bed.

"OK, suit yourself then." She wasn't being a smart-ass, she just hadn't realized how exhausted she was until she had sat on the bed.

After a moment he spoke again.

"So what? You were just gon' leave town without discussing it with me first?"

Jadyn sighed loudly before turning onto her back. "No, Taji. I was going to tell you the other night, but you know what happened. Actually, I wasn't gonna tell you anything, I thought I was going to break up with you. But now, I don't know. I want us to try to work things out."

"Oh, you want to work things out? Gonna be kind of hard for us to do that when you in one city and I'm in another, don't you think?"

"No, I don't think. Look, ain't no need in even talkin' about all this right now, anyway. I haven't got the part yet. Can't we talk about it after we find out for sure?"

"Why the hell not? You done already made up your damn mind anyway." He pulled the covers over his head and scooted as far away from her as he could without falling on the floor, like he always did when he was angry and done talking.

She sighed loudly again before rolling over onto her stomach and closing her eyes, waiting for sleep to come.

15

The phone rang and when Jadyn answered it, Taji's aunt Toki was on the other end.

"Hi Jadyn. I wanted to call and check on you after all the drama that went on last night. Are you doing OK?"

Jadyn was surprised to hear from Taji's aunt. After all, she was his father's sister and they were very close. Even though Jadyn liked her, she really didn't know her that well. And despite all the praise that she had heaped upon Jadyn's dance skills, she just wasn't sure how much she should say to her.

"Hi Toki. I'm doing OK. I guess some people in your family are upset with me though."

"I wouldn't worry about that so much, Jadyn. After all, it's not about what my brother likes or doesn't like, it is about what you and Taji work out. It is your life and his life. You both have to live it out in a way that is best for each of you."

That made sense. She was a bit surprised to hear Toki say anything that might even remotely resemble criticism of her brother. But Jadyn wasn't going to comment one way or the other on what she had just said. It was one thing for your sister to say something about you, and a whole other thing for your son's girlfriend to do the same. She wasn't stupid.

"I want you to know that I really enjoyed your dancing the other night. God has truly blessed you with a gift. You know, Jadyn, when God blesses us with a gift, we have an obligation to share it with the world in the ways that we can. It's almost like it's a sin to waste a great gift or to keep it to ourselves. What I'm trying to say is follow your heart, Jadyn, and everything else will fall into place. Live out your dreams while there is still time. Don't worry about how it might look to others. When talent meets purpose there is nothing that can stop you. Do you understand what I'm saying to you?"

Jadyn thought about it for a moment before answering.

"I think I do. Don't let the opinions of others prevent you from using your gift to reach your dream?"

"Yes, that's pretty much it in a nutshell," Toki said with a giggle. "But I want you to know that I believe in you and I believe in my nephew whom I love very, very much. You both are young and have some growing up to do. Growing can only come through time. It cannot be rushed, no matter how we may wish otherwise. Give yourself time to grow, Jadyn. Give my nephew time, as well. And remember I am here for you if you should ever need someone to talk to. OK?"

Toki was nice and seemed to be sweet, but she just didn't think she would ever confide anything to Taji's aunt. Mostly because she was his dad's sister. She would never be able to get past that.

"Thank you for the offer, Toki. And for your words of encouragement. I really, really appreciate it."

"I meant every word. And Jadyn, if you get the part you auditioned for, please let me know where your first performance will be. I would love to come see you."

"I will, Toki, and thanks again."

16

Jadyn had to rush home after work. Selena hadn't dragged her ass in until after two, so she had been stuck there until then. Selena's lateness was beginning to wear on her last nerve. It would be different if it wasn't just the three of them working there. If Selena was late, or just didn't show, she would be fucking up Jadyn's plans for the day. She hoped that Caroline's weak ass would check her before she had to. She was glad that she had prepared everything the night before and all she had to do was cook. It had taken a lot of planning and preparation to pull off Taji's special dinner.

She planned to have an intimate evening with just the two of them. It would serve two purposes: The first was to celebrate the fact that she had gotten the role in *STOMP*. Oh, they hadn't announced it, but the way they were drooling over her after her performance, she knew that shit was as good as in the bag. The second reason was she'd decided that tonight would be a fresh start for the two of them. She was going to tell him that she had changed her mind about marrying him. He would ask her again and she was going to tell him yes. She realized that she loved Taji, and didn't want to lose him. He didn't need to know that she planned on having a long engagement, at least one year. The time she would be on tour with *STOMP*.

She had made all of Taji's favorite foods, a chef's salad with apples and raisins, beef Stroganoff from scratch with extra beef and sour cream, and homemade rolls. She was going to cheat a little on the rolls, though. She was going to buy yeast rolls at the supermarket that tasted remarkably similar to hers. You still had to bake them and the kitchen would be filled with the aroma of fresh baked bread, so Taji wouldn't know the difference. For dessert she was making her famous red velvet cake with sour cream frosting.

She had also bought a special outfit, especially for him. They had been looking through a magazine together one night, and Taji had commented on how sexy he thought nylons and garters were. So Jadyn had gone out and bought this sexy, sheer red silk nightie, with a matching garter and red hose. She had it all planned. After dinner she would slip into the lingerie before bringing him the dessert. Then, she would see which dessert he'd like to indulge in first, the red velvet cake or red silk her. She smiled slyly to herself. Maybe he could enjoy them both at the same time. Jadyn imagined feeding Taji a bite of cake and him enjoying it with a big smile on his face, and then returning the favor by giving her a treat every bit as delicious as the cake. She smiled again thinking about the last time he'd made love to her. Just the mere thought of it sent a shudder through her body and made her press her thighs together. Yes, he had made her beg for mercy for sure.

But she still couldn't quite figure out why, or even how Taji had managed to turn into such a sensitive type man all of a sudden. One who understood exactly what she needed. And she really wasn't trying to figure that out right at the moment. Not while her body was calling for him. Yeah, and like the group TLC said, she "Ain't 2 Proud 2 Beg" if it came to that.

Ha! Where had that come from? She wasn't about to beg nobody for nothing. Not in this life or the next. Not for sex.

Still, he had blown her mind when he had told her how much he loved her "tiny feet," and "perfect little toes." Then he had shown her by kissing and sucking on each one . . .

On second thought, a little groveling never hurt anyone. Did it?

17

Right before it was time for Taji to walk through the door, she had a moment of panic. What if he didn't want to propose to her again? What if he was still too hurt? Or still too upset with her for not talking to him about the possibility of going on tour with *STOMP*? No, that was silly. Taji had gone out and bought that expensive ring and gone to all of that trouble with the flowers and the dinner a few nights ago. If he loved her enough to propose then, before he had shown her the way to paradise, then he must still want to marry her. Or at least, she hoped so. Oh well, it was too late to worry about all that now. She couldn't just disappear with all the food and decorations. He would be home from work any second.

OK. Where should she greet him? Should she stand beside the door and leap into his arms as soon as he opened the door? No. Maybe she should stretch out on the sofa, propped up on one elbow with a sexy expression on her face? She hopped up on the sofa and arranged herself in what she hoped was a very inviting pose. No, that wasn't going to work, either. He might get the idea that she was ready to get busy right then and there and even worse, if he wanted to have some makeup sex, she might not mind a bit. Then the food would get cold and that would spoil everything. The problem was solved, though, because Taji walked through the door just as she was raising herself up off the couch.

As soon as she saw him, she broke into a smile.

"Hi, baby!" she said as she rushed into his arms.

"Hey, sweetheart!" Taji said, sweeping her up with one arm and trying to keep the other hidden behind his back.

"What are you trying to hide behind your back?" she asked, throwing her arms around his neck and trying to peer behind him at the same time.

"I'm not telling you, nosy," he teased as he reached up and pulled her arms down, capturing her lips with his own. She relaxed and closed her eyes as he brought his other arm around and enveloped her. She enjoyed the kiss for a moment longer before pulling away, as he lifted her up and carried her to the sofa. He sat, pulling Jadyn down onto his lap.

"It's a surprise. Now, would you mind tellin' me what this is all about?" He smiled at her.

Jadyn smiled back. "Well, I can show you better than I can tell you." She said, mimicking the words that he had used on their anniversary. Then she kissed him again before climbing off his lap.

"Come on, I have a few surprises for you, too, and you don't have to wait, neither, at least, not for this first surprise, anyway."

"Oh, so I get more than one?"

"Maybe, maybe not, who's to say?"

Taji grinned and gazed at her with his pretty, tea-brown eyes. Jadyn's pulse raced and she flushed hot, just as she had the first time he had looked at her that way. He pulled her close and kissed her deeply, making his tongue dance around hers, heating her up even more. She forced herself to pull away, though she didn't really want to. She calmed herself with thoughts of what would happen later.

"Come on, Taj. Stop. You're gonna ruin the surprise!"

"OK," he said and allowed Jadyn to drag him into the kitchen.

He stopped right at the doorway and stared. Jadyn had decorated the kitchen so beautifully, he was speechless. The thing that really caught his eye was the huge banner that hung over the table and read, "I love you, Taj!" It was decorated with red balloons and hearts, with a single red rose making the exclamation point. There were more red roses in a vase on the dinner table. And a little black velvet box tied with a single red ribbon sitting in a saucer next to his plate.

He broke into another grin and made a fist that he brought up to his mouth. "Awwww heellll, naw! What did my baby get me?" He began to walk over to the table, but Jadyn pulled him back by his shirttail.

"Not so fast, boy," she teased. "That's for later! Now go on up and take your shower while I finish setting out the food," she told him, pulling him around by his shirttail and pointing him toward the steps.

He gave her another kiss. "OK, but this is gon' be the quickest shower I ever took, because I can smell the food and it is bangin'!" Taji raced up the steps, still talking: "Mmmph, mmmmmmmmmmmph, mmmmmmmmmph! Woooooo! Smells *too* good!"

Jadyn smiled to herself when she could still hear him talking as he turned on the shower.

As Taji showered and she busied herself taking the food out of the fridge and the oven, Jadyn couldn't help but wonder how she was going to begin the *real* conversation that she knew she and Taji needed to have. Right now, she wasn't even sure that she should. They were both so happy at the moment, maybe she should just let the evening play out and if the opportunity arose for them to talk about their problems, and her getting the part in the musical and leaving town for a while, she'd take it. If it didn't, well, she just would worry about it some other time.

Taji came down wearing a pair of jean shorts and nothing else, smelling like a fresh ocean breeze. Jadyn took in his damp, unruly hair, the strong curve of his jaw, and his light chocolate skin. His chest rippled naturally and the hair on his chest was wavy and lay flat against the clearly defined six-pack abs he was sporting. She smiled. Her man *knew* he looked good!

"What do you think you doing? Where's the rest of your clothes?" she asked as Taji moved forward and swept her up in a big hug, swaying slightly from side to side.

"What? Don't front, you know you like what you see," he said, grazing her ear with his lips and tongue.

A little moan escaped from her lips involuntarily, and once again Jadyn found it hard to pull away. She summoned all her will-power to do so.

"Taj, you keep on and both of us are gonna end up missin' out on all this good food I made for you."

"Right, right," Taji said releasing her, walking over to the table and pulling Jadyn's chair out for her.

Jadyn smiled. "Thank you, baby." She reached across the table and picked up the little velvet box that sat in the saucer next to Taji's plate.

"Aw, hold up. I thought you said that we wasn't gon' do this 'til later?"

"Well, I changed my mind. You actin' all hot and stuff and you keep trynna make me all anxious and things, so we better do this while we are both cool, calm, and collected."

"OK, but I gotta run and get mine so hold on."

Taji ran back upstairs, and returned holding a small gift box, neatly wrapped in pink paper, covered in hearts and tied with a little white satin ribbon.

He walked over to Jadyn. "Hello, baby, I missed you," he said, ending his sentence with a kiss.

Jadyn handed Taji his gift before opening hers.

He opened the velvet box as she tore off the wrapping paper. Taji pulled out the gold chain at the same time Jadyn unleashed the tennis bracelet. The bracelet was beautiful, with what appeared to be diamonds and rubies. She hid her disappointment that it didn't contain the ring. They both began to speak at the same time.

"How could you afford this?" he said. Jadyn blushed.

"Sorry. I don't have a rich dad, so I got it at the pawnshop."

Taji gathered Jadyn in his arms. "I love it because it came from you. It doesn't matter where you bought it."

18

Taji piled his plate high with food before finally taking a spoonful of the beef Stroganoff. He closed his eyes and hummed as he chewed.

"Mmmmmmmm, babe. Now *this* is perfection!"

Jadyn blushed. "I'm glad you like it, baby."

"Like it? Baby, that don't even come close! This is crucial!"

"Aw baby, you makin' me blush. So how was your day?" Jadyn asked feeling the need to redirect the conversation.

"It was good, Jay. Except . . . you remember last week when my grandfather was here?" Taji was looking down at his plate, but Jadyn stared directly at Taji. Jadyn knew that he had been working hard, trying to take the family business to the next level. To create opportunities to show his father that his new ideas were a viable way to bring more value to what it had taken generations for the family to build. He was trying to bring new technology in to improve the company's ability to compete in the global marketplace that was just beginning to open up. He had told her that his father and uncle were resisting, trusting in tradition and the way they had always done things.

"Yeah, Taj, what about it?"

Taji took another bite of his food, chewing slowly.

"Girl, you know you can throw down in the kitchen, don't you?

It's one of the reasons I'm keeping you around," he said and gave her a crooked smile, pointing his fork at her as he spoke.

"Will you stop playin' around?"

"OK. Look, when my grandfather was in town, he said that he wants me to work with his team. He said that he believes in the direction I want to take the company and he is behind me a hundred percent, but he wants me to get a better handle on the corporate end of things."

Jadyn ran around the table and sat on his lap.

"Taji, that is wonderful! Now your dad and uncle are gonna have to take you seriously! I'm so happy for you!"

Taji's grandfather had the final say in everything. That's just the way it was. The Hietkikko family had very traditional Japanese values, so the elders were still revered and their opinions were given the ultimate respect. And honor was everything.

Then it was her turn to gaze into Taji's eyes in the way that always made her weak in the knees. Jadyn could feel his erection begin to poke her in the behind. She tried to rise, but he pulled her back down on his lap.

"Taj, you gonna mess up our dinner . . ."

"It can wait. That's why they invented microwaves," he said, between kisses.

Then he scooped her breast out of her bra and ducked his head under her shirt. He flicked his tongue lightly over her nipple before sucking it into his mouth. She let her head roll back into her shoulder and moaned softly, losing herself in the motion of his tongue.

"Ahhh, Taj . . . Taji . . ."

"Yes, baby?" he asked, only releasing her nipple for a moment to speak, before capturing it between his lips and ravaging it more savagely.

"Taj . . . wait, baby, please . . . stop . . ."

"Why, baby? Hunh? I don't want to . . . ," Taji said, his voice growing hoarse with desire and he released her other breast and applied his tongue there.

"Unh, Taj, baby . . . I . . . I . . . Oh! Taj . . . I got . . . I . . . got a . . . surprise . . . please . . ."

Taji brought his head up and locked his eyes on hers. "You sure you want me to stop?"

"Hell no, I don't *want* you to stop. Is you crazy?" They both burst into laughter.

"Girl, you somethin' else. This surprise better be worth it," he teased, giving her behind a light spank as she rose from his lap.

"I'll let you be the judge of that," she said, smiling, and crooking her finger to signal that he should follow her up the stairs.

In the bedroom, Jadyn grabbed something out of the drawer and scooted into the bathroom closing the door behind her.

"Jadyn," he protested.

"Chill Taj, this ain't gonna take but a hot second," she said, opening the door and peeking out.

She watched as Taji eased his shorts off, his erection bounced down and back, finally standing straight up as he laid on top of the bed. He picked up the remote to turn on the TV, and then turned it off again. When he picked up the remote for the CD player she knew that he had decided music would be better. He turned on the CD player and immediately Joe's smooth voice began to fill the room.

"Baby, I wanna do
All of the things your man won't do . . ."

She stood in the bathroom doorway watching Taji, fascinated by what he was doing. She couldn't help but smile as he frowned at the words of Joe's song. He shook his head, and she could tell he wasn't trying to put thoughts of another man in her head. Especially not tonight or any other night for that matter. He flicked the button to change the CD player to another selection. The harmony of Silk drifted into the room and he smiled.

Here we are, just the two of us together

Yes, Yes. That was more like it. Jadyn agreed with his selection. Silk would definitely set the right mood and tone for what she had in mind. She closed the bathroom door and hurriedly changed into the outfit she had so carefully selected for the night's festivities. She could hear Taji's voice as he joined in with Silk and sang the next line of the song loudly.

" 'Don't keep me waiting, I've waited so long! I want to be right inside your arms, baby! Don't make me wait for you . . .' "

Jadyn opened the door at that moment and stood in the doorway briefly before she strolled over to the bed. Taji stopped singing and his mouth fell open. Jadyn had let her long auburn hair down and it flowed softly around her shoulders. The sheer material she was draped in did nothing to hide her bangin' body. The material hugged the deep curve of her waist and she knew that he still couldn't believe how tiny her waist was. He had told her often enough. She could almost see his body tremble as he drank in the way the ruby-red silk clung to her waist and the matching garter stretched across her beautifully shaped thighs. The red silk stockings caressed the curve of her finely chiseled calves accentuating them nicely. Jadyn had always loved the way silk felt so luxurious against her skin and could make her feel absolutely drop-dead gorgeous. His hard-on grew even more as he drew her close and made contact with the soft material. He touched her lightly and her skin grew warm under the contact of his fingertips. He seemed speech-less as he knelt before her, took her around the waist and lifted her up on the bed. Taking one of her feet in his hands, he began kiss-ing the soles of each one, as she enjoyed the thrill of his tongue against the slick fabric. *"Slow down, baby please don't rush . . ."* Silk sang softly in the background and Jadyn had to agree with them. Her body was on fire, she wanted Taji so badly, but if tonight was going to be anything like the last time, she knew that he was going to control himself, take his time, and give her all the pleasure his imagination could conjure.

He ran his tongue over her toes and she shuddered as a soft moan escaped her lips. He traveled upward, igniting a flame with his lips all the way. Lifting her leg onto his shoulder, he buried his face in the satiny, soft flesh behind her knee. He inhaled deeply, and she knew that he must be enjoying the sweet smell of her, be-fore sucking and kissing her there. Jadyn moaned louder and lifted her hips off the bed.

"Ohhhhhhhhhh, Taj . . ."

"Yes, baby?"

Jadyn loved the pleasurable feeling of Taji's tongue there. She couldn't understand how the spot behind her knee could bring such pleasure.

He played there a little while longer, kissing his way down her thigh before dropping his head between her legs.

As he continued to explore her intimately, he took his fingers and opened her up more, fully exposing her. He licked and lapped and sucked hard, alternately gently pulling on her clit with his lips. She relished in the way Taji moaned as she pushed her hips up and back.

Oh, the man in the boat! It had taken Taji a while to locate him but now that he had finally discovered his hiding place and nudged him out of his spot, he was worrying that man to death every chance he got.

And Jadyn was loving every single minute of it!

19

Jadyn didn't know how long she had slept, but she awoke to the sound of Taji speaking in a low whisper. She stirred and sat up, already feeling a little sore from the mad lovemaking they had engaged in.

Taji was in the bathroom with the door closed. She glanced over at the nightstand beside the bed and saw that the cordless phone they kept there was missing. Why had he felt the need to go into another room to answer the phone? Jadyn strained her ears toward the sound of Taji's voice drifting from behind the bathroom door. She could barely make out what he was saying.

"Listen, Rome, I keep tellin' you I don't know what you talkin' about. I haven't told anyone to fix shit with some woman. What woman are you speaking about? The other woman? What woman? The shit is a mystery to me, I haven't spoken to my father about nothin'. Matter of fact what's my father have to do with what you talkin' about? You're making no sense whatsoever, man!"

"What the fuck?" Jadyn said under her breath. Who the hell was he talking to? She felt her temper rise. She just knew that he wasn't cheating on her and talking about some woman on the phone after making love to her the way he just had. How could he?

She threw the covers back, eased out of the bed, and tiptoed down the stairs. She picked up the extension in the living room, pressing the MUTE button as she did.

". . . I don't understand, Rome. You said you took care of things?"

"Yeah, man. Thangs is cool. Thangs went down, just like they was supposed to. I made a few calls, slashed a couple tires . . . the part in STOMP is no longer a possibility for your girl . . . So when do I get my dough?"

"Man, what the fuck are you talkin' about?"

"Whatchu mean what the fuck I'm talkin' 'bout? What the fuck is you talkin' 'bout playa? The shit is taken care of so pay me my money and I'm ghost!"

Jadyn's anger bubbled over. She released the mute button. "What services you did you pay for, Taji?" she couldn't help but asking.

She heard a loud "fuck" on the other end and then the dial tone.

"Jadyn? What the . . . ," she heard Taji's voice break in. "Hang up the damn phone!" he ordered.

"I ain't hangin' up shit! How could you do this, Taj?" She felt her anger turn to an overwhelming hurt as disbelief clouded her mind. Would he be this dirty and low-down? Would he fuckin' mess up her dreams just to get what he wanted? Tears welled up in her eyes.

"This is some straight-up bullshit!" Taji said before she heard a *click* as he hung up the phone.

Jadyn heard Taji's footsteps running down the stairs.

"Just what do you think you doin'? Hunh? What gives you the right to fuckin' eavesdrop on my calls?"

"You are fuckin' jokin', right?" Jadyn couldn't believe her ears. Just like a man to try to flip the script when his ass has been caught in some scandalous shit. Jadyn walked right up to Taji and stood toe-to-toe with him although in her bare feet she only came to his chest.

"Oh, no! Unh-unh. The real question is, what the fuck were you and that damn thuggish ass Rome talkin' about just now? Hunh? I know he wasn't talking about fuckin' around with the people who run *STOMP* now was he? Tell me I'm wrong, Taji. Tell me that that muhfucka didn't just tell you you owe him money for messin' up my part in *STOMP!*"

Taji stared at her in disbelief.

"The fuck's the matter with you, Jadyn? Why do you always think you know what's going on without asking? You have no fuckin' idea what the hell you just did, who the fuck I was talkin' to, but because you think something in your damn silly-ass head, that's automatically the way it is!"

Taji's voice was rising with his anger.

"What I think? What else am I supposed to think when I wake up and you're talking on the phone behind a closed door in the middle of the night? And it happens to be some damn scandalous ass thug!"

"You ain't supposed to think shit! You supposed to ask me what the fuck is going on, not assume your silly ass know shit! 'Cause you ain't got a fuckin' clue!"

"I don't have a clue?" Jadyn flung her hair as she spoke. "I got more than a clue. Seem to me your ass is the clueless one. I don't speak to thugs about my life. Especially thugs like that scum of the earth Rome, who would cut his own grandmother's throat for the right price. So tell me this: How in the fuck would he know anything about me and my audition for *STOMP?*"

"I don't know! That is what I was trynna find out before your ass decided to play that sneaky ass spy shit, eavesdroppin' on my gotdamn calls and shit!"

"You know what, this ain't about you and your fuckin' right to privacy shit. You always trynna make shit about you!" She shook her head and threw her hands up as she tried to move around him.

"I'm done, Taj. I'm done. Finished! There it is! I am finished with this relationship. I am tired of this shit. I say something and you take over. You make every fuckin' thing about *you*. You couldn't care less about the real issue here."

Taji stepped in front of her.

"Oh, is that right? If you don't like the shit I do, there are plenty of women out there who will! There ain't no pleasing a bitch like you."

Bitch? Did he just call her a bitch?

"Take your ass on down the road then. I guaran-damn-tee yo' ass that another bitch ain't gon' have no problem with puttin' this shit on and wearin' it!" He began ripping open boxes and pulling out designer jeans, blouses, and shoes and flinging them across the room.

"Yeah, I'm sure that they will. So go ahead and go for yours," Jadyn said as she tried to move around him again. "Ain't no need to froth at the mouth and shit. Go get yours, I'm out!"

Taji again blocked her path.

"No need to what? Didn't you hear me tellin' that nigga that I didn't know what the fuck he was talkin 'bout? I'm as much in the dark about the shit as you!"

"Then why would he even know to call here? The shit makes no sense! So don't try to play me like some slow, lame broad who can't think on her own, OK?"

It was Taji's turn to throw his hands up in frustration as he stepped aside.

"That what you think of me? That's what you want? Fine. You want to leave? Go! Go on . . . get to steppin', then."

Jadyn stared at Taji, suddenly unsure if he was really letting her go. But she wasn't prepared to leave right that moment. Where would she go? She had thought that she would continue to live there until she left with the dance company for the first stop on the tour. But how could she tell him that now? How could she tell him that after he may have ruined all her plans for his own selfish reasons? His eyes held so much pain, she wanted him to explain this mess to her. To make it right, or make it disappear. But he couldn't and neither could she. It was what it was.

"What you waitin' on? I said get the fuck out my face!"

"Let me get my stuff," she said and began to walk toward the stairs.

"Yeah, you do that, you get your shit and get the fuck out my house!"

She moved past him and ran upstairs. Suddenly realizing she had to pee, Jadyn stormed into the bathroom, started to sit on the toilet seat, but noticed the pee splashes, in the nick of time, and did a little whoopsie swivel to avoid sitting.

"Damn that, Taji! I told him a million times to put up the fuckin' seat when he take a piss!" she mumbled to herself as she grabbed the end of the toilet paper roll and snatched a piece off to wipe the seat.

As she sat relieving herself, she contemplated the circumstances of her life. Every man she ever knew always let her down. Was always fuckin' up her plans.

Jadyn stood, flushed the toilet, and stepped to the sink to wash her hands. As she soaped her hands, she rubbed them together until they were white with lather, trying to scrub away the troubles she and Taji were having. Or maybe it was the nightmare that was her life that she was trying to wash away.

In the room she had shared with Taji for eight months, she pulled out the biggest piece of luggage from her Versace set and flipped it open. She had just begun filling it with her belongings when she heard something move outside her door. Taji entered the room.

"I ain't even goin' out like this! You ain't playin' me for no bitch-ass nigga like this! You gon' keep yo' ass here and you gon' keep doin' the same shit you been doin'. Takin' those fuckin' dance classes and goin' yo' ass to work!"

Taji began taking Jadyn's things from the suitcase and tossing them back into the drawer and Jadyn kept taking them out and flinging them back into the suitcase. Finally, Jadyn grabbed on to a pair of jeans at the same time Taji did. Taji kept trying to snatch the jeans out of her hands but Jadyn held on tight, even though she was being slung back and forth as Taji tried to wrestle them from her hands. Jadyn suddenly released her hold and Taji fell back against the dresser drawer.

"What is up with you, Taj? Didn't you not five minutes ago tell me to get the fuck out? Am I trippin'? That was you, wasn't it?"

"I don't give a fuck about that. I'm tellin' you now your ass ain't goin' nowhere!"

"Oh yeah? I'm goin'! I'm leaving and you might as well get fuckin' used to it! You can't stop me. There ain't a muhfuckin' person on this planet that can stop me. Now, we can do this easy or we can do it hard! It makes no damn difference to me!"

Taji moved closer to her and pointed his finger in her face.

"I said, you're not goin' nowhere."

Jadyn pushed his finger away from her face.

"And just how you plan on stoppin' me?"

She glared at him, reaching up and pushing that stubborn lock of hair out of her face again before propping her hands on her hips.

"A'ight, then," Taji turned on his heels and left the room once again, slamming the door after him.

Jadyn stared at the door for a moment before she went back to packing her bags, making sure that she only packed the things she had bought for herself and not taking anything Taji bought her. Although she hated leaving some of the jewelry, especially the gold chain with her name inscribed in diamonds and rubies on a charm and the matching bracelet that was also diamond-inscribed with *"Taj and Jay."* It was the first nice piece of jewelry he had bought her. But she left both pieces on top of the dresser. She didn't want or need the drama that taking it might cause with Taji feeling the way he did right about now. She thought she heard the doorknob jiggle and prayed that Taji wasn't coming back. She was tired of arguing and she just wanted to leave. She didn't quite know where she was going, but she knew she had to get out of there. When he didn't enter the room, she took her box of jewelry from the dresser drawer and placed it on top of the clothing in the large suitcase.

She heard the doorknob jiggle again and glanced in that direction.

"Taj?"

He didn't answer, so she walked over to the door and tried to open it. The knob spun in her hands, but didn't engage the catch. The door wouldn't open.

"What the fuck?"

She grabbed the knob with both hands and twisted.

"Taji, open the fuckin' door! Open it, now! What the fuck is this? You a kidnapper now?"

"You can't be a kidnapper in your own home," he said from the other side of the door.

"Taji, what is this gonna solve? You know you can't keep me locked in here forever. When you do open the fuckin' door, I'm out! So quit playin'!"

"Ain't nobody playin'. I'm just givin' you a little time to think about what you doin'. Make you realize all you about to give up. Really, love. It's for your own good."

Jadyn's temper was rising as she beat on the door with her fists and kicked it with her feet.

"Let me out of here!"

"Not 'til you get your mind right."

Jadyn kicked the door again. She beat on it with her fists and kicked it again before leaning her back against it, tears of anger and frustration running down her cheeks.

She couldn't even call the police because Taji had the handset for the cordless phone they kept by the bed. She couldn't use her cell phone, either. It was still downstairs by the door where she had dropped her bag as she had come into the house.

She turned and grabbed the knob with both hands, as if she could make the door open.

"Damn you, Taji! Let me outta here!"

She glanced around the room at all of Taji's things. The big screen TV, the Dolby surround sound stereo system, his framed autographed Michael Jordan and Shaquille O'Neal jerseys, and assorted other valuable items.

She pulled a chair from her dressing table and climbed up on it so that she could remove the framed Michael Jordan jersey from the wall. She did the same with the Shaquille O'Neal one. She knew he loved his stuff more than anything in the world. Maybe even more than he did her.

"If you don't open this door, I'ma start bustin' up shit in here! And Michael Jordan is going first!" she yelled through the door.

Silence.

"I'm not fuckin' playin' with you!"

More silence.

She flung the jersey against the wall, shattering the glass. Following that with Shaq's jersey.

More silence.

Her anger boiled over as she karate kicked the stereo and sent it crashing to the floor. She tried kicking the big screen TV but it didn't budge. Bracing her back against the sides, she began trying to push it over, but all she could manage was to rock it back and forth. She heard a scraping sound outside of the door and imagined that Taji was moving whatever he had pushed in front of the door out of the way.

She picked up one of the heavy metal vases and raised it up in the air. Just as she was about to hurl it at the screen, he burst through the door.

"No, Jay, no!" He held his hand in front of him as if the motion could make her stop.

She still held the vase in the air, tears streaming down her cheeks, breathing hard from all the destruction.

"Baby, don't! Don't . . . you can go . . . for real . . . I'm not gon' try to stop you this time."

She began to lower the vase. "Don't fuckin' play me, Taji, I ain't jokin'."

"Ain't nobody trynna play nobody . . . Jay, you just don't trust me! You really don't trust no one. That's the bottom line. And without trust, we ain't got nothin' anyway."

She dropped the vase and picked up her bags. She threw one over her shoulder and took the other one by the handle. Dragging the heavy suitcase behind her, she eased past Taji.

"Ain't nobody ever given me a reason to trust."

He just stood there, motionless. Even as she bumped the heavy suitcase down the steps and out the door. Even as she loaded it into the car.

She reentered to get her last bag and saw that Taji had finally moved from the bedroom to the top of the stairs. She picked up her bag, which held her audition clothes, and her purse. She glanced up at him as she flung the bag over her shoulder.

"Oh yeah, don't even bother to come lookin' for me tomorrow or ever. I'm leaving town first chance I get. I don't ever want to see your face again!"

She closed the door a little too hard without another word.

20

"What's up, Nite? You got plans for tonight?" Jadyn quizzed her cousin, knowing all the while what the answer would be.

"What? You mean besides being heated that I broke up with Justice last week, and trying to figure out a way to make him take me out tonight without sounding like I'm beggin'? Absolutely nothing, cuz. Why? What's up?"

"Want to do something that will take your mind off of all that and help your favorite cousin out at the same time?" Jadyn smiled, hoping she could transmit her feelings through the telephone and they would land in Nite's heart. She didn't think she could carry out her plans without her cousin's help.

"Tell me that you are *not* about to ask me to run you nowhere this time of the night? Please tell me I'm trippin' and that you can't *possibly* be for real?"

Jadyn's smile faded and her heart began beating faster. "Aw, come on, Nite. What I need you to ride me around for when I got my own car? Don't be stupid."

"Well, your shit coulda broke down or somethin', how the fuck would I know? So if that ain't it then what's up?"

Jadyn swallowed hard. It was crazy that she had actually left Taji. Now that she was really away from the house, she was beginning to feel the loss. Had he really paid someone to mess up her chances at getting the part in *STOMP*? She wondered if she had done the right thing, especially after the way he had made love to her tonight. Could he make love to her so good and then do something so dirty? How had it all gone so bad so quickly?

"I left Taji and I got no place to go."

"Whaaaaaaaaaat? You for real?"

"Yes, I'm for real. You know me and Taji been having problems lately. We . . . had a fight and I need to crash at your crib for a minute."

"Damn, Jay. I can't believe you did that. Taj is fine as hell, got money and money's mammy. And didn't mind spending it on you, neither."

"Look, I feel bad enough right about now, Nite. I don't need you pointing out alla Taji's virtues right at this moment, OK?"

"My bad, cuz. It's just that all the women be lookin' at him like he's a juicy steak, and they are some hungry wolves that ain't had a meal in a year."

Jadyn sighed. "I know that, damn. I need you tonight, Nite! Look, I don't know if me and Taji are going to be able to make things work if we keep going on the way we are. That's why I needed to leave. At least I thought it was a good idea at the time. But now . . . Look, can you just tell me if I can crash there for a while? I'm worn out as hell from all this fuckin' drama . . ."

"You know you ain't even gotta ask that shit. Bring your ass on over here."

"Open the door," she said, popping the lock and climbing out of the car. "I'm already outside."

"Well damn!" was all Nite could say as she opened the front door.

"I'm here for you, Jay. You know I'm crazy about you and I don't have a problem with you stayin' with me anytime you need to, but I need to know what happened with you and Taji."

Nite walked over to Jadyn and handed her a cup of tea. Nite always had some type of tea handy. She generally thought that a hot cup of tea could cure anything.

"That buster didn't put his hands on you did he? 'Cause if he did, I'ma get Dad to go over there and show him a little sumpn' sumpn'."

Jadyn laughed.

"You know better than that. Taji is anything but a woman beater. To hit a woman wouldn't even enter his mind. And what Uncle Earl gon' do? Yeah, he was considered gangsta, back in the day. But don't you think he gettin' a little old for that shit right about now?"

"Your moms won't tell you he's gettin' old after he kicked off in Zane's ass a few years ago."

"Yeah, he did break that fool off some, didn't he?" she said, giving Nite the high-five.

"Sure did. Beetlejuice didn't have shit on him when dad got through."

Jadyn stopped laughing. She never had much liked her mom's boyfriends, but Zane had been the worst one of all. Introducing her mom to freebasing cocaine and then crack. And ultimately bringing that fuckin' murderous Quin into their lives. Quin was the one that visited her in her damn nightmares every night. She would never forget how he had aimed the gun at her and fired, but ended up shooting her mother instead before the police gunned him down.

She took a sip from her cup of tea before setting it back down on the table. Nite noticed the change in Jadyn and was sorry she had brought up the hurtful memories.

"My life back then was a trip. I still have nightmares about that fool trynna kill me and Mom."

Nite tried to redirect the conversation.

"So what happened with you and Taji? What made you want to leave him?"

"This shit has been building for a while now. It ain't just one thing, it's everything. Shit, he wasn't even a good lover most of the time we were together. Not until the last few times, anyway. His ass must have known that I had made up my mind to leave him or some shit, 'cause his ass been gettin' busy. That nigga pulled out every trick in the book and then some. I mean he set my ass on fire and then hosed me down better than ever!"

"Girl, hush!"

"Yeah, the shit had me confused as fuck! He had me twisted after the way he made love to me. I was ready to give us another try. He even bought me a ring."

Nite leapt out of her chair and ran over and pulled Jadyn out of her chair almost knocking the hot tea over. She started dancing Jadyn around in a circle.

"He asked you to marry him! He asked you to marry him!" Nite squealed. But then a thought hit her and she stopped spinning them around.

"Hold up. If his ass gave you a ring, why in the hell would you leave him? Shit! I been tryin' to get Justice's ass to buy me one for damn near a year!"

Jadyn sat back down in her chair and picked up her tea again, taking another sip.

"Yeah. Well, I ain't trynna get married. Like I told you, I had a a callback for my audition for *STOMP* last week, and—"

Nite jumped up from her chair squealing again. She started toward Jadyn but she stopped in her tracks when Jadyn gave her a look.

"Don't come over here spinning me around and shit no more! My ass is still dizzy. Just sit your ass down and listen."

"I know, I know, but damn! Did you get the part?" Nite asked.

"Not yet, girl. But if I get it I'm gonna be leaving to travel anyway. So I guess I thought now would be as good a time as any to break up with Taji. But that was before he made love to me the way he did, and got me all confused an' shit. Now I'm not so sure breaking up is what I want."

"Then why did you?"

"'Cause . . ."

Nite walked around the table and pulled a chair close to her cousin. She no sooner had placed a hand on her shoulder than Jadyn buried her face in her shoulder and began sobbing.

"This part is everything to me right now, Nite! I want this more than I have ever wanted anything! I'm sick of this town, I need to leave here."

Nite held her cousin tight and tried to give her comfort, trying hard not to cry her damn self.

"Jay, don't cry. You just got too much shit coming at you all at once. Those judges ain't no fools. They recognize talent when they see it. You got hella talent, cuz, don't you ever doubt that! You gonna be the star you was born to be. Believe that!"

Jadyn pulled away from her cousin and stood to her feet, wiping her face hard with the palms of her hands to dry the tears.

"You don't understand, Nite. I'll never know now whether I was good enough or not, because Taji paid somebody to scare the judges into not hiring me."

Nite's eyes grew huge and her mouth dropped open.

"What? Why in the hell would he do some shit like that?"

Jadyn sat down hard. "I can't figure that shit out. If he loved me, he had to know that it would be over for us if I ever found out. So why would he take that chance?"

"Jay, you sure? That is some extra foul shady shit. He just don't seem like he would be that low-down and dirty."

"Yeah, the heart is an evil thing. Given the right situation even angels can turn into devils. But I'm not gon' lie, Nite. The shit makes no sense and if I hadn't heard the shit with my own ears, I would never have believed the shit, either.

"After that, we got into a bad argument. And Taji wasn't trynna let me leave and I ended up breaking up some of his shit. Some of his treasures and . . . the shit is just all fucked up!"

"Yeah, you shoulda at least waited to see if you was gonna get the part or not."

Jadyn gave Nite another look.

"Whose side are you on anyway? You really know how to make me feel better. *Not!* Look, it don't seem like we gonna be able to work it out. And if he pulled that shady shit, ain't nothin' to work out."

"Right! That's the exact same damn thing I was thinking about me and Justice. Maybe we need some time apart, too."

"Nite, you know you ain't gonna stay broke up with Justice. You know you ain't gonna do nothin' but sit around waiting for him to call and make up with you. You know Justice knows that, too. You know he gon' be all spiteful and shit and he ain't even gon' call for a while to teach you a lesson and try to . . ." Jadyn didn't get to finish her sentence because Nite burst into tears.

"Jay! You didn't even have to go there. I'm not strong as you, Jay. I miss Justice too much. I knooow Justice ain't gonna call and I'ma end up giving in and calling his ass first. I can't help it! I'm a weakling when it comes to him. I ain't gon' sit here and lie about it."

Jadyn sighed. She couldn't help but feel sorry for the way she had spoken to Nite. There was no reason to make her miserable, too.

"Don't cry, Nite. I'm sorry. I didn't mean to get you all upset or anything. . . . It'll be all right, you'll see. Justice doesn't want to be away from you any more than you want to be away from him."

Nite sniffled as she spoke.

"You really think so, Jay? You think he'll call me?"

"Yeah, Nite," Jadyn told her. "You know that boy can't stand not having that 'whip appeal' of yours for very long!"

Nite broke into a smile through her tears. "Yeah, you probably right. Me and Justice ain't never had a problem there."

Jadyn got up and put her cup in the sink, glancing at the clock on the range top. Damn! Three a damn clock in the morning. She had to get a least a few hours sleep. She was planning on getting up early to try and talk to the judge, to see if Rome had really fucked with one of them.

"Where you want me to sleep, Nite? I need to crash. I gotta get up early and try to find out what's going on with the audition."

"You know you got the other bedroom, Jay. Why you keep askin' crazy questions?"

Oh, I'm the one that's been asking crazy questions?

"OK, I'll see you in the morning."

"All right, cuz. Clean towels in the guest bathroom, if you want to take a shower."

"OK. Thank you. That sounds good. Maybe a good, hot shower will help me get to sleep quicker."

21

Jadyn couldn't understand why Taji would pull some foul shit like interfering with her future.

The judge told her that the part had gone to Madoline.

Jadyn's world spun.

"Wait . . . there has to be some mistake. You liked my performance—no, no you *loved* my performance. You couldn't even contain the excitement you felt over my dancing. Even Madoline felt it! Why? I just don't understand . . ."

"Yes, well, I believe I told you that there were other things that we had to consider, besides talent. You were both talented, but we had to weigh . . . other factors."

Jadyn began to cry. She didn't even try to hide it.

The judge softened. "Look, Jadyn, I'm going to go off the record and tell you this: You had the part, we all think that you are more than talented. You have that certain something that separates stars from the rest of us. But quite frankly, we don't take threats and intimidation very well."

Just like that her fears about Taji were confirmed.

"Wait, sir, I can explain. You can't hold something against me that I knew nothing about. Please, give me a chance to explain," she begged tearfully.

"I'm sorry but explanations are no good at this point. Madoline has already been given the part. I do hope you understand. Goodbye, Jadyn. I wish you well."

And then she heard the dial tone. She had been living with a lying, lowly snake. Too late she had found out how full of venom his bite had been. He had sunk his fangs deep and poisoned all her dreams.

Just like her stepfather Ian had.

She buried her face in her hands and tears streamed down her face as her past and present collided. Visions of Ian sneaking into her room late at night and sliding under her covers, naked. Whispering in her ear, making her so afraid as she whimpered in the darkness, helpless and alone, as his hands fumbled inside her panties.

Jadyn wept at the loss of her childhood. She wept because once again she had been betrayed by a man who was supposed to love, cherish, and protect her.

And she wept because once again she had been betrayed by a man who had only pretended to love her.

22

That evening at Nite's apartment, Jadyn shut herself up in her room, climbed in bed, and pulled the covers up over her head. When Nite got home from work and came to check on her, she just pretended that she was asleep.

But she couldn't sleep. She was feeling overwhelmed by all of the recent events in her life. From breaking up with Taji, to finding out what a fucking, no good nigga he really was, to wanting to find her real dad, and most of all, being cheated out of what could have been her one big chance to break into the type of dancing that she craved: the respect and validation that came with dancing in an off-Broadway production and traveling around the country at the same time.

Her heart was breaking under all the pressure and she felt that somehow, somebody had sneaked into the room while she wasn't looking and injected lead into her veins. Her body was suddenly so heavy, she could barely pull herself out of bed to go to the bathroom.

She cried so much, her eyes were aching and burning from her wiping them with Kleenex. She could find comfort in nothing.

Nothing seemed to matter any longer. At the moment, she didn't care if—when she was finally able to fall asleep—she never woke up again.

She didn't emerge from her room for two days. Didn't shower, didn't brush her teeth, didn't change her clothes, nothing. She just lay under the covers. She couldn't even remember when she had eaten last or what that last meal had been. And she didn't care because she wasn't hungry.

On the third day, Nite had had enough. She didn't even bother knocking, she just barged into the room.

"Get up, Jay, we're going to church!" she announced.

"What? Get the fuck outta here. I ain't goin' nowhere. I'm not gettin' out of this bed. And who told you to come in my room anyway?"

"The last time I looked, my signature was the only one on the lease on this bad boy. So I do believe I can walk into any part of this place that I see fit."

Jadyn pulled the covers up over her head. "Well, see fit to walk your ass in some other part because this part is occupied right now."

Nite snatched the covers off her head.

"Come on now, Jay, get your ass up! It doesn't take a rocket scientist to figure out that you are depressed, and I'm not gon' just sit around and do nothing while you lay up in here marinating in your own funk and slowly starving yourself to death."

Jadyn slowly sat up in bed, angrier than ever.

"Would you please just get the hell out of here and leave me alone?"

Nite fanned her hand in front of her face. "Pee-yew! Your ass ain't the only thing that's funky! God, your breath is ripe!"

"I told you to leave!" Jadyn said, presenting her back to her cousin.

"No I won't, troll! Now get your ass up! If you don't, I'm gon' make the biggest pitcher of ice water I can find and pour it all over your ass."

Jadyn twisted the upper part of her body and turned her head toward Nite, narrowed her eyes, pursed her lips and gave her cousin the most evil look.

"Oooooooooooo! I can't stand you! Always messin' with somebody! What in the hell makes you think I want to go sit in church with a bunch of crooks and hypocrites?"

"It ain't about that and you know it. You are at a low point in your life and you need someone to pray for you. Even I can figure that out!"

"Oh now you playin' that Christian role, hunh? I been inside a church since your sinful behind has!"

Nite put her hand on her cousin's back and made her voice soft for the first time since she had entered the room.

"You are carrying a load way too heavy for one person, Jay. I don't know how to help you and I don't want it to make you snap. I'm worried about you, cuz. Come on, now. We could both use a little prayer, don't you think?"

Jadyn looked at Nite's face and could see all of the worry and concern. Her eyes were filled with tears and she was trying hard not to let them fall.

Jadyn hugged her. "I guess it couldn't hurt to go and get some of the Word inside me. I feel like shit, that ain't no lie. I'm going to go with you just because you need it just as much if not more than me."

They both smiled.

"Well, you need to get up and get in the shower. It's eight forty-five and the church we going to starts at ten o'clock or ten thirty."

With much effort, Jadyn threw her legs over the side of the bed and sat up.

"What church are we going to? And how are you going to wake me up to go somewhere with you and not know exactly what time we gotta be there?" She stood up and as she did, caught a whiff of her own funk. "Pee-yew! I stank!"

"See, that's what I'm saying. So we're going to this little church called the Remnant Church. It's not one of those big mega-churches that we both don't like. The pastor is kind of young, only about thirty-nine or forty-one or something like that."

Jadyn shed the three-day old T-shirt and sweats that she had slept in all that time, and dropped them into her laundry basket. She grabbed a towel from the linen closet and walked over to the bathroom. Nite followed.

"To tell you the truth, I could care less who the pastor is, or how old he is, either. I told you before, I'm only doing this for you. What are you wearing anyway?" she asked as she turned the taps and lifted the knob for the shower. She held her hands under the spray as it sprang from the shower head to gauge the temperature, adjusting the knobs until it felt just right.

"Shoot, the jeans and T-shirt I have on. That's the good thing about this church, when they say come as you are they mean come as you are. They ain't on that dress-for-success-type crap."

Jadyn was glad of that. She didn't even feel like dressing up today. She dropped her bra and panties and stepped into the shower. As she stood under the spray she started to feel a little better. The steamy jets felt good as they massaged her body with the soothing spray.

"That's good to know. I think if you'd said anything else I would've jumped back into bed. Be ready in about fifteen minutes."

23

As they walked up the three steps to the church and entered the hallway that led to the sanctuary, Jadyn was glad to learn that her cousin hadn't lied to her about either the dress code or the fact that the church was relatively small. As they walked in, an usher hugged them both and handed them a bulletin that contained offering envelopes.

"Welcome, sisters. Please, help yourself to some refreshments, eating *is* allowed in the sanctuary."

Jadyn and Nite both spoke to each other with their eyes.

Well, this is new and different, their eyes said. They were used to ushers saying just the opposite.

"Please no chewing gum or candy allowed in the sanctuary" was what one was more prone to hear when entering church on a Sunday morning.

As they walked past the continental breakfast that was spread out across a long table, Jadyn's stomach rumbled loudly and did a little flip. Her appetite had suddenly returned. The delicious aroma of coffee lured her over to check out the breakfast fare.

There was bottled water, orange juice, tea, bagels, both apple-cinnamon and cinnamon-raisin muffins, banana-nut bread, and an absolutely heavenly looking fruit salad that almost made her mouth water. There were peaches, ripe red strawberries, pineapple slices, grapes, and several types of melon. Oh yes, Jadyn didn't know what Nite was going to do, but she would definitely accept the usher's invitation to help herself. Reaching into her purse, she pulled out her handy travel-size bottle of hand sanitizer and stepping away from the spread momentarily, squirted a small amount of liquid into her palms. Her cousin was suddenly right at her side and stuck her hands out for a squirt.

Jadyn looked at her and smiled.

"Oh yeah. You know I'm 'bout to get my grub on, too," she said.

She and Jadyn turned back to the table and picked up foam plates. Jadyn dug into the fruit salad and added a slice of banana-nut bread. She picked up a plastic knife and fork and grabbed a bottle of water before standing off to the side to wait for Nite. Nite filled her plate with two bagels and cream cheese and she held a cup of orange juice in her hand instead of bottled water. They both entered the sanctuary together.

Never one to sit in the back, Jadyn chose to sit in a row of seats closer to the middle of the sanctuary and Nite followed her. As they took their seats and balanced their food on their laps, Nite nudged her cousin in the ribs.

"Why did you sit here? Almost in the front of the church?"

Jadyn nudged her back. "We ain't in no front. Since when did the middle become the front?"

"Well, it might as well be. If we want to leave early we can't now."

Jadyn glanced around the sanctuary, which was filling up pretty quickly. "You're right. Let's move back a few." But just as they were getting up to move, a group of young people filled the seats on either side of them. They looked at each other, but sat back down.

They still had their plates full of food and didn't want to take a chance of spilling it on someone.

They ate their food in silence. A little while later, a teenage boy walked down the aisle with a trash bag collecting used plates and cups.

Shortly after that, a young, skinny, white guy got up and spoke into the mic.

"Good morning."

"Good morning," most of the congregation responded. Nite had spoken with the rest of them, Jadyn kept quiet.

"How's everybody doing this morning? I hope you all had some of the food that the ladies prepared for you this morning. Those who haven't had an opportunity to have some, please feel free to help yourselves. There is still plenty of food left. Oh and by the way. In case you didn't notice, we do allow food in the sanctuary. We don't believe in letting people go hungry just to prevent a few spills. That's why God invented mops, brooms, and other cleaning equipment. Amen?"

The remarks brought laughter and applause along with a few "Amens."

"I promise you God won't fall off His throne if a few crumbs get smashed into the carpet or a little juice stains it. We just clean it up again. Amen?"

"Amen," the congregation chorused.

"Well, now we are going to get things started with prayer this morning. Every head bowed and every eye closed, please."

"Father we pray Your blessings down upon us today, dear Lord. If someone is here today who is broken-hearted, or down in spirit, or even feeling like they can't go on another day, Lord, would You let them know that there is healing in Your name. Would You let them know that You are the Lord of the breakthrough and that You sent Your only son to die for Our sins and that through Him we can have life and that more abundantly. That all those who will come to You will in no way be cast out and You have everything we need. We forever give Your name the praise and all the glory forever and ever. And we all say . . ."

All the congregation finished the prayer with "Amen."

And this time Jadyn joined in, too, because in her heart, she felt that somehow the man was speaking directly to her. She felt that God knew her heart had been broken in a million pieces and that through the prayer He was letting her know that He was here to mend the pieces and make her whole again.

The young man was speaking again and he said that the mime ministry was going to come and minister to them.

Two young women took the stage. They had painted their faces clown white and wore all black, except for a pair of white gloves, and stood quietly with their heads bowed and arms at their sides. The house lights went down and can lights shone on the pair.

As the music began, one of the mimes became animated.

"And what do you say when your friends turn away, and you're all alone . . . alone . . . ," Donnie McClurkin's voice sang.

Jadyn could definitely relate to that one. Alone was exactly how she felt now. Even though she knew that Nite had her back no matter what, that knowledge wasn't doing anything to take away the deep loneliness and emptiness that she was feeling.

The other mime became animated and began to answer the first mime with silent motion.

"You just stand, watch the Lord see you through . . ."

As the two moved silently around the stage acting out the

words to the song, Jadyn could feel them in a new way. Their spirits were conveying a message to hers.

They were telling her no matter what you had to go through in life, God was with you and you only had to trust Him to light your path and lead you not only into your purpose, but His purpose, as well. And you didn't have to go through a bunch of phony rituals to get God's attention. You just had to acknowledge Him in everything you did and accept His great sacrifice, the greatest gift anyone could ever give: His life for ours. He would be faithful to forgive us of our sins and lead and guide us into all truths.

As Jadyn watched the mimes minister in their quiet yet dynamic way, she realized that your silence can sometimes speak many more volumes than your words ever could. She knew when she left church that day she would leave behind some of the weight she had been carrying.

By the time the preacher came on to do his morning sermon, she had to admit she was starting to feel better. Her mood was improving and she didn't feel quite as hopeless as she had when she woke up that morning, that was for sure.

Nite had been right, the preacher did look young. And he was kind of easy on the eyes, too. Tall. Very Tall. Maybe around six foot four or so. Husky build. Jadyn thought he could use a haircut though. His hair looked kind of like a mini-Afro to her. But let his wife worry about that—if he had one.

"Good morning, everyone. I want you to know that God just dropped a word in my spirit for somebody today. And that word is, He never closes a door that He doesn't open a window. And sometimes in order for God to take you to that next level in Him, you have to be willing to change your environment. Nothing wrong with where you're at right now. There's not a real problem there. The people in your arena may be good people. Notice I said *may* be good people. Because we all know that just because someone, be they a man or be they a woman—not talking to young children right now. This is for the adults. But just because you have been going to church for ten . . . fifteen . . . or even twenty-five years does not mean that you are right with God. That same one who is the first one inside the church each and every time the doors open, and the last one to leave; that same person who sings in the choir every single Sunday, and got their hands in everything that goes on in the church, and call themselves gatekeepers. Some of those very same people just come to church every single Sunday to stir up mess . . ."

The preacher's last sentence was greeted with a whole bunch of "Amens."

"And if they can't find any mess to stir up they will be sure to do everything in their power to create some or bring some mess with them to stir, while many pastors are looking the other way. Pretending that they don't see those troublemakers . . . making excuses for them to keep right on doing the dirt they do! Hurting people, walking up and down in the congregation wearing that pious and righteous mask of the sanctified perfect Christian, when in reality underneath all of that they are perusing the aisles, searching for that unsuspecting person to pounce upon like hungry, roaring lions—looking for someone they can eat alive!"

A young woman in the front row wearing jeans and a T-shirt that had "The Remnant" inscribed across the front in bold red letters, leapt from her seat and waved her hand toward the pastor and said, "You better tell the truth, Pastor."

"Yes, they pretend to be Christians. Wearing their false holiness and pious faces all the while acting ugly, in the name of the Lord! But now, I must also remind you, that is only *some* Christians. That is not an indictment of all Christians. For you see, there is a remnant in the church who won't give in to that fleshly need and desire to make themselves feel big and important by attempting to make others feel small and unimportant. There are those dedicated few who come to church with a purpose and one purpose only. And that is to serve the Lord our God with all that is within them! To lift up those who are hurting, not box them in and heap more hurt upon their already wounded souls. There are those who come into the sanctuary first thing in the morning to pray and seek God's face. They don't come to the service empty-handed, or to stir up mess, but they bring a fresh anointing with them. You see they have spent time in the presence of the Lord at home, where we spend most of our time. They seek the Lord's will without seeking something in return and ask Him how they may serve Him day-to-day. You see, they are about the Father's business seven days a week, not just on Sunday mornings!"

More of the congregation stood to their feet with loud "Amen"s and "Speak the word!"

"They wake up early on Sunday morning and fill the sanctuary with prayer and praise unto our God, so that when I come into the sanctuary I am greeted with the sweet-smelling savor of the Lord's precious Holy Spirit, instead of the stench of those who do nothing but create and stir up mess inside God's house!"

Preacher, it ain't just the Christians who like to keep mess stirred up, Jadyn thought, about Taji and his father. And yes at times even her own mother.

"But in every house God has placed a remnant who won't sell out to the flesh . . . who won't give in to the group mind-set of 'that's how we've always done it and that's how we will continue to do it!' No matter who falls by the wayside, no matter who it hurts! But there is a remnant whom God has set aside, who knows how to reach God, who knows how to fall on their faces and cry out to

God not just on Sunday mornings but every day of the week! They know how to reach God with their prayers. And when God speaks from eternity and says change your environment, you do it without question, because that is what the Father has commanded from the beginning. What He demands is your obedience! And it is your obedience to Him that will always set your feet on the right path! Who is that one that God is speaking to today? I'm speaking to someone this morning. And God is telling you to change your environment now! And do it quickly!"

Jadyn began to feel a stirring inside of her. And the more the preacher spoke about doing God's will, and changing your environment, the more that she felt that God was speaking directly to her. If indeed she was the one that God was speaking to this morning, she had heard Him loud and clear!

24

Jadyn awoke the next morning, and as she rose from the bed, she knew two things: She was leaving Columbus and she wanted to find her real father.

Jadyn didn't know much about the man who had fathered her. Only that he had impregnated her mother when she had gone to visit her older sister one summer. And that even though her mother had cut him off when she had married Ian, he still sent Jadyn birthday and Christmas presents and cards. Charles Ivery had wanted a relationship with his only child, but when he had asked for Jadyn to come visit him on vacations from school, during spring break, and in the summer, her mother had always said no. After years of rejection, her dad had remarried and stopped calling. Jadyn never understood her mother's thinking and had grown to resent the fact that she had kept her and her father apart. She didn't understand why her father had given up on her, either.

She knew in her heart that it was her mother's fault for putting Jadyn's life in jeopardy when she was young. How could her mother have allowed some man to get her all caught up and hooked on crack, when she had three children to care for? An addiction that also caused her to get involved in some crazy shit with a lunatic who had ended up trying to shoot both of them. Jadyn relived it almost nightly. Her mother's ex-boyfriend, Zane Blackmon, all beat up in one corner of the basement, tied to a chair and unconscious. Zane's psycho-ass friend Quin intent on making her mother pay for stealing dope from him. Something her mother had no part of, but he had been too crazy to listen to that. And then how he had aimed the gun at Jadyn and fired. Her mother should never have gotten them involved with that crazy shit in the first place. Jadyn's mind began to drift back to that night in Zane's basement.

"Quin, this is between you and me now." Jadyn's mother jabbed her finger into her own chest as she spoke. "Just you and me." Then she had proceeded to inch toward Quin, trying to put distance between him and Jadyn. Her mother pointed back toward her as she moved closer to him. "She ain't got nothin' to do with this. You can do whatever you feel you need to with me. But she ain't got nothin' to do with this."

"The fuck she don't!" Quin had roared, fixing his gaze on Jadyn as he spoke. His eyes had terrorized Jadyn. They looked empty and fierce at the same time, like he didn't give a fuck about anything or anyone. His eyes continued to pierce her as he continued speaking. "I told you . . . up there," Quin said pointing over his shoulder with the gun to emphasize his point, "you mess with mines and I'm definitely gon' fuck yours!" He had leered at Jadyn before finally turning his eyes back to her mom. "I told you that shit, didn't I? So don't be acting all surprised." Then Quin had started laughing an evil, eerie laugh that almost caused Jadyn to pee her pants. Her mother had frozen in her tracks as Quin went on.

"Oh this shit is funny as hell. When I told you I would fuck yours, I bet you never in a million years thought I was talkin' about your daughter."

"No!" Jadyn screamed. "Mom, don't let him hurt me!"

Jadyn's mom snapped her head in her direction. "Quiet Jadyn," her mother had shushed her. "Not as long as I'm breathin'." And Jadyn tried to shrink back against the wall even more, tried to become invisible as her mother tried to draw Quin's focus back on her.

"That can definitely be arranged!" Quin threatened, his face darkening. "Who you thank you is, bitch?"

"Quin, you right, you right, you absolutely right! Whoever messed with your stuff should have to pay. But that's me, right? Right, Quin? You got those other ones good. Now I'm ready to take my medicine. I deserve everything I get. I mean, you already got Gloria and Zane, right?" Her mother nodded her head toward Zane.

Quin looked over at him. "Yeah, stupid muhfucka! I definitely got his ass. We go way back, fool! Why did you try to fuck me? We was brothers! And you let somethin' I was put-in' the rod to fuck with your head like this?" Quin strode up to Zane and grabbed him by his hair, pulling his head back. "This what you get, nigga! This is what you get when you try to step to me! I woulda gave you the shit you stole, you bitch-ass punk! If you'd a asked for it! But yo' bitch ass gon' try to steal from me? Hunh, bitch? Don't nobody *fuck with King Quin! You hear me, muthafucka?*"

Quin had slammed Zane's head down so hard, Jadyn had thought his neck would break. And after all of that, Zane still didn't utter a sound.

"Naw, you don't hear me. You can't hear a muhfuckin' thang!" Quin had glanced from her mother to Jadyn and back to Zane. Samai eased backward trying to make sure her body was between Quin and Jadyn.

"I'm gon' handle the rest of this shit! Then everybody gon' know that Quin ain't nothin' nice and I ain't *nothin'* to be *played with!*" Quin took a few steps toward them. But before he could reach them, there was a loud knock at the door, stopping Quin in his tracks.

"Open up, this is the police!" one of them called loudly.

Quin's face became a fierce mask of purple rage.

"What the fuck! You called the police?" Quin raised the gun and cocked the hammer. "Say yo' goodbyes, bitches! If I'm goin' down for murder, two more dead bodies ain't gon' make a damn bit a difference!"

The pounding on the door upstairs got louder. Quin locked eyes with her mother and he had the look of a crazed maniac intent on murder on his face. Everything seemed to go in slow motion after that. Quin bared his teeth and began turning the gun toward Jadyn as his finger squeezed the trigger and her mother stepped in front of the bullet that was meant for Jadyn. Jadyn thought her mother was dead.

She heard a booming crash as blood splattered into the air in a spray that splashed her mother's face. As she began to fall backward, Jadyn screamed and began running over to cradle her mother in her arms; a policeman's voice was yelling something as loud footsteps clattered down the stairs. Quin's face still held an evil grin as he took aim at Jadyn once again, and suddenly his face became a mask of pain and confusion as the policeman's bullets ripped into his body. Jadyn's soft, cool hands gently stroked her mother's face as Jadyn's tears splashed down on her as she pleaded with her mother not to leave her. . . .

Her mother spent more than three weeks in the hospital recovering, and of course Jadyn was overjoyed that she had survived. But that didn't stop the nighmares that plagued her almost every single night. Nor did it stop the anger that she felt over her mother's bad choices that landed her in trouble almost her whole life.

She knew, too, that she had to confront her mother about that, sooner or later. KeMari Reynolds had told her that there would be no true healing for her or her mother unless she faced her anger and directed it toward the one who had really hurt her. Her stepfather Ian, mostly, but her mother, too, along with the fears that plagued her since the shooting, and all the questions that perhaps would be better answered from within. She hadn't really quite understood what KeMari had meant by that. She knew she didn't really like being angry at her mother all the time. She just couldn't help it right now. That's just how it was. Eventually she knew she would deal with it, but she couldn't bring herself to do that right now.

The first thing to do was to find out where her real father was. She was tired of all the crazy, ignorant men who had been around her all her life. Beginning with her stepfather Ian, then her mother's boyfriend Zane and that crazy maniac Quin, and then ending with Taji. All of them were heartless schemers. Incapable of loving anyone but themselves. In the end they only worried about what they wanted and what made them happy. It didn't matter what price others had to pay for their pleasure.

She wanted, no *needed* to find out if her father was different. If he loved her, unconditionally. She had always wondered what it would feel like to have a father who would love you no matter what. Maybe her dad would, if she could find him.

She wanted to find out what he was like, what his mother, her other grandmother, was like. Did she look like her grandmother? Would she care that she existed? Was she alive? Did she have a grandfather? Did she have more brothers? What about a sister? Aunts, uncles, cousins?

She could have a whole other family. One that wasn't fractured and messed up like the one she had now. Jadyn loved her younger brothers, E and Devon, but she hadn't seen them in almost a year. She rarely saw them because she couldn't bring herself to stay around her mother for long periods of time. She wanted to find her father, but where would she begin?

Though she wasn't looking forward to it, she knew that it was a conversation she and her mother had to have. So she picked up her cell and punched in her mother's number.

"Mom, do you have an address or phone number for my real dad? I want to get in touch with him."

There was silence on the other end.

"Mom, did you hear me?"

Her mother finally spoke.

"Yes, I heard you. But why do you want to speak to him after all of these years?"

Jadyn sighed, rolled her eyes, and changed her cell phone from one ear to the other. As she clenched her jaw tightly and ground her back teeth together, it was all she could do to suppress the anger that simmered deep inside at the sound of her mother's voice. She couldn't believe how much it irritated her and sounded like a lot of noise in her ears lately. Talking to her just really got on her *last* nerve. Couldn't she just give her a straight answer?

"Mom, you were the one who decided Ian should be the only father I ever needed. I didn't have any say in your decision back then. Things have changed. I'm a grown woman now, and I've decided that your ex-husband wasn't the father I needed. I want to speak to my real dad. Is that so hard for you to understand?"

"There is no need for you to be nasty with me, Jadyn. I just don't know if it's a good idea to stir up mess. I mean, what if your dad doesn't want to see you? Will you be able to handle that? And do you have to have such a nasty attitude?"

Jadyn was trying desperately to hold on to the message that she had heard in church yesterday. She had to remember to forgive. She realized that she needed to somehow end the love-hate relationship that she was carrying on with her mom. She had to find a way to grow the part of her that loved her mother and wanted to have a good relationship with her until love was all that she felt. She had to find a way to let the old stuff die. But how? How? When everything that her mother said seemed to get on her nerves every time they spoke?

"First of all, Mom, I'm not trying to be nasty, and I'm sorry that you feel that way. I just want to find my dad. And I was hopin' that you would be able to help me do that. Can you do that for me, please?" Jadyn struggled to keep her voice even and as pleasant as she could.

"Jadyn, I'm not going to talk to you if you want to keep disrespecting me the way you are . . ."

Jadyn cut her short. Her mother had a habit of turning situations around and making them all about her. That was one of the things that irritated her so much about trying to have conversations with her.

"What do you mean, I'm being disrespectful? I asked you a simple question about my dad! How is that being disrespectful? Why can't you just tell me what I need to know?"

Jadyn heard her mother sigh before speaking.

"I'm hanging up the phone, Jadyn. Why don't you call me back when you can control your tone better? I don't know how to talk to you anymore. How to reach you. Everything I say seems to make you mad . . . Maybe if you would come to church with me, God would . . ."

Jadyn was losing the battle to keep her anger in check. "Now is not the time to try to talk to me about God and church. We're not talking about Him. We were talking about my dad. But just so you know, me and Nite went to church yesterday. I just don't feel like hearin' that every time I try to talk to you. Why don't you just wait for the right time to—"

"When is the right time? You say that all the time, Jadyn. It's not like you don't know the Lord and His Word."

Why couldn't her mother just talk to her without all that? Always talking about God this and God that. Yes Jadyn believed in God. She just didn't believe that you should pull Him out like a weapon any time you didn't like something somebody said. Or to prevent people from asking you questions that you didn't want to answer, like her mother was doing right now.

"Can't you just answer a damn question? Hunh? Can't you?"

Jadyn flipped her phone shut before her mother could answer. Forget this weak-ass shit. She would find her father on her own.

25

"I understand that, Jadyn, but I depend on you. I don't know if I can run this place without you," Caroline Van Horn said, tears forming in her eyes.

"Don't you start cryin', Caroline. You gonna make me start cryin', too," Jadyn said, as she reached her arms around her soon to be ex-boss and gave her a hug.

"You know you've become my right hand, losing you is like losing my sister." She reached into her jacket pocket and pulled out a Kleenex to blow her nose.

Jadyn took her hand. "It might not be forever. I might be back in a couple of months or so, if things don't work out for me. And I promise you will be the first person I come see about getting my job back."

"And you know you can have it. You'll always have a position here if you want it. I'm just going to miss you so much!"

"And I'm gonna miss you, Caroline."

"I'll miss you, too, Jadyn." Selena stepped out from the dressing room. She looked pale, her dark blond, medium-length hair hanging limply around her shoulders. Rushing over she gave Jadyn a hug.

"Me, too, Selena."

Selena leaned close and whispered in Jadyn's ear, "Now I have to be here on time every day because I'm not going to have you to cover for me!"

Jadyn whispered back, "I never liked covering for your ass anyway, so I'm not gonna miss that!" They both laughed. Selena had tears and the heavy black mascara she always wore running down her pale pink cheeks.

Caroline came up and handed her the envelope she had been holding in one hand.

"Well, here's your last check for now." She smiled and embraced Jadyn again. "You take care of yourself. And if you ever need *anything* don't you dare hesitate to call me!" She planted a kiss on Jadyn's cheek.

"I won't. I promise. Thank you, Caroline."

Back in her car, she opened the envelope and gasped. Not only was her last paycheck there, but so was a personal check from Caroline for five hundred dollars, and one from Mrs. Lichty for two thousand dollars! Jadyn opened the door and was about to run back inside and tell her friend that she couldn't accept a gift like this when she saw the note.

Jadyn,

Don't get your panties all in a bunch. The check is from me, but when I told Mrs. Lichty you were leaving she insisted that she write a check for you, too. Please, don't let your foolish pride prevent you from accepting the gift. You know that woman has money to burn! As for me, it's just the bonus I was planning on giving you anyway for Christmas.

Take care and I hope to see you again soon!

Love, Caroline Kennedi Van Horn.

Jadyn closed the car door. The extra $2500 would come in handy. She would call Caroline and thank her once she got settled. She opened the glove compartment and pulled out the little box that had held the last gift her father had ever given her. The box on which was written his last known address. She looked at her father's scrawled handwriting, with the exaggerated loops in the "l"s and read: "Charles William Ivery, 1219 Hunter Street, Cocoa Beach, Florida."

"So . . . you're gonna let one disappointment cause you to give up on your dreams? All of the work you've done and all the hours you've spent honing your talent, you just gonna throw it all away? Over one moment in time?" Ms. Deborah Rashad asked as she pulled her glasses down the bridge of her nose and stared over the frames at her. Jadyn knew that Ms. Rashad wasn't too happy with her at the moment, she always moved her glasses down her nose that way when she was about to deliver a lecture. Despite her petite five-foot frame, Ms. Rashad never had any trouble maintaining the respect of her pupils. Jadyn took in her wavy, fine black hair, pulled back into a ponytail that was pinned on top of her head—the same style she always wore when she taught class—her captivating hazel eyes, and a complexion the color of honey. She definitely had Jadyn's attention now.

"Ms. Rashad, you don't understand. It's not just the fact that I didn't get the part . . . I mean that is part of it," Jadyn told her and felt the frustration resurfacing and choking off her words. She sat down in the overstuffed armchair that sat opposite Ms. Rashad's huge oak desk.

Ms. Rashad peered at her, narrowing her eyes until they were tiny slits that seemed to peer into Jadyn's soul.

"Child, haven't you learned anything during the years that I've spent with you? What have I always told you, what have I always told all the children who come here to learn dance?" Ms. Rashad raised her hand and pointed toward Jadyn, her bracelets jingling.

Jadyn glanced up at the ceiling and down at the floor, basically anywhere else to avoid Ms. Rashad's penetrating eyes, feeling more like a ten-year-old than the adult she had become.

"You . . . you always told us never to let anything but God cause us to give up on our talent or our dreams. And that if we believe in ourselves, the places our talent will take us are limitless." Jadyn paused for a second, unwilling to let Ms. Rashad's mantra change the point she wanted to make. She turned away from her teacher as she spoke. "But you don't know what happened. You don't understand what Taji has done. Sometimes you get bombarded with a lot of things at once. And you feel like you're breaking inside. People always letting you down." She turned back to face her mentor. "Men using you and throwing you away whenever they feel like it!" Jadyn stood to her feet and faced the wall, as tears formed in her eyes that she struggled to hold back.

She heard Ms. Rashad rise from her seat and felt her gently touch her arm. Jadyn turned toward her.

"Oh Jadyn, how I wish that life didn't hurt so much. Sometimes there is a special pain to bear when God blesses you with special talent. The bigger the talent, the bigger the pain. I don't understand why that is, but it just is. My grandmother always told me that the pain is never sent to break you, no matter how harsh it may seem. It's meant to make you strong, to mold and shape you into the person you are meant to be."

She opened her arms and Jadyn folded herself into her embrace, allowing her emotions to overtake her.

"But how, how do you deal with the hurt and pain when life keeps adding salt to old wounds and opening up new ones? It's just too much . . . it's too much . . ."

"It's all right, honey. I know life can deal us some pretty low cards sometimes and there's nothing we can do about it but play the hand we're given. But God gives us a way to beat the odds and win with what others may think is a losing hand."

Ms. Rashad pulled away from her and placed her hands on either side of her face.

"You might have had to endure the ugly side of life so far, Jadyn, but from where I stand I only see a winner. You're a winner, because God has blessed you with outward beauty, a mighty talent, and that special something that lights up a room when you walk in. I saw it the first day I laid eyes on you, and it's only gotten brighter as you've grown older and your talent has only grown bigger and better."

She reached over and pulled a box of tissues off her desk and handed them to Jadyn. She wiped her eyes and blew her nose.

"When you are on that stage, you feel it, that's obvious, but you make your audience feel it, as well. Now, there are a lot of good dancers in the world and they can *hold* an audience's attention. But you *command* their attention. And more than that, you carry them along with you when you dance. Only a handful of dancers can do that."

"I hear what you're sayin' and I know that God gave me this talent. And I don't plan to waste it. But, I can't stay here right now, Ms. Rashad. I have to get away. Now, I don't know if it's forever, but

I just know I gotta go. And I'm not running away from my problems. How can a person run from themselves?"

"Oh, they can and they do. They certainly do. Listen there's nothing wrong with taking a vacation from your problems. As long as you understand that they aren't going anywhere just because you do. And the reality is, if you are gonna fly to pieces every time you don't get a role you have auditioned for, no matter what the reason, well you may as well hang up your dancing shoes right now. And I know much as you love dancing you're not about to do that! Now, where did you say you're going?"

"Palm City, Florida. My great-uncle lives there."

"Go with my blessings. But if you decide to make your vacation permanent, give me a call. They have dancers and teachers in Florida just like they do here."

Then Ms. Rashad snapped her fingers like she had just remembered something. "Did you say Palm City? That's close to Orlando, isn't it?"

Jadyn looked puzzled. "I'm not sure, Ms. Rashad, but it could be. I remember back in the day, my grandma took me and my little brothers to Palm City to visit her brother and they ended up driving us to Disney World. That's in Orlando, right?"

"It sure is! How long did it take you to get there?"

Jadyn perched on the edge of the huge desk, frowning as she strained her memory.

"Wow, I don't remember. We were little, and it was a long time ago." She threw up her hands in frustration as she spoke. "Why are you asking all these questions about Orlando?"

Ms. Rashad lifted her hand and rubbed her cheek as she spoke.

"I don't really want to say right this minute. I have a friend down there I need to speak to before I say anything else." She dropped her hand back to her side, and strolled around to the other side of her desk. She rummaged around the top of her desk for a bit, mumbling to herself before finding what she was looking for. She picked up her heavy day planner, which was barely holding together with all of the extra papers she had stuffed into it hanging out everywhere. Pushing the planner toward Jadyn she said, "Here, write down your cell phone number, and the number of that cousin of yours that you are so tight with. If anybody will be able to find you, that child will. Y'all two are tighter than Aunt Fanny's panty girdle and last I looked, she weighed a good three hundred pounds, so you know that girdle is screaming for mercy, it's so tight!"

Ms. Rashad cracked herself up and Jadyn couldn't help laughing right along with her, as she wrote down the numbers.

"If you haven't heard from me by the time you leave, you make sure you call me once you get down there."

Jadyn stood to her feet and handed the planner back to Ms. Rashad. "I'll do that. But can't you just tell me what all this is about?"

"It ain't about anything, yet. And might not ever be. But if it is, you'll be the second one to know." Ms. Rashad winked at her. "Right after me."

26

"Flight 2339 to Palm Beach International Airport now boarding at Gate 57," the anonymous voice announced over the loudspeaker.

Jadyn stood, took hold of her carry-on luggage, and headed for the terminal, ticket in hand. There was no changing her mind now. She was headed into the unknown and was more than a little apprehensive about what would greet her on the other side.

She had no idea how she could find her father, all she had was his name and the box that held the last gift he had sent her with his return address printed in a neat scrawl in the upper right-hand corner. The box had held the solid gold necklace that he had sent her for her sixteenth birthday. She still wore it around her neck.

Nite had a fit when she found out she was leaving and wanted to come along, but she couldn't get any time off from her job with such short notice. But she had given Jadyn the name of an agency that helps you find lost loved ones that she had seen on *Oprah* one day. Once Jadyn got settled, she was going to give them a call. It just so happened that the home office of the organization was located in Florida.

. . .

She was glad that she got a window seat and she stared out of it, watching everything getting smaller and smaller, as she absently wondered what in the world was holding something so heavy in the sky.

"It gets better," said a deep baritone voice beside her.

Jadyn turned her head to face the man who had taken the seat next to her.

"Excuse me?"

"I said it gets better. The view from the window. If you like clouds that is."

He continued, as Jadyn gave him a look that anyone in their right mind could read: *Fool, what is you talkin' about?*

"I always get nervous when we take off and the houses and cars keep getting smaller and smaller and I start thinking about how far above the earth we're gettin' and start thinking what the hell is holdin' this big-ass plane not to mention all the people and everything else inside up in the air!"

Mystery man started to chuckle, but even though he had practically read her thoughts she failed to see the humor in his weak-ass conversation. He was nice looking enough, in a retro sort of style. He looked older than her. His gear wasn't cheap, but kind of corny and a little young for him with his FUBU jeans outfit, and tan FUBU shirt. She glanced down at his feet. At least his Timberlands matched his outfit. She had hoped when he sat down beside her that he was just going to keep his mouth shut and read a book or listen to some music. Anything but hurt her ears with his nonsense.

She threw him her weakest smile and turned back to the window, hoping he would catch the hint. He didn't.

"So is Palm Beach your final destination, foxy brown, or are you connecting to parts unknown?"

Foxy brown? Damn! It was going to be even worse than she had imagined. Jadyn saw that she was going to have to tell this man in plain English that she wasn't interested, since subtlety seemed to fly right over his head.

"Look, no offense, but I don't get down with long conversations with strangers. I'm tired, I have a lot on my mind, and I just wanna chill and quietly enjoy my flight. In other words, I don't know you and I ain't curious. OK?"

Jadyn knew that she was lying to herself. She couldn't help noticing his LL Cool J lips. But she cautioned herself to remember Taji and the real reason she was on the plane. It wasn't to start up no bs with a stranger. No matter how fine he was. And the words of a song came into her head unbidden. "I promise to never fall in love with a stranger" by K-Ci and JoJo. She turned her head just as LL Cool J Lips spoke to her.

"Excuse me, I won't bother you after this, but do you see the restroom? I looked in the back where it usually is but I didn't see it."

His voice definitely matched his lips, and all the rest of him for that matter. He had smooth, chocolate-caramel skin, and she noticed his pretty, straight white teeth when he smiled at her. She allowed her gaze to leave his lips. There was the neat mustache and trim goatee surrounding those lips, deep dimples in his cheeks, soulful dark brown eyes framed by dark, lush eyelashes, and coal black waves of hair pasted tightly to his head in a neat fade. The booming bass in his voice as he spoke shook her from her perusal.

"I'm sorry, but I really need to go, do you see the sign for the bathroom? Because I just can't seem . . ."

Jadyn was embarrassed that he caught her checking him out but tried to cover her embarrassment with indifference. She curled the corners of her mouth in a smirk as she raised her hand and pointed a finger toward the sign near the front entrance of the plane.

"I guess you don't see that red sign with the little stick drawing of the man and woman all lit up right there in front. Even a child can recognize that!" she said a little too sharply and swallowed her regret at being so harsh to someone who looked so damn good! She gave him her most disinterested stare as he spoke again.

"Sorry to have troubled you," he said as he unbuckled his seat belt and stood to his feet. "It won't happen again. Believe that." His face showed no trace of the beautiful dimpled smile this time. She drew one corner of her lips up hard, gave her head a little shake and said, "And? So what?" before turning her face to the window.

As the stranger stalked off, Jadyn pretended not to care that she had pissed him off, but she knew that she was lying to herself again. The truth was she had been extra mean so she wouldn't have to admit to herself that she was attracted to him. She even pretended that she was still looking out of the window instead of turning her head ever so slightly and slanting her eyes just enough to catch the powerful swing of his thighs, the way his jeans hugged his cute little butt, and the way his shirt clung to a tight waist, muscular back, and perfectly molded shoulders. She allowed herself a little smile. Oh yeah! He was definitely fine as hell. From head to toe. But she would never let on to him that she knew this.

When he came back to his seat, he made no effort to hide the fact that she had pissed him off. He clicked down the table from the seat in front of him a little too hard. He took the laptop from the little black bag beneath his seat, and pulled the zipper so hard it broke.

"Ah damn!" he said. Jadyn pretended not to notice, even though she was laughing inside. She still faced the window, but allowed her head to remain slightly tilted so that she caught everything with her peripheral vision. She saw him sneak a peek her way before opening up his laptop. He pulled some papers from the brief-case and balanced them on his lap, before leaning over and shoving the briefcase back under his seat. As he came up, he somehow bumped his luscious lips against the edge of the tiny, makeshift desktop. The pain made him jerk upright, causing his knees to bump up and joggle the laptop. He made a mad grab for the laptop before it could crash to the floor and the papers that were in his lap went flying. He looked so funny trying to juggle everything that Jadyn burst into laughter.

He gave her a stern look. "This shit ain't funny!" he said, making sure he held on to the computer and letting the papers fall where they may.

Jadyn continued giggling. "You just saying that because you can't see how funny you look with your long legs all scrunched up beneath that little bitty tray, and every time you move you just messing things up more! And the look on your face is funny as hell!" she managed to say before breaking into laughter again. He tried not to, but in the end his face lit up with that gorgeous dimpled smile again.

"OK, OK, glad I could entertain you. I'd much rather see you laugh than have that funky attitude."

Jadyn stopped laughing. "Say what? Attitude—"

The stranger hurriedly added: "I only meant that your face is much prettier when you smile."

Jadyn was transfixed by his expression as he spoke and extended his hand.

"My name is Julian. Julian Locklin the third, at your service." As he reached toward her, his knees caused the tabletop to shift, and he had to catch his laptop again. Jadyn smiled and took his hand.

"Nice to meet you, Julian. I'm Jadyn Collins." And because she was curious she added, "What type of service do you provide?"

"Well, that would depend on what kind of service you need." He continued to stare into her eyes as he held on to her hand.

Jadyn blushed, realizing too late the double meaning in her question. She withdrew her hand and qualified her question.

"I was asking about your work. What is it you do for a living exactly?"

Julian reached into his shirt pocket and handed her a business card. "I guess you could say I'm in entertainment."

The card read: "'JL Promotions. Promotions, Singers, Dancers, Rappers and Special Venues by request.'" Jadyn flipped the card over and read the other side. "We make your business streetwise!" She flipped the card faceup again. *Dancers*. Jadyn's gaze stuck there. For real, though?

"What kind of dancers you looking for?"

"All kinds, baby, all kinds."

Oh really? We'll see about that.

"Well, I'm a dancer," she said tucking his card inside her purse. "Maybe I'll give you a call sometime, after I'm settled in."

"You do that. You never know what can happen."

"You got that right," Jadyn said as she turned and stared out the window again.

27

Jadyn's great-uncle, BruhJay, lived in Palm City, and when his only sister, her grandmother, had called and told him that she was coming he had said that she was more than welcome. Jadyn had only told her grandmother that she was taking a vacation. She saw no reason to tell her the whole story.

"Hey, looka here now. You grown now, ain'tchu, little girl?" Uncle BruhJay's voice broke into Jadyn's thoughts. She smiled when she saw him. She knew him right away because he had her grandmother's face, the only difference between the two was her uncle's face was light brown and freckled where her grandmother's was dark brown and perfectly flawless. They had the same curly hair, except her grandmother's was longer. Her uncle was much taller, too, about six feet even.

"Hey Unc!" she greeted him as he grabbed her in a bear hug and swung her around.

"How your grandmama doin'? Y'all ain't up there runnin' her crazy are you?"

"No sir, Unc. We ain't trynna have you come up there and beat us half to death!"

He let out a loud laugh that sounded like a male version of her grandma. "And you know I will dust every last one of y'all down, for messin' with Sista! That's my only sister and she is my heart!"

Uncle BruhJay took both her bags. "Lawd, I'm gonna have to sleep with one eye open and my gun by the door 'cause you sure are a pretty little thing! You look just like yo' grandmama when she was your age! I got the truck right outside. Let's go. You hungry?"

"Starvin'! You know they don't give you anything but some little bitty half-empty bag of stale pretzels or peanuts."

"I know that's right, little girl. You like seafood? 'Cause you know we the seafood capital of the world! I cooked you up a little snack. Some smothered crabs, some fresh scallops, some crab legs, and some buttered pasta."

"Stop it, Unc, you makin' my stomach growl even worse. I'm ready to throw down!"

"Aw girl, what you talkin' 'bout? That ain't nothin' but a little predinner snack! I got my grandson Flash down here. He gon' make sure you have a good time and keep a eye on you. Make sure you stay outta trouble." He gave Jadyn a wink as he loaded her things into the back of the truck.

"You ain't gotta worry about that. Trouble is one thing that I hope keeps its distance from me."

As they turned down the street her uncle lived on, Jadyn was pleasantly surprised. He lived on a street that was lined with palm trees and all of the houses were ranch-style, and made of brightly colored stucco. People in Ohio would collapse and die if they saw this many orange, purple, yellow, and even pink buildings in their neighborhood. Shoot! They would probably petition the governor to either make the owners paint them a nice quiet brown, tan, or brick color, or force the owners to sell to someone more conservative.

It seemed as if most of the neighbors were her great-uncle's age or older, from what she could see. It was pretty quiet, everyone kept their lawns neatly manicured, and each one of them had flowers or some type of garden in front of their homes.

As they pulled up to his house, one of his neighbors waved and called out a greeting. She was short, dark-skinned, and you could see as she spoke, that she had a gold front tooth. She was very slender and had her long hair pulled up in a ponytail.

"Hey, Robert. How you doin' today? Who's that you got with you?"

"Hey RachelJean, what you doin' out heah this time of the afternoon in all this heah heat? You gon' mess around and catch a heat stroke if you ain't careful," he called out in response, right before he leaned in closer to Jadyn's side of the truck and explained. "That right there is one of the nosiest, most gossipin' old biddies on the block. Now if you want your business all in these streets while you here, you just tell it to her."

"Robert, don't you be lyin' on me to that young woman. Honey, don't you believe nothin' he tells you 'bout me."

Her uncle winked at her and whispered under his breath, "See what I'm talkin' bout?" Then he said loudly, "Aw, RachelJean, ain't nobody talkin' about you. You are trippin'. Now come on around here and meet my great-niece from Ohio."

28

Her cousin Flash was well over six feet tall, with dark chocolate-brown skin and a gapped-tooth smile with a gold crown shining from one of his canines. His hair was long and wavy and he had it cornrowed, but his baby hair peeked out and lay flat around the edges.

"What up, little cousin?" he said as he picked her up and swung her around before taking a seat on one of the patio chairs around the table in the backyard. Her uncle had not lied about all the food he had prepared.

"You kinda changed since we went on that trip to Disney World when we was little. You was a cute kid but you done grown into a fine young woman. Shole did. My little cousin is lookin' fresh!"

Jadyn took a seat as her mind wandered briefly back to the long-ago Disney trip. Though the memory was a bit fuzzy, she could plainly remember how Flash had taken charge of her and her little brothers, even though he was only a few years older than she. He had been very protective of her even back then. Telling her which rides were safe, and not allowing anyone to diss them as they stood in line for the rides. Even offering to black one guy's eye for accidentally bumping her arm, causing her to drop her candy apple.

Flash spoke again, breaking up the memories of her first meeting with him.

"You don't worry about nothin'—Flash gon' show you a real good time while you here," he told her, giving her a smile before bringing a crab to his mouth and cracking the shell with his teeth. "Pretty as you is, I know I'ma have to keep it locked and loaded, to keep these niggas offa you!"

Jadyn laughed out loud, thinking how funny it was that Flash was acting just the same as she had remembered.

"Whatever, cousin. I'm feelin' you. Just don't try to smother me. I'm a big girl now and I ain't got no trouble standing up for myself."

Flash gave her a look as he cracked another crab with his teeth. "I heard that! I'll keep my distance. But just remember, long as you here, I got you. You don't worry about a thang."

She pushed herself back from the table. She never knew until now how stuffed you could get off crab legs. Now that her stomach was full, she suddenly realized how exhausted she was. Flash wanted to take her out to a club, but she really didn't think that she was feeling that tonight. Maybe she would feel differently after she took a nap.

"We'll have to wait and see, Flash," she told him. "I'm about wore out right now." She excused herself, retiring to the room her uncle had shown her earlier. She didn't quite know why, but as she closed the door behind her, she made sure it was locked.

As she unpacked her bags, she came across the picture she had packed of Taji. She wasn't sure why she packed it, but she set it on top of the dresser, stroking the frame as she drew her hand away. Her heart ached for what they had begun before he had betrayed her. But she had some unfinished business with him.

She picked up the phone and dialed her home number.

"Hello?"

"Hey, Taj."

"Hey, baby! You all right?"

"I'm fine. I was just calling to tell you where you could go and pick up the Toyota."

"Now, what do you mean 'pick up the Toyota'? That is your car. I bought it for you. I mean just because we are like we are . . . I'm not a Indian giver."

"We are like we are? You destroyed my dreams and that's all you got to say is 'we are like we are'?"

"Jadyn, I miss you so much. Come over here. Let's talk. Let me explain. The shit is fucked up, for real, but it's really not what you think. I'm not the one who—"

"Be kinda hard for me to come over when I'm in Florida."

"You're where? In Florida, what the hell?"

"Yes, Florida. I only called so you could go to the airport and pick up the Toyota, so it doesn't get towed. I parked in the short-term yellow lot on the second tier."

Jadyn was quiet and a little uncomfortable at the way she could be so easily taken there when she heard the sound of his voice. She had to admit that despite all the shady shit, she missed Taji, too. No matter how much she wished it could be otherwise, that she could just feel nothing. She missed the smooth tenor of his voice. The way it would get soft and mushy when he said her name. How it could turn husky and sexy when he was stroking her . . . She shook the thoughts. If she kept dwelling on things like that she would be on the next flight home. And that wouldn't change the fact that he was a snake that couldn't be trusted.

"Listen. I gotta go."

"Jay, wait. Let me talk to you, please. When are you coming home? I mean, back to Ohio?"

"Take care of yourself."

"Jadyn, I . . ."

Jadyn hung up the phone. She held it to her heart briefly, before putting it down. She pulled one of Taji's extra large T-shirts from her suitcase. She had brought it along just to feel him near her, as crazy as that seemed. She truly felt the meaning now of having a love-hate relationship with someone.

Burying her face in its folds, she inhaled deeply. Though it had been laundered, she could still smell the faint scent of the Armani cologne that he loved so much. It reminded her of the last time he had made love to her. The way he had kissed every inch of skin on her body, inside and out. Playing for a long time with the inside of her thighs and using his tongue on her until he had her stuttering and begging. Suddenly, she wanted to be where he was, sitting on his lap, having him hold her in his strong arms.

Walking into the bathroom she laid the T-shirt on top of the toilet seat. As she glanced around she was amazed at how totally spotless everything was. The sink gleamed pearly white and the large mirror above it was perfectly spotless, not a water spot in sight. Her uncle was just every bit as much of a neatnik as his sister was.

The yellow towels, which were a perfect match for the shower curtain and throw rugs that lay neatly in front of the tub and the toilet bowl, were immaculate and folded in meticulous rectangles of equal size. She found that the towels and washcloths in the linen closet were folded just as neatly as she pulled a pair from the shelf.

Picking up Taji's shirt she inhaled his scent again as she shed her clothing, pulled back the yellow shower curtain, and turned the shower on. As the water sprayed from the showerhead, she held one hand beneath it checking to make sure that it was just the right temperature. She again pressed the shirt to her face, inhaling Taji's scent, holding it there, hoping that the action might in some way help ease the loneliness and regret she felt over the arguments and her abrupt departure.

Dropping the shirt down on top of the toilet seat, she stepped into the tub and stood under the steaming jets, replaying the scenes of their lovemaking over and over in her head. At the moment she wanted to forget about the distance and all the other shit that separated them and focus on how good Taji had made her feel. How he had loved her so tenderly and just so damned good! She immersed herself in the soothing comfort of the warm droplets massaging her body and leisurely soaped her body. A sigh escaped her lips when an errant stream found her nipple and played there. She knew she should draw away from the tantalizing sensation, but instead she shifted her shoulders so that the errant spray could tease her other nipple. Before she knew it she was lost in the mo-ment as she gave in to the thrill that was like an invisible tongue lapping at her body. Reaching up she discovered that the shower-head was the handheld type. Taking it from the clip that held it in place she adjusted the shower massage to a single, more steady stream, spreading her legs apart as she did so, positioning herself so that the waterfall was directed between her legs. Suddenly nothing else mattered except the warm water massaging her most intimate parts. She conjured an image of Taji giving her a tongue lashing and this only intensified the feelings. Leaning her head back against the shower wall and enjoying the water play, she moved the showerhead back and forth, her hips following the rhythm smoothly, rocking up and back. Her movements became more frantic and she softly called Taji's name as her climax jerked her forward with surprising intensity. She closed her legs allowing her head to rest against the shower wall as she slowly recovered. The quick fix over her loneliness for Taji had been good while it lasted. But it was doing nothing to ease the longing for his presence she felt now. She closed her eyes and silently whispered his name over and over.

29

Jadyn heard a knock on the bedroom door. Glancing at the clock, she was surprised she had been asleep for a few hours. She heard Flash's loud voice through the door.

"You still sleep? Cuz, if you is you needs to get on up. You on vacation—this ain't no time to sleep." Jadyn smiled and rose to open the door.

"Hey Flash, what's goin' on?"

"I forgot to tell you that this dude name Steele Money havin' this party tonight at the club. If you ain't too tired, we can go check it out. It'a give you a chance to see how we do it up here in "Da City," he said with a grin.

Jadyn was tired, but she also felt the need to let go and have a good time. It would be nice just to relax, have some fun, and forget about all that drama with Taji and the audition.

"Cuz, that sounds like a plan. But who's Steele Money?"

"He this cat that be hangin' out with all the rappers and singers and shit that be comin' to town. His parties is live as hell. But check it, cuz, at the end of the night he be doin' them cattle calls for the chicks that they want to take back to they hotel room and sex up for the night, and fine as you is, I know they gonna try to pull you into that shit. So don't make me hafta bus' a cap in some of them niggas asses tonight," he said, giving her a look that was playful and serious at the same time.

"Cuz, please. You didn't even have to break on me like that. I ain't into being no-damn-body's plaything, and I'm not no damn groupie, neither. So you can get that shit straight right now. And I told you, a while ago, I know how to take care of myself, too, so chill with all that noise."

Flash watched her for a second. "Unh-hunh, well we'll see. You came down here at the right time, li'l cuz, we gon' be partyin' left and right! My dude Steele, he is about to set it off! There's a buncha rappers coming down here in two weeks, and Steele is the one that be gettin' them bitches together for the after parties that I just got done tellin' you about."

Then he seemed to relax as he gave her a smile. "Everythang's cool, cuz, I ain't trynna spoil your first night here and shit. I'm trynna make sure you have fun without havin' to deal with all that dumb-ass extracurricular shit that I know them knuckleheads gonna try to put on you."

She rubbed Flash's arm. "Yeah, Flash, it's all good. I know you just trynna look out for me and things."

"A'ight then, cuz. Granddaddy down 'ere cookin' us up some more crabs, and crab legs, and some hamburgers, and whole buncha other food, so I'ma let you freshen up and thangs. You'll have time to lay down and rest a while later after we eat. Clubs don't close here, so we'll prolly head out 'round ten or 'leven or so."

"Sounds good!" she said as Flash closed the door.

30

"Daaaaaaaaaamn, Flash! How in the fuck did you manage to hang a dime like that?" Judge, one of Flash's friends, called out as Flash stepped up into Calhoun's with Jadyn by his side.

"Man, shut the fuck up and wipe the slobber off yo' muzzle, dog. This here my cousin Jadyn. She visitin' from Ohio. Yeah, she fine as hell, I know alla y'all dying to trade places with me, but let me assure you that shit ain't—"

Jadyn felt it was time to cut Flash's speech short.

"Look, Cousin Robocop, quit playin' bodyguard and introduce me to the rest of your friends, please?"

Laughter broke out among the group. A petite fair-skinned girl, top heavy with big hips and long curly black hair, came forward dragging a short, buff dude along behind her.

"Girl, you know Flash always playin' that guard dog role with alla us. I am so glad you told him to tone that shit down! I'm Mani and this my dude Jarrell. Him and Flash like brothers, so you gon' be seein' a lot of us while you here." Mani began pointing to the rest of the crowd, continuing the introductions.

"This is Dawn and Malachai, and that's Sharae and Leon. Y'all this is Flash's cousin Jadyn. She from Ohio."

While Mani talked, Flash appeared by her side once again, and taking her elbow, guided her over to an area that had ten or twelve tables set up in rectangles on a raised platform. It was dark and very smoky, so she was glad that Flash knew where he was going. She could barely see a few feet in front of her at a time. The music was so loud that their voices barely carried even though they were practically yelling. They definitely had the pound pound of the bass going on.

The dance floor was huge and took up one whole section of the room. Suspended up above the floor at opposite corners were two young women dancing in neon-lit cages. They were about the same size and height, both dressed in Daisy Dukes and wife-beaters. One of them wore cowboy boots on her feet and a cowboy hat on her head. The other had on pumps and a visor covered her neatly bobbed hair. Jadyn watched them move for a few moments. They could dance OK, but she could tell they weren't real dancers. She could get up there and show them what dancing was really about if she wanted to.

Jadyn, Flash, and his friends quickly filled the tables and the fun began. A skinny girl with surprisingly big boobs, wearing a tight, short black skirt and a white, low-cut, V-neck T-shirt that showed her ample cleavage, came over to their table. She had her hair up in a ponytail and Jordans on her feet.

Flash leaned in close and grabbed her around the waist. "What's up, lovely? Now you know you too fine to be workin' in this here spot, 'round all these thuggish, ruggish bones. Why 'on't you let a nigga like me take you away from this here joint?"

The waitress gave him a wry smile before gingerly plucking his hand from her waist.

"Unh-hunh, and how do you plan on takin' me outta this piece when your ass practically need to start payin' rent here you in here so damn much!" she told him sarcastically.

Flash leaned back and looked her up and down, as his cohorts burst into laughter, giving each other fives.

"Oh it's like that, hunh?" he asked the girl. Jadyn could see the shadow of a smile playing at his lips.

"Yeah it's just like that. Now you gonna order some drinks or what? I am workin' and I do got other people in here to serve."

"Aw, slow your roll, baby, I got this," Flash told her before asking, "What you drinkin', Jay?"

"Tanqueray and Seven," she answered.

"Gin, hunh? You know gin'a' make ya sin and I ain't trynna have none a' that shit up in here tonight. I don't wanna hafta cut a nigga!"

Mani spoke up, "There go ol' Pitbull Sewell trynna be all protective and shit again! Leave 'er alone, Flash! Let the girl drink what she wanna drink!"

"All right, All right, I ain't trynna hear all that noise!" Flash gave Jadyn a wink and ordered what she wanted along with a Grey Goose and cranberry and a Corona for himself. After the waitress took all the orders at the table, Flash grabbed her around the waist again, leaned in and whispered something the rest of them couldn't hear. This time the girl smiled and whispered something in Flash's ear that caused him to grin and watch her walk all the way back to the bar. She looked like she was swinging her hips extra hard as she went.

"If you want to get your swerve on, cuz, don't let the pitbull babysitter in you squash your mood," Jadyn told him.

He gave her another wink. "Oh don't you worry 'bout that, li'l cousin, I'm definitely gon' take care of mine and still have time to keep one a' these eyes on you at all times. Believe that!"

A guy wearing a Miami Dolphins warm-up suit with a matching cap came up and asked her to dance. Flash started to object, but she stood up so fast, there wasn't much he could say.

Once they were on the dance floor he tried to spit game at her, but she wasn't really feeling him, so she made small talk or pretended the music was so loud she couldn't hear him until the song was over. He wanted to dance to another song, but she was ready to move on. He couldn't keep up with her anyway.

Jadyn was hardly back in her seat before someone else came and asked her to dance. She danced a couple of songs with the new guy. He was cool and funny, and she liked the way he held his arm out and walked her back to her seat. You would never get that from a man in Ohio. This went on for a while before she was so exhausted that she turned the next comer down.

"Baby, I'm tired," she told him. "I have to catch my breath . . ."

"I'll wait," he said. And though it was dim and noisy, she thought she caught something familiar in his voice. He turned toward her and at that same instant the strobe light lit his face and his features came into focus. It was Julian, the guy from the plane. What in the hell was he doing here?

"What's goin' on, Jadyn?"

"No the real question is, what are you doing here?"

He laughed out loud and took a swig of his beer before he answered. "What, a brother can't just happen to come out for some fun and run into a new acquaintance? That's how it happens in the movies, ain't it?" She just gave him a look and he could tell she wasn't buying what he was trying to sell.

"Look, I ain't no damn stalker if that's what you thinkin'. I was invited."

Jadyn didn't know if he was or wasn't, but she was happy that

Flash was on the floor getting his dance on right about now. Julian looked at the empty seat and asked, "Mind if I sit down?"

"Well, the person whose seat it is is on the floor at the moment . . . but I guess you can sit here 'til he gets back."

Julian didn't need to be told twice. He moved into the seat. "It's all good. I'll move when the time comes."

He stared at Jadyn. "I don't mind telling you, you even finer tonight than you were on the plane and that's goin' some. 'Cause you definitely looked damn good then, too."

Jadyn blushed, but didn't say anything.

"Can I buy you a drink?"

Jadyn looked down at her glass, which was still a little less than half full. The ice had melted and it tasted even weaker than it had when the waitress had left it. She suspected now that what Flash had whispered in her ear had more to do with how to fix her drink than any secret rendezvous between the two of them.

"Sure can, I'm drinking Tanqueray and Seven."

Julian signaled the waitress. He ordered another Bud for himself, as well.

"So Miss Lovely, who you here with?"

Mani walked back to the table with Jarrell.

"Wooo, girl! That DJ is playin' all the jams tonight, ain't he?"

"Girl, you know you don't even care what song the DJ play, it could be fast, slow, in between, you don't give a fuck as long as you can be out there shakin' that ass!" Jarrell said.

Mani slapped him playfully.

"Oh shut up. 'Rel, you know you like to show off on the floor more than anybody, so you ain't got no room to talk!"

Jarell just leaned toward her snapping his fingers and singing, "'Shake ya ass! But wwwatch ya'self!'" he sang, doing his best impression of Mystikal the singer.

Mani started laughing and so did she. Then Mani asked, "Who is this fine specimen of a gentleman? Ouch!" Jarrell smacked her thigh. "Well, he is fine, damn I ain't blind!"

Jadyn laughed again and then Flash was standing over her.

31

"Who dis nigga sittin' in my seat?" Flash asked, sounding playful but serious, too. Julian began to rise from the seat.

"Aw, it's cool, man. I was just—"

Flash stepped in a little closer. "Just what, nigga?" he said a bit more ominously.

Jadyn interrupted, "Stop it, Flash, I know him."

Flash relaxed a little and took a step back. "Know him from where?"

"He from Ohio," she lied. "He friends with Nite. We hooked up on the same flight on the way here. This is Julian. Julian Locklin."

"Julian, hunh?"

Julian reached out a hand to Flash. Flash reluctantly gave him the pound.

"Nice to meet you," Julian said before turning Jadyn's way. "I guess I'll have to wait on that dance."

"Naw, dude, sit down. Join us. You cool with my cousin, you cool wit' me." Flash seemed to relax a little more, reached for an empty chair behind him, and scooted it over a little to make room for Julian.

Flash turned toward Jarrell and began speaking to him in a low voice. Julian leaned in to say something to Jadyn, but before he could speak, a large dark-skinned man in a black tee, Timberlands, and black jeans, began to speak into a microphone.

"All right you pahty people, it's time to git this here pahty stahted! Alla y'all that been here before know what time it is when Steele Money take the mic. It's time for the dimes to shine and the nickels and pennies to whine!"

Laughter broke out in a wave at Steele Money's last remark.

"A'ight, y'all nickels and pennies ain't gotta whine but you damn sho' ain't gonna step up in this line!" More laughs from the crowd.

"This line is for the true dimes! Those that are fine as wine, and just as sweet. If you think you can get on, then come on up here. But I'm warnin' y'all, don't play yourself, 'cause y'all know I'oun't have no problem callin' out the fake from the real! Y'all know the deal!"

Jadyn was surprised by how many girls began standing up and practically running up to the front. Mani started to stand, but Jarrell immediately grabbed her hand and pulled her back down.

"Man, sit your narrow ass down and quit playin'!" he said.

Mani pouted. "First of all, my ass is anything but narrow. And second, you heard the man, he say he want all the dimes to come up front. What, you don't think that's me?"

"Hell yeah, it's you. And you know you definitely got a fatty on you." He leaned back and rubbed his hand over her rear. "But you wit' me and you ain't goin' nowhere, girl!"

Mani smiled and Jarrell pulled her close and gave her a kiss.

"You know I ain't goin' nowhere, baby, I was just playin'."

"I know."

Flash, who had been trying to speak with their waitress, was eyeballing Jadyn and giving her a look like *Don't even.* She smirked and made a face at him. He smiled and tipped his beer toward her before taking a big gulp, not moving his eyes off her. Jadyn just looked away.

She glanced over at the line of the wannabe dimes that was growing longer by the second. As far as she could see some of the ladies that were getting in line were setting themselves up to be clowned because they damn sure weren't no dimes. She wasn't trying to be cruel or nothing, but hell some of them weren't even pennies, they weren't even registering on the radar of good looks! Jadyn shook her head and laughed to herself as she twirled the straw around in her drink before taking another sip. She made a face because the melting ice had diluted the drink down to where it was almost all water with no kick. She pushed her glass away and placed her elbows on top of the table.

"What's funny?" Julian asked.

Jadyn tilted her head to one side and gazed into Julian's eyes.

"What's funny is you. You happening to be here tonight, alone. You happening to find me, outta all the women up in the joint. I mean look at 'em." She nodded her head in the direction of the dime line.

"Yeah, I'm lookin'. I don't see no women up there though. All I see is a bunch of chickens trying to snare the prize rooster. Lining up like Steele about to give away a million dollars instead of maybe a chance to get star fucked. And a slim chance at that."

Jadyn broke her gaze and watched the action. Steele was walking up the line perusing the "beauties." He walked past one that had to weigh at least a good three hundred pounds. Steele paused for effect and then brought the microphone to his lips and said, "Hold up," before taking two steps back and landing in front of the plus-size chick.

"What in the hell is you doin' in the dime line? I asked for the dimes not a truckload of Chuck E. Cheese tokens!"

The whole place roared with laughter. Jadyn glanced over at Flash, who had just taken another swig of his beer and then spewed it out all over the waitress he had been trying to holla at all night.

"Fool, look what you did, you asshole!" she cried, jumping back a little too late. Flash set his beer on the bar, still laughing and took one of those little square napkins off the bar and began trying to wipe the beer off her, dabbing at the wet cleavage that rose above the tight V-necked tee she was wearing.

"Ah, now, baby, you know I didn't mean to do that, but that shit was funny as hell and I couldn't hold it back," Flash said, rubbing the little square of paper against her nipples. She'd had enough, she slapped his hand away from her breasts.

"Ain't shit funny, nigga! Git yo' hands *off* me." She picked up her tray and started to elbow her way past him. Since her hands were busy holding the tray, Flash took the opportunity to rub her ass and grab a handful as she passed by.

Her eyes pierced him as she flung an insult at him. "Low-life punk!"

"Aw baby, lighten up. You know you want this," he threw back at her, grabbing his crotch.

"Save it for ya mammy!"

"Oh I got a mammy fo' yo' ass! You'll be hollerin' for ya mammy and ya grandmammy before I get through wit' you!"

Jarrell stood up and gave Flash dap and they both cracked up laughing.

Steele Money was still having fun at the big girl's expense. She didn't have sense enough to sit down.

"Lawd ha' mercy, baby, you got more cakes than Duncan Hines. I mean, you done *ate* all the cakes at Duncan Hines."

The girl finally started making her way back to her seat.

"Fuck you, muhafucka!" she threw over her shoulder.

"Aw, gon' somewhere and find yourself a swimming pool, ya fuckin' beached whale. Betta yet, find yaself a ocean! Two oceans!"

The crowd was going crazy. Steele turned back to the line.

"OK, now alla y'all ain't got the hair you was born with, sit ya asses down."

Not one of the women moved, so Steele took out a wide-toothed comb. "Don't make me have to prove it. I know all y'all bitches wasn't born with hair down to ya asses, so quit trippin'!" He walked up and stood next to a chick that everybody could see had weave and weave's mammy. She had so much weave she could have been Diana Ross's twin sister.

Steele raised the comb up in front of her. She knocked it away with her arm.

"Aw kiss my ass, punk," she said, tossing her weave as she sashayed to her seat.

"All the rest of ya'll with horse hair gone with her!" The line got about ten women shorter. One of them threw up her middle finger as she marched by him. Steele raised his foot and threw a fake kick at her ass.

"Man, that's some bullshit!" Jadyn said. "Why do broads be puttin' their shit out there like that? Don't they have more respect for themselves than that?" The shit wasn't even funny to her. "I bet if it was a woman up there lining up men, y'all wouldn't think the shit was so fuckin' funny."

Flash had come back to the table.

"Wouldn't think what was so fuckin' funny?" he asked, looking from Jadyn to Julian and back again. Jadyn stared blankly at her cousin. She doubted if he would understand. She hated the degrading things that Steele Money was saying to the women. How he was clowning and disrespecting them, treating them like they were less than human. Like they didn't deserve to be treated any better than this, like they were supposed to be treated like cattle. The best of the herd to be plucked and screwed and then thrown away after the bull was done. It was sad and pitiful that the assumption was that black women had no value, not even to those who should treasure them.

Steele was dissing those who didn't have straight white teeth now, and Julian and Flash were still laughing. Jadyn glared at them. Flash caught her look first.

"What's wrong wit'chu?"

Jadyn stared at him for a few more beats before rising from her chair.

"Forget about it. You could never feel what I'm feelin'," she said. "I'm goin' to get me another drink."

Jadyn went and sat on an empty bar stool and ordered another drink. A double.

She felt a hand touch her lower back and turned slightly to see who had touched her. It was Julian.

"You all right?"

She glanced up at him and then back at the man fixing her drink. "No, I'm not all right. I think that it's pretty fucked up that y'all are!"

Julian sat in the seat next to her and ordered another drink for himself.

"I'm payin' for the lady's drink, too."

He leaned toward Jadyn. "Maybe if you told me what's got you so pissed, a brother could begin to understand."

The bartender set their drinks in front of them. Jadyn picked hers up and swung her legs so that her stool swiveled and faced the dime line. She took a sip of her drink and nodded as she pointed toward the line.

"Can you tell me why this freak show doesn't bother you? I mean, how in the hell do y'all even laugh at shit like this?"

Steele only had six women still standing and he wasn't done. "Oh, no. We ain't lettin' Da City go down like that! Where alla y'all real dimes at? Don't stand in the shadows like you don't know. Brang ya fine asses on up here," Steele said, as he lifted his hand to his brow and scanned the crowd.

The crowd was speckled with feminine voices murmuring "Hell no!" and "Fuck that shit." But Steele wasn't to be denied.

"Gimme the spotlight, fellas," he said. "If y'all don't want to come to me then I'ma just have to bring the line to you."

The spotlight began rolling around the club. Catching a pretty face every now and then.

Jadyn was smirking because she knew the ladies who had kept their seats were just that—real ladies and they weren't about to be put on display for none of this dumb shit. Fuck the dumb!

Jadyn spun around in her seat and faced the bar again.

"That shit is for the birds. Who in the hell does that dude think he is to decide what's fine and what ain't? I mean look at him all decked out in some old jean outfit. I mean it ain't even name-brand shit like Kanai or FUBU. But he gon' call himself fit to judge others? What a freakin' joke! Give me a fuckin' break! And on top of all of that, he ain't even fine himself!"

Julian laughed. And Jadyn noticed his LL Cool J lips once again. The skin was smooth and soft as it stretched across his gorgeous white teeth. She was unable to pull her eyes away.

"You might have a point there," Julian said. "But why do you care? If silly bitches want to put themselves out there like that it's on them, it ain't on you. They should school themselves on the game. And if they're too dumb to figure out the real deal, then that is also on them. Why should you try to carry their burdens?" Julian spoke in an even tone with not even a hint of sarcasm.

Jadyn sipped her drink and listened. She was starting to feel the buzz from the gin. It was making her feel loose and carefree. Julian's words sort of made sense, but part of her was still angry about the way the women were allowing themselves to be treated.

Julian continued speaking. "Anyway, not only are you the finest babe in here, but you know how to think for yourself, too. You didn't go running up front to show off and shit. Even though you would definitely have had every right to!"

Jadyn blushed and smiled.

"Oh yeah, see what I'm sayin'? Look at that smile. It's corny as hell but you light up this corner when you do that. Your skin got that pretty red brown, and seems to be made of satin. It begs to be touched, and this man is dying to oblige. Your hair, I ain't seen its equal in a long time. It's so thick and coarse, yet shiny and beautiful at the same time. And those eyes of yours . . . it makes my heart play the drums against my ribs, just to look at them. It feels like my whole body is being soaked up like a sponge every time you look at me the way you are now."

Jadyn looked away. "You trippin'. I'm not lookin' at you no special type way."

"That's the point. You don't have to." Julian reached up and turned her face toward his. He locked eyes with hers and she felt her heart pound. He began bringing his lips toward hers and at the last possible second, she ducked her head so his lips landed on her cheek.

She could tell Julian was disappointed, but he just picked up his drink and took a sip before he spoke to her again.

"What you doin' tomorrow afternoon?" he asked.

"Why you askin'?"

Julian smiled and spun her stool around to face him. "Why am I asking? What do I have to do to let you know that I want to get to know you better? I thought maybe we could go to the beach or somethin'. Why don't you give me your number so I could call you?"

Jadyn smiled and on an impulse scribbled her cell number down on a napkin and handed it to him.

She was about to say something to him when suddenly the spotlight shone on her.

"Whoooo-wee! Now that is what I call fine. Fuck a dime baby, you way off the meter! Youse a bona fide ten-karat gold piece. *Damn!* Now I know you gon' brang your fine ass up here!"

"Oh shit! Flash gon' lose his damn mind! You know he playin' that overprotective role with me," Jadyn said.

"Yeah I caught that earlier. Want me to check dude and get him to back off?"

An idea popped into Jadyn's head as Julian began to rise from his seat.

"No, wait a minute. I'm cool. I got a surprise for your boy," she said as she stepped down from the stool and took two steps without really meaning to. Julian instinctively reached out his arms to steady her.

"I'm cool," Jadyn said brushing his arms away from her.

"What's going on in that pretty little head of yours?"

Jadyn smoothed her skirt and ran her fingers through her thick locks.

"Just watch," she said as she walked away, glancing back over her shoulder and loving the fact that Julian couldn't seem to keep his eyes off the sashay of her hips shifting to and fro and she strode purposefully up to Steele Money.

32

"Damn! Somebody wake me up 'cause I got to be dreamin'!"

Flash was in the back trying to make things right with the barmaid after spilling the drink on her so he didn't see what Jadyn was up to.

She stepped closer to Steele Money and flashed her brightest smile. It was one she used when she wanted her way and usually got it.

"Mmmm-mmmp-mmmp baby, don't do me this way," Steele Money fake-whined, grinning, showing-brown, uneven teeth.

Jadyn whispered something in his ear, and he handed her the mic. "Do your thang, baby, do your thang!"

Jadyn walked over to the line and looked over the remaining women standing there. She motioned for them to come over to where she was standing. They crowded together like football players in a huddle getting plans for the next play. A few of them giggled, a couple went back to their seats not willing to go along with Jadyn's plan.

Jadyn spoke into the mic. "OK, y'all came here tonight to get your party on with some dimes, right? Well, here we are!" Jadyn and the ladies struck a few poses, hands on hips and swinging their hair around. This brought a round of whoops and catcalls from the men in the bar.

"Y'all ready to party down with us?" Steele Money stepped up to Jadyn smiling and tried to envelop her in a bear hug, but Jadyn lithely sidestepped him and he grabbed air instead.

"Unh-unh Mr. Sir. This is our game, our rules. Right, ladies?"

"Yeah, that's right. We the ones runnin' things now!" one of them shouted.

"Now we gonna pick some fellas to party with us. But we want the true *dimes* only, don't we, ladies? We want y'all all to come up here and line up in front right across here, but we only taking the best with us, hunh girls?"

The fellas broke their necks trying to be the first to head to the front of the club. The bouncers stepped up to make their presence known. Jadyn noticed Julian was still at the bar, but he was standing on his feet sipping his beer. She still didn't see Flash but guessed he must be busy with the barmaid.

She walked up and down the line of guys, looking them over as Steele Money had done earlier with the ladies.

"Now you know us ladies love a man with a pretty smile. So if any of y'all have teeth so yellow they look like you could throw them in the air and make sunshine, sit your asses down!" The bar went wild with cheering and laughter once again. Steele suddenly wasn't smiling anymore, but Jadyn was just getting warmed up. Some of the men, getting where she was going, began walking back to their seats shaking their heads. A few brave souls and Steele were still standing.

"Now if you wearing wack ass no name brand jeans and you're wearing Lumberlands on your feet instead of Timberlands, sit your ass down!" She eyed Steele before she turned back to the crowd. She was playing the crowd strictly for laughs now. "If your ass is so damn big that I got to grow an extra set of eyes to look at your whole body, sit your fat asses, down!"

"Oh hell no she didn't! That's fucked up!" came calls from the crowd.

"If your ass smell like cologne and funk—"

Jadyn didn't get to finish her sentence because Steele walked over and wrestled the microphone from her hand.

"Unh, yeah, you thought that shit was cute, hunh? That shit wadn't funny," he said as he covered the mic with his hand. "Go sit your ass down before I lose my temper. Don't nobody make Steele look like a fool and live to tell it!"

"Aw, whatever. We was just havin' some fun. Showin' y'all how it feels to be put on blast like that."

"Yeah, I'ma show you how my foot feel in your ass if you don't get the fuck out my face, bit—"

Steele's insult was cut short because Flash suddenly appeared next to Jadyn and plowed his fist into Steele's mouth. Steele flew backward and fell, sprawled on his back on the floor. "Nigga, you done lost yo' fuckin' mind threatenin' my li'l cousin like that!"

Mani ran up and grabbed Jadyn and started pulling her out of the way. Steele jumped up and charged Flash, knocking over tables, sending drinks and beer bottles flying as Flash crashed to the floor. They punched and pummeled each other, tussling for position. Jarrell and Steele's boys were trying to pull them apart as the bouncers came up, dragging them apart.

"I'ma kill you and that scrawny, squirrelly-ass, trick bitch cousin of yours. You wait and see. I'ma bus' a cap in yo' fake ass, playa!" Steele screamed.

Flash tore away from the two men that were holding him, pulling his Glock out of the waist of his jeans as he did. He ran up on Steele and shoved the gun in his face.

"Yeah, nigga, who you gon' kill now, bitch? Who you gon' kill? I will split yo muhfuckin' wig, nigga!" Flash cocked the trigger as Jarrell ran up behind him and pulled him away from Steele. Flash and Steele's crews pulled their guns and pointed them at each other.

"*No!*" Julian pushed through the crowd and when he spoke the guns disappeared. Julian stepped to Steele and whispered something in his ear and he immediately sucked it up and his face became a blank mask.

"No, nigga, no! Is you crazy! Alla these people in here?" Jarrell continued to pull Flash back, pushing his gun hand down. "Man, let's get your cousin and bounce! It ain't worth this shit!"

Flash and Steele eyeballed each other, but Flash began backing away.

"It's on, nigga. You gon' remember this night, nigga," Steele told him.

"Fuck you, bitch!" Flash said, reaching behind him and jamming his piece inside his waistband. "You rather run through fire with gasoline draws on than step to me!"

"What were you thinkin', Jay? What made you do some dumb shit like that? You don't know these people! You don't know nothin' about these fools and what they capable of! Do you? Do *you?*" Flash yelled.

"Leave her alone, Flash," Mani started. "She just had a little too much to drink that's all. She just wanted to—"

"She just wanted, my ass! She shouldn'ta done what she did!"

Jadyn only moaned.

"Pull the car over! Oh God, oh Jesus, I'm gonna throw up!"

Flash pulled over and Mani opened the door. Jadyn slumped

over and leaned out of the open door, spewing vomit all over the ground.

"Yeah, that's what your lil' drunk ass git! Damn, I knew I shoulda kept my eye on you. I knew that shit!"

"Oh, please. Oh Lord, my head! Don't talk to me right now. My head hurts!"

"I hope your head fall off! It'a teach your ass a lesson."

Mani held Jadyn's head in her lap and stroked her hair.

"Leave her alone, Flash, you see she don't feel good. You can fuss at her tomorrow."

Flash looked at them in the rearview mirror and frowned, rubbing a spot over his eye.

"Yeah, well whatever. That shit was fucked up and y'all know it. Somebody's ass was 'bout to get blowed away over some ol' dumb ass shit. That ish shouldn'ta never happened! Who know what the fuck is gon' go down after this. I know one damn thing, it ain't gon' be me!"

33

The next day Jadyn had the house to herself since her uncle and cousin had to work. Flash was still pissed and not treating her as warmly as he had that first night.

The phone rang and she picked it up.

"Hello."

"What's good, Jay? It's Mani. I'm just callin' to check on you and whatnot. You was really high last night, wasn't you?"

"Yeah, girl, I don't know what was up with me. I usually don't get drunk. I can usually handle mine."

"Well, you sure as hell wasn't handlin' yours last night. You was wil'in' out."

"Damn, was it that bad?"

"That bad and worse! You was all over the place and then on the way home you almost threw up in Flash's ride. He woulda been pissed!"

"Yeah well, he's pissed enough as it is. He was all givin' me the cold shoulder and shit this morning before he went to work."

"If I was you I would be happy that the cold shoulder was all he was givin' me. Don't you know you was all up in the club talkin' shit on the microphone to Steele Money? Of all the people up in Palm City to start some shit with, you had to pick him."

"I vaguely remember that shit. I don't know, it just pissed me off the way his ugly ass was up there dissin' the ladies and all those dudes laughin' at them and things. I guess I just lost it."

"Yeah, but why did that bother you so much? I mean if those broads wanted to get up there and make fools of themselves, why the hell should you give a damn?"

Mani had echoed Julian's words to her last night almost to a tee. Why had she cared? What had made her so upset?

"I do not know. I guess the thought of men treatin' women like shit just 'cause they can just irritates the hell out of me."

She heard Mani sigh on the other end. "Yeah, I guess I can understand you feelin' that way. But girl, watch your back while you here. I know Flash got your back and all, but that nigga Steele . . . He be clownin' up in the clubs and things, 'cause that's what he do. But trust me, he ain't no joke. And when you cross him, he don't forget."

"Yeah, OK. Thanks for calling, Mani and givin' me the 411."

"You welcome, girl. I'll probably call you later to see what y'all getting into tonight. I gotta get outta here right now, 'fore my ass is late to work."

Jadyn thought of something else. She liked Mani, she seemed cool as hell.

"Hey, Mani, what you gonna be doing Saturday morning?"

"I'm probly gon' have my ass in bed sleeping late for one thing. It's my day off. Why?"

"I need a ride someplace. If I give you gas money, do you think you could take me?"

"What time you talking about?"

"Early, but not too. Maybe nine or ten o'clock."

"Nine or ten? Girl what you think is not too early about that on somebody's day off? I usually sleep at least 'til noon!"

Jadyn sighed. She didn't sleep 'til noon ever. Between work, practice, and auditions, she almost always had to be up well before.

"OK, OK, then will you take me when you get up?"

"Yeah, Jay, I can do that. Look here, I gotta run. I'll talk to you later."

"All right, talk to you later!"

No sooner had she laid the phone down, it rang again.

"Hello?"

"Hello, Jadyn? It's Ms. Rashad."

"Ms. Rashad, hi!"

"Listen, baby, I'm taking a short break from class so I can't talk long, but I talked to my friend and I wanted to tell you right away."

Jadyn leaned back in the chair and glanced up at the ceiling. She wished Ms. Rashad would quit playing games and tell her what was up.

"OK, Ms. Rashad. What's up?"

"Well, she'll explain everything to you once you see her, but anyway, she wants to see you dance. She's holding auditions for some little something she's putting together. Don't worry about the what right now, just worry about the how. Can you get your uncle or your cousin to take you to Orlando to see her?"

Jadyn leaned forward and stood on her feet.

"Orlando?"

"Yes, darlin', don't you remember me telling you my friend lived in Orlando? Well, even if you don't remember, she told me that Palm City is about a two-hour drive from where she is. This is very important, so I want you to dance for her like your life depends on the outcome. I want you to perform that number you choreographed to 'I Still Believe in Me.' "

Jadyn smiled, it was one of her favorite dances. It was a very special piece because Ms. Rashad had written the music, had choreographed it, and had been there with Jadyn the first time she had performed it.

"OK, Ms. Rashad. But you're asking a whole lot from me without really givin' any details. I mean, can't you even give me a hint?"

"No, not now, child, I told you I don't have much time. In fact I just have time to give you my friend's address before I have to go. But I will tell you that she is looking for dancers for a very special project, OK? You got a pencil and paper?"

Jadyn walked over and picked up her purse from the dresser, opened it up, and took out her wallet. She always had a pen and paper in there.

"Yes, Ms. Rashad, I have them, go ahead, please."

"Her name is Henrietta Hollister, you are to meet her at two o'clock sharp on Tuesday. Her address is 8122 Lake Baldwin Lane and in case you get lost her number is 407-555-1016."

Jadyn wrote as quickly as possible. "OK, got it."

"All right, sweetheart. Now I gave Henrietta my recommendation; my highest, in fact so you betta not make me look bad!"

Jadyn laughed. "I'll try not to do that Ms. Rashad."

"And Jadyn, have faith in me. Know that I believe in you and I wouldn't waste Henrietta's time or yours if I didn't think you were good enough. Believe that. Have a little faith."

34

Friday evening, Jarrell and Flash said they had some business they had to take care of, so Mani called Jadyn.

"Hey girl, you want to go get something to eat or somethin' since 'Rel and Flash gon' be busy all evening?"

Jadyn didn't hesitate. She needed to talk to Mani about taking her to Cocoa Beach tomorrow, anyway. She knew she would have to confide in her about wanting to find her father, so this would give her time to read her a little bit better.

"Yeah, that sounds like a plan to me. What time you wanna go?"

"I don't know. I was thinking around six thirty, seven. Somewhere around in there."

"Sounds good to me."

"All right, I'll be by to get you about then."

"What you wearin'?"

"Probably some shorts or a skirt or something, I'm not trying to get dressed up."

"Yeah, I'ma probably throw on a pair of shorts myself. OK, I'll see you after while."

. . .

In her hands was the empty box that had once held the sweet sixteen necklace from her dad. She kept staring at the address on the label, wondering if she would be able to find it on her own if she couldn't convince Mani to make the two-hour long drive tomorrow.

She could get on a bus and head to Cocoa Beach. Once there, she figured she could get a cab and have the driver take her to the address. But the question that always pressed her and made her afraid made itself known once again. What are you going to say to him when you see him? She sighed and leaned her head back in the overstuffed chair in the living room. Such a simple question, not even particularly scary when you just looked at it on its own. But when you attached it to a situation like hers, it took on a whole new dimension. Jadyn shifted in her seat and stared out of the large window directly across from her. The view was picture perfect and soothing, with clear blue skies and lush greenery that only Palm City could offer. She rose from her seat and walked outside into the bright sunshine. Squinting against the sun's rays, she took a seat on one of the chaise lounges her uncle had set out on the patio and waited for Mani.

They decided they wanted Chinese. Mani knew of a nice buffet-style restaurant that wasn't too far from her.

The setup was nice and family casual. After using hand sanitizer, they stepped up to the bar. There were the perfunctory selections you would find at any buffet: salad greens and black olives, cheese, mushrooms, onions, boiled eggs, raisins, sunflower seeds. The greens looked fresh and crisp, so they must have just been put there.

The pungent odor of shellfish and shrimp mingled with the

fruity, spicy aromas of the sauces and dips that were arranged neatly along the highly polished stainless steel buffet table. The zesty fragrance of orange, sesame, and General Tso's chicken, along with black pepper scallops filled the air, while little vapors of steam rose from the trays of white and fried rice. The egg drop soup, beef, and vegetables added their sharp, pungent odor to the mix.

"Everything looks so good. I think I'll start with the salad and crab legs, with steamed rice and the shrimp and scallops."

Mani laughed. "If that's a start, I'd hate to see how you finish. I can't believe somebody as small as you are could eat that much."

Jadyn laughed, too. "I like to get my grub on, for real."

Mani helped herself to some crab legs and a salad topped with everything available.

"I see you don't have any problems getting your eat on either!"

"Hmph. Not hardly."

Once they had taken their seats, Jadyn wondered what would be the best way to approach the subject of why she had come to Florida. Luckily Mani saved her the trouble by bringing it up first.

"So what made you decide to come to Palm City? You just wanted to visit your family, or what?" she asked as she opened up her paper napkin to its full size and spread it delicately over her lap. She forked up a bite of her salad before placing her fork back down on her plate as she chewed.

Jadyn picked up a crab leg, placed it in the cracker, and squeezed. The crab shell made a loud crunching sound as it gave way to reveal the reddish pink, sweet crabmeat inside. Picking up the little fork specially made for this purpose, she speared a chunk and pulled it out onto her plate. Jadyn picked up another leg and repeated the process as she thought about Mani's question. To be honest, she would never have even thought about coming if Taji hadn't done the snaky things he had and ruined her audition, so that was the real reason she had come: to get away from all of that. But it was also an opportunity to find her father. And she really did need him in her life after all the shit she had been through. Since she needed Mani's help with that, she'd just begin and end her story there and not tell Mani about her and Taji. She didn't think it was necessary to bare her soul to the bone to Mani.

"Yeah, that's really it. I wanted to visit my family. I only met my Uncle BruhJay a few times, but he always treated us good, and he is my grandma's only brother. The only other living relative my grandma has is her Aunt Hattie, and she got to be over ninety years old, 'cause my grandma is in her sixties. She always told us that her Aunt Hattie raised her and she was old then."

"Both my great-grandparents are alive and kickin'. My mother's grandmother is livin' with my parents. She got Alzheimer's, bless her soul. Mama and Daddy always fighting about it, because Daddy don't really want her there. He thinks my grandmother should be takin' care of her. But Mama thinks her mother's not strong enough to care for her. She'd rather do it."

"Your father ain't happy with that, hunh? Well, to be fair it must be hard for him to care for your great-grandmother, your mother, and you, too."

"Trust me, Daddy ain't hurtin' for no money. Even before I moved out of the house, he made sure we had what we needed and wanted. Daddy owns his own trash collection company, and believe me when I tell you that around here, there is always somebody moving in and building a new house or rebuilding their old one after a storm, so there is always a bunch of trash to haul away. My daddy ain't hardly hurtin' for no money."

"I hear you," Jadyn said and as Mani talked about her father, it stirred up the same old longing for hers.

"Daddy spoiled us all rotten. He even bought me my car when

I moved out, and paid the deposit on my apartment. He always doing shit like that." Mani smiled as she picked up her fork and ate another bite of salad.

Watching Mani like she was, Jadyn couldn't help but wonder how somebody who ate like a bird could be as thick as she was. She wasn't fat at all, but she had wide hips—which wasn't a bad thing—and big thighs and legs and big boobs. She looked like all of the cartoon drawings of a sister. She wore her long hair pulled up into a ponytail, which accented her perfectly arched eyebrows and huge, round, almost bulging eyes. Her dark hair was a stark contrast to her full lips and light brown skin.

Since Mani had opened up to Jadyn about her family, she decided now was a good time to tell Mani about her dad.

"I want to tell you something, Mani. Something that I don't want Flash to know about right now. So the only way I'm gonna tell you what it is, is if you promise not to say nothing to Flash or Jarrell."

"I know you don't know me all like this, but you ask anybody here, if they don't tell you nothing else, they'll tell you that I can keep a secret. What's going on?"

"Ain't nothin' goin' on really. Look, Mani, one of the reasons I'm here is to find my biological dad," Jadyn blurted out before taking a bite of her scallops and chewing slowly.

"No shit? So Flash and them . . . your uncle . . . they don't know this?"

Jadyn shook her head without speaking.

"Why is it a secret, Jadyn? Why don't you want nobody to know?"

Jadyn stared at Mani without speaking. How could she explain that her father had stopped calling her years ago and might not want her? That if that was the case, she didn't want her family feeling all sorry for her and shit. Or even worse, getting mad and going and trying to get some kind of stupid revenge on her father. They wouldn't understand that if he rejected her, it wouldn't stop her from loving him. It would hurt like hell, but she knew the loving and the wanting would continue, no matter what.

"I don't know, Mani. I guess I just want to keep it simple if things don't go the way I think they will or they should. I don't want everybody's feelings gettin' involved and things. Can't nobody understand what it's like not to really know your father. They think they can replace your real father with an uncle or by marrying another man. They don't understand that that won't happen, that part of you will always be missing if you don't have your dad. You don't know, anybody who's grown up with their real dad, can never really know what I'm feeling. And trynna explain it only makes it worse. If things don't go my way, even if things do go my way, this is something I just want to keep private between my dad and me. For now anyway."

Mani reached across the table and squeezed Jadyn's hand for a second before telling her, "I think I do get it, Jadyn. I won't tell nobody. I promise."

Jadyn looked up and smiled as she picked up her fork.

"That's good. I'm glad you understand because that's where you taking me tomorrow. But can we change the day to Tuesday evening?"

"What? What are you talking about?"

"Look, I'm a dancer and I have an audition with this woman who might be able to get me into a Broadway show." Jadyn twisted the truth. She didn't want to tell Mani that she didn't quite know what she was auditioning for. And besides, she thought throwing in that she had a chance to dance on Broadway might help convince Mani to change the date of the trip to Tuesday. "So now you know the whole story. I need to get to Orlando on Tuesday afternoon, for the audition. See, I thought I could try to kill two birds with one stone. Do the audition and check out the last address I have for my dad at the same time. The address is in Cocoa Beach, outside Orlando."

"So you expect me to take a day off from work and drive you all the way to Cocoa Beach?"

"I know I'm asking a lot, seeing how we don't know each other all that well yet. I'll drive if you don't feel like it. I'll pay for all the gas and I'll make sure it's on full when we get back, too."

Mani stared at her. "You gon' what? Fill up my gas tank? Who gonna pay for the day I'm losing at work?"

Jadyn gave her a blank stare. "You can't get your man to cover one day's pay? Shi-it! You need to fire him, then!"

Mani was shocked at Jadyn's question at first, but then she began laughing and so did Jadyn.

"Look, I'll pay you the same amount it would cost me to take a bus there. OK? And if I ever get to Broadway I'll give you free tickets to the first show I do," Jadyn told her, grinning broadly.

Mani rolled her eyes, glanced down at her plate, and sighed. Then she looked at Jadyn and smiled. "OK. I'm game," Mani said, picking up a crab leg from Jadyn's plate and cracking it open. "And I'll just get my girl Sandy to switch her Tuesday off for my Thursday, that way neither you nor my man got to worry about payin' me for my work time. But you gon' do all the drivin' there and back, no matter what."

"I said I would, didn't I?"

"And I'll be 'round there around ten to pick you up."

Jadyn rose from her seat to give Mani a hug.

"All right already! All that ain't necessary. I'm gon' sleep the whole trip and don't try to keep me woke trynna talk to me, nei-ther."

"OK, you can get your sleep on while I drive. I ain't hatin'."

"Unh-hunh, we'll see."

Jadyn had all of the crabmeat pulled from the shell. She then began piling the crab meat on top of her salad.

"That looks good. Can I taste it?" Mani asked.

"Yeah, go ahead, take some," she said, pushing her bowl toward Mani's side of the table.

"I can't believe you haven't tried this before, since you living up here in the seafood capital of the world."

"Who said I never tried it before? I just want to taste some of yours. Be ready when I get to your house on Tuesday, because I don't like to be kept waiting."

Jadyn glared at her for a brief moment. She was about to tell Mani to watch how she spoke to her. Sometimes the girl could speak to you like you were beneath her or some shit. But she bit her tongue since she was supplying the transportation.

"Yeah, I'll be ready, don't worry."

35

Mani was true to her word and slept the entire ride. She even brought a blanket and pillow with her. She only stayed awake long enough to direct Jadyn to the interstate. Luckily there was only one turn she had to make and then it was a straight shot to Cocoa. Once they were on their way, Mani made herself comfortable and had fallen asleep almost as soon as her head hit the pillow, snoring softly.

Jadyn put in a Maxwell CD and sang along softly with him all the way there, willing herself not to think about all the possible repercussions of finally seeing her father face-to-face after so much time had passed.

Popping out the Maxwell CD, she replaced it with the one she would be using for the audition, and pressed the REPEAT button. As the music began, she mentally worked her way through her performance. She loved the piece so much and had performed it so many times that she could do the dance in her sleep. Even so, she had spent the entire weekend refining the choreography and perfecting the arm movements. The dance was a wonderful blend of ballet and modern and, if done correctly, usually brought some in the audience to their feet. She was so caught up in the music and performing the piece in her head that, before she realized it, she had reached the Cocoa Beach exit.

Glancing down at the sheet of paper upon which Mani had written directions, she made a quick right turn off the exit ramp and continued in that direction. According to the directions, she only needed to make two more turns: straight ahead for five miles, make a left. Follow that road another three miles, make another left, and she would end up on her dad's street.

Her heart began to pound at the thought of maybe seeing her dad for the first time. The old fears resurfaced and mixed with new. What if he didn't want her? What if he got mad at her for showing up at his door unannounced? What if the way he treated her affected her at the audition? What if it made her blow the audition? Taking a deep breath through her nostrils, she blew it out slowly through her mouth and repeated the process to try to calm herself down. It was too late to think about that now. She wouldn't dare wake Mani up and tell her that she was too chicken to go through with her plan after convincing her to take a day off work.

Too quickly, she found herself pulling up in front of the house that was the last known address for her father. She sat there, staring at it for a while before reaching over to rouse Mani from her long nap.

"Hey, we're here."

Mani stretched and yawned. "You found the house by yourself?"

"Yeah, these directions you pulled off of MapQuest ended up being easy to follow."

Mani rubbed her eyes, stretched again, and pooted.

"Ewwww! Stinky ass!" Jadyn immediately pressed the button to let her window down and stuck her head outside.

"So girl, that is a normal bodily function. I ain't shame."

"You don't have to be shame, but you could have opened your

door and stuck your butt outside. Those type things is deadly in close confines like this."

Mani giggled. "Wherever you may be, let the gas run free, the way I look at it. But it was foul, wasn't it?"

"Foul ain't the word." Jadyn pinched her nostrils together before bringing her head back inside.

They both settled down and stared at the house.

"You goin' up there and ring the doorbell?"

Jadyn sighed. Was she? Was she really prepared to deal with things if they didn't go the way she hoped?

"Yeah, I guess."

"I would go with you, but I think one of us should stay in the car in case a crazy person lives there. I can call the police on my cell."

Jadyn rolled her eyes at her. "Whatever," she said before opening the door. "You do that."

Jadyn's heart was beating extra hard against her chest like a jackhammer, the way it always did when she was excited or nervous. She wondered if one day her heart would just give out on her since she seemed to overwork it so much.

She took deep breaths to calm herself down as she walked up the front walkway. Quicker than she realized, the door loomed right in front of her. *Here we go.* She lifted her hand and pressed the doorbell, hearing it chime somewhere behind the door.

Her heart skipped and thudded as she waited for the door to open. One minute . . . two minutes . . . Glancing over her shoulder at Mani, she shrugged her shoulders. Mani made a sign for her to push the doorbell again. She pushed the bell again and leaned on it for a couple of seconds before letting go, hearing the harsh chimes sounding somewhere inside the house. Even if they were still asleep, that was certainly enough to wake them. And Jadyn had a fleeting thought that it might not be a good thing, waking people up on what could be their day off.

Her heart thumped and skipped some more, but it was for no reason. No one came to the door. Mani got out of the car and walked up to join her at the front door. She pounded on the door with her fist before Jadyn could stop her.

"Girl, don't do that! If somebody is in there, they are gonna think we are crazy or somethin' and call the police."

"Well, go over there and look in that window and see what you see."

"No, girl, what if he in there gettin' busy or somethin' and just don't want to answer? What if they right there in the livin' room gettin' off? I don't want to see my father naked and doing stuff. You look."

Mani let out a deep sigh and tipped up to the front window and peeked in. Then she put her hands up to the window so that she could see a little more clearly before she announced, "Don't nobody live here, Jay. It's empty."

Jadyn's shoulders slumped and a lump formed in her throat, her frustration threatening to overtake her. She walked back to the car with Mani close on her heels.

Once she had taken her place behind the driver's seat, and she had placed the key in the ignition, a tear rolled down her cheek. She brushed it away in frustration, but another took its place.

"You want me to drive?" Mani offered.

The tears were flowing in a steady stream now. Jadyn leaned her forehead against the steering wheel.

"No, I'ma be all right. I just need a minute, that's all. I'm OK. I'm just so damn disappointed I just don't know what to do now."

"Jadyn, it's gon' be OK. You'll find him. I know you will." Mani rubbed her arm. Jadyn rubbed away more tears with her hands.

"You right. I'ma find him. It's just gonna take some time." She sniffed back the tears and cleared her throat as she glanced at the clock on the dashboard. Twelve fifteen. "You hungry? We got about two hours to kill before the audition."

Mani stretched and scratched her head. "You know, come to think of it, I really didn't eat much of a breakfast. Just a slice of toast and coffee. I could use a li'l sumpn' sumpn'."

Jadyn leaned forward and turned the ignition. "OK, let's find a restaurant or a mall food court or something. The least I can do is treat you to lunch for helpin' me out today."

Mani and Jadyn sat in the studio in Henrietta Hollister's condo and waited for her return. After ushering them downstairs, she had suddenly remembered a call she had to make and rushed back up the steps.

After a few moments she returned, carrying a tray that held bottled water, juice, and cookies.

"I apologize for that, but the call couldn't wait," Ms. Hollister said, her refined voice carefully enunciating each word.

She looked as regal as she sounded. Jadyn estimated that she was around six feet tall and wore her short cropped Afro like a crown. Though Ms. Rashad had said that she and Ms. Hollister were about the same age, somewhere in their fifties, she had the body of a much younger woman. With long lean legs and slender arms that showed not a trace of fat or cellulite anywhere. Her dark, ebony face was as unlined and lean as her body and gave no hint of her age. The oval face was defined by a finely bridged nose that flared suddenly and fully around her nostrils. There was something about her eyes and lips that reminded Jadyn of the old school movie actress, Diahann Carroll. They were equally beautiful. As she set the tray on a table in a far corner of the room, you couldn't help but notice how she moved with such grace, anyone could see that she had been trained in some form of dance.

"Well, Jadyn, I am so happy that you have agreed to dance for me. You come highly recommended by one of my dearest friends, so I can't express to you enough how I anticipate seeing you perform."

Jadyn stood to her feet. "Thank you so much, Ms. Hollister, it is my pleasure. I owe Ms. Rashad so much, I could never refuse her anything." She glanced over at Mani before she continued.

"I hope you don't mind, but I don't have a car, so my friend offered to bring me."

"Not at all, Jadyn, your friend is more than welcome."

"I'm so sorry, Ms. Hollister, this is Mani . . ." Jadyn stared at her friend. If she had ever told her her last name, she couldn't remember it now. Luckily her friend noticed her gaffe and stepped in, rising to her feet.

"Mani Hunter, pleased to meet you, ma'am," Mani said politely. Ms. Hollister seemed to float across the room as she stopped to shake Mani's hand.

"Nice to meet you, too, Mani," she said before turning to face Jadyn. "There's a changing room just to your right and around the corner there. I don't mean to rush you, but I have another appointment in ninety minutes, so we really should begin."

"Yes, ma'am," Jadyn said as she picked up her bag and headed in the direction in which she had been pointed. "I'll be right back."

Once she made it to the room, she closed the door and leaned against it, blowing out her breath, trying to focus and prepare herself mentally for the audition. The space was large, and surprisingly roomy with a barre running along one wall. Jadyn imagined that it was probably a training room of sorts. As she began to shed her street clothes she couldn't shake the feeling that she had seen Ms. Hollister's face somewhere before, though she couldn't quite place her, and it bothered her slightly. Once she had dressed in her leotard and shorts, she pushed the nagging question aside. She would think about it later. She jiggled her arms and legs to begin loosening up her muscles and rotated her head a few times to loosen her neck. She did a few squats and stretches, and took a few deep, cleansing breaths before she opened the door and walked back into the audition room. She handed her CD to Ms. Hollister before going to stand in the middle of the floor.

As the music began, Jadyn came to life as she raised her right arm and leaned her body in the same direction while lifting her left arm behind her as she raised her body up on her toes. She moved across the floor, holding that position. Coming down off her toes she kicked out her right leg in a perfect right angle holding it there for a moment, perfectly balanced, before bringing it down and leaping into the air, tucking her right leg under her and kicking her left leg out behind her as she gracefully unfolded her arms, allowing them to flutter like the wings of a bird. The music caught her and carried her along with each note. Bending, twisting, and spinning to the rhythms, she floated across the floor, as weightless as a feather and flexing her leg muscles in intricate spirals. She could tell by the crescendo that the song was building to a finish. Back on her toes, swaying back and forth, following the graceful movement of her arms. Folding herself in and pressing her body down until she was resting on the floor sitting on one leg, the other splayed out in front and her arms and head rested on top of that leg as the music ended.

The room was quiet as Jadyn rose to her feet. Neither Mani nor Ms. Hollister had uttered a sound during the performance but Ms. Hollister broke the silence.

"Jadyn, I am impressed. And believe me, I am not easily impressed."

"Thank you, Ms. Hollister. I'm glad you enjoyed it."

"Enjoyed it? My dear girl, your dancing is almost impossible to describe. A dancer such as you comes along only very rarely. Your poise and grace are astounding. Words cannot adequately describe your talent . . . but listen to me, babbling on and on."

Jadyn drank in the praise. She was always surprised when people spoke of her in such glowing terms, but was pleased just the same.

Mani, who had remained silent, was suddenly standing next to her.

"Woo, Jadyn. Who knew you could move like that? You're good! Really good." Jadyn turned toward Mani, smiling, but her smile faded as she caught Mani's expression. Her face didn't match her words. She didn't look happy for Jadyn at all. But her expression changed like lightning and she smiled as she hugged Jadyn. "You got skills, girl! What other secrets you keeping?"

"Jadyn, why don't you get dressed and then we'll talk," Ms. Hollister told her, and from the way she was looking at Mani, Jadyn knew that she had caught the insincerity in Mani's remarks, too.

Jadyn walked back to the changing room without a word. She was trying to figure Mani out. One minute she could be as friendly as a sister, and the next second she was making some rude comment that a real friend would never make.

When she had changed back into her street clothes and reentered the room, Mani was nowhere to be found.

"Where'd Mani go?" she asked Ms. Hollister.

"Oh, she said to tell you she'd wait for you in the car. Jadyn, I want you to know that I'm going to try to set up an audition for you with someone very influential. Someone who can do a lot for you in your pursuit of a career in dancing."

"Really? Who is that?" Jadyn asked, the prospect exciting her beyond words.

"None other than Ms. Judith Jamison herself. The creative director of the Alvin Ailey American Dance Theater."

Jadyn couldn't wait to call and tell Ms. Rashad her good news. She dialed her number right after Mani had dropped her off at her uncle's house.

"Ms. Rashad, can you believe it? I might get to dance in front of Ms. Judith Jamison! Now I never in a million years woulda thought somethin' like this would happen to me!"

Jadyn's excitement had boiled over, despite Ms. Hollister's telling her that she couldn't promise her anything. She was definitely going to do everything in her power to get her an audition.

"Jadyn, that is wonderful news! But I wouldn't get too excited just yet. You know, Henrietta only told you she *might* be able to get you an audition."

Jadyn sighed before speaking. "Yes, Ms. Rashad, I know, but just the thought of havin' a chance. That's what's exciting."

"I know, darlin', but I want you to try to keep this in perspective. 'Might' is a long way off. So let's leap one hurdle at a time. That's why I didn't want to tell you too much about this, and I wish Henrietta hadn't said anything to you until we had more information."

Jadyn grew quiet as Ms. Rashad continued to speak. "I'm not tying to burst your bubble, Jadyn, or minimize the possible opportunity here. It's just that we just don't know if Henrietta will be able to pull this off. Ms. Jamison is a very busy woman and there are many, many excellent dancers, some of them students at Alvin Ailey School of Dance, who would love to dance in one of her productions. I believe you are every bit as talented as any of them. If I didn't I would have never set you on this course. It will be an amazing opportunity should it pan out, but let's not get ahead of ourselves."

Jadyn understood what her mentor was trying to tell her. There was nothing really to get excited about just yet. There was no need to set herself up for possible disappointment.

"I get what you're sayin', Ms. Rashad. And I appreciate it," Jadyn told her. "Don't build this up into something it's not, be patient, and take it slow, right?"

"That's exactly what I'm saying. So you just go on about your business like nothing's happened. Keep practicing your dance. That's important, Jadyn. So if you're not coming back here anytime soon, I could get Henrietta to work with you while you're there."

Jadyn perked up. "That would be so good if you could do that for me, Ms. Rashad."

"I'll call her as soon as we hang up. You take care, honey, and keep in touch!"

"Thank you, Ms. Rashad. I will."

36

Jadyn thought she had developed a case of insomnia or something, because she just couldn't seem to sleep. The night after she had danced for Ms. Hollister, she had The Dream again, she awoke and she hadn't been able to go right to sleep since. Sometimes, she would lie in bed wide awake 'til the crack of dawn.

It wasn't just the nightmares, it was all the disappointments she'd had of late. She'd even called KeMari Reynolds after one sleepless night to talk, but her answering service had told her that she was with a client. When they asked if she wanted to leave a message, she had told them no. She knew KeMari was more of a face-to-face type therapist. So she would undoubtedly ask her to come in to see her. And of course she couldn't do that right now.

She was just dealing with too many problems right now. Ms. Rashad had been right when she had told her you can't run from your problems. Traveling all these miles hadn't put one inch of distance between her and her problems. They were still right here. The problems with her mother and stepfather, the lost audition, Taji's deceit and their breakup, not being able to find her father. All these problems sometimes seemed too much for her to bear alone. That's why it was so important to find her real father right now. She needed him to help her get rid of this heavy load. Or at least help her carry it.

Maybe he was looking for her, too. Maybe he wanted her just as much as she wanted him.

And she did want him. She wanted to look into the eyes of the man who had helped create her. She wanted to know that missing part of her. Most of all she wanted the love. She needed the love that only a father could give her. She needed to know that the love of a father could be good and clean. Not the sick and twisted shit that she had grown up with. And just like that she knew that she had made the right decision. Finding her father was the right thing to do. Since the only lead she had had taken her to a dead end, she knew she needed help to continue her search.

She took out the card that Nite had given her and looked it over. "Finders Keepers. Reuniting lost loved ones." She was out of ideas so maybe she'd give Finders Keepers a call.

When it came to tracking down her dad, two heads had to be better than one.

37

"Finders Keepers, Anthony Eisley."

Jadyn looked down at the card Nite had given her again and couldn't help but wonder why, if he was the owner, he was answering his own phone. Maybe he wasn't as good at finding people as he claimed if he didn't even make enough money to pay a receptionist.

"Hello. I-I'm looking for someone I haven't seen in a while. Someone told me that you might be able to help me. . . ."

Jadyn rolled her eyes and made a face at how lame she knew she sounded. Why had she said that?

"Why don't you come down to the office and let's talk. You tell us what you know about the person and then we'll tell you what we're able to do for you."

Jadyn cleared her throat, which had suddenly gone dry.

"What I need you to do is tell me about your prices first. I need to see if it's something I can afford. Then we'll go from there. If your fees are too high for my purse, then there's no need to waste my time or yours."

"I totally understand. Our fees are actually based on how much legwork we need to do, whether or not we are successful in our search, and a number of other factors. May I ask who you're searching for?"

Jadyn felt awkward. She never thought about how the fact that she was looking for her father might sound to a perfect stranger. But then again, if he was in the business of finding people, she imagined it could be something he was used to hearing.

"I'm looking for my birth father. I mean, my natural father. My real father. My mother married some other man who wasn't my father and . . ."

"Yes, I see."

Thankfully, the man on the other end cut her off. She was feeling more than a little awkward.

"This is one of the most common requests that we get so please, don't be embarrassed. Like I said, before we can give you a quote, we'll need you to come in for an interview. We need to make sure that you are related to the person you want to locate, that there are no restraining orders against you by the person, that you aren't wanting to find them to do bodily harm to them. That kind of stuff."

"Yeah, I understand. It's good to know that not just any old body can use your service to find somebody. What do you have available?"

"Let me see." Jadyn could hear the person flipping pages. "I have this morning at ten thirty, or tomorrow afternoon at two. Then Thursday is open. What time would you like?"

She didn't have a rental car. She hadn't wanted to waste money on one. Her uncle had told her she could borrow his car anytime, but she would need a few days to familiarize herself with the streets. Maybe she could take a cab. She glanced at the clock on the wall: 9:05 A.M.

"This morning is fine. Ten thirty, you said?"

"Yes, that's right. All right, what is your name, please?"

"Jadyn Collins."

"OK, Ms. Collins, we'll see you then."

"Do you know where your dad was born? When his birthday is?"

Jadyn took out the papers she had brought with her and un-folded them.

"Yes, he was born in Indianapolis, Indiana. November tenth, 1962. His full name is Charles William Ivery."

"His mother's name?"

"Ellaree Johnson."

"Father?"

"I don't know."

"Brothers and sisters?"

"Yes, but I don't know their names. I think he had one sister and two brothers."

"Last known address?"

"1219 Hunter St. Cocoa Beach, Florida."

"Well, this might not be as hard as you think. How current is that address?"

"The last contact I had with him was about four years ago. He lived there then. I've been there recently and the house is vacant. That's really all the information I have on him."

"Right. OK, what I'm gonna do is search public records and do a background check. Many times that's all it takes to locate a per-son, unless they don't want to be located. If it's a simple search, it'll run you about fifty dollars. Anything more extensive and the price will vary. The most I've had to charge is three hundred."

"Mr. Eisley, three hundred is out of my budget. So you'll let me know if you need to go beyond fifty before you do anything else, right?"

"Absolutely."

He stood and came around to shake her hand. "Don't worry, Miss Collins. I'll do everything I know how to help you find your father. If I have any information to pass to you or if I need to clarify something with you, do you have another number where I can reach you?"

"Well, the number I gave you is my cell, you should be able to reach me there if you need to."

"I hope you understand that I can't make any promises or guarantees. That even if I don't find your father, I will still expect you to pay me at least twenty-five dollars, maybe more depending on how much effort I have to put forth."

"Look, I understand that you're not doing this for free. But I need you to understand that I have a limited amount of money so I need you not to add any charges beyond fifty dollars unless you speak to me about it first."

"Yes, well I think we both understand each other." Mr. Eisley extended his hand again toward Jadyn. She stood, opened her hand, and took hold of his. He shook it firmly.

"It was a pleasure meeting you."

At that moment, his cell phone rang and he picked it up, taking a quick look at the caller ID. "Sorry, this is my wife and I need to take this call. I'll be in touch. OK?" he said, stepping over to the door and opening it for her as he answered the call.

"Hello, love . . . yes I remembered the tickets . . ." Jadyn heard him say from the other side of the door, as she walked away.

38

"Hey, lady. You ready to go for that swim?"

It was Julian. She was hoping that he would forget that she had told him they could go to the beach today.

"Not at the moment, but I can be by the time you get here."

"Well, let's get it crackalackin' then. All I need is the time and the place and I will be there to pick you up."

She gave him her uncle's address before hanging up.

There was no denying that Julian was a fine specimen of a man, like Mani had said that night at the club. She couldn't stand having those lips so close to hers. And though she hadn't mentioned it, she hadn't forgotten how he had stepped in between Steele and Flash's boys and with one word had put a stop to the fight before somebody ended up with bullet holes in them. She wanted to know how a man who seemed to be all about business, with seemingly no interest in the streets, could command the attention of dudes on the verge of murder. There was obviously more to Julian than he was revealing.

He got to her uncle's house pretty quickly, and when he arrived he came up and rang the doorbell. That was a plus for him in her book. Too many men would just sit out in the car and beep. She wasn't going to spend time with him alone in her uncle's house, though, so she grabbed her bag and met him on the porch.

"OK, if we're going to the beach we better get goin' now. I want to get back in time to make dinner for my uncle." She was rushing out so quickly that her bag fell off her shoulder and onto the porch. Julian automatically bent down to pick it up for her.

"I got it," he said as he scooped up the bag.

Julian straightened his back and handed her the bag as he reached for his phone. "Just let me notify my answering service that they need to forward calls to my cell phone. I forgot to do that before I left the office."

Jadyn snatched the blanket off the chair on the porch, rattled the knob on the front door to make sure it was locked, and began walking down the steps toward the street, with Julian close on her heels.

39

Jadyn walked beside Julian, looking at the cars and trucks lined up at the curb trying to pick out the one she thought might be his. She settled on the coal-black Jeep Cherokee with the moon roof on top, slightly propped open. That ride was tight! But when Julian took her elbow and steered her across the street to the car that was actually his, her jaw dropped. The only thing she had gotten right was the color.

Julian pressed a button on his key chain and the door locks popped open as they stood next to the black on black 2001 BMW X5 SUV. Damn! It was funny how both him and Taji had black on black BMWs, even though Taji's was a car instead of a truck. He held her door open for her as she slid her backside across the buttery soft leather seats. Beside her, she noticed the gearshift looked as if it were made of real wood, nestled in a bed of the same smooth leather she sat on.

Julian shut the door and did a little jog around the front of the car to the driver's side. He slid in, put the key in the ignition, and pressed a button that made a hidden panel slide apart and reveal the moon roof as it smoothly slid back to let in the sunlight.

"Nice ride," Jadyn said and hoped her voice hid the excitement she felt.

"Yeah, this is my baby!" he said as he moved the gearshift into reverse and backed out of the parking space.

"You going to take this to the beach?" she couldn't help asking. If she owned a ride like this, there would be no way she would drive around in the sand in it.

"Of course," he said smiling. "Wherever I'm going, you best believe I'm going in style."

40

The scenery was so beautiful. Jadyn couldn't help smiling as she took in the view. The palm trees looked amazing with their limbs swaying in the breeze. The tree trunks were equally astonishing in their glory, with the wood intricately carved, in a beautiful crisscross design that reminded her of a pineapple skin. When the beach suddenly burst into view, the magnificent expanse of water with the bright sunshine glinting off the surface gave the appearance of a huge, square-cut diamond. The sparkling tan sandy beaches created a sharp contrast to the crystal blue of the ocean.

Having never swam in the ocean before, Jadyn was a little wary. She had heard the horror stories about sharks swimming regularly in the ocean and sometimes snacking on human arms and legs. She wasn't trying to be lunch for Jaws.

"So, how do you know if there is a shark swimming in the water with you or not?" she asked.

"When the person swimming next to you is missing a limb and the water around you starts turning to blood," Julian said, matter-of-factly.

Jadyn turned her face toward him and all the blood drained

from her face. Her brows knitted together and her eyes grew wide as her mouth flew open.

"Don't get your panties in a bunch, love. I was just teasin'," he said, laughing.

Jadyn swung her beach bag and hit him upside the head.

"That shit wasn't funny! Don't play. You don't want me to change my mind and have you take me back home, do you?" She rolled her eyes at him to emphasize her point.

"Aw lighten up, girl. I said I was just teasing you," he said and gave her an air kiss the next time she looked his way. "So tell me something. Are you just here for a little vacation or is there another reason for you visiting our fair city?"

Jadyn kept her eyes on the scenery as she contemplated just how much she should tell him. Should she tell him about the fact that she had felt betrayed by her mother and had been devastated by her stepfather? The more she pondered what she should reveal, the more she knew the answer was clearly not a damn thing.

Turning her head to face Julian she asked, "Wasn't it you who said that we were coming out here to just chill? Or are you just being nosy?" Jadyn flashed her most charming smile and Julian must have been totally disarmed.

"Sorry, baby. I really wasn't trynna get all in your business or anything. Just curious is all," Julian said while stealing glances at her as he drove.

"Well, how about you? I'm curious about you, too, so if you want me to spill my guts to you, you have to go first."

Jadyn smiled again and Julian started talking. She knew that he couldn't help it. She realized that when she smiled, she could ask for anything and damn if a man wouldn't try to get it for her.

"Ain't much to tell. I was born and raised here, my mother died while she was having me and Pops never remarried, so I don't have any brothers or sisters. He's a financial planner and never got over his disappointment about me not following in his footsteps. I was never good in math, but loved the English language. I was the best writer in my school. That's what I wanted to be, a writer. Pops thought different. Said that his son wasn't going to be no fag writer. Said every last one of them was sleeping around with other men, even if they tried to front like they weren't. So he crushed that dream for me. I was in college at the time. I didn't want to do anything else, so I dropped out."

Julian gripped the steering wheel more tightly and stared straight ahead.

"Why did you let him tell you what to do? You were already in college, so why didn't you just tell him that it was your life and you weren't going to let him take over?"

Julian glanced over at her and winked. "If only it were that simple. See Pops's family had money. My grandfather lived in New York and faithfully played the lottery for years. Every payday, he played twenty dollars' worth of numbers, and one Friday he finally got lucky. The pot had gone up to $324 million and Granddad had all the numbers."

Jadyn sucked in her breath. "Three hundred and twenty-four million? Good golly, Miss Molly!"

Julian burst into laughter. "What did you say? 'Good golly, Miss Molly'?" He laughed again. "Now where in the world did you get that from?"

"My grandfather used to say it all the time when he heard something unbelievable. I guess you talking about your grandfather made me think about mine."

"I guess," Julian said. "Anyway, that set Granddad and Pops up for life. Or so Pops thought. But Granddad told Pops that he had to work hard all his life and he wasn't going to watch him get soft living off his winnings. He gave Pops five hundred thousand and set up a trust fund for me that I can't touch until I'm thirty-five. Although I get to live off the interest. Pops was mad at Granddad for that. He thought he should have gotten more of the money."

"Whaat? Your grandfather gave your dad five hundred thousand and he was mad about that? Umph! I wish somebody would give me a little piece of that. I would be grinning from ear to ear."

"I know, right? But since Pops was his only child, he thought Granddad should have been more generous."

Jadyn suddenly had a thought. "How many people did your gramps have to split with?" she asked, mentally trying to divide that much money by four, six, eight, and twenty. Even if he'd had to share with twenty people he was still filthy rich. Fifteen million dollars apiece! Damn!

"Grandad only had to divide the money by two. Him and the IRS."

Jadyn blinked hard and sank down in her seat. She couldn't even imagine one person having that much money! Julian had turned up the music, so she guessed he was done talking about it for now.

41

Jadyn still wasn't trying to swim with any sharks so she played at the edge of the beach, splashing her feet in the water and allowing the little eddies of water to splash against her ankles, while Julian dived in and swam out a ways.

"Come on out here, girl!" he called to her. "Ain't no sharks out here. I was just teasin' your ass, I told you!"

"No, I'm fine right where I'm at. The water is cool on my feet and it feels just fine," she told him, kicking a little water in his direction to emphasize her point.

"Unh-unh, girl. I'm not lettin' you get off that easily. We coulda went to Wally World and got a kiddie pool if that's all you wanted to do. Now are you comin' out here where I'm at or do I have to come and get you?" Julian swam a few strokes and then stood up in the shallow water, which only came up to his chest.

Jadyn tried not to laugh as he made his way toward her.

"Quit playin', Julian. I said I'm fine where I am," she said, backing away from him and giggling in spite of herself.

"Oh, you think I'm playin'? If I have to chase your butt I'm gon' take you way out where the sharks swim and leave you!" He was moving toward her as quickly as the current would allow as the water ebbed and flowed against his chest.

Jadyn screeched, "No, leave me alone! Don't you dare!" She turned to flee but didn't get very far before running into a barrier of human flesh.

"Well, well, looky here, looky here now," Steele Money said, as he wrapped his arms around Jadyn. She immediately began to struggle against him, trying to free herself.

"Get your hands offa me!" she yelled.

"Aw, now you can be a little more friendly than that cain't ya?" He stuck out his tongue and gave her a big lick from her chin to her eyelid. He put his lips close to her ear and whispered.

"That's my mark, Ms. Lovely. I always mark the bitches before I use and abuse them. Remember what I told ya . . ."

Jadyn turned her head. "Get offa me!" she managed again, but Steele had grabbed her ponytail and was holding her head in place as he tried to kiss her.

Julian caught up with them.

"Man, what the fuck? Didn't you see that she is with me, fool?"

Steele glared at Julian before pushing Jadyn toward him. Julian reached out and grabbed her before she could fall on her face.

"What the hell is you thinkin', dawg? Didn't yo' mama teach you how to treat a lady?"

"She sho' in the fuck did, and when I see one I'll show you."

Julian's face contorted and flushed an angry red brown. Jadyn, not wanting to be caught up in the middle of a fight, pulled Julian's arm. Steele just laughed.

"Oh you want som'a this? You want some?" he taunted Julian.

"Bring it on, nigga. Let's go! I been wantin' to get in that ass!" Julian said loudly.

"It's OK, Julian. Let it go."

Steele's face became a cold, hard mask, but Jadyn could see the muscles flexing and releasing in his jaw, a silent testament to his anger.

"Oh yeah, muhfucka? Whatchu waitin' on then? Here I am," Steele yelled back at him. "You startin' to believe you bad because of that shit you did at the club the other night? We both know what that shit was really about and it damn sho' wasn't about you!"

Steele's words made Julian lurch in his direction.

"No, Julian! No!" Jadyn was having a hard time holding on to his arm because he kept trying to shake loose. A couple of officers patrolling the beach stopped and got out of their cars. They started walking toward them with their hands perched on their gun butts.

"What's the problem, fellas?"

Julian and Steele continued to stare at one another, neither of them moving away. Jadyn continued to tug on Julian's arm.

The larger of the two officers stepped up. "I asked if there was a problem here?"

Jadyn spoke, "No, officer, no problem here. Just a slight misunderstanding. We were just leaving."

"Let's go, Julian. Let's just go," she said, and Julian relented, beginning to follow Jadyn.

"This ain't over!" he threw over his shoulder as he passed Steele.

"No doubt!" Steele spat back at him.

42

Jadyn and Julian picked up their things and walked back to his car in total silence.

Jadyn was trying to figure out the deal between Steele and Julian. She didn't think it strange that Steele had shown up at the beach, after all it was a public place and anyone was free to come and go as they pleased. But the tension that flowed back and forth between them was palpable. Jadyn wondered how seemingly casual contact between them could generate such raw anger at the drop of a dime.

Julian spoke first. "I don't know what's up with that buster, but I'ma fuck his ass up if he keep steppin' to me like that."

Jadyn continued to walk in silence.

"How is that muhfucka just gon' think he can disrespect me like that, I can't figure. But he 'bout to find out that ain't happening! Not one more time!"

He was getting so worked up that Jadyn finally spoke for fear he might run back and confront Steele.

"It's not worth it. And anyway, you promised to have me home before my uncle got home from work. Now how you gonna be able to do that if you sitting on top of that big old, rhinoceros ass lookin' nigga, gettin' your fight on?"

Jadyn had run ahead of Julian and stopped in front of him with hands on her hips, and a funny pout on her face. Julian grinned.

"Rhinocerous? Woman you just don't know," he said, shaking his head.

"Well, maybe I don't. But I'm not trynna find out neither," she said smiling, too.

Julian pulled her close and before she could stop him, he kissed her long and deep. When Julian pulled his mouth away from hers, her head was reeling. She knew she should have done something to stop him and was embarrassed that she hadn't.

43

Jadyn had Mani drive her to the grocery store so that she could pick up some things for dinner. She was going to grill steaks and make some of her famous spaghetti.

Once she had the steaks grilling and the spaghetti sauce simmering, she went upstairs to take a quick shower. Suddenly she wanted to share her good news with Taji.

Taji had been a lot of things, selfish, self-centered, spoiled, and maybe even a little controlling. But he had never been cruel or heartless toward her, or anyone else for that matter. Would he really have sabotaged her audition or paid someone to do it? What reason would he have had to do that? Yes, he had been upset about her plans to tour with *STOMP* but would that push him to do something so dirty?

Yes, they had had their problems, but he had been trying to work on that. And she had been very pleased about it. She could at least give him the chance to explain. She had cut him off before when he had tried to tell her his side of the story. Maybe she could just hear him out, she thought, as she dialed the number.

As she held the ringing phone to her ear, she kept his picture in her hand, remembering again the way that he had surprised and thrilled her the last time they'd made love. The phone stopped ringing; someone had picked up on the other end.

"Taji?" she said.

There was a long pause before a female voice responded. "No, not Taji . . ."

Jadyn's surprise turned to resentment. It was obvious that Taji wasn't thinking about her.

She swallowed her anger, refusing to allow it to control her actions.

"I have no idea why you feel comfortable enough to pick up the phone in my man's home, but I need to speak to Taji, can you give him the phone, please?"

Jadyn thought she detected a bit of smug humor in the woman's voice as she answered, "I'd love to do that for you dear, however, he's in the shower right at the moment. Would you like to wait until he's finished?"

Despite her best efforts, the woman's attitude sent her over the edge.

"No, bitch, I do not want to wait. And you better pray that I never run into your trynna be funny in my man's home ass. 'Cause if I do, you'll think twice before you answer anyone else's phone again!"

Jadyn slammed the phone shut so hard she wondered if she'd broken it. She jumped up and threw Taji's picture back on the dresser and began pacing back and forth.

The shit is on now! How in the fuck is Taji gon' let some woman answer his phone. And why in the hell was he so comfortable that he would get in the damn shower and let that bitch have free rein in his home? She was probably going through his personal belongings right this moment!

She had to admit to herself that she was hurt. She hadn't even been gone a month and he was with somebody else. Bitch!

OK. OK. She would deal with Taji's bullshit in time. All the lying and all the deceit. If Taji wanted to play those games, she would teach him not only how to play, but how to win!

After Jadyn had calmed down, she went downstairs, flipped the steaks, and turned the spaghetti sauce down to low. Then she got on the phone and dialed Nite's number.

"It's about time you called somebody, with your stank ass. What's good, cuz?"

"Well, I got some good news! I might get to audition for Alvin Ailey American Dance Theater!" Jadyn said, then held the phone away from her ear as Nite began screaming.

"Jay, that is so good! I'm so proud of you!" Nite said, and Jadyn could hear the genuine joy in her voice.

"Thanks, cuz," she said, unable to crank up her enthusiasm as high as it had been earlier.

"OK, what's wrong?" Nite asked. "You sound down and you should be spinning cartwheels. So what up?"

"Well, I got so happy about the audition that I got to feelin' sentimental about Taji, and me not really letting him tell me his side of the story about what happened to my audition for STOMP. So I called home, well, Taji's house, and some snotty heffa answered his phone."

"Oh no, she did not!"

"Oh yes, she did, too. So you know my ass is heated!"

"I know you are."

"But that ain't it. So I'm trynna act all like the shit ain't fazed me, right. You know, never let a bitch see you sweat."

"I feel you, cuz! And you know this!"

"Yeah, so I tells her to put Taji on the phone. This broad gon' tell me, Oh, he's in the shower right now but you can wait if you want to."

"Nunh-unh. Where Taji live? You want me to roll over there and see if her ass is still there and tap that ass for you?"

"No, gangsta boo!" Jadyn cracked up laughing.

"What did you say to her?"

"I said, 'No bitch, I do not want to wait.' And I forget the other shit I said 'cause my ears was roastin'! All I know is I slammed that phone shut so hard I almost broke it. I hope her ear is still ringing from the noise."

"I know! That shit would have me burnin' up, too. I told you the bitches was hiding out in the wings like hungry wolves panting like Taji was a juicy steak, didn't I?"

"And you ain't neva lied!"

"I know Taji called you right back, did you cuss his trifling ass out?"

"Hell yes he been ringing my phone off the hook. But I am not answering his calls. Let his ass wonder what is up with me for a change. You know I ain't forgot about that scandalous shit he pulled."

"Did you ever talk to him about why he did that shit?"

"No, but I mean, what is there to say, really? Couldn't nobody else have done that shit but him." Jadyn suddenly caught a whiff of smoke in the air.

"Oh no! Hey cuz, I'ma have to call you back, I think somethin's burning!"

"OK, call me back!"

"I will."

She hated to hang up the phone, because hearing her cousin's voice made her realize how much she really missed her. She had a lot to catch her up on.

Jadyn ran down the steps just as her uncle burst through the door.

"What's all that there smoke coming out tha backyard, gal?"

Jadyn continued past her uncle and out the back door. "I'm so sorry, Unc! I was tryin' to surprise you by having dinner all ready for you and now it's ruined!"

"Aw now, looka here. Don't you worry about that. That meat ain't burnt, it's just a tad bit well done! Now I'ma let you in on a little secret. That damn Flash will eat any-damn-thang. And he love him some barbecue. So you just put a whole lotta hot sauce and barbecue sauce on that and serve it up to him. Trust and believe baby girl. I guaran-damn-tee you. Flash will eat the shit out of it!"

Jadyn took the tongs and picked up one of the steaks. It was pretty crispy on the one side, although the top still looked fresh and juicy. Jadyn shook her head in disbelief. "I don't know, Unc. This meat looks pretty bad to me. . . ."

"You mind what I tell you now. Watch and see. Let old Unc change outta these work clothes and I'ma fix them steaks right on up!" Her uncle forked the steaks over to the side so that they were no longer sizzling on the grill.

Jadyn shook her head again and walked back into the house with her uncle. Luckily for them, she had put the spaghetti sauce on low and it was still simmering lightly. And when she stirred it, she was relieved to find that it hadn't stuck to the bottom of the pan.

Flash burst through the front door.

"Yo yo yo, little cousin! What up! Somethin' is smellin' mighty tasty up in here!"

"What it be like, cousin!" Jadyn greeted him back.

Flash walked up and gave her a bear hug and a wet smack on the cheek.

Jadyn smiled. "Oh, so you ain't mad at me anymore, hunh?"

"Mad? I was never mad. I was *pissed*! Pissed, do you hear me? But naw, I ain't pissed no more. I figure that shit was partly my fault for not keeping my eye on you mo' better." Flash grinned and let her know that he was teasing.

"Well, that is so good to know."

"What you done cooked up in here smellin' all good and shit?" Then after a beat he added: "Did you cook or did Granddaddy?"

"I did!" Jadyn slapped his hand away as he grabbed a slice of bread from the counter and tried to dip it in the spaghetti sauce. Since Flash was so much bigger he managed to dip up some sauce anyway.

"Mmmmmmmmmm! This is slammin'!" he said as he walked down the basement steps to the spare bedroom.

Jadyn put on a pot to boil the pasta. She tried not to, but her thoughts drifted back to Taji. They had their problems for sure, but deep down inside she loved him. She had believed that he loved her, too, until tonight. She knew for a fact that he loved her more than he sometimes showed, so she couldn't figure out why he would have some bitch at their house answering their phone. Probably gettin' his freak on right now. So what if she had left him. Didn't that fool know that he was supposed to fight to get her back?

Her uncle came downstairs and headed straight out to the patio.

"I heard Flash down 'ere, I hope he didn't find the steaks before I had a chance to work on them a little bit."

She couldn't help but smile when she saw the sneaky look on her uncle's face.

"No, Unc, he went straight for the spaghetti sauce before going downstairs to get cleaned up for dinner."

"Good," he said, opening the cabinets and pulling down barbecue sauce and a few different ingredients to blend together. He poured everything into a large bowl and carried it out back. He turned and put a finger up to his lips, making the "sh" sign as he gave her a conspiratorial wink before disappearing through the patio door.

Flash came up the steps two at a time.

"I hope that food is ready 'cause I needs to get my grub on. I'm hongry enough to eat up the world!"

"Well I hope I made enough spaghetti for you, because I definitely didn't put the world on the menu tonight."

"Say you didn't, hunh? Well, what else you got to go with that, then?"

"I made a salad, baked some garlic bread, and . . ."

"And we gon' eat these here steaks and them leftover crabs from the other day, boy. So I know that'a fill up that bottomless pit you call a stomach," Unc said.

"Itta be a good start, anyway!" Flash said, walking out to the screened-in porch. Jadyn had set the table outside since there was a nice breeze stirring. She wanted to soak up more of Florida's dynamic outdoor life. Even the birds were more exotic than anything she'd ever seen. The yard birds at home were plain brown sparrows and maybe a few blackbirds and robins every now and then. But the birds that flew around the little man-made lake out back looked like little miniature storks, and the ducks were the most colorful she had ever seen. They even had swans swimming around, showing off their long graceful necks. And of course there were loads of luscious palms, some with a mile of trunk before the leafy fronds branched out like the blades of a ceiling fan.

Unc was right. Flash put two of the charbroiled steaks on his plate and immediately tore into them, before heaping the pile of spaghetti onto his plate. Amazingly enough, Unc had worked some kind of magic on those steaks, because the meat didn't appear to be tough anymore. She watched Flash's knife glide through it just like butter. Unc put a steak on his plate, too, as he kept staring at Flash's plate in an exaggerated manner and back at her. He mouthed "I told you," and quickly glanced back down at his plate when Flash took a break from shoveling food into his mouth.

"You a good cook, li'l cousin. Who knew that a city girl like you could throw down like this?"

"Now that ain't no mystery to me. She got Sista's blood runnin' through those veins of hers. She couldn't help but to burn!" Uncle BruhJay said before he guffawed at their private joke about the steaks.

Flash looked from one of them to the other. "What's so funny?"

"Nothin'," Jadyn and her uncle said in unison.

44

Taji had been blowing up Jadyn's cell phone since that night she'd made dinner for her uncle and cousin. She just ignored him and deleted his messages without even listening to them. She wasn't trying to hear Taji's lame excuses for what had happened. Once again she had caught him in some shady shit! And once again there wasn't a damned thing he could say to make the shit right. Sneaky ass! Maybe sneaky and dirty was who he really was. And if that was true, then it was good to find it out now.

Then again, who was she to be passing judgment on him, when she was running around with another man? She had left him. . . . So really, he had the right to do whatever he was big enough to do and have whoever he wanted at his house. And if he was such a rotten snake, why was the shit pissing her off so much?

What the hell. They were both free to do what they wanted. She needed to focus on what was going on here and forget Taji and all the madness back there in Ohio right now.

Julian and Jadyn had begun spending most of their free time together. When he got off work, he would usually come by and they would go to the beach. Julian was closing shop early today to take her to Universal Studios. She dressed in a pair of red shorts, a red and white striped tank, a red cap, which she pulled her ponytail through, and the red and white Jordans that Taji had bought her for Christmas. She didn't even have the slightest twinge of guilt about wearing his gift on a date with another man.

Flash walked in as she was lacing up her shoes.

"Goin' out with that Julian punk again?" he asked, not cracking even the slightest smile.

Jadyn returned his blank look with one of her own.

"I don't appreciate you doggin' him like that, Flash. What do you got against him anyway? What'd he ever do to you?" Jadyn tied an angry bow on her shoe, pulling the strings just a little too tightly.

"Muhfucka ain't done a muhfuckin' thang to me. I just don't trust his bougie, sneaky ass, that's all. And anyway, I know you got a nigga back home. Ain't you still kickin' it with him?"

Jadyn stood up and grabbed her bag as the doorbell rang.

"Look, Flash, I'm not all in your business like that, so I would appreciate it if you stayed outta mine, OK?" She tugged the drawstring on her bag and cinched it shut.

"No problem, li'l cousin. No problem. If you cool wit' it I'm cool wit' it, too. I ain't lettin' no dumb shit cause problems between us. So everything is copacetic, a'ight?"

Flash opened his arms for a hug. Jadyn smiled and walked into his embrace. "OK, cousin," she said.

But Flash held on to her. "But if your boy ain't all that he pretending to be, I'ma have to get wit' him and break him off some."

Jadyn gave him a fake punch in the chest and a playful shove. "Sure, if he don't break you off some first," she said, before making a mad dash for the door, laughing.

"Yeah, when palm trees grow in Ohio," she heard him say as she flew out the door.

She was laughing and pulling on Julian's arm. "Let's go!"

Julian allowed Jadyn to pull him along. "What's goin' on?" he asked, smiling himself.

"Nothin'. Flash just lightweight trippin' as usual."

Julian rolled his eyes.

"Yeah, well let's give him something to really trip about," he said, sweeping Jadyn up in his arms and spinning around with her before planting a wet one smack-dab on her lips.

Flash, who was standing in the door taking it all in, sucked his teeth and flipped Julian the bird before disappearing inside.

Julian stared after him not even flinching.

45

"So what is the beef between you, Flash, and Steele? And please don't try to tell me there ain't one, because I know there is. Y'all niggas are all tense and shit every time you see one another. You don't even need to speak, you just set eyes on one another and it's like somebody done lit a stick of dynamite." Jadyn had never been one to beat around the bush.

Julian sighed and kept watching the road as he spoke. "OK, it's like this. Me and Flash grew up together. We wasn't really friends, but we were cool, you know? Never had beef, kicked it every now and then at the clubs and shit like that."

Jadyn thought back to that first night at the club when she called herself calming Flash down about Julian by telling him that Julian was from Ohio.

"Oh shit! You mean Flash knew I was lying about you that first night in the club?"

Julian nodded.

"Damn! No wonder he felt he had to keep an eye on me. He musta thought you were running a game on me and I was lame enough to fall for it. Why didn't you tell me then that y'all knew each other?"

"Look, how did I know that we was gon' start kickin' it like we are? I was thinkin' that it was just gonna be a 'let's dance at the club tonight' type thing. I heard you were Flash's cousin. I wasn't trying to cross him by gettin' over on you. I definitely wasn't planning on getting caught up with you, since you only here for the short term. So wasn't no need for long explanations and thangs since me and him knew the real.

"Flash was always talking about he wasn't gon' hook up with no gangbanger and slang no dope, because he was too smart for that and he wasn't trynna end up grindin' on the block while some other joker got rich and then end up getting busted and doing hard time and trynna choose a punk to be his wife."

Jadyn folded her arms over her breasts and sighed loudly. "That's the most disgusting shit I have ever heard," she said.

"Well, disgusting or not, it's the real of doing time in jail. It's only so much jaggin' off a nigga can do. I ain't sayin' that I'm down with that shit, or even that your cousin would be down with that shit, either, I'm just saying it's a choice that a nigga does have to make if he doing that long stretch. Anyway, like I said, me and Flash was cool, but when my granddad won all that dough and I went off to college, everything changed. When I would come home on visits Flash started crackin' on me, asking me how come a bougie nigga like me still wanted to associate with the common folks and dumb shit like that. So after a while we just wasn't cool no more."

Jadyn glanced over at Julian. "OK, that explains what up with you and Flash. What about you and this Steele Money character?"

Julian didn't answer, but Jadyn could feel the change in him at the mention of Steele's name. He seemed like he was trying to cover it up.

"Ain't nothing goin' on with me and Steele. I did some work

with him a few times, that's it. But I can tell you this, we ain't really feeling each other anymore, either, that's for damn sure."

Julian laid his hand on Jadyn's thigh and she promptly removed it back to his side of the car.

He smiled sheepishly. "Can't blame a cat for tryin'. So anyway, your turn. Tell me about Jadyn."

"OK. I was born in Columbus, Ohio. Been there all my life. In fact, this is the first time I been out of the state since I was a kid. . . ."

"You jokin', right?"

"No, I am not," Jadyn said, catching a slight attitude.

"Sorry, baby, I just can't imagine staying in one place all the time, that's all. I wasn't trynna signify or anything."

"Anyway, as I was saying. I don't really know my birth father, that's one of the main things that brought me here. I was raised by my mother and stepfather and she had two kids by him, my brothers. E is fourteen now and Devon is twelve. I don't get to see them much because me and my mom's relationship is for shit. I don't have any sisters. My mother works at a bank, though she had some issues when we were younger."

"Issues?"

"Yeah, issues, just leave it at that, OK?" Jadyn was uncomfortable now talking about her mother and her family. She didn't know why, but she still wasn't ready to tell Julian about Taji.

"My mom divorced my brothers' sire, and she hasn't remarried so far."

Jadyn's phone rang and the caller ID showed it was Finders Keepers.

"Sorry, I gotta take this. Hello?"

"Jadyn, listen, I may have a pretty good lead on your dad."

Jadyn perked right up. "You do? What did you find out?"

"I didn't find out anything solid yet, I said I got what may be a pretty good lead. I might have found out where your dad works."

"Where he works? What's the name of the place?"

"Look, I can't tell you until I confirm a few details, OK? I just wanted you to know that I'm on it and to let you know you're still in the fifty-dollar range right now."

Jadyn was quiet.

"So far there are no extra charges. I'll call you when I have somethin' more for you."

"OK. Thanks, Anthony."

"You're welcome. Oh and Jadyn?"

"Yes?"

"If this should turn out to be a good number for contacting your dad, how do you want me to go forward with this? Would you want me to give him this number to call you, or would you prefer I just call you back and give you the contact information?"

Jadyn soaked up the question and let the fact that it was now in the realm of possibility that she could soon be speaking to her father marinate inside her for a moment. If she wanted to speak to her dad as quickly as humanly possible, the logical thing to do would be to allow Anthony to give the number to her dad. On the other hand, if her dad were to be a little less enthusiastic and more apprehensive in making first contact with her than she was with him, his feelings might delay the opportunity for their reunion as she envisioned it.

"Both. You can give him my number, but I also want you to call me back and give me his phone number, too."

"Will do!" he said before hanging up the phone.

Julian pushed a CD into the player and Mary J's soulful voice floated into the car. He didn't ask her who called so she didn't feel the need to tell him. As she listened to "No More Drama" she let her mind drift away.

She thought about all of the drama that had been in her life from as far back as she could remember. Not even including the foul things the pervert who had the nerve to call himself her dad had done to her. Right there at the top of her list was her mother's drug binge after they got rid of him. Instead of being happy and making her life better, making all their lives better, she went and got involved with some pretty boy playa and wound up hooked on crack.

Those thoughts were bringing Jadyn down, so she shifted her focus back to finding her real dad. What if Anthony did find him? What would her next move be? Would she call him up? What would she say? "Hello, Dad, remember me?" Or "Hi Daddy, guess what happened to me while you were gone?" Yeah, that would really make her dad happy that she'd found him.

How would he react? Would he be happy that she had found him? Would he sweep her up in a bear hug and burst into tears, telling her how much he loved her and how sorry he was, over and over again? Yes . . . that's how it would go. And she would end up comforting her dad. She would tell him that she forgave him for everything. She would tell him that she loved him, too.

". . . you planning on staying?"

Julian's question drew her back to the present. "What did you say?"

Julian glanced over at her and then focused on the road again.

"I asked you how long you were planning on being in town."

"I'm not sure. There's nothin' pressin' me to go back to Ohio right now. I'm havin' a pretty good time here, except for a few people gettin' on my last nerve."

"You mean your cousin Flash jammin' you up all the time every time you move a half an inch out of his sight?"

"No, not Flash. He can be a little irritating at times, but I know he really is acting the way he is out of love for the fam. Love for me. He ain't bad," Jadyn told him.

"So you say," Julian said appearing slightly agitated.

"Yes, so I say. Flash has a good heart. He's mad cool. I'm not so sure about your boy Steele Money, though. Some'n ain't right about him."

"Fa sho'! I peeped that shit the first time we hooked up," Julian said, his voice sounding even more irritated.

"You knew, but you still go ahead and kick it with him anyway? I don't know who is worse, him or you."

"Well, allow me to help you out on that one—it's definitely him. Hookin' up with him wasn't crazy on my part because we had business to take care of and we did that. Nothin' crazy about that."

"Maybe not at first, but somethin' crazy musta happened since then. That boy seems like he is one king shy of a full house," Jadyn said laughing at the same time.

Julian laughed, too. "What? One king shy of a full house? Girl you don't even play no cards, do you? You shoulda said something you know a little something about like he was one egg shy of a dozen, or two pints short of a gallon . . ."

Jadyn laughed harder. "Oh you sayin' I only know about that barefoot and in the kitchen type shit, hunh? Well then your ass need to be sayin' somethin' like he one kick short of a field goal, 'cause you so full of game!"

They both laughed.

"No, seriously though, Steele all right on the business tip. His social skills may be lacking a tad bit, but he knows how to make bank."

"Yeah, well you'd never know it by the way he dresses," Jadyn said thinking about that night at the club again.

46

When they got to Orlando, instead of going to Universal Studios, Julian took her shopping.

"Hey, I thought we were going to Universal Studios?"

"I wanted to surprise you," Julian told her, giving her a wink and a peck on the cheek before he jumped out of the car and walked around to let her out.

The first store he took her to was Fendi to pick out a new purse. Jadyn couldn't believe how expensive the bags were. She saw a little tan-colored straw Dior bag for $3,500, Fendi bags started at $900, Dolce & Gabbana bags on sale for $1,695!

Taji had been more than generous. But he was also a bit conservative, too. He would lay down a lot of cash for a car, or a coat, or something that you had to use over and over again, but a purse? She couldn't see plopping down that type money for a purse either. The most Jadyn had ever spent on a purse was three hundred dollars for a Coach bag and at the time she had thought that was a lot.

"Come on, baby. Pick out something, we have other stores to hit," Julian told her.

Jadyn fingered a tag and then glanced back at Julian.

"Just get what you want and let me worry about how much it costs."

Because Julian kept insisting, she finally picked up the $900 Fendi, a $600 pair of Dolce & Gabbana metallic sandals, and a $1,200 mint-green satin D&G sheath that hugged her curves in exactly the right places without being tight, and fell just above her knees.

After they left that store, Jadyn stopped looking at the price tags. Julian would just tell her not to worry about it, so she just relaxed and shopped. She had never felt so outrageously extravagant in her life. Yes, Taji and his family had money, too, and he never told her that she *couldn't* spend this way, but he had never taken her on a sky-is-the-limit spree like Julian was, either.

By the time they had finished, Jadyn had six bags full of designer duds, from Michael Kors and Dior, to Cavalli and BCBG.

They had lunch at an upscale Japanese hibachi restaurant, where the chef performed tricks with the food as he prepared it on an elongated hot plate that was built into the table.

"So, how do you feel?" Julian asked her after lunch as they strolled back to the car.

Jadyn smiled. "I feel special for sure. But what is this about? Why are you dropping major coin on somebody who may be here today and gone tomorrow?"

"Baby, like the old folks say, you can't take it wit'chu and you only live once, right? Besides, a woman that is as fine as you only deserves the best that life can offer. I thought you knew."

"Yeah, maybe so." *But old folks say ain't nothin' in life free so you better count up the cost!* "But just because it's the best doesn't mean it's good for you," she said.

47

"Hey Jadyn, what y'all gettin' into tonight?" Mani's voice sounded bright and chipper.

"Girl, Julian took me shopping and bought me some new outfits! I'm talkin' shoes, bag, dresses, shorts, jeans . . ."

Mani's mood seem to instantly change, once again catching Jadyn off guard.

"He did? Where did y'all go?" Mani asked unenthusiastically.

"He took me to Orlando and then we went to all these designer shops and things. He spent a pretty penny, today," Jadyn told her, ignoring Mani's flat tone.

"Umph. Does Flash know?" she asked even more flatly.

"No, he don't know and ain't gonna find out. Is he, Mani?"

"Don't 'is he, Mani' me. You know your cousin thinks that Julian is pushin' up on you too quick. And if you want the truth, so do I. You ain't even been here, what? Four weeks and dude already trying to buy your ass?"

Mani's last comment got on Jadyn's nerves. Couldn't nobody buy her. She wasn't for sale.

"Ain't nobody trynna buy me. You trippin'. Like Jarrell didn't buy you stuff when y'all first started talkin' to each other. And if he didn't, that shit's on you," Jadyn said sharply.

"Don't you worry about what 'Rel and me was doin' back then or right now. You need to be worryin' about what Flash gon' do if pretty boy don't back the fuck up."

"Look, did you call to pick a fight or did you call to talk?" Jadyn could feel herself getting angry.

"Neither one, I called to ask you what you all was doing tonight. Y'all goin' to the club with us or y'all goin' on your own . . . again?"

"Flash told me he got other plans tonight, that he ain't goin' to the club. So why don't you lose the funky attitude and you and Jarrell can hang with me and Julian?"

"You and Julian? I don't know, I gotta check with Jarrell about that one."

"OK. You do that and call me back."

Jadyn was tripping about the day she had spent with Julian, and all of the gifts he had showered down on her. She loved each and every outfit that she had picked out. One was just a casual two-piece short set with matching shoes. The other was a mint-green sheath with thin, almost invisible straps. It fit Jadyn's body like a glove and the color was perfect with her hair and skin tone.

After dropping her home to change, he was taking her to this fabulous oceanside restaurant that specialized in steak and ribs.

Mani had called her back to say that Jarrell wanted to come over to Mani's apartment and watch some movies, so they were just going to chill, which was cool with Jadyn. The more she thought about it, the more she didn't want to be bothered with Mani's ass tonight.

She had just stepped out of the shower and wrapped a towel around her to begin her skin care routine when her cell phone rang. Thinking that it was Mani calling back to let her know that she and Jarrell would be joining them for dinner after all, she frowned as she flipped open her phone.

"Look, if you and Jarrell have changed your mind about going with us, it's too late. We've made plans to be alone tonight."

"Hello, is that you, Jadyn? This is your dad."

Jadyn's heart thudded against her chest and her body filled with nervous energy. Her mouth went dry as cotton and tears unexpectedly filled her eyes.

"Daddy? Is this really you?" She didn't know what to feel. The moment that she had anticipated and hoped for, yet feared at the same time, was upon her. Her father was on the other end of this phone call. With her emotions bubbling over, she took a few deep cleansing breaths in an attempt to calm herself. As she held the phone to her ear, she said a quick prayer: *Jesus, please help us.*

"Yes, sweetheart, it's me."

Though her father spoke tenderly and gently, his deep bass voice boomed through the phone.

Overwhelmed by unexpected emotions, she was momentarily speechless as tears streamed down her cheeks.

Her dad continued to speak after a brief pause. "Baby, I pray to God that you can one day find it in your heart to forgive me for dropping out of your life the way I did. I have cursed myself every day for leaving you like that. But please believe, I love you with all my heart and I never meant for things to happen the way they did. I don't believe your mother did, either. We made some terribly bad choices back then and I'm not going to try to make excuses for neither one of us."

"I have so much to tell you, so much I need to tell you about, to share with you . . . so much has happened . . . I don't know where or how to begin," Jadyn told him.

"I have missed you so much, baby. Not a day has gone by that I haven't wondered what's going on with you and prayed that everything is good with you," her dad said, his voice filling with emotion.

"But why didn't you just call me, Daddy?"

"The numbers I had for your mother and her family were all no good. I even made a trip to the last address where I knew your mother lived, but of course y'all had moved away. I know I should have done more, baby, and though it's not an excuse, I have been crazy busy at work. I was just about to look into hiring a PI to track you down. But you found me first."

"Daddy, I missed having you in my life. So much."

"I can't wait to see you, love."

"I can't wait to get together with you, too," she said.

"Where are you, baby? That dude that you hired said that he couldn't give me that information."

"I'm in Palm City."

She could almost hear her father's smile.

"That is great, baby, I'm not too far away from you. I live in Viera, only about a thirty-minute drive away."

Jadyn's heart started pounding again. Was her father going to come and see her tonight? That would surpass any fantasy that she had ever had about finding her real dad.

"When are you coming, Dad?"

Her father grew silent on the other end. Jadyn suddenly grew apprehensive. "Or I could come to you."

Her father finally spoke again. "Well, sweetheart, we might have to hold off on our reunion for another couple of weeks."

Jadyn's heart fell to her shoes.

"A couple of weeks?" she spoke slowly, unable to hide her

disappointment and not totally sure she wanted to. Let him feel the pain he was causing her yet again.

"Yes, I have a business trip that I have to take and my flight leaves in a couple of hours."

A business trip.

"Jadyn, baby, I know it's disappointing to have to wait a little while longer for us to see one another. I hate to do this to you but please believe me when I tell you it can't be helped. I wish I could take you with me, but you wouldn't enjoy yourself even if I could. I'm going to be in back-to-back meetings all the while I'm there."

He should have just asked her to go anyway. Maybe she would have been happy just to sit next to him on the plane, no matter if the ride would be long or short. Maybe she just wanted to touch him and spend time with him. Maybe it wouldn't have mattered if that time ended up being twenty hours or twenty seconds.

"I love you, baby, and I promise you that you will be the first person I call when I get back in town. Soon as the plane hits the tarmac I'll call you."

"I am disappointed, Dad. But I understand. Really. You can't be expected to drop everything without notice. It's fine," she said, as she choked back her disappointment. "We waited this long, a few more weeks won't kill us."

"OK, baby, I have to run. I love you," he said warmly.

"I love you, too, Dad," she told him, her heart overflowing.

She flipped the phone closed and threw it on the bed. The tears flowed again as the disappointment overtook her. It was the story of her life. When she expected good things to happen with family in her life, all she got was empty promises and excuses. After a few moments she wiped the tears and rose to wash her face with cold water so that her eyes wouldn't swell from the salty tears. As she splashed the cool refreshing water on her face, it soothed her frustrations. She had a date to get ready for.

When Julian picked her up, he was dressed in a suit, which didn't surprise her. He had asked her to wear the dress he had bought her, so she had expected him to dress well, too.

Once they were seated at the restaurant, they began having the most amazing conversation. With the candlelit table nestled in a cozy private corner of the restaurant, Jadyn was beginning to lose herself in all that was Julian.

"I know you get sicka hearin' it all the time, but you are fine! I mean you look like a movie star in that dress."

"Yeah, it does get on my nerves sometimes when you keep harpin' on the shit, but I'm cool with it comin' from you. 'Specially since you lookin' pretty fine tonight yourself."

"OK, we make a fine lookin' couple, how 'bout that? We both super sharp and can't nobody get to us."

Jadyn was laughing.

"You know you can be funny when you want to be," she said, still smiling.

"I can be, most definitely when I'm with the right one."

Jadyn frowned. "What makes you think I'm that right one? You don't really know me. I haven't really told you much about my life. Who I am."

Julian lifted his glass and took a sip of wine before asking, "So what is it you want me to know?"

Jadyn again hesitated about how much to tell him.

"Tell me something first," she said.

"OK."

"How come you don't have a woman?"

"How do you know that I don't?"

"Well, you don't really know me from Eve, you been talking to me almost every single night since I got here. You spendin' all this money on me, taking me out to all the best restaurants. Need I go on?"

Julian put his hands on top of the table and leaned toward her. "I'll admit that I have been on you. Been on you a lot but so what? How do you know I don't treat all beautiful women the same way?"

"You might. So then it comes back to why me?"

Julian took her hands in his and gazed into her eyes. "OK, I admit it. You ain't just another pretty face. You are definitely something different. I can't lie. From that first time I saw you that day on the plane, it's like your image was branded in my memory. No matter how hard I try, I just can't seem to shake it."

Jadyn took a sip of her chardonnay before she spoke. "Maybe you just haven't tried hard enough."

Taking one of her hands in his again and stroking it lightly he said, "That's just it. Maybe I don't want to."

Jadyn pulled her hand away and pretended she needed to use it to pick up a forkful of salad.

"You know, Julian, you've never really told me about your business, and I'm curious to hear more about it."

"You are? Why is that?"

"You said on the plane that you were looking for dancers. I'm a dancer."

Julian leaned back in his chair and tilted his head to one side. "Really? What kind of dancing you do?"

"Well, I do modern, jazz, hip-hop, ballet . . ."

"Whew! For a second there I thought you were about to tell me you were a stripper." He grinned.

Jadyn frowned. "And why do you find humor in that? Frankly, I find that insulting."

"No, please, don't take it that way."

"Well, I don't know how else you want me to take it. Why would that be your first thought about the kind of dancer I might be? Is that the kind of dancer you deal with in your business?"

Jadyn laid her fork down rather hard beside her bowl. She could feel her face flush and her anger rising.

"Whoa, whoa, whoa, Jadyn. Calm down. I apologize. I had no intention of insulting you. I'm sorry. Forgive me, please."

He took her hand again and gazed into her eyes.

"It's nothing that you've done or said. You know sometimes a thought will just pop into your head out of nowhere, no rhyme or reason for it, it just happens. Has that ever happened to you?"

She smiled at the thought. "Yeah, I guess it happens to all of us at one time or another."

"You know, it's funny that you should ask me about my business. I have a video shoot coming up for this hip-hop artist and . . ."

Right. Just the kind of dancing Jadyn wasn't interested in doing.

"Thank you, but I'm not really interested in that kind of dancing. I don't want to be shaking my ass all up in some camera and simulating sex onscreen, like some desperate ho."

Julian cleared his throat.

"Well, that's not the part I envisioned for you, you know, not at all. See, not every music video is about shakin' your ass in a camera lens. There will be some choreographed pieces, as well."

Jadyn was embarrassed by her outburst. "Oh. Are you holding auditions soon?"

"As a matter of fact I am in a few days. But ain't no need for you to have to wait. Come to my office tomorrow, bring your music and show me what you workin' with. If you can dance half as good as you look, you definitely in."

Jadyn just smiled.

48

After dinner they walked down to the beach and strolled hand-in-hand. Jadyn slipped off her sandals so that they could walk closer to the water. Julian followed suit and slipped off his shoes and socks and rolled up his cuffs. Julian took her gently by the elbow, and they veered off of the beach.

"Where you takin' me?"

"Don't worry, we'll still be on the beach. I just want to show you my private cove."

They walked a little ways down a sandy strip and through a stand of trees before coming out on the most beautiful, picture-perfect little paradise.

Julian hadn't lied, the beach was still there, but this particular area was surrounded by lush palms and ferns. And straight ahead was a mini-cliff with a waterfall trickling over the rocks and flowing out to the ocean. The sound of the water rushing over the rocks was very pleasant and soothing.

Julian kissed her again and Jadyn didn't pull away this time. She lost herself in the sweet taste of Julian's lips and tongue and the way he moved his tongue inside her mouth as he pressed his lips against hers. He darted his tongue, in and out, and back and forth, gently sucking and teasing hers. It was almost as if he were using his tongue to make love to her. She savored every moment of it and she didn't want the kiss to end.

Sinking to the sand he pulled Jadyn down on top of him, briefly breaking the kiss, but then he captured her lips again.

"Wait, Julian . . . my dress . . ."

"I'll buy you another one even better than this one," he said, kissing her more deeply.

He rolled in the sand and was on top of Jadyn, massaging her breasts through the clingy material, making her nipples spring tautly against its restraints. Julian definitely noticed and took the opportunity to duck his head slightly and lick the impressions her nipples made. Jadyn moaned and turned her head to one side. His tongue flicked back and forth, his saliva wetting the fabric. She felt Julian's hand dip down inside her dress and scoop out one of her breasts and immediately sucked the nipple into his mouth. She moaned again as he continued to suckle her breast and flick his tongue over and around her nipple. Julian shifted so that his hard-on lay heavy between her legs as he began to slowly grind his hips, making her legs open. Her dress hiked high above her hips and Julian pressed his hard-on against her, rubbing it up and down against her tender flesh until she was pulsating against him. As he freed her other breast and began circling it with his tongue, his hand moved inside her panties and began pushing them down her legs. He had Jadyn in a spin and she shuffled her legs to move the panties down around her ankles before kicking them off. He nibbled her nipples lightly with his teeth before loving and licking them with his tongue and then repeated the process on the other one and then back to the first one again. Jadyn moaned and thrashed and opened her legs wider. Julian moved down until his head was beneath her dress. Without hesitation, he began kissing her there, as he placed her thighs on his shoulders and his palms beneath her behind and lifted her slightly. He buried his lips in the moistness between her legs and groaned at the taste of her. Her aroma appeared to be driving him into a frenzy as she felt his hard-on stretch tighter against the crotch of this pants. She heard a sigh escape from his lips as her fingers fumbled with the button at his waistband and then slid his zipper down, allowing his penis to spring from its confines. Jadyn wrapped her hand around it and squeezed. She thought he was going to lose it, but he must have willed himself not to as he continued to taste her sweetness.

Plunging his tongue more deeply he found the prize and went to work on it, taking his time alternately licking and sucking it at the same time.

"Oh Julian, oh please!"

Her moans caused him to lick her ever more slowly and lightly, tantalizing and teasing her unmercifully.

It seemed he was doing everything in his power to make sure that she wanted, no craved, more of this. He switched the stroke of his tongue as he applied more pressure and began moving his tongue up and down, never leaving contact with the tender, pulsating skin, sucking hard and pulling downward with his lips at the same time.

"Oh yeah! Oh yeah, baby, do it just like that, oh. My . . . yeaaaaaaaaaah, yeahhhhhhhhhh. That's it, baby, right there!"

She didn't need to tell him twice. He kept up the steady pace, applying even more pressure with his tongue. Lick up, lick down, suck, pull down. Lick, suck, pull down. She was losing control. She began to squirm around and couldn't stop rubbing herself against his tongue as he licked her. He grabbed her hips and helped her move up and down against his tongue.

Jadyn couldn't believe the way he was making her feel. She was moving toward her orgasm and nothing was going to hold it back. She pushed her hips closer to his magic tongue and moved them up and down. Each stroke of his tongue pushed her closer to the edge. She felt a glowing ember between her legs getting hotter and hotter, and still he licked and lapped and sucked her. And then it was unbearably good.

"Oh yes, baby," she whispered. "There it is, there it is . . ."

And the ember caught fire and exploded in a flood of hot molten pleasure.

She arched her back and called out his name. Julian was feeling around in his pockets for something. Jadyn hoped it was a rubber.

She was both surprised and embarrassed by her reaction to the explosive orgasm she had just experienced. She should have been relaxed and calm, instead all she could feel was shame. At the peak of her pleasure it was Taji's face that came to her mind.

Julian gave up his search for whatever he was looking for and rolled over on top of her.

"You protected, baby? You on birth control?"

All of a sudden, making love to Julian was the last thing she wanted.

"No," she lied. "I'm sorry . . . and anyway, I can't do this unless you have a rubber."

"Aw, *damn!*" Jadyn felt him go soft against her leg.

Jadyn pulled her dress down to cover herself, and scanned the beach, searching for her panties. Spotting them she scooped them up and stood to her feet. Julian was caught completely off guard as she strode back in the direction from which they had come.

He stood up quickly trying to pull up his boxers and pants at the same time.

"Jadyn! Hold up! Baby, wait! What the fuck, woman? I know

this ain't gon' happen. Trynna run off without letting me get mines off? Naw, that shit ain't cool. Not cool at all."

Catching her by the elbow he turned her toward him.

"Oh so that's how it is? You get yours and leave me hangin'?" he said, sounding breathless.

"I can't do this . . . It wasn't s'posed to happen like this. I'm sorry . . . I was wrong to let it get to this." She pulled her arm away from him and continued walking down the beach. Julian caught up with her, jogging in front of her as he blocked her path.

"What are you talking about, Jadyn? What's not right? I thought we were diggin' each other. . . ."

"I do dig you, Julian, and that's what makes this so wack! You don't really know me. There are things I ain't even told you about and that I don't want to talk about right now. . . . I . . . can't talk about this right now . . ."

"What? What is this? I . . . I just gave you probably the best orgasm your ass ever had and you trippin' on me like this? This is some bullshit!"

Jadyn couldn't blame him for being upset. She shouldn't have let things get so out of control.

"You don't understand," she said.

"You damned right I don't understand. So like I told you before, why don't you make me understand."

Julian stared into her face and she was suddenly self-conscious about the tears and mascara streaking it. She opened her purse and began fishing around for a Kleenex and turned away from him as she spoke.

"I can't do this right now, I can't! I can't!"

Julian stared after her as she ran the last few steps to the car and got in.

"I don't believe this shit! I just don't fuckin' believe this shit. It's fucked up is what it is! It's just not natural."

Jadyn remained silent.

It was going to be a long ride home.

49

Jadyn was quiet all the way home. Julian had tried to get her to talk, but she just kept her head turned toward the window.

He turned the car off when they pulled into her uncle's driveway. He reached for her but she was completely stiff. He pulled her into his arms anyway, stroking her hair.

"I'm sorry about . . . everything. I don't know what happened back there, but if I rushed you, I'm sorry. Don't feel bad. Don't blame yourself. Ain't no need."

Jadyn burst into tears.

"It's not your fault either, Julian. I wanted you just as much as you wanted me. At least I thought I did. It's just the timing . . . the place." *The man.* "It just wasn't right that's all. I'm sorry."

He wiped her tears gently with his thumbs.

"Shhhhh. Now ain't no need for tears. You want your cousin and your uncle to come out here and kick off in my ass?"

She laughed in spite of herself.

"No."

"Well, come on then. Dry up those tears. Brush your hair and get yourself looking decent so I can walk you to the door and leave with my head still attached to my shoulders."

They both grinned. She straightened her dress and smoothed it out. Ran her fingers through her hair and took some Kleenex out of her purse and wiped the makeup streaks off her face.

She opened the door, but Julian touched her elbow.

"You all right?"

Jadyn nodded.

"You still coming to my office for the audition tomorrow?"

"I don't know about that. I'll call you."

She opened the door and disappeared into the house without a backward glance.

She was glad that Flash wasn't home and her uncle appeared to have already gone to bed because the house was quiet as she closed the door behind her and climbed the steps to her bedroom.

She immediately walked into her bathroom and turned on the shower. She wanted to wash the sand off her skin and out of her hair.

Before tonight she had only willingly given herself to Taji. Taj had never made her feel bad when he made love to her. The thought of Taji made the tears silently flow again. Taji was really the only person in her life who had loved her for who she was. She knew this, and now he could be loving someone else.

She shed the mint-green sheath, balled it up, and stuffed it inside a trash bag. She would take it to the cleaners in the morning.

She didn't know how it had happened. She had enjoyed Julian's kisses, part of her had wanted him to stop and the other part wanted him to keep thrilling her. Had wanted him to keep going. He had played her body like he had known exactly what she needed. He was definitely good at what he did. She stepped into the steaming shower and let the jets splash down over her head.

She had allowed him to get carried away with the foreplay. She had to admit what she'd done. She hadn't meant for it to go as far as it had. But the way he kissed her body, the way he used his hands and tongue on her, she had lost her self-control. She just wanted him to make her feel good. So why did she feel so bad about it?

She took the bar of soap and began lathering herself.

Her tears wouldn't stop. She had betrayed the man she loved. She had gone further than she had intended with Julian. The reasons why didn't matter. She wondered if Taji was loving someone else, too?

Jadyn was awakened by the ringing of her cell phone. Though she was groggy, she threw back the covers, grabbed her purse, and began fishing around in it for her cell phone.

She finally grabbed hold of it.

"Hello?"

"Hey lovely, I called to see how you doin' this morning."

Jadyn let her head fall back on the pillow.

"I'm doing all right, Julian. I feel better than I did last night, I guess."

"Good, good. Glad to hear that. You get you some rest?"

"I guess so. I don't remember when my head hit the pillow so I'd have to say I did. What time is it?"

"Nine o'clock. Look here, the reason for my call is we are gon' skip that audition at my office today. You say you a dancer, I'm just gon' take your word for it. See, that hip-hopper is coming to town this evening and he moved the shoot up a day. So I'm short a dancer."

"Really? So how much does it pay?"

"A honey like you will make top dollar if you can follow directions and if you a quick study on pickin' up the moves."

"I haven't had any problem picking up choreography in the past, so it shouldn't be a problem. Just remember, I'm definitely not doing any hoochie dancing, so if that's all this is about, don't even set yourself up to be clowned," she told him sternly.

"Yeah, well about that, Jay. The boss kinda changed his mind about that, too. Everybody gotta wear swimsuits in this one scene, even the stars."

Jadyn groaned. "Oh here we go! What did I just say! I'm not trynna do that! That is the one thing I have always told myself, not to mention my family and friends, that I wouldn't do!"

"Look, Jay, everybody can't start at the top. Sometimes you have to start low and work your way up. You know that. And not all the women in the video be getting all down and dirty like that. Like I told you some pieces will be choreographed. And even the ones that aren't, some of the women will still look classy, just dancing cute with a glass of Rémy in their hands. If you help me out, I'll make sure that that's what's up with you. You won't have to do none of that other shit. I promise."

Julian's pleas were having very little effect on her. She was still trying to sort out her feelings about what had happened the night before. Right at the moment she was leaning toward just ending the call and going back to sleep.

"Unh-hunh. Let's say I agree to do it, how much does it pay?"

"Oh you will get top dollar, no doubt. I promise you that for sure. You will leave the shoot with no less than five Gs. I guarantee it."

No less than five grand?

"Impressive. I'll tell you what. I'll go with you and everything. If it's like you say, I'll do it. But if it's not . . ."

"Don't worry about a thing, baby. I got this."

50

"Hey Jay, you rollin' with us tonight, or you gon' hang out with that busta Julian?"

Jadyn was excited about the music video, but Julian had told her to be sure not to tell Flash where they were going that night.

"You know how it is, baby," he had explained to her. "When these rappers come to town, everybody and they mama think they got the looks to dance in a video. You remember all those chicken heads that thought they were dimes when you and I both know it was maybe two or three out of the fifty chicks that ran up there that were true dimes."

She had to admit that Julian had a point.

"If word gets out about the shoot, and all those wannabes run up on the scene, they gon' cancel the shoot and move it somewhere else. Maybe to another town. And you would be out of an easy five Gs for nothing."

His words rang in her head when she told Flash, "Julian's taking me to that concert tonight. You know Li'l Bri and them."

"Whaaaaat? That fool got tickets to that? They been sold out for months."

"Yeah, he said he got them when they first went on sale 'cause he knew they would sell out fast."

"Yeah, that's what's up. Look here, li'l cousin, when y'all get back, have him bring you up to the club. That's where the party at."

"You mean, you gonna show up at Steele's party even though y'all got beef?"

"Shit, we squashed that shit. Everybody was drunk. Steele cool wit' it. And I don't give a fuck if he ain't. I'm not missing the livest party of the year because some nigga trynna sweat me."

Jadyn didn't know how to feel about that. She hoped that Flash wasn't going to look for trouble.

"Anyway, everybody gonna be so jammed up in there, and it's gonna be so dark and smoky up in there. Ain't nobody gon' be able to see a muhfuckin' thang. You mind what I tell you and have dude bring you up there."

Jadyn turned her head away without answering and Flash grabbed her face and turned it back toward him.

"You have him bring you to the party after the concert, hear?"

"Okay, cuz, no worries. I'm cool."

"I'm dead serious, don't make me have to come looking for you and your boy."

Jadyn looked her cousin straight in the eye. "Quit trippin', cuz. Everything's cool. For real."

"A'ight then, I'll see you later on at the club."

51

Jadyn hadn't wanted to call attention to herself, so she had dressed simply in a nice pair of jeans, a dressy tank, and high-heeled pumps with a matching belt and some light jewelry. A gold bracelet, the tennis bracelet Taji had bought her, a gold necklace, earrings, and rings on all of her fingers, including her thumb. She did love her jewelry and Julian had been showering her with more gold than she had had in her life.

Julian had told her not to worry about bringing any extra clothes because they would have the outfits for the girls to wear already there.

"How do they know I'ma be able to fit any of the things they picked out?"

"Are you for real? Baby with a body like yours, they ain't going to have any trouble at all dressing you! You so fine, the clothes will be wearing a grin just 'cause they get to be next to you! Trust and believe."

Jadyn smiled.

.   .   .

When they turned onto the paved driveway leading up to the mansion, Jadyn was amazed by how monstrously big it was. If she had thought that Taji's parents' home was huge, the difference between their home and what she was looking at now was extreme. It was like comparing a yacht to the *Titanic!*

Jadyn suddenly felt self-conscious about the way she was dressed, despite the fact that she was supposed to have a change of clothes waiting for her. The winding driveway came to a dead end at a huge, black-barred gate that had to be at least eighteen feet tall. There was a guard shack directly behind and to the left of the gate. They pulled up to the black callbox next to the gate.

"Good evening. I need you to give me the pass code for tonight, as well as your pass for the evening. When I am finished speaking, press the user buttons and key in your code on the buttons on the callbox. You may enter it one time and one time only, so take your time. If the code is correct, the gate will open. Please remove your guest pass and have it ready to hand to me once you enter the gate. Please note that you may exit the grounds at any time during the evening, but you will not be allowed to reenter for any reason. Do you understand these instructions or should I repeat them?"

Julian pressed the TALK button on the box. "Understood," he said and proceeded to enter the pass code into the box. Jadyn heard a metallic *click* and the oversize gate immediately began to swing open. Two guards exited the shack with metal detectors. The guards were tall, both stood well over six feet. One appeared to be more muscular than the other, but both were well-built.

"Please step out of the car, place your keys and jewelry in the container, and stand spread-eagled, please," the more muscular of the two instructed, while the other stood back with his hand on the pistol he wore at his side.

Jadyn studied the guards' faces as Julian stepped out of the car and handed one of the guards his pass. Then he held his arms out to the sides. Floodlights lit the stone driveway behind the gate and Jadyn could see their faces. The one who took Julian's pass had a medium brown complexion, and bushy eyebrows that seemed to run together. The other guard with the metal detector in his hand was a white guy with his hair long in the front and shaved close to the scalp in back, his long nose was crooked and looked like it had been broken a time or two. She removed her jewelry and stepped out of the car. She dropped the jewelry into the bin and stood with her arms out to the sides as she had seen Julian do. The guard waved the security wand over her body as he had Julian's.

"Open your purse, please," he instructed after waving the wand over it. The metal detector had most likely picked up her tube of lipstick.

"OK, you're good to go. Enjoy your evening," the guard said casually as Jadyn and Julian climbed back into the car.

"All of that just for a video shoot?" Jadyn asked as they continued down the driveway toward the mansion.

"Baby, don't forget these are rappers who are coming here tonight. You know the owners aren't taking any chances with these fools shooting up all their goods."

"Yeah, I know that's right!" she agreed.

52

As they rounded a curve in the driveway the mansion came into view. Jadyn sucked in her breath at the sight of it.

It was a sprawling expanse of buildings that looked as if two or three families could live there comfortably. The driveway was lined with gigantic palm trees that ran the length of the front of the house and ran down a path that led to a covered walkway. As Julian pulled to the side and parked, Jadyn could see that the stone drive had become marble. The same sand- and brown-colored marble formed a row of huge pillars that stood side-by-side around the front of the house. Julian came around and opened Jadyn's door for her. Jadyn tried not to show how impressed she was. She didn't want Julian to think that she was intimidated by her surroundings, though intimidated was exactly how she felt.

"I knew they had booked a mansion for the shoot, but I had no clue that it was all like this." Julian's words echoed Jadyn's thoughts. "I mean, don't get me wrong, I have been on video shoots in mansions before, but none even came close to this."

"I know I definitely wasn't expecting *Lifestyles of the Rich and Famous* when you invited me to this party, for sure."

Julian took Jadyn's arm and led her between the marble pillars, up the marble steps, and into the foyer that led to the front doors. There was track lighting everywhere they stepped. Julian looked over at Jadyn, he gazed at her so long that he made her uncomfortable. She reached up and ran her fingers through her hair.

"Is something the matter?" she asked.

"Not at all. I was just thinking how damn perfect you are. You really don't have any idea how good you really look, do you? Steele got it right when he told you you were more than a dime!"

Jadyn blushed. "That may be true, because I damn sure never thought my looks could earn me five Gs in one night. Just for being in a video."

Jadyn smiled at him, but caught a glimpse of concern cross his face that vanished quickly.

"You ready for this?" he asked her.

"If I'm not, I just ought to be, right?"

Julian smiled.

The door opened and a tall, skinny, dark-skinned chick stood on the other side. She wore minimal makeup on her smooth ebony face and a toothpick dangled from her glossy, full lips. A gold earring sparkled from her brow and another from her nostril. Another twelve or so studs dotted her right ear. Her hair was cut very short and permed bone straight, from what Jadyn could see showing under the ball cap she wore tilted to the side. She sported a white wife-beater, and about a dozen chains slung around her neck. One of the chains had a large pendant with what appeared to be diamonds encrusted across the entire surface. One of the legs on the sweats she wore was pushed up to her calf, and on her feet were the requisite Jordans and white ankle socks. There was a Corona in her hand and as she stepped aside to allow them to enter, she tipped it up and took a long swig, a loud "Ahhhhhhhh" escaping her lips.

"What's crackalackin', Ju?" she said and as Julian stepped through the door, she grabbed him in a bear hug and patted his back like a homeboy would. Jadyn took that in and also the way she wore her sweatpants with one leg rolled up like that. Even the way she stood was more like the way a dude would. She felt right away that she was most likely a lesbian. No matter what her status was, Jadyn made a mental note about her. Not that she had anything against gays—she didn't care one way or the other about another woman or man's preference as long as they didn't bring it into her world. Live and let live was her motto. Though she knew that her mother would say different.

Her mother had remarked on more than one occasion that God had not made men and women to lay down with the same sex, that he thought it was an abomination. But Jadyn thought that would be between them and God.

"What up, Li'l Bri?" Julian greeted her back.

"Well, well, well, and who do we have here?" Li'l Bri released Julian and turned her full attention to Jadyn, checking her out from head to toe.

"Uh, Li'l Bri, this is Jadyn Collins. Jadyn Collins, Li'l Bri, rapper extraordinaire."

Jadyn knew who Li'l Bri was. She had the hits "Put You on Lock" and "Fool's Gold."

"Nice meeting you," Jadyn said, trying not to sound starstruck, as she reached her hand out. Bri took it and enfolded it inside both of hers.

"A pleasure to meet you, I'm sure, with your fine ass." She held on to Jadyn's hand so long it was beginning to get on her nerves, star rapper or not.

Pulling her hand away, she turned toward Julian and said, "Where are we shootin' the video? Shouldn't I be getting dressed?"

She hoped that Li'l Bri caught that the reason she was here was strictly business.

It was Li'l Bri who answered.

"Oh hell yeah, baby. By all means. But in your case it's gon' be more like undressing."

Li'l Bri licked her lips and leered at her once again, looking her body up and down.

Jadyn looked from her to Julian and back again.

"Julian, what is she talking about?"

Julian looked down at the floor and back up again, clearing his throat and rubbing his forehead before he spoke.

"It's Li'l Bri's shoot. You and the others gon' be dancing around the pool for Bri. So you gon' be wearing bikinis."

Li'l Bri was grinning now, flashing gold crowns across both sides of her teeth. Only the two front teeth were gold-free. *Ugly mouth*, Jadyn couldn't help thinking.

"Look here, walk down that hall and turn right, the patio is there. Go on out back to the pool house with the other ladies, you'll see the bikinis laid out. You can take your pick. Get dressed and wait for us by the pool. We gon' narrow down our picks of who's in and who's out then."

53

Who's in and who's out? Julian had made it seem like it was a done deal, that she was already in. She couldn't conceal her frustration about this whole situation.

She slung her purse over her shoulder and began marching down the hall, throwing a "Whatever, man" over her shoulder as she walked away. She heard Li'l Bri ask, "What's up with your girl, Ju?" and Julian mumble something she couldn't quite make out.

That damned Julian was full of shit. He knew she wouldn't have anything to do with a video shoot for a lesbian if he had been straight up with her. She had to be honest, he hadn't exactly lied about it, but at the same time he hadn't told her what was up. She contemplated calling Flash and telling him to come pick her up. The trouble was, she didn't exactly know where she was. She supposed if she really needed to she could walk back to the guard shack and ask. On the other hand, there was still a chance that she could make a lot of money for a few hours' work, so maybe she should just let it play out. If she didn't get chosen, she would call Flash then.

As she stepped out onto the patio, she was amazed at the expanse of water that lay before her. The same marble that paved the front entryway was echoed here and ran around the entire pool. Cascading fountains and waterfalls spouted around the sky-blue waters and the sultry lighting made everything look cozy. There was a warm breeze rustling the leaves of the palm trees that framed the back edge of the pool, and a building loomed in front of them. It had to be the guesthouse because she saw a couple of young women emerge, already clad in bikinis. They both wore pumps, but she noticed that neither of them were wearing cover-ups. They walked with such confidence, it didn't seem to bother them one bit.

"Hey lady, you here for the shoot?" the darker of the two called out, waving her hand in greeting.

Since they were walking in Jadyn's direction, they soon met each other on the walkway. The one who had called out to Jadyn was extremely beautiful, with dark brown skin and hair cornrowed finely to the back, with two long skinny braids dangling on either side of her face that ended in beads. She wore a pale blue two-piece suit, the strapless bra cups held together by a large round silver hoop. The bottoms were barely a scrap of material, a small triangle that covered her privates, connected on both hips by silver hoops like the one connecting the bra cups. The pumps were the same shade of blue. Jadyn had to admit, the girl was wearing the hell out of it, with her tiny waist, round hips and butt, and shapely legs.

"What's up, ladies? Yeah, I guess that's what I'm here for. Are the suits back there?" Jadyn asked, just for the sake of conversation.

"Yeah, girl. There are so many suits in there, o' girl might as well open her own boutique!" the other girl answered. She was equally as stunning as her companion, with her caramel-brown skin, bone-straight blond hair, green eyes, and the longest legs Jadyn had ever seen. The pale green halter style bikini accented her eyes. She wore silver strappy four-inch sandals that wound halfway up her calves.

"Good thing you came early so you don't get the leftover coochie cutters that's been on some other broad's ass first. My name is Chalice, and this is Tia."

"I'm Jadyn. Nice to meet you and good lookin' out."

Tia spoke again. "When you get your suit picked out and you get changed, come back up to the house. We been on these shoots before, so we'll let you know what's up. Girls be seeing the videos on TV and they think that you just show up, the rapper does his thing while you shake your ass like it's a party while the cameras be rollin'. In reality, it don't go down nothing like that. You might get picked to be in the scene with the rapper, or you might shoot first and get sent on your way, you never know."

"Yeah, well I kinda figured there was a lot more to it than it appeared. So anyway, I'ma get changed so I'll see y'all back up at the house."

Chalice said, "Yeah, make sure you get with us, 'cause ain't but two or three of us going to get chosen to be in the shot with the rappers. You seem cool and you look good. Damn near as good as us!" She cracked up and Tia said, "That was cold-blooded."

"Be quiet. I wasn't being cold, just stating a fact. You know I'm not ever gon' say another broad looks better than me."

"Ya heard?" Tia and Chalice began walking toward the house.

"Peace out," Chalice said, throwing up two fingers.

Chalice had been right. There were enough suits to open up a store. They weren't cheap, either. She imagined that a lot of the designers gave away the suits just to get the exposure that a pretty girl wearing their gear would give them.

Jadyn wondered what was up with those two and why they had been trying to be so friendly. She knew she couldn't take those bitches seriously. Especially since there were just a limited number of spots with the star. You could bet that the ones who won the spots with the rappers would be the ones to make the real cheddar. They wouldn't be paying no five Gs to every face in the crowd, for sure. She would let Tia and Chalice think that she had fallen for their bs for the time being.

54

The first suit that caught Jadyn's eye was the one she decided to wear. It hung on the back of the rack, a splash of yellow with green and blue swirled through a clasp buckle that fastened the suit together on either hip, and the same clasp joined the bra cups together. The halter straps began with yellow and narrowed into skinny straps that had the identical swirls of color as the buckles. It was skimpy, but not as bad as what Tia and Chalice wore. She smiled to herself as she pulled the suit from its hanger and examined the inside of the panties to make sure those two asses hadn't been inside. When she was sure it hadn't been tried on, she hung it back up and began removing her T-shirt and jeans. She decided that she would be a little more clean-minded than the two before her, leaving her panties on as she tried on the suit.

Stepping in front of the mirror Jadyn was mesmerized by her reflection. This suit was made for her. As she turned to look at her behind, yes her cheeks hung out a little, but it looked sexy, not nasty. The bottom hugged hers in such a way that it actually made her cheeks look rounder and the "toot" more pronounced, which in turn made her waist look tiny. The color was perfect against her copper skin. She couldn't help but grin as she thought about Tia and Chalice with their blue and green suits. Yes, they were stunning, but they would look like they were just there to make her shine, since the colors of their suits would bounce back and make hers stand out.

Mess with a playa, ya ass gets played . . . , she thought to herself.

She found the paper inserts that were meant to be worn inside the bottom, the ones they kept inside boutiques when you tried them on. She quickly slipped the bottom and her panties off and pulled the bikini bottom up around her hips again.

Looking over the selection of shoes, she chose a pair of bronze sandals that laced up around the ankles. Taking a hair clip out of her bag, she brushed her hair away from her face and gathered it into the clip, so that her curls cascaded down her neck in a tumble, setting two long tendrils loose on either side of her face.

She finished with a little gloss to make her lips look moist. It wasn't necessary to add anything else. She didn't need it. She also figured they'd have someone on the set to make up their faces if necessary. She folded her jeans and T-shirt neatly before placing them inside her bag on top of her bra and panties, then looked around for a place to stash it until after the shoot. It didn't take long for her to find a spot beneath a dressing table in a corner away from where the swimwear was hanging. Satisfied her bag was safe, she strode out of the guesthouse just in time to run into twenty other girls.

"How y'all ladies doin' tonight," she called out casually, not slowing her steps as she maneuvered between the group. She saw in their eyes that she looked fly.

Tia and Chalice, watch your backs!

Jadyn made her way down the path, thinking about the money she would have once the night was over. Definitely enough to fly to New York and stay for a week or so if she got the audition with

Judith Jamison and the Alvin Ailey troupe. She hadn't heard back from Ms. Hollister yet, but it would be great if she was totally prepared and all she had to do was pack her bags and go. When she thought about it that way, doing this video could be a good thing. But she still wasn't going to do anything that might come back and bite her in the ass later on.

55

The music was loud, live, and the party was jumping when Jadyn entered the house from the patio. There had to be at least fifty people inside. Some were getting their dance on. Jadyn noticed that there were other women who didn't have on bikinis. She wondered if they just hadn't bothered to change yet, or if they were there to dance in the video at all.

Beyoncé's voice could be heard above the pound pound of the bass. "All the women who are independent . . . throw your hands up at me. All the honeys who makin' money throw your hands up at me . . ."

"That's the jam!" Jadyn shouted as she joined the crowd and began dancing around.

"Oh, baby, don't do it like that!" a dude called out and immediately stepped in front of her and began gyrating his hips, mimicking her dance moves.

"Make me wanna holla!"

Someone tapped her on the shoulder and she turned, still laughing and dancing.

It was Julian.

"Hold that down, girl. You know you got to keep it fresh for the camera."

Jadyn kept right on dancing. "Baby, I'm always fresh, don't you worry about that!" She turned around, gave her hips a little shake, rolled her stomach, and broke Julian down.

"Well damn! Let's go!" he said as he began moving to the beat.

Jadyn had the men staring and panting as she moved around the floor. Other women who had on their swimwear were also dancing around.

"I'm 'bout to have a heart attack up in here!" Julian said, winded and holding Jadyn around the waist.

"Come on, baby, for real. You need to chill out. The camera catches everything and I know you don't want to look all wrung out on screen, now do you?"

Jadyn stopped moving. "Yeah, you got a point there. But you don't even know if I'ma get chosen."

"Baby, the only way you ain't gon' get chosen is if the ones doing the choosin' is blind, retarded, or dead!"

Jadyn laughed.

"You are rockin' that swimsuit and you know it!" Julian told her, still grinning.

All at once, a group of about eight men entered the room. The shortest one of them began barking out orders.

"Come people, posse up! We only have so much time to get in, get this video shoot in the can, and raise up outta here! So this is what I want you to do. Now, I believe I can use each and every one of you in this one, so for the time being, no one is getting cut."

The room broke out in applause and cheers. From the way the man had walked in and taken control, Jadyn assumed that he would be directing the video and the rest were a part of his crew.

"All right, all right! Calm your asses down!" The clapping and cheers began to die down as he continued speaking.

"Now having said that, some of you will be seen more than

others." His comment was greeted by moans, groans, and complaining.

"Quiet! Now y'all know that you can't all be stars in here. Let me back up for a moment and introduce myself and my crew. I'm Darren Michaels, I'm the director, this is Coleman Bates, assistant director, he'll be the one that most of you will be taking instructions from. Chico Martinez, he's my choreographer, and he's going to take a very small group of you, maybe three girls and two guys, and actually teach you a short routine. I hope whoever he chooses are quick studies, too."

For the first time since Julian had asked her to be a part of this video, Jadyn grew excited. She was going to make sure she was one of those chosen few. She wasn't going to miss the opportunity to be seen dancing onscreen by maybe millions of people. Who knew, maybe one or two of the potential millions of viewers just might be someone who could advance her career. It had happened more than a few times. One minute you saw someone in a video, and the next thing they were either doing cameo appearances on the big screen or dancing on stage at the Grammy awards. Either was definitely cool with her!

". . . and my cameramen, R. J. Saunders, Lamar, and Bootsy Genovese." The crowd gave the crew a round of applause.

"Now, what I need first, is for all the ladies who have a professional background in dancing to step forward. And if you are unclear about what I mean when I say 'professional background,' let me just clarify. If your only dancing experience includes a stage with a pole attached to it that you wrapped your legs around and slid down before you proceeded to remove any of your clothing . . . I'm not speaking to you! You'll have an opportunity to do what you do best later when I need someone to drop it like it's hot!" There was a mix of laughter and groans from the crowd. "Now, all the rest of you ladies who paid for dance lessons, please step forward."

Jadyn and about five other young women stepped forward. "I need y'all to step over to my choreographer, introduce yourselves, and follow his instructions to the letter," he said, dismissing them as he turned back to the crowd. "I need professional male dancers next. The definition I gave to the ladies applies to you as well minus the pole dancing part . . . for most of you." More muted laughter. The director picked three of them.

"OK, this way ladies, over here." Chico Martinez stood in a far corner of the room and was waving them over. After the introductions he explained the deal. "Now I'm telling you, if you know that you are not a quick study and you have never been one to pick up the moves after watching your instructor once or twice, please do not waste my time or yours. Excuse yourself now and move back into the large group. If you remain and you can't keep up with me, you will be sent home."

"But Darren said no one would be cut . . . ," said one of the girls.

Chico turned toward her. "Do I look like Darren to you?"

Anyone with eyes could see that the two men looked nothing alike. Where Chico's body was well-defined and chiseled, Darren's was a little on the soft side. Where Darren was a deep chocolate color and had a fine-boned, handsome face and sported a clean-shaven head, Chico was very fair, kind of plain, and had his long wavy hair pulled back in a ponytail. The girl got his point: He was in control right now and she and all the rest would do well to recognize that fact.

Nobody returned to the large group and two young men walked up to join the female dancers. Chico repeated his admonition to them, and they both chose to stay.

"All right then, here's what I need."

Chico moved around the floor, doing a few pop-and-lock moves before breaking into some serious dance steps.

"Let's go!" he said, stepping back and expecting them to mimic what he had just done.

The two guys, Jadyn, and one of the other girls had no problem. However, the girl who had spoken up was seriously lacking. It didn't look like she had had any type of formal training.

"Oh no! Unh-unh. Kick rocks, girl!" he said, pulling her out of the group.

She began moving toward the crowd, but Chico wasn't having that.

"Where you goin', girl? I think I made it clear that anyone who wasted my time was out. Now, get gone right out that door."

"But I didn't drive!"

"So? That would be your problem. Look, this is a big place, you ain't gotta go home, but you gotta get the hell up outta here! In other words, lose yourself in another part of this muhfucka!"

The girl flounced out of the room, showing big attitude, and Chico turned back to them. "And the rest of you can wipe those grins from your faces, because a couple of you are real close to joining her. Don't get it twisted. I will do this part by my damn self if I have to! Now step it up!"

In the end, everyone else got the choreography so no one else got the ax.

Jadyn and her group stood off to the side rehearsing their routine, while Darren and Chico began to work the big crowd.

"I need pole dancers next. All you ladies step it up. Come on, move it!" Darren yelled, clapping his hands.

During their part of the video shoot, Jadyn danced hard and

furiously. She could have sworn the cameraman had zoomed in on her. He stood almost directly in front of her and she noticed he adjusted the lens. It couldn't get any better than that! She was happier than she'd been in a while.

56

Jadyn walked up the stairs and entered the room that Julian had told Jadyn all the dancers were meeting in to collect their cash. She had to climb the winding stairs that had been the focal point of one of the major scenes for the video, then walk about halfway down the carpeted hallway.

She hesitated for a moment in front of the door, feeling a bit uneasy that she was still wearing only the bikini. It was one thing to dance around half-naked at a party where most of the people were dressed the exact same way, but it was another to collect cash from a man in a separate room. Something inside was warning her that something wasn't right. She couldn't put her finger on it, so she pushed the thought aside, lifted her hand, and knocked.

"Come on in," someone said, and she was surprised that the voice behind the door was female. *Good,* she thought and relaxed as she entered the room. Her mouth flew open.

On the bed were Tia and Chalice. Naked as the day they left the womb. They were so caught up in giving pleasure to each other that they didn't notice Jadyn open the door.

Jadyn spoke to herself more than to the two cavorting on the bed. "I obviously have the wrong room."

Li'l Bri emerged from behind the door, holding on to it with one hand so that Jadyn couldn't close it. Leering at Jadyn while staring her straight in the eyes, she told her, "That depends on what you looking for." Li'l Bri allowed her gaze to rove over Jadyn's body and then over the two on the bed before connecting with Jadyn's eyes again. "If you here to get paid, you got the right one."

57

"What the fuck?" Jadyn was stunned at first. She hadn't seen anything like this before. Heard of it, just never been in that world. She recovered quickly.

"I'm here to get paid for the work I did in the video. Nothin' more, nothin' less," she said, returning Bri's stare.

"Oh, you only want the crumbs? I thought somebody who look as good as you would want to make some real cheddar," Bri said, strolling over to the dresser and pulling out a wad of cash. She walked back over to Jadyn counting out one-hundred-dollar bills. Once Bri had counted out fifty bills she handed them to her.

"Now you can take this, and be on your merry way. Or . . ." Bri walked over to the bed and began rubbing one of the girl's behinds. "You can stay here and party with us. If you wanna join the party, I might double, maybe even triple your dough," she said, rising to her feet and walking back over to stand in front of Jadyn.

Jadyn shook her head, glanced down at the floor and back up again. She couldn't believe what she was hearing. This broad had her twisted. She had never wanted to be a star-fucker. And she wasn't about to become no ho for anybody for any amount of money. Some people would sell their souls for the right price. Jadyn wasn't one of them.

"Look, what you do with them or whoever, that's your business, OK? But I'm not the one. I am strictly dickly and I don't get down like that." She glanced over at Chalice and Tia. Chalice had moved to the edge of the bed, with one leg propped up on the mattress and the other on the floor. Tia was on her knees in front of her with her face buried between her legs. Chalice had her fingers entwined in Tia's hair, her face twisted in pleasure.

Jadyn turned to leave, but Bri grabbed her arm.

"Hold up, hold up now. Let's talk this over. Think about it. I got endless bank here tonight, and baby, it's all for you." Bri started spreading the remaining hundred dollar bills out like a fat, green fan and waved it in front of her face. "Just say the word. When will you ever get another chance to make this kinda money this fast, hunh? You gonna pass up an opportunity like this?" Bri was moving closer to Jadyn with each word she spoke until she was standing toe-to-toe with her. "Don't you want Bri to love you right, hunh? Can't no man give you what Bri can, let me teach you what making love is really all about."

She leaned in for a kiss and Jadyn threw her arm in front of her.

"Bitch, you need to back the fuck up! What part of 'this ain't my type of party' don't you understand? Was it the 'no' or the 'way'?" Jadyn gave Bri a push and Chalice leapt naked from the bed.

"Trick, you put your hands on my woman again and I'm gon' kick your muhfuckin' ass!"

"Sit down, Chalice," Bri said.

"Your woman?"

Would the surprises never cease?

"Yes, my woman, you got a problem with it?" Chalice said.

"I told you to sit your ass down, Chalice!" Bri said more force-fully, holding up her arm to prevent her from lunging at Jadyn.

Tia, who was up on her knees on the bed, spoke. "Throw that hood rat out on her ass, she messin' up our party. Come on back to bed, baby, don't let that pigeon spoil our fun." She lay back on the bed fondling herself. Chalice joined her, stroking and kissing Tia, before looking back at Bri. "Don't keep me waiting too long, Bri. I might just get caught up in something new," she finished, giving Tia a deep tongue kiss before moving down to her breasts.

"Quit beggin' that bitch to take your money, if she too dumb to have some fun with us and get paid for it, fuck her. Get rid of the troll," Tia said.

"Beggin'? You watch your mouth. Bri don't beg." Bri got mad and tried to snatch the five grand from Jadyn's hands, but Jadyn was too quick and moved it out of reach.

"What the hell? This is mine! I earned this."

Bri moved so fast that Jadyn didn't see it coming. She back-handed Jadyn and caught her in the nose and part of her mouth, drawing blood.

"Don't get that shit twisted. You ain't earned shit of my money unless I say so. Now give it up!"

Bri threw a punch and hit Jadyn in the face, and she stumbled backward, falling into the dresser. "No you did not!" she yelled as she dabbed her nose and looked down at her bloody palm. Jadyn balled up her fist and popped L'il Bri in the mouth and blood began flowing from there, too.

Chalice was off the bed in seconds and plowed into Jadyn, landing her naked body on top of her. Tia sat on the bed laughing.

"Get your stank ass up off me!" The bitch had the biggest titties in the world and they kept flapping around like giant water bal-loons. Jadyn had to maneuver her body to keep them out of her face, while she pummeled the girl with her fists and bucked her hips, trying to shake Chalice's naked ass off her. Chalice was digging her nails into Jadyn's skin. Jadyn twisted her body to the side and kicked her legs, sending Chalice flying. She jumped up and drove the heel of her sandal into Chalice's ass as she crawled on the floor trying to get her balance.

Chalice screamed savagely and charged at Jadyn again, full speed with boobs flopping.

"I'ma kill you, you fuckin' bitch!" she bellowed.

Jadyn scanned the room for a weapon and her eyes fell upon a brass lamp on the table above her head.

She reached up and snatched it from the table, swung hard and connected with Chalice's head. She fell backward like a ton of bricks, out cold. Jadyn rose to her feet as Li'l Bri stepped toward her, her mouth still bloody.

"Stay the fuck away from me! Or I'ma clock you in the head the same way I did your girl," Jadyn warned as she backed up until she had reached the doorway.

"I don't know what in the hell is really goin' on up in this piece. But I ain't havin' it! I am not on this!"

"Take ya funky ass on down the road then, tramp. Just leave my muhfuckin' money! 'Cause if I gotta come find it, it's gon' get real ugly real fast. And trust and believe you don't want none a this!"

"What the fuck-ever! Like I told your ass before, I earned this shit!" Jadyn kicked the door shut and ran down the hall, looking over her shoulder every few seconds. But there was no one behind her.

58

She continued down the steps thinking if she made it outside she would be all right. She would call a taxi from her cell phone and tell them to pick her up at the Bently Davis Mansion. Lucky for her, she had overheard Darren, the video director, say the name of the mansion during the shoot. She was sure someone who drove for a living would know where it was.

Downstairs, the crowd had grown even larger and it was hard for Jadyn to push through. She was still clad only in the bikini, and the men kept trying to get in her face and hold her up. Once she made it to the patio, she ran out to the guesthouse to retrieve her bag and change her clothes.

She grabbed her bag, dug out her cell phone, and punched in 411 for information.

"Yeah, give me the number for a cab company . . . no I do not know which one . . . Merritt Island . . . the Bently Davis Mansion . . . Bently Davis Man . . . Yeah, on Merritt Island. OK, yeah I can hold." Jadyn waited for the operator to connect her to the cab company. She repeated where she needed them to come, breathed a sigh of relief that they knew where to find her as she flipped the phone closed.

After she changed out of her suit, she opened the door a crack to see if Li'l Bri had sent anybody to look for her.

She didn't see anyone on the patio, but a few people were lounging around the pool. She could see a couple of them had shed their suits and were either about to get busy or go skinny-dipping. Either way, she knew they wouldn't be thinking about her. Just as she was about to ease out onto the walkway, Julian rounded the corner. He was on his cell phone and he had two dudes on either side of him. She was sure he knew the whole time what Li'l Bri wanted her to do. She had to leave without Julian spotting her.

"Shit!" Jadyn frantically glanced around the room for a place to hide. Her eyes landed on the closet, but that would be the first place he would look.

Walking over to the swimsuit rack, she looked up and saw a door in the ceiling. She had seen one like that before and knew that it probably led to a crawlspace.

Praying she would be able to get it open, she began climbing the shelves behind the rack of swimsuits. Thoughts of spiders and worse that could be hiding behind the door crowded her mind and almost made her want to throw up, but fear propelled her forward. She could hear Julian's voice getting louder as she pressed against the door with her hands.

"Hell fuckin' no, I didn't know about this shit," Julian said, his voice sounding angrier by the second. "Why in the fuck would I settle for some chump change like that when I make more than that in five minutes at a party like this with all the bitches I brought up in here . . ."

The door wasn't budging and Jadyn frantically shoved with her shoulders. "Please . . . open . . . come on . . ." She gave one last push and the door gave way. A ton of dust showered down on her head. Ignoring the grime and the ugly images of what awaited her, she pulled herself up and was easing the door back down as Julian and his crew burst through the door. Pressing an eye against the little finger hole that was used to pull the door open, she could make out Julian and one of the men, searching for her.

Julian was still speaking. "That little fool don't know who in the fuck she messin' with, but she 'bout to find out quick, fast, and in a hurry. Look in that bathroom, I'll check the closets, you go out back and see if that skank is hiding out there. And if you find her ass, don't neither one of you touch her. You bring her to me. She still got work to do."

Work to do? What was he talking about? If he was talking about Bri and her girls, he could forget that shit. Wasn't nobody gonna turn her out that way. Not while she had breath. She thought about Chalice and Tia, remembering how stunning both of them were. And they obviously loved what they were doing. Why wasn't that Bri bitch satisfied with what she had? Greedy ass . . .

She didn't get to finish her last thought. Julian stepped into the room below her and had picked up her discarded bikini. At the same time, the dust in the room began to irritate her nose and throat. She had to fight a sneeze and a dry cough that was pressing against her tonsils trying to force the noise past her lips. Even if she managed her usual inward sneeze and a quiet little throat clearing "ahem," the guesthouse was so quiet, Julian would hear her for sure. She couldn't risk that. *Oh Lord, I know I ain't prayed as much I should, but please don't let me sneeze!*

59

She was frozen in time. The minutes seemed to pass like hours as Julian stood only a few feet beneath her. Her nose trembled from trying to hold in the sneeze. She didn't dare move a muscle, lest she make a noise. Sweat began beading on her forehead, a little stream was making its way down her cheek. She knew how scared she really was because she'd never busted a sweat before unless she was dancing. She worked her mouth to make her nose twitch, trying to will the sneeze to go away. Her entire body and mind was concentrating on holding back that sneeze. Her body began trembling from the effort.

Julian looked around, then up. He peered, seeming to contemplate if he should look behind the door, but his cell phone rang.

"Hello? No, it ain't like that . . . Yeah, he's payin' and I mean the knot . . . What? That fool tripping . . . right . . . nothing but dimes? I got dimes plus . . . Man, whatever . . . tell him he got my price and if it moves anywhere, it's gonna be on my side of the decimal point, not his! Fifty Gs for the whole night and that's a bargain 'cause the nigga is a good, steady customer. Hell yeah, he pays for the mansion! Listen if he don't like it he can get to steppin' and hire some old lame, who ain't gonna have honeys half as fine as the ones I got. Shit, I got one special one that could easily charge five Gs an hour all by her damn self. Hell yes, I'm talkin' about Jadyn. Flash? Get the fuck outta here. Fuck a damn Flash and his crew. His cousin is a grown-ass woman. What he gon' do? How I know she down? It's like this, son. He who has the money rules the girls! I ain't had a bitch turn down a grand for a night's work yet! Ho or not." Julian flipped his phone shut and ended the call, but then flipped it open again and pushed redial.

"Hey, I forgot to ask you, did you remember to put that ad in the paper, too? Yeah, the one about the video shoot at Worthing Manor? Man, you trippin'! Since when do we give a fuck as long as the fine bitches show up?" He flipped the phone shut.

Jadyn couldn't believe this shit. She had to admit he was way too good at running game on the broads at the club and getting them to believe they were going to be stars in some rap video instead of just a disposable girl for a night for one of the rappers that came to town. Or one of their bodyguards, or just one of their boys. Shit, his slimy ass probably didn't even feel guilty about the shit he was perpetrating. It sickened her to know that all she represented to him was money. What had he called her? His prize beauty, the one that was going to bring him the most money for the night once his best-paying client got a look at her.

One of Julian's boys came in.

"Man, that was some coldblooded shit you had planned for your girl, Jadyn. As fine as her ass is, I wouldn't want nobody busting that ass before I could. Male or female," he said with a grin on his face.

Not in this life or the next, punk, Jadyn thought.

"Yeah, at first I thought about makin' her my woman or some shit like that. But that kinda thinkin' will get you outta this game quick, fast, and in a hurry. You could never have one woman in this game. You gotta be free to do ya thing. All you gotta do is remember this number one rule: A bitch ain't good for nothin' but fuckin' and makin' money. I just make sure that they do the two together and that all the money comes to me. I don't give a fuck how fine they asses is."

"That bitch ain't out here. If she had any sense she's long gone," his other boy said, sticking his head through the door.

"Yeah, there's only one thing wrong with that scenario. I drove her ass here. So if she did leave, her ass is walking. But what I'm wonderin' is how she got past security."

"Oh, they work for the broad that owns this joint, they don't work for Li'l Bri and them. So if she did get out there it ain't gon' be much you can do."

"Yeah, it's all good. I'ma get with the bitch, sooner than later. You can believe me when I tell you."

"Man, fine as she is, you really gonna fuck her up?"

"Listen, muhfucka like I just told you the only thing fine bitches is good for is fuckin' and makin' my pockets deep. And this one ain't done neither one. So what I need her for?"

The other dude snickered as they walked out the door. She could hear Julian call for the other member of his crew and then their voices faded in the distance.

She sat up, buried her head in her lap, sneezed twice and cleared her throat. Then she just sat and waited for her heart to stop beating so hard and so loudly.

Once she was relatively certain that Julian and crew were gone, she eased open the door and slid down from her hiding place, gingerly feeling for the swimsuit rack with her toes.

Deciding that a rear exit might be her best move, she opened the door a crack and peered out. Loud noises, grunts, and groans of ecstasy floated up from someplace nearby. Figuring that they would be too caught up to care about her even if they had a mind to, Jadyn slipped through the door and began a very fast walk toward the front of the mansion and the safety of the guard shack.

"Hey." She tapped on the glass door. One of the guards was watching a small portable TV. She didn't know where the other one was.

The white guard looked up and opened the door.

"What's the problem?"

"My ride left me and I called a taxi. Has one been here yet?"

"Yeah." The guard shined a light down the driveway a few feet. "It just pulled up and I told him to wait over there. I told him if his fare wasn't out in ten minutes to beat it."

He was talking to Jadyn's shadow because she was sprinting the few feet to her escape.

"Take me to 2303 Sineca Bay Drive, Palm City . . . ," she commanded, jumping into the backseat and slamming the door.

"This address is many, many miles away. You are having enough money for this far drive?" the cabbie said with a thick East Indian accent.

"Hell yeah, I got the money, now do your fuckin' job! Let's go!" she said turning her neck and peering out of the back window. She could see three men standing on the mansion steps. It looked like Julian and his boys.

"Such vile language coming from the mouth of such a beautiful girl." The cabdriver spoke as he started up the engine. "Your father would be so ashamed. Such a dirty potty mouth. Even the devil would be trembling and running away . . ." He pulled away down the drive just as the three began walking toward them.

Jadyn stared out the window, watching Julian grow smaller and smaller as the cabdriver continued talking. She couldn't help thinking it was going to be a long ride home.

60

"Shut up! Will you please just close your frickin' mouth? God! Here, here, take this money and let me up out of this damn ride!"

The cabbie had been reciting the evils of using foul language all the way to her uncle's house, with a few adjectives sprinkled in of how beautiful she was. It had been a nonstop trip!

"Learn to speak words of achievement to yourself. This will make your head clean, veddy clean. If your head is clean, clean thoughts will fill up your brain and that is how you will speak clean language and rid yourself of a foul mouth!" he had shouted after her as she sprinted up the walk.

Unlocking the door she let herself in without so much as a backward glance.

As soon as her feet touched the floor inside her uncle's home, she remembered that she was supposed to meet Flash at the club. *Damn!* She glanced at the clock on the wall. 3:30 A.M. They might still be there. She snatched open the door to see if the cab was still out there, but it was pulling away from the curb. She almost yelled for him to stop, but then decided not to. Her uncle was most likely asleep in bed, no use in waking him up. Not to mention the fact that she would go completely insane if she had to listen to dude telling her how to get her mouth *veddy veddy* clean. The shit might have been funny if she wasn't so pissed.

"Fuck it, I'm tired as hell," she muttered to herself as she closed the door again. "I'm getting in the shower and then taking my ass to bed!"

She hoped Flash wouldn't really come looking for her. She would worry about that drama tomorrow.

Jadyn's head had just hit the pillow when her cell phone rang.

"Hello?"

"Where you at, Jay? Didn't I tell you to have that busta bring yo ass to the club?"

"Yeah, Flash, but I rode with somebody else," she said and immediately thought, *Damn! What did I say that for?*

"You what? You rode with somebody else? Who in the fuck did you ride with and where was that fool at? What was he doing that he couldn't bring your ass home like he took you away from here?"

"Look, Flash, I caught a ride with some girl." She knew that sounded lame and weak.

"Some girl? Some girl, hunh? Where you at now?"

"I'm at home."

"You at home. Where was your ass at?"

"Flash, I'm tired as hell, I don't feel like you drilling me like this . . ."

"This ain't drillin'. Where in the fuck did that nigga take you and don't even lie to me. I know y'all wadn't at no muhfuckin' concert. Now where in the fuck did he take you?"

Jadyn sighed. Flash was mad as hell, so he had to know something. She didn't know exactly what though.

"OK look, Flash. We went to a video shoot and . . ."

"A video shoot? What the fuck . . ."

"Flash, I know I shouldnt'a lied about where we were going, but Julian said that I could make a lot of money and—"

All Jadyn heard was a loud *click* followed by silence.

61

The ringing doorbell woke Jadyn up the next morning. She got up to answer, but her uncle beat her to it.

"Gal, what you doin' up this early on a Sunday morning? I know you ain't goin' to church are you? If you is you need to take Flash's ass—I mean 'scuse me Lord for cussin' on the Sabbath—Flash's *behind* right on with you."

"No, sir, Unc, I'm here to see Jay, but quiet as it's kept, I think we gon' skip church this Sunday," she heard Mani's voice reply.

"Quiet as it's kept? Shooot! Even the red devil in hell done been before God since any of y'all heathens have. She upstairs. Go on up."

"Good morning, Uncle BruhJay," Jadyn called down.

"Good mornin'. Y'all want some breakfast?"

"Yes sir," both Jadyn and Mani called.

They knew he would fix them breakfast no matter what they said.

"What's goin' on, Mani?"

"That's what I should be asking you. Trouble seem to follow you wherever you go girl. What did you and Julian do?"

Jadyn pulled her into the room and shut the door.

"What do you mean?"

"Flash came by late last night, or early this morning, and picked 'Rel up."

"So what you think is going down? What . . ."

"You tell me! What the fuck is up, Jay? I heard Flash tell 'Rel to grab his strap. I know it had something to do with you and Julian. Now what's goin' on?" Mani stepped closer to her and she was frowning.

"Chill, why are you goin' off on me like this?" Jadyn took a step backward to keep some space between them. She didn't appreciate Mani stepping into her face, but she was trying to keep her cool.

"Because I don't want my man gettin' shot or killed over some dumb shit. I wanna know what's up!" Mani had stepped nose-to-nose with her and poked her finger into Jadyn's chest.

Jadyn pushed her back.

"Quit trippin', damn! OK, look." Jadyn sat down on the edge of the bed and pulled her legs up beneath her. "I lied to Flash about Julian taking me to a concert last night, OK?"

Mani flopped down on the bed next to Jadyn.

"Tell me somethin' I don't know."

"What?"

"Girl, we all knew that y'all wasn't goin' to that concert. The tickets was sold out that first day, and didn't hardly nobody in Palm City get tickets. Maybe one or two people and they drove down and stood in line all night to get 'em. So what happened, Jay?"

"Julian told me that this rapper, Li'l Bri, was shootin' a video and that he thought I could make a lot of money if I went with him. So naturally I went. Who wouldn'ta?"

Mani sighed deeply. "Yeah, you right. Anybody would have wanted to make some easy swiss, if it was legit. But how did you know that he just wasn't trynna play you?"

Jadyn stood up and ran her hands through her hair and gazed out the window as she spoke.

"He tried to."

"He tried to? What you mean he tried to?"

Jadyn turned around and faced Mani. "Yeah, that's what I said. He tried to, but I when I found out the real deal I didn't go through with it."

"You found out the real. You ain't found out shit. Julian been playin' your ass from day one."

"No, he only thought he was playin' me. I peeped that his shit was fake from day one. I knew his business was just a front for whatever else he had goin' on," Jadyn told her with a bit of an edge to her voice.

Mani stood and walked over to the window and stared out. Taking a cigarette and lighter from the pack that she had pulled from her purse, she lit up and inhaled the smoke deeply into her lungs before blowing it out. She continued to stare out of the window as she spoke.

"You don't have a clue about how deep this shit is."

"I know more than you think! I know that after we shot the video, Julian's ass tried to set me up to freak some lesbian shit and I wasn't down for that. He sent me to Li'l Bri's room to get my money and she was up their gettin' her freak on with two of the chicks that were in the video with me and—"

"Like I said, you don't get it. There was never a video shoot for Li'l Bri, not the kind you think anyway. Don't you understand? The shit was fake. All of it. Julian was settin' you up to star in a muh-fuckin' sex video from day one."

"What? What the . . . ?"

"Yeah, but the shit gets even deeper."

"What in the hell can be worse than that?"

"Julian's ass is dead and Li'l Bri and her crew are missin' in action."

62

"Dead? What do you mean Julian's dead?" Jadyn stood to her feet and walked over to the window by Mani.

"That's what I heard Flash tell 'Rel when he came to get him." She inhaled from her cigarette again before flicking the ashes out the window.

Jadyn walked back over to the bed and sat down hard. "How did this shit happen? What's goin' on, Mani? Tell me what's really goin' on. Don't be handin' me these little bullshit bits and pieces. What the shit is goin' on?"

"No . . . no . . . I'm not tellin' you nothin' else. Let Flash tell you . . . I'm done. I probably said too much already."

Mani stood up and marched toward the door. Jadyn grabbed her arm and yanked her back.

"Mani, I got a right to know what the hell is going on. Now Julian's dead and Flash and Jarrell are out there with guns. I need you to tell me. What in the world is goin' on here?"

"All right. OK, I'll tell you."

Jadyn held on to Mani's hand and they walked back to the bed and sat down together.

"The real deal is that Julian and Flash are makin' big money shootin' pornography. It was Julian's idea, but Flash went along with it because him and Julian been boys since middle school. Julian's grandfather hit the lottery for four million dollars. . . ."

"Four million? Julian told me that it was hundreds of millions. And that his dad and his grandfather fell out because he only gave him a half a million and his dad wanted more."

"That part is true. The part about his granddaddy and daddy fallin' out over the money. But it was nowhere near that amount. But let me get to that later.

"Julian's grandfather gave Julian a lot of money, nobody knows how much exactly, so that he could start a business. Julian took it and was blowing the money on new cars and jewelry and shit, and wasn't trynna do what his grandfather told him—start a business. So his grandfather cut off his flow and put the money in a trust fund for Julian, which he can't touch 'til he's in his thirties."

Jadyn threw her head back and ran her fingers through her hair before she spoke.

"At least he told the truth about that," she said.

Mani took one last drag on the cigarette and a final sip from water that she had brought with her before dropping the cigarette butt down into the bottle.

"Yeah, but Julian still had some of the money that his grand-daddy had originally given him, so to get back on his good side, he started JL Promotions."

"Flash had got into some trouble slangin' dope and wanted to get out of the game, so that's why your uncle let him move here and got him a job where he work. But Julian and Flash hooked up and Julian told him about this idea he had for makin' loot off the porn business because wasn't a lot of good black porn out there and the young rappers and some others with money burning holes in their pockets was craving to see some hot black chicks getting their freak on like the white girls do," Mani told her as she pulled the ponytail holder from her hair. Then she looped the band around her fingers, and smoothed her hair flat with both hands before pulling it up in a ponytail again.

"Damn, Flash and Julian in business together. I was thinking that it was Julian and Steele, all this time," Jadyn said, as she pulled her feet up under her on the bed, thinking how so much shit could be going on right under your nose. If it was out of your sphere of reality, you would never figure the shit out without somebody who was in the know hipping you to what was happening.

"Well, you was thinking right," Mani said, looking her straight in the eyes. "Steele was in on it, too. Because you know both Flash and Julian are fine, like two fine sides of the same coin, right? They both got a way with the ladies. But the two of them couldn't pull enough fine broads to make the kind of movies the boys with the cheese was payin' top dollar for."

"OK, I got you. That's where Steele comes in, right? He does those dime cattle calls for the rappers that come to town, so they can not only get their freak on, but they can make videos with pretty women freaking the rappers or some of their crew. Maybe even the body guards, so they can have their own personal collection of porn," Jadyn said, her stomach turning at the thought of women being used that way.

"Yeah, and the more freaky the girls can get, the more they make in a night. And if they extra gorgeous, like you, and freaky, too, they gets paid double or triple. That's why Julian was on you so hard. You were goin' to be worth a lot if you were down."

Jadyn put her head in her hands as she asked the next question. "So did Flash know what Julian was trynna do to me?"

"No, Jay. No." Mani knelt down in front of her and held her hands. "That's why Flash was on you like he was. Why he was watching you. He didn't want you to get caught up in Julian's game."

"Well, why didn't he just tell me what was up then? Why did he let me think that he didn't even know Julian?"

"Because Julian got something on Flash. None of us, not even 'Rel, knows what it is. But it must be something serious because Flash and Julian fell out behind it and things ain't been cool between them for a while."

"So what's the deal with Steele Money?"

"You called it about the cattle calls. But Steele felt like he was doin' all the real work, getting the girls and settin' up the places to shoot the porn and making the deals with the rappers because he was the one with all the connections since he worked the club scene and made the VIP sections available for the rappers and actors when they came to town. So he was making noise like he wanted to buy Flash and Julian out and run the business on his own. Flash was down, because he was liking his job and he had made the knot with the porn business. He wasn't trynna go back to jail for no dumb shit. But Julian wasn't ready to get out. He wanted things to stay like they was until he turned old enough to get his trust fund. But he couldn't handle Steele one on one, without Flash. Oh, he could make noise and Steele would listen to him as long as Flash was around. But without him, Steele would punk Julian every chance he got."

Jadyn had witnessed that shit so she knew that to be true.

"The picture becomes quite clear now. That's why Flash and Steele got beef."

"Julian is crazy for real. I mean really unstable. His grandfather ended up getting murdered and his father went to jail, because five-oh said that he hired somebody to kill his own daddy to get his hands on the millions. Julian ain't been right in the head since the shit happened."

"So who you think offed Julian?"

"I don't know. It coulda been Steele. Coulda been Li'l Bri or somebody who worked for her. Who knows? All I know is whatever you did or didn't do, you cost their little company one of their biggest clients. He came to town to see and star in a movie with what Julian said was the hottest, finest chick ever, which was you. He paid something like a hundred grand to see you freak with three other pretty broads, get it on film and then to be in the movie with the three of you freaking him. He saw you in the fake music video and chose you personally, just like Julian knew he would. But when you ran out, he wanted all of his money back. Every penny. Nobody knows what happened after that. Julian turned up dead, so I guess Flash and 'Rel think whoever did it gon' come after them, too. Maybe even come after you. So I guess they gonna get them first. I don't know."

Damn! The shit was getting crazier and crazier. Suddenly all Jadyn wanted was to go home.

"I need to talk to Flash. I need to find out what's really going on and if he's gonna be all right."

"Then what?"

"Then I'm taking my ass back to Ohio."

63

Jadyn kept dialing Flash's cell phone number, but it kept going straight to voicemail. He probably hadn't charged it and it had gone dead. Dead. Like Julian. She was still trying to wrap her mind around that shit. Yeah, Julian was a little weird, but wasn't every-body? We all got our crazy shit to deal with in life. She knew she did. Some people just kept their crazy side in check better than others could.

Mani said that they should chill 'til later on. If Flash and Jarrell didn't turn up by then, they would ride down to the club. They had to turn up there sooner or later, since that's where Steele would be. And he would most likely be the one with answers about what happened to Julian.

Jadyn sat out on the patio sipping on lemonade laced with some of her uncle's gin. She still had a few hours until Mani would be picking her up.

She heard the patio door slide open and looked up to see her uncle step out onto the patio.

"Hey, Uncle BruhJay."

"Hey, niecy. What you doin' sittin' out here all by your lone-some? Where that grandson of mine? I ain't seen him all day."

Jadyn looked at her uncle and took another swig of the lemonade to give herself time to think of an answer.

"I don't know, Unc. I think Mani said him and Jarrell drove down to Titusville to visit his mother. They should be back any time now."

Her uncle stared at her then walked closer to the screen around the patio, gazing at the brilliant colors the sun was painting against the sky as the sun began dropping out of sight.

"You know, Jadyn, this here is a pretty town, Palm City is. Most folks that come here are lookin' for a slice of Eden. A slice of the lost paradise. A lot of the time they find it. Beautiful weather, mostly. Some of the prettiest scenery with the palm trees, and exotic plants and birds you ever seen in your life. And don't even mention the beaches. Whooo-wee! You talkin' about pretty!" He turned back to face Jadyn, his happy carefree voice turning serious to match his expression.

"But sometimes . . . sometimes there's something hard and ugly hiding up under all that beauty. Yes sir. Underneath pretty pictures can sometimes hide the soul of a lizard or even a gator. Both them creatures just as cold as ice. Layin' quiet. Waitin' to tear you into pieces and eat you alive. You gotta watch out for snakes, too. Them old poison snakes be hidin'." He placed his hand on Jadyn's shoulder. "They be hidin' right under your own house sometimes. Them old snakes just hidin' bidin' their time. Trynna fool you into trustin' they ain't really no snakes here. Then when you least expect it, they chomp down on you real quick, and before you know it, they done spread poison all through your body. Poison that goes straight to your heart and kills ya quick."

Her uncle's eyes pierced her with age-old wisdom that spoke volumes. They told her that he knew she had lied and knew there was something else going on. She almost wanted to tell him everything.

Almost wanted to confess that Flash was in danger and maybe she could be, too. Before she could her uncle's mood changed again.

He stood to his feet. "Yep, watch out for lizards, gators, and snakes while you out here. I shoulda told you that the first day you got here. But I figgered Flash would watch out for you and teach you about 'em and make sure you stayed away from 'em." He stepped through the sliding door. "You say Flash went to visit his mother in Titusville? Flash's mother ran off with a drug dealer 'bout ten years ago. Ain't neither one of us seen or heard from her since."

Her uncle slid the patio door closed without another word. Jadyn stood and peeked through the glass. She saw her uncle pour a cup of coffee, pick up the newspaper, and walk into the living room where he laid his cup down on a coaster on the coffee table. He flopped down on the sofa and reached for the remote. He just held it in his hand, not moving, just staring into space.

Jadyn felt bad for her uncle; she wanted to go to him, to hug him and let him know things would be all right. But she couldn't because she didn't know if it was true. She sat back down and picked up her lemonade and sipped on it waiting for Mani to come by, needing to talk to Flash more than ever.

64

"So Mani, you telling me that Jarrell called you and told you to meet him? Meet him for what? Where is Flash?"

"This shit is crazy, girl, the whole thing. Jarrell said that him and Flash decided to split up for now and then hook back up later on at the club. He said we need to lay low, too, 'til they can figure this shit out and whatnot. See who trynna tightrope who and shit."

Jadyn noticed that Mani was acting strange. Looking out of the side of her eyes, and apparently talking out of the side of her neck, too. Why would Mani need to lay low? She wasn't in none of this shit. She wasn't at the video shoot. But maybe it was because she was Jarrell's girl. Everybody knew Flash and Jarrell were like brothers, so whatever came down on Flash could come down on Jarrell. Maybe it could trickle down to his girl, too.

"What's the matter with you? Why you actin' all nervous as fuck?"

"'Cause my ass is scared, dammit! That's why! You still don't get it, do you? This ain't no muhfuckin' joke. People turnin' up dead and others gon' be on a milk carton and shit. Hell fuckin' yeah my ass is nervous and yours oughta be, too, if you got good sense!"

"Yeah, whatever. I might be, but I ain't gonna send myself into cardiac arrest over it like you doin'."

Mani gave her a dirty look before she asked, "So you got the five Gs on you that you took from Li'l Bri?" She did a sharp turn with the car and all of a sudden they weren't on a main road any longer. They were going at a pretty fast speed down a dirt road.

"Where we goin' now? I thought we was goin' to the club?"

"Nah, I told you. 'Rel said we gotta lay low. Him and Flash got this old cabin they used to take bitches and players to back in the day when they first started shootin' X-rated videos."

"'Rel and Flash? I thought you said it was Flash and Julian that started the shit."

At first Mani looked shocked at her slip-up, but then began looking smug.

"Did I say 'Rel? I meant to say Julian. What the fuck ever, it don't make no difference, they all in it together now. Steele, Julian, Flash, 'Rel . . . so it don't matter. They all used to come out here."

Then a question Mani had asked her a moment earlier suddenly smacked her in the face like a bucket of ice water.

"You got the five Gs on you that you took from Li'l Bri?"

How in the fuck did she know about that? She hadn't mentioned that to anyone. Jadyn's heart raced and her face flushed hot. Whatever was going down, Mani knew all about it. More than what she had told Jadyn. She had the ear of someone close. And now she was taking her to God only knew where. Would they kill her over five Gs? She wasn't trynna find out.

She reached down as cautiously as she could and began feeling around up under her seat for something, anything she could use as a weapon, while trying to keep the conversation going. Not letting Mani know she had figured out the game.

"That's some crazy shit. Why would they bring broads way out here? Like they was scared they would try to run away or some shit?"

Jadyn's fingers traveled across the carpet and found something hard and smooth. It felt like a bottle of some sort.

"No, they wasn't scared of no shit like that. They just didn't want nobody else to get hip to the game before they could set it off. And they didn't want to attract attention from five-oh, neither."

Jadyn played and replayed different scenarios in her head of how she was going to escape danger yet again. She could bring up the bottle and clock Mani upside her big old head as hard as she could, before she even realized what was happening, carjack her ride, and get the hell out of there. But what if she veered off this old dirt road and landed them in a bog or swamp? Jadyn didn't know anything about shit like that. Her uncle's words came back to her about gators and snakes. She knew he had been warning her about the human kind, but there were real ones to be dealt with, too.

The road took a sudden dip and then curved sharply, causing the bottle to roll away from Jadyn's fingertips. It didn't matter anyway. As the road straightened, in front of them sat a dimly lit dilapidated cabin.

"This is it," Mani said as she cut the motor.

"What the hell? They expect us to chill in some shit like this? I'm not taking my ass in there."

"Look, I been out here before, it ain't that bad inside. They fixed it up in there. They just left the outside lookin' tore down so anybody who happened up on it would just keep going."

Mani pulled the keys out of the ignition and stepped out of the car. "You can stay out here if you want to but I'm goin' inside."

Jadyn looked around, trying to make her eyes adjust to the darkness. There were no other cars as far as she could see, which more than likely meant that she and Mani were the only ones out here at the moment. She could still clock Mani's ass in the head, take the car, and leave her ass for Jarrell to find. She felt around under the seat again and this time her hand touched cold hard steel. A crowbar! Even better. She pulled it from its hiding place, opened the car door, and stepped out. A light came on inside the cabin and slightly illuminated the outside. In the dim light, the ramshackle cabin looked more like a shack than anything else.

"Are you comin' in here or not?" Mani's voice floated out from behind the cabin door.

"Yeah, here I come!"

Jadyn shoved the crowbar down the back of her jeans, pulling her shirt out, and letting it fall over the top of it. She hoped it would stay in place.

The inside of the cabin did look way better than the outside but considering the shape the outside was in that really wasn't saying a whole lot. They had moved in some nice furniture, painted the walls, restored the cabinets. It still didn't look like any place that Jadyn would want to spend long periods of time, but she could tolerate it for a few minutes. She didn't think it would take longer than that to knock Mani upside the head, take the keys, and get the hell outta there. Mani stood over in the kitchen part of the cabin. She pulled a bottle of wine from the fridge and poured herself a glass.

"You want some?" She held up the bottle toward Jadyn as she spoke.

"Might as well," Jadyn told her as she walked over.

She stood next to Mani as she poured wine into another glass. "You got any ice?"

"It might be some in here," Mani said, giving her a smirk before turning toward the fridge and opening the freezer. As she turned

Jadyn reached into the back of her jeans and pulled out the crow-bar. She had pulled it back and was about to swing it when a voice froze her arm mid-swing.

"I wouldn't do that if I was you . . . ," the male voice warned.

Mani spun around and caught sight of the crowbar in Jadyn's hand.

"You fuckin' bitch!" she said as she grabbed it from her hand before punching her in the face.

Jadyn fell backward onto the floor and Steele Money chuckled loudly.

65

"Ouch! I felt that shit way over here," he said as he moved farther into the cabin.

Mani stood over her waving the crowbar menacingly.

"I'ma show this bitch how it feel to be coldcocked in the brain like she planned on doin' to me!" Mani said, her voice filled with anger.

Mani raised the bar over her head.

"Hold up girl, slow ya roll. You can't damage the merchandise. You know the clients don't pay top dollar for damaged goods."

He walked the few feet across the floor and took the bar from Mani's hands.

"Silly-ass, lame-ass bitch!" Mani spat at her as she turned back to Steele. "I brought the bitch to you, now where is my damn money so I can raise the fuck up outta here?"

"You'a get yours as soon as I gets mines," Steele said, still looking amused, though the amusement never reached his eyes. They were as cold and lifeless as a dead snake.

"No, I'm not waiting around here. I wanna leave now! So give me my damned money so I can go. I don't want nothing else to do with this shit!" Mani had her hands on her hips and her face was contorted into a frown as she spoke.

Steele glanced over at Mani as he pulled a thick roll of bills out of his pocket, any trace of amusement gone from his face.

"You ready to go? You can't wait? Hunh? Here, get to steppin' then. Get the fuck on up outta here." He peeled off the bills and flung them in Mani's direction. She caught some of them but others slipped through her fingers. She didn't care. She just stooped and snatched up the others that had fluttered to the floor. Then she hurried out of the cabin without a word or backward glance at her former friend, grinning foolishly and counting the bills as she went.

"Trick-ass, fake-ass, phony-ass, scandalous bitch!" Jadyn yelled after her. She couldn't believe how she had trusted Mani, told her all her secrets, treated her like a sister. And she turned on her for a little bit of money? It made no sense. But then when she thought about how quickly she had given Mani her trust, she really couldn't blame her at all. Lesson learned. If she got out of this she would never again trust a jealous bitch. No matter how friendly they pretend to be. They pretend to love you and like they got your back, all in your face like they're your biggest cheerleaders and shit. All the while they're plotting in secret on how to stab you in the back like the two-faced bitches they are. And then laugh about it.

Steele walked over and stood in front of her, shaking his head.

"Damn shame, ain't it. Really fucked up. Ya think ya know somebody . . . think they somebody you can trust and bam! They put a knife in ya back and twist it."

He took a Black & Mild from his pocket and began carefully unwrapping it. Taking the paper that he had just removed from the little cigar, he held it carefully between his fingers and began rolling it back and forth, causing the tobacco to drop down into the cellophane wrapper. "Just go to show you. Only one muhfucka in the world you can trust, and that's ya own damn self. 'Cause everybody else on this planet is out for theirs. Believe that!"

He then took all the tobacco that he had tapped out into the cellophane wrapper and began pouring it back into the cigar shell.

Jadyn moved away from him. "What do you want from me? Where's my cousin?" Panic was rising inside her. She didn't like being stranded out in the middle of nowhere, especially with somebody like Steele.

Once that was done, he lit it up, inhaling deeply, and blowing smoke rings before he went on.

"Oh Flash? Him? Hmmph. Let's say he got more troubles than you do right about now. Somebody is givin' his ass the blues for real. See, Flash got skills fa sho'. He just put them to use with the wrong people that's all," Steele told her, his voice cold and unemotional.

"Flash know how to take care of his. That's for sure," Jadyn said, trying to tame her sense of panic with a bit of bravado.

"Think so? Then why is your ass out here wit' me, all by your lonesome? Hunh?" he asked her sarcastically, looking her right in the eyes. "You know, that cousin of yours thought you was too good for me. His ass didn't even want me to speak your name. But here we are, just the two of us," he said, spreading his arms out wide as he spoke.

"What do you want from me?" Jadyn repeated the question. "I know you ain't still pissed because I got drunk and dissed you at the club."

Steele walked over to the counter, picked up the bottle of wine, and took a long swallow. He leaned against the counter with the wine in one hand, a .45 in the other, and the Black & Mild clenched between his teeth. He crossed his legs at the ankles as his cold dark eyes pierced her.

"Yeah, that was some foul shit. But that was just some petty dumb shit. Didn't really faze me. Naaaw. See . . ." He paused for a moment flicking ashes on the floor and reaching up with his right hand to scratch his head. "What fucks with me is when somebody fucks with my pockets. And you. You dug down deep when you flipped out on Li'l Bri." He jabbed the Black & Mild in her direction as he spoke. "See when you took from her, that's the same as takin' from me."

Steele raised the wine bottle to his lips and drained it before setting it down on the counter and walking back toward her.

"Now I hope, for your sake, you brought the loot with you. Things will go a lot smoother for you if you did."

"I didn't bring nothin' with me, 'cause wasn't nothin' to bring. I don't know what you talking about."

Jadyn racked her brain for a way to placate Steele and make him release her. She wondered if she tried to make a break for the door if she could outrun him.

"Oh so now you trynna play me, right? You gon' try to stand there and look me dead in my face and lie? That shit ain't gon' do nothing but make your time with me so much worse." He dropped the Black & Mild on the floor and crushed it under his boot. "Now, what the fuck did you do with my money?"

"The only money I got is the money Bri gave me. For dancin' in that video. I haven't stole nothin'!"

"You know the real. I know Mani hipped you to the real happ'nins so don't play that naïve role with me! That shit is over. You didn't make the movie, so you got shit owed to yo' ass. You see, in case you still don't get it, you didn't deliver with Bri. And on top a that, you disappointed our best payin' client. So now he don't wanna do business wit' us no more."

"That shit ain't on me. Julian's ass shoulda told me what was really goin' down. Then he woulda known I wasn't the one to get into that freaky deaky shit. That shit is on his ass! There's plenty of bitches out there that love to get their freak on with whoever, whenever, but I ain't one of them. So if your shit got fucked up that's between you and Julian."

"You think so? I see you think you still in a position to call the shots around here don't you? You still trynna play that siddity role. Let me break it down to you like this: You ain't got shit coming. You owe me five Gs and . . ."

Steele unzipped his fly and pulled his dick out at the same time.

"You gon' suck me off for all the trouble and grief you done caused."

He began walking toward her, stroking himself, making himself rigid.

66

"You got me bent. I'm not suckin' shit!" Jadyn said, backing up, her panic level rising to the top.

"Oh but you is. And that's just the beginning. After you done with me, I'm taking you to meet with my client. See, I gots money to collect and you got unfinished business with him."

"What?"

"You heard me. You gon' service me, then I'm gon' make you a star!"

Jadyn whipped around and made a mad dash for the door, but Steele could move fast for his size and seized her by the hair just as she made it to the door. He grabbed a handful and pulled her backward so hard she thought her neck was about to break. Her hands flew up to her hair automatically, trying to minimize the painful pulling. She quickly brought her hands back down as he pulled harder. Holding her by her hair he pushed her down until she was kneeling on the floor in front of him. He placed the gun to her temple.

"I got nothin' to lose, baby, so please don't test me. But you, on the other hand, got everything ridin' on how well you perform, now and later on. See, I could bust a cap in yo ass and leave the same way I came, none the worse. Yeah, I would be out a good payin' client, but there's more where he came from. Your ass will be just another bitch gon' missin' that nobody would ever find once I dump yo ass in the Everglades and the gators eat you for muhfuckin' breakfast, lunch, and dinner."

This fool was even sicker than she had ever imagined in her wildest dreams. Her eyes darted across the room, desperately searching for a way to escape.

"If the money and your client don't mean shit to you, then why you even bother? Why you doin' this to me?"

"Easy answer. Because I want to. And because I can."

He poked his erection against her face as he spoke, trying to position himself against her lips. Jadyn turned her head from side to side.

"Don't do this to me, please . . ." Tears were forming in her eyes as she began to feel trapped and destined to die out here in this godforsaken place. The worst thing was that everyone would be looking for her, but they'd never find her. Even if Flash figured out where she was, it would be too late. They would never find enough of her to identify.

Either the alcohol or the anticipation of what he was about to force her to do was clouding his judgment, or Steele was just caught up in what he was feeling and got careless. Whatever the reason, he laid the gun down on the back of the sofa and wrapped both of his hands in Jadyn's hair so that she could no longer move her head while he pressed himself hard against her lips, pushing them apart. Jadyn gritted her teeth together.

"Don't make this hard, come on, open up for Daddy. I might change up and let you go, if you do me right. Open your mouth. . . ." Lust had taken over, making Steele's voice whispery and full of desire. Jadyn stole a look up at him and saw that his eyes had glazed over.

Steele began to pull Jadyn's hair hard in both hands. It felt as though her scalp was pulling away from her skull.

"I said, open your mouth . . . ," he growled.

Jadyn's mouth sprung open as tears streamed down her face. She felt Steele's rock hardness slide inside her mouth.

Then the memories flooded her and her survival instincts kicked in. She thought of the nightmares that plagued her almost every single night and filled her with fear. She thought about the man in the shadows with the gun in her dreams and she knew Steele would never let her go. She could either go out like a helpless weakling or she could go down fighting. She wasn't a helpless little girl anymore and she wasn't going to be forced to do something she didn't want to do, not ever again.

She brought her teeth together and bit down hard. As hard as she could. She heard Steele scream.

"Let me go! Let go!" She saw him reach for the gun but instead he knocked it to the floor. Jadyn bit harder and tasted blood. At the same time, feeling Steele's hard-on wither as he squealed like a bitch, pulling her hair, but he quickly let go of that idea, because it only caused him to stretch against her teeth that were clamped down like a vice.

"*Aaaaaaaaaaaaaaaaahgh!* You bitch! I'ma kill you! Let go 'a me!"

She only bit down harder, feeling the skin beginning to split beneath the force of her teeth.

Then Steele began to beat against her skull with his fists. "Stop it! *Aahhhhhhhhhhhhhhh!* Stop it! Let go! Let go, *ahhhhhhhhhhhh*, you fuckin' bitch!"

The pain must have been unbearable as he rained blows on the side of her head. One final blow to the top of her skull and the room began to turn dark and her ears buzzed. She felt her mouth go slack and Steele dropped to the floor like a ton of bricks.

Blood streamed from the gash on Steele's privates as he writhed on the floor in pain, holding it cupped between his hands.

"Oh you skank! You bitch! I'ma ki' you bi . . . Oh God, oh God! I'ma kill you! I swear . . . on my mama's . . . grave . . ."

Jadyn still felt faint, so she pinched herself hard to keep herself from blacking out. She had to get out of there. She dragged herself up off the floor and tried to move toward the door, but she stumbled and fell.

Steele was still writhing on the floor in a ball, but she had no idea how much longer he would remain so.

One of her eyes was beginning to swell shut, but she frantically scanned the room with her good eye, trying to locate the gun.

She finally spotted it beneath a table near Steele's foot.

Swish swish. She heard the noise and thought she caught a flash of movement in the corner near the door. What the fuck? What had made that noise? She strained her good eye in that direction, trying to bring the dark corner into focus. She couldn't see anything. She must be hallucinating.

Again focusing on the gun, she tried to decide if it would be better to try to get to the gun, or to get out the door. Steele began to unfold himself, still making threats under his breath.

Jadyn decided to go for the gun. There was nowhere for her to run once she got out the door. She could try to hide, but she was almost as afraid of the creatures that could be lurking out there as she was of the monster that lay on the floor in front of her.

Swish Swish. There was that noise again.

The room began to spin and Jadyn knew time was running out for her. She was either going to pass out cold or Steele was going to recover enough to make good on his threats. She stood and stumbled the few feet to the table and fell onto her stomach. Stretching her hand as far as she could she reached for the pistol. She almost had her fingers on the butt, right before Steele drove his boot into her ribs.

As she doubled over from the pain, her hand swiped the butt of the gun and sent it spinning farther away as she squirmed from the pain that shot through her body like it was on fire.

Steele wrapped his fist around Jadyn's ankle and began to pull her toward him.

"Your ass is mine bitch! I'ma fuckin' snap yo' neck with my bare hands. Fuckin' choke you 'til your eyes bleed."

As she felt herself being pulled toward Steele, she began to pray as she clawed the bare wood floor with her fingers, trying to stop her backward progress. "Dear Jesus, please! Oh God, please help me!"

And suddenly she saw it. *Swish. Swish. Swish.*

The alligator moved out of the shadows and shot toward them with a quickness that belied its size.

"Oh Lord! Jesus have mercy!" Jadyn screamed. She fought to remember any prayer, any Scripture that her mother had taught her when she was a child.

"The Lord is my shepherd, I shall not want. He maketh me . . . ," she began mouthing the Twenty-third Psalm as she heard the *swish, swish* of the gator's tail as it moved swiftly toward them.

"Unh-hunh! Yeah, bitch! Jesus ain't gon' help yo' ass now!" He wrapped his other hand around her ankle and tugged, but Jadyn had wrapped her hands around the table leg and held on. It moved with her, but it was so heavy it kept her from moving more than a few inches. *Swish swish.* The gator paused a few feet from Steele. And locked eyes with Jadyn.

If alligators look fierce and scary on TV and in the movies, it pales in comparison to literally coming face-to-face with one in real life. It looked like something out of the darkest pits of hell and nothing like the chic alligator shoes and purses made from their skin. The scaly slimy beast was as ferocious looking standing there staring as he would have been had he continued the charge toward them. His teeth resembled hacksaws that ran along both sides of its mouth.

Jadyn began kicking her legs frantically trying to get away from Steele's grip. She still mouthed the words of the only Scripture that came to mind.

"Yea though I walk through the valley of the shadow of death I will fear no evil . . ." Her eyes remained glued to the gator as he inched closer. "For Thou art with me!"

Swish, swish. She heard Steele scream as the gator clamped its mighty jaws down on his leg causing him to release his grip on her ankle.

The gator was dragging Steele to the opposite side of the room, shaking its head as it went. As big as Steele was, he was like a rag doll in the gator's jaws. The shock of it all froze Jadyn in place.

"Help me! Help me!" It was Steele's turn to call on the Lord now. "Oh God, please, oh God oh God! . . ." he called as the gator continued to shake him to and fro, dragging him back and forth.

When Jadyn saw Steele's leg being brutally shredded in the gator's mouth, she was shaken out of freeze mode. She got up and grabbed Steele's keys from the table and ran out the door.

She could hear his frantic screams as she made her way toward his truck. She was running on pure adrenaline. She tripped and fell off the porch and crashed all her weight down on her left leg. Suddenly, she was terrified that the gator had left Steele and was now coming out the door to get her. She crawled frantically along the dirt road, trying to find something to pull herself up on. Finding nothing, she dragged herself up off the ground and hopped the rest of the way toward Steele's Jeep.

"Come back here, bitch! Help me, don't you leave my ass! Help me. Help! Get the gun! Oh dear Jesus! Oh God, please just give me the gun so I can shoot this bastard. Please!" Steele pleaded.

She heard him scream the most bloodcurdling scream, just as she opened the door to the Jeep and jumped in, slamming the door and locking it.

Though she knew it was impossible, she looked down at her feet and over behind her in the backseats, fearing a gator may have somehow made its way into the vehicle.

Her hands were trembling and blood roared in her ears as her vision began to cloud.

"Jesus! Please . . . ," she prayed some more. "Please, not now, don't let me pass out now! Please . . ."

She remembered there was another prayer that her mother would sometimes read to her and her brothers at night. She struggled to remember it now.

"The Lord is my fortress and my shield. Who shall I be afraid of . . . He is . . . my strong tower . . . He is my strong tower . . ."

She fumbled with the keys, dropping them on the floor. She could still hear Steele screaming, so she clapped her hands over her ears as tears streamed down her face. "He is an ever present help in the time of trouble . . . Jesus *please* dear Jesus don't let me die here tonight . . ." Her head was spinning and pounding as she struggled to stay anchored to this side of consciousness. "If You just get me through this, Lord, I promise, I will never . . . I will go to church every Sunday, I'ma pray every night . . ."

That was when the screaming stopped.

Jadyn had visions of the gator coming after her, using its razor-sharp teeth like a can opener and splitting open the car door. Leaning down, she frantically felt around the floorboards for the keys, but couldn't feel them. It was impossible to see anything in the pitch darkness.

Finally her baby finger bumped against the keys and she wrapped her hand around them and brought them up. She didn't know which key was which. Shoving the first key into the ignition she tried to spin the switch. Wrong key. She pulled it out and shoved in the next one. Suddenly a thought slammed into her heart and made it pound against her chest. What if she'd grabbed the wrong keys? What if they weren't to the Jeep after all? She wouldn't be able to go back into the cabin with that alligator doing God knew what to Steele. She twisted her wrist and breathed a sigh of relief as the switch turned and the engine roared to life. She pulled the gear into reverse and stepped on the gas, the tires spitting up gravel. She turned the wheel and careened down the path, full speed, not slowing down until she saw headlights and knew that she was about to hit the main road.

She reached a traffic light but kept up her speed, barreling through the red light.

She breathed a sigh of relief as she heard the police siren and saw the flashing lights in her rearview mirror.

Pulling the car over to the side of the road, she sat and waited for the cop car to catch up to her.

The policeman kept the flashing light on as he pulled up behind her. Glancing in the rearview mirror, the scenery seemed to sink underwater, everything beginning to look wavy, like a watercolor painting, or steam rising from a sidewalk on a hot sunny day. Her head was pounding, and the same rhythm seemed to beat in her midsection around her heart. With each thump the pain seemed to grow more intense. The sweat that was running down into her eyes was making her scalp itch, but she couldn't muster the strength to raise her hand to wipe it away.

Time seemed to stand still, the cop taking forever to step out of the squad car. Jadyn tried to rehearse in her head what she would say to him. She would tell him . . . What? . . . what the hell had happened anyway? . . . Mani picked her up to take her to . . . Flash? Hold up . . . not Flash . . . her head was hurtin' something fierce! She let her head rest on the steering wheel. It seemed to her that it was swelling up like a balloon. She needed an Advil or Motrin . . . something to make it stop hurtin'. She couldn't take all the pain any longer. She would just get out of the truck and ask the officer if he had anything for a headache. Maybe if she just took a nap . . . the pain would go away . . .

The world lit up like it was on fire and she heard a muffled voice asking her a question that she couldn't quite understand.

She lifted her head and saw the policeman standing next to the Jeep, shining his bright flashlight into her eyes. She tried to focus.

"Officer . . . I can't . . . I don't . . ."

"Ma'am, I asked you for your license and registration! What have you had to drink tonight?"

Jadyn tried to sound coherent. She couldn't think straight.

"Step out of the car, ma'am."

Step out of the car? OK. She could do that.

Jadyn opened the door and stepped out onto the pavement and promptly fell flat on her face.

The policemen stepped over to her and rolled her over, shining his flashlight directly on her face.

"Holy shit!" he spoke directly into the microphone that was clipped to his collar. "This is 3599 requesting an ambulance stat. Victim is a black female approximately twenty-two years of age . . ."

67

"Hey shawty. How you feelin' this mornin'? You been sleep for quite a while now. And the way you was sawin' them logs, I know you was sleepin' good, too!"

Uncle BruhJay looked down at her with a twinkle in his eyes, but the twinkle did little to mask the concern in his voice.

"The doc said you need to get up from here and walk around some, to keep your muscles from getting stiff. So come on now. I can't let you sleep your life away."

Jadyn managed a smile and immediately regretted it, as the smile caused the split in her bottom lip to break open again. She winced as she spoke.

"Unc, that doctor musta been talking out the other side of his mouth. There ain't a spot on me that's not hurtin' right about now. I feel like I been trampled by a thousand bulls!"

Her uncle laughed. "That may be true, but you gon' get outta this heah bed today and get some fresh air and exercise. Even if that means just walking around this bed. You been in this bed for nearly a week now."

A week? Had it been that long?

"Aw Granddaddy, leave her alone, now. She say she still sore.

Ain't nothin' wrong with layin' in bed when you sore and you got a concussion. Not to mention a dislocated shoulder, and all them other assorted bumps and bruises."

"Flash! Flash, they had me thinking you were dead."

Flash perched carefully on the edge of the bed.

"Who told you that shit? I mean *ish*," he said remembering too late that he was in his grandfather's presence.

His grandfather just rolled his eyes. "Don't put up no fronts for me. I know botha y'all be cussing like a broke sailor. But I'ma leave y'all be for now." He bent down and moved her bangs out of her face and planted a kiss on her forehead before whispering, "You need old Unc to bring you anything? You hungry?"

"Yes sir, I am, kinda. You got any grits? I got a taste for some. And some juice, please."

"Do I have any grits? Girl, now you know this is the grits capital of the world. Not only that, grits is my middle name. I'ma go on out in the kitchen and whip up the best grits you done evah tasted. And Flash, don't you be in here upsettin' her with no wild talk, neither. She ain't well yet, so don't think I won't take my belt to you, you upset little bit and you will find out different today. Try me if you think I'm lyin'," he continued fussing as he walked out of the room.

"Unc is somethin' else, aint he?" Jadyn managed.

"Yeah, he talk a good game, fa sho'," Flash answered.

Jadyn began sitting up in the bed and Flash immediately stood and moved her pillows to help prop her up.

"That's good. Thanks, cuz."

"It ain't nothin'."

"How do I look, cousin? Don't lie to me neither. I been askin' Unc to let me have a mirror and he keeps saying he's gonna bring me one. But every time he come back in here, he claims he forgot. Now I know I don't look that damn bad, do I?"

Flash looked her over. "Well, you really swollen up still and you got two black eyes, one is yellow, purple, and blue, and the other is just black. Your bottom lip is split and . . ."

"Never mind, cuz. Damn, I asked you not to lie, I didn't say you had to be fuckin' brutally honest."

"Sorry, little cousin," Flash said looking down at his feet. If she wasn't mistaken, he looked troubled.

Flash walked over to the dressing table and brought back a little makeup mirror.

She tried to lift her arm to reach for it, but the shoulder that had been dislocated was her right one so it was hard to do. Flash helped her out by holding the mirror for her.

"Damn! I look like a beast!" Jadyn moaned. "Would you look at my hair? Flash, please, get a brush or a comb and put my hair up in a ponytail or something. Please."

"OK, but I'm warning you, it might look even worse when I get through."

She stared at her reflection. It wasn't all that bad. She did have two black eyes and a busted lip, but at least her nose wasn't broken and she hadn't lost any teeth. She looked better than the picture Flash was painting in her mind anyway.

Once Flash managed to brush her hair up and get the rubber band on it, she looked more like a beast with neat hair than a human being.

By that time, her uncle was carrying in a tray piled high with food that smelled like heaven.

"Now, don't you eat too much of this. You need anything else you just holla. Or send Flash after it. You hear?"

"Yes sir, Unc."

Then he happened to see the mirror.

"Now Flash, what in the world you hand that child a mirror for. You ain't gon' do nothin' but get her all worked up and upset . . ."

"It's OK, Unc. I asked him to do it. I'm OK. Believe me, after escaping the jaws of that gator . . . you know I'm just thankful I'm still here."

"We glad you still here, too, little girl."

Her uncle kissed her on the forehead again and walked out of the room, then poked his head back through the door.

"Oh, I forgot to tell you. Nite is on a plane comin' to see you. They'll be here in a few hours. Your mama and grandmama gon' have your uncle Earl drive them and the boys down here on Saturday. Meanwhile, they want you to call them when you up to it."

"OK, Unc. I'll be glad when Nite gets here so she can help me take a shower and do my hair."

Her uncle started to disappear again.

"Uncle?"

"Yes, darlin'?"

"You said 'they' will be here in a few hours. Who's coming on the plane with Nite?"

"Somebody named . . . uhhhh . . . Tajine or Tajid or somethin' another."

Taji!

68

"Flash, where were you that night? Where were you and Jarrell? Did you know Mani set me up for Steele to rape me and try to kill me?"

"Hold up, li'l cousin. Slow down, now. I can only answer one question at a time. But you sure you ready to talk about that night?"

Jadyn glanced out of the window. The sun shone brightly against a beautiful pale blue sky. The palm trees outside her window cast their shadow against her side of the house. A gentle breeze caused the fronds to sway slightly, as it tickled the surface of the blue waters in the pond just beyond the backyard. She saw ducks, geese, and some exotic white bird with a bright orange beak that she'd never seen before.

She thought back to the night that the alligator killed Steele. The gruesome sounds and pictures, the *swish swish* of the gator's tail as it had moved around in the dark corner before attacking him, all visited her nightly without help from anyone. The images constantly played and replayed in her head. The things Steele had tried to force her to do, the way he beat her as she was biting him.

She brought her gaze back into the room and focused on Flash.

"I guess there are things about that night I don't ever want to remember. But how can I not? It's in my head. I think about all that happened and I don't understand. How could somebody that barely knew my name hate me so much?"

"That buster was just a crazy fool. Er'body knew he had a screw or two loose, but didn't nobody think he was crazy enough to try the shit he did that night."

"What was really goin' on? Where is Julian? What happened to him? Is he really dead?" Jadyn asked, getting agitated, unsure if she really wanted to know.

"Ain't nothin' happen to that nigga, but he took all the money and left town. When I catch his scandalous ass, he gon' wish it had though," Flash said angrily.

Jadyn stared at him blankly, needing him to explain things more clearly.

"You haven't told me about you, Steele Money, and Julian. Mani told me how y'all was all in on this together. And Jarrell, too. She said alla y'all set up those broads at the club. Got them to believe they was going to party with the stars. Maybe even be in a video with them. All the while you knew. You knew you was settin' them up to be in those X-rated movies." It was hard for her to keep the disdain she felt for her cousin out of her voice.

"Hold up, cousin. Now didn't nobody hold a gun to none of their heads. It was their choice. They chose the money. They got paid for what they did. They knew we was filming them," Flash told her, sounding a bit irritated.

"So you telling me what Mani said was true? You were part of it?"

"Come on now. Don't look at me like that. Er'body got a hustle. Them broads is grown-ass women . . . All I did was help set up the parties at the clubs. I didn't have nothin' to do with that other shit. Me and Jarrell just set up the parties, I swear to God. It was Steele and Julian that come up with that other shit. Yeah, we took a cut of the money, I ain't gon' lie about it. Those fuckin' rappers paid big money to get naked in the videos with some fine honeys. I'm talkin one hundred Gs or more. Dependin' on how freaky they was."

She looked away from Flash. "That's not how it was, Flash. You're fooling yourself. They get the girls drunk, maybe even slip something into their drinks so they don't care. Then they send them up to a room to collect their pay for dancin' in some fake-ass video. And they already sexin' each other up in that room. I know, 'cause damn Julian and Steele tried to set me up the same way, with Li'l Bri when she was in town. Did you know about that shit, too, Flash?"

Flash stared at her, his eyes flashing angrily as he answered.

"Hell fuckin' no, I didn't know about the shit. How you gon' even fix your mouth to ask me some shit like that? Hunh? When all I been doin' since you got here is try to keep yo' ass away from the shit? Think about it."

She had to admit he was right. She remembered the talk that he had with her the first night she had gotten there. Before he had taken her to the club.

"I'm sorry, cuz, you're right. You have had my back from day one."

"It was that damn Julian and Mani that was tryin' to set you up. Mani and Julian had been fuckin' around behind Jarrell's back. Yeah, that shit is fucked up. I bet her ass is with Julian right now, 'cause ain't nobody seen her since Julian's ass left town. Muhfucka knew he fucked up, takin' all that money and not deliverin' the product. So his punk bitch-ass call me talkin' 'bout he need help squarin' shit with Li'l Bri and them. Shit, fuck alla them niggas! I ain't helpin' him with shit. After what he done to you. He done set off some shit that he ain't gon' be able to get his snaky, sneaky ass out of."

69

"Nite, where ya'all at?" Jadyn spoke into the cell phone. She had turned it to speaker phone since she couldn't hold on to it too well.

"We at the car rental place at the airport. Taji is at the counter getting a car for us. Why you ask?"

"Listen, when you and Taji get here, don't let him see me until you come in first."

"Why not, girl? You trippin'. The man is worried about you, just like the rest of us. He just wants to make sure you're OK. I had a long talk with him on the flight over. I call myself gonna set him straight on a few things. But Jay, we was wrong. You was dead wrong. Things ain't what they seem. He told me who that trick was who answered his phone that time."

"You know what, Nite? I ain't even on that shit no more. You know when death is starin' you in the face and you just know that you knockin' on heaven's door, it's strange. The way that you used to look at things really shifts and your entire viewpoint changes." But then Jadyn said, "But who was the bitch?"

Nite laughed out loud and Jadyn tried not to, because she didn't want her split lip to break open again.

"Well, here he come. So you want to keep talkin' or what?"

"No, just remember, when y'all get here, just come and get me together first. I don't know when the last time I had a bath, but my ass is ripe!"

"Oh, I see what you sayin'. Don't worry, I got you, cuz. See you in about fifteen or twenty minutes."

"OK, Nite."

"What did that slimy piece of shit do to you!?" Nite breezed into the room carrying a big teddy bear and a vase of flowers.

She walked into the room and laid her bags at the entrance, rushing to Jadyn's beside to cradle her in her arms and give her comfort.

"I'm all right, Nite. Just remember, at least I'm alive."

"I know, baby. I'm so glad to see you, I don't know what to do," Nite said, her voice full of emotion.

Jadyn allowed her to hold on to her a bit longer before she spoke. "Well, I know what you can do. You can help me into the bathroom and help me get into a nice, hot bath," she teased Nite, trying to make her feel better.

"You got it, love," Nite said as she kissed her on the forehead. "You just sit tight. I brought you some spa balls to put in the water. I'll have it fixed right up!"

Nite dragged her suitcase over to the bathroom.

Jadyn heard her turn on the water in the tub and busy herself walking back and forth between the bathroom and the bedroom, getting her new sleepwear out and her towels ready.

"OK, cuz, are you ready? Before we start, what is hurting you so I don't make it worse?" Nite questioned, her face showing pain as she took inventory of Jadyn's injuries.

"My right shoulder is dislocated, but it's getting better, my ribs are broken on that side, and that's about it. Well, let me back up, my whole body is kind of sore."

"OK, you'll feel better once you get in that nice hot bath with those spa balls in it. You'll be all right. You want me to wash your hair, too?"

"Please do! My head has been itching like crazy!"

"I don't wish evil on no one, but it's a good thing that bastard didn't survive, because I'd kill him for what he's done to you!"

"You don't know the half. I'll tell you all about it while I'm soaking in the tub."

Getting a bath and her hair washed, though it felt wonderful, really took a lot out of her. By the time Nite had dressed her in a nightgown and settled back in bed, all she wanted was a pain pill and some sleep.

"Jay, I know you tired, but Taji just wants to come in and see you. You don't have to talk tonight if you don't want to. He just wants to see how you feel. Can I tell him it's OK to come in for a little bit?"

Jadyn lay her head back on the pillow. So much had happened it was hard for her to believe that it had been a little over two months since she'd last seen Taji.

It seemed like a lifetime.

"Yes, he can come in, but Nite, tell him I'm tired, too."

"OK, cuz."

When Taji walked into the room, he stood in the doorway and stared for a moment before bringing his knuckles to his mouth and biting down on them.

One look at Taji, just having him in her presence, sent all the hurt and pain away. All she wanted was for him to hold her. She didn't care about anything else.

"Baby," she said and tears filled her eyes.

Taji slowly walked over to her bed. He looked at her broken and bruised body and tears filled his eyes, as well.

"Can I just hold you, baby? I'll be gentle, I promise."

Jadyn nodded.

He looked around the room for a chair and spotted a big soft rocking chair in one corner of the room. He dragged it over to the side of the bed before he bent and gently lifted her into his arms.

Holding her as if she would break, he sat in the chair and lowered her into his lap.

"Are you OK, baby? Am I hurting you?"

"No, Taji, I'm fine."

Taji began to rock the chair back and forth as he buried his face in her hair and wept silent tears.

"Jay, I'm so sorry about this. It's my fault. If only my father hadn't called Rome . . ."

Jadyn lifted her head and stared into his eyes.

"Your father? Why?"

"It's a long story but when my grandfather came to town, you already know that Dad had lied about us being married. But he also told Grandfather that you were pregnant."

"I knew something crazy was going on. But why would a man like your father need to lie like that?"

"I guess because of how he had disappointed Grandfather those many years ago, it really wasn't about him marrying my mother. I mean, that was part of it. But he and Grandfather had problems long before that. Father flunked out of college for one thing. Wasn't interested in the family business for another. But he liked to spend Grandfather's money. So it was just a big mess. That's why Grandfather was so happy when Dad had me. And why he has always insisted that I make good grades and learn the family business."

"No wonder your father didn't like me. He knew my wanting to have a career in dancing would mean I wouldn't want children right away. So if we stayed together he couldn't give your grandfather what he wanted almost more than anything in this world— a great-grandchild. It's all beginning to make sense now."

"Yeah. He was always asking me when I was gon' find the 'right' girl, get married, and have children to carry on the family name. I told you, my paternal relatives are all very old school, very traditional. To them, family is everything. I told him that I didn't know, that you were about to go on the road for your dancing career and we would talk about it when you got back. If you ever came back."

Jadyn thought back to the barbecue and even before. How his father could barely stand to speak to her with a civil tongue. How he was always looking at her as if she had done something to him. When in reality the only thing she had done was try to live her own life the best way she could. She couldn't help it if what she wanted didn't connect with what he wanted for his son. Sometimes parents needed to learn to let go and stop trying to control their children's lives.

"This is so deep. It doesn't even seem real. It seems like something out of a movie or something." She really felt those words when she said them. Her life over the past few weeks was more like a bad dream than anything else.

"My grandfather wasn't happy with that. He said a woman should decide when children should come into the world, not the man. I guess he and my father had a big argument about that. And about all of the lies he had told. I guess my father was embarrassed by everything. Believe it or not, honor is still above all in Japan. And my father had not done the honorable thing in Grandfather's eyes. My father was desperate to find some way to please Grandfather and to regain some of that honor. So he wanted to make sure you stayed home. In his desperation he thought that the key to everything was making sure you didn't go away."

"So wait a minute, baby. You're sayin' your father called Rome? But how did he know how to contact him?"

"Jay, you didn't know this, but me and Rome went to high school together. Rome wasn't always the thug he is now. He had dreams and goals like the rest of us. He used to play basketball and football. He ran track."

"But what happened?"

"He couldn't make the grades to qualify to stay on the team. That made him bitter, because the man was good. And everybody knew it. You know the drill. After that he just didn't care anymore. Anyway, Dad kept in touch with him over the years, tried to help him, you know get his head on straight, but it didn't happen. Some people just give up on life and Rome is one of 'em."

"Wow. What did your dad do when you figured it out?"

"Nothing. No apology. He said he wouldn't apologize for doing what he thought was best for his only son."

"Oh baby, I'm so sorry. I'm so sorry this came between us. You're right, I should have trusted in you more. I should have talked things over with you before jumping to conclusions. Always cutting you off when you tried to explain. But you know, I was really ready to listen to what you had to say that evening I called you and that little heffa answered the phone."

"Don't upset yourself, baby. It's my fault, too. I shouldn't blow up all the time over nothin'. And that woman was nobody. Or I should say 'girl.'"

Jadyn moved slightly so that she could see his face. "Girl?" she asked.

"Yes, girl. A high school senior. She was interning around the office. There were a couple of checks that needed my signature right away, so they had her run them over to me. I had some papers that I needed to send back to the office with her, but I had left them upstairs. I couldn't locate them right away, and I guess you called while I was searching for them."

"Oh she really was a little fast tail heffa. Bold, too. Did you know she had a crush on you?"

"No baby, I had no idea. I barely knew she existed. But when I caught her with my phone in her hand, I wanted to light that ass up, and then fire her. But she apologized and said that she was sorry. And she looked so pitiful after I bawled her ass out, I felt sorry for her, so I didn't do either. I just had her little ass transferred to a different position in another part of the building."

Jadyn laid her head against his chest. "Well, I guess I can understand how she could develop a crush on you. I'm glad you took it easy on her."

"You are?" It was Taji's turn to sound surprised.

"Yes, we all make mistakes when we're growing up. Most kids should be given a second chance, don't you think?"

"Yes, I guess that's why I didn't fire her. I'm glad you agree with my decision though."

They both were silent for a moment, as Taji held and rocked her.

It was Taji who spoke first, breaking the comfortable silence.

"I have to say though, I think Dad must have felt bad about the things he'd done. Aunt Toki told me that he'd tried to contact those judges and get them to give you another chance, but they wouldn't do it."

Jadyn shifted around in his lap, trying to get more comfortable.

"Well, I just have to get well and dance even better at the next audition. And if I don't get that one, I just have to keep practicing and going to auditions. Until hopefully one day someone decides

I'm good enough and gives me a chance to prove that I'm worth the risk."

"Whatever you want to do, I'm gon' be with you all the way. It's me and you against the world, baby."

They both grew quiet again for a long moment.

Jadyn spoke first this time.

"You know what I've learned, baby?"

"What's that, love?"

"It's like I told Nite earlier. When you feel like you're going to die, all of that stuff just doesn't matter. All you think about is how you wish you could see the ones you love just one last time. How you just want the chance to tell them how dumb all that crap was that seemed so important that it kept you apart. It goes away. And all you want is the chance to hold them close and tell them how much you love them just one more time."

"Baby, the one who thinks they are losing the one they love, they feel all those things, too. Just like you just said."

"You do?"

"Yes, I do."

Jadyn rested her head against Taji's chest.

Her great-uncle rapped softly on the door before poking his head around the corner.

"You still woke, little girl?"

She raised herself up but didn't try to get off of Taji's lap.

"Yes Uncle BruhJay, I'm still awake. Is everything all right?"

Her great-uncle stepped into the room.

"Everything is just fine, love. But can you stand another visitor?"

"Well, that depends on who it is. I am gettin' kind of tired."

"I think you'll want to see this person. It's your daddy."

Jadyn stood to her feet with Taji's help and her heart began to pound again.

"My dad is here? In this house . . . right now?"

Her uncle laughed.

"He sure is. Standing right out yonder in the livin' room waitin' on word from you to come see his baby girl."

Jadyn smiled as wide as she could, and as carefully as she could, so as not to split her lip again.

"Uncle, could you please tell him to come on in?"

"You got it, love," he said as he closed the door.

Jadyn moved toward the bed.

"You want to get back in the bed? Let me help you, baby."

She allowed Taji to effortlessly lift her back into bed.

He fussed over her, fluffing her pillows and straightening the covers around her, making sure to tuck in the ends.

"So, are you ready to meet my father?" she asked him as he busied himself trying to make sure that she was comfortable.

"I was thinking about, you know, going downstairs so you two can have some time alone together."

"Unh-uhn. No way am I gonna let you miss those same warm loving feelings from my dad that your dad shared with me! Not a chance."

Taji smiled, but still managed to look as nervous as she had felt the day that she was going to meet his grandparents for the first time.

He leaned over her to give her a peck on the lips, but she kissed him more deeply.

"Relax, baby, it's going to be all right. I think you'll like my dad."

"Yes, but will he like me?"

"Don't worry, I got you," she said.

Taji stood at her side and reached for her hand, entwining his fingers in hers, before bringing it up to his lips and planting a kiss on it.

"I love you, Taji."

"I love you, too, Jadyn."

Epilogue

It had finally happened! Ms. Hollister had convinced Judith Jamison to give her an audition for the Alvin Ailey American Dance Theater. Auditions were open to students and the public, so there was a large crowd out front.

Jadyn was offstage, waiting for her turn, nerves making it impossible for her to sit still. She peeked around the curtain for about the tenth time and smiled as she looked out at her family.

Taji was there of course, along with his mother his father, and his aunt Toki. His grandfather and grandmother had even flown in for her. They sat next to Taji. Her mother was seated next to Taji's, and E and Devon were sitting next to them. She couldn't help laughing at them when she saw Devon punch E in the arm and E punch him back. Though they were teenagers now, they still picked at each other. She smiled as Taji admonished them. They elbowed each other the moment he took his eyes off them.

Nite and Justice were seated in the row just behind her mom and brothers. Nite's face was beaming with pride not only for her cousin, but for herself, as well. She kept trying to position her hand in such a way that everyone could see the diamond engagement ring on her finger. She kept trying to convince Jadyn and Taji that a double wedding would be oh, so marvelous!

Her father and his wife, Aubrae, sat directly behind Taji. Their relationship wasn't going smooth as silk, like she had fantasized it would. The residual trauma she had suffered with Ian was making it difficult to relax and trust her dad. But his patient, loving kindness, and rock-steady presence in her life was going a long way in helping her to heal. Jadyn had to admit, she was a little disappointed to discover that her dad didn't have any other children besides her. She wouldn't have minded having a sister.

Rushing down the aisle, looking so handsome dressed in suit and tie, were her Uncle BruhJay and Flash. They had told her they didn't know if they would make it. She was so glad they did. They paused and looked around, unsure of which way to go. Nite stood up and waved them over.

Ms. Rashad and Ms. Hollister sat side-by-side on the front row, chatting with Judith Jamison herself. KeMari Reynolds and her date sat in the second row to the left of the stage.

Her life wasn't perfect, but then whose was, really? And she was working hard on making hers better.

She had continued her counseling sessions with KeMari. Taji had even started coming with her, so that he could understand the trauma she had endured as a child and young teenager. KeMari helped find a family counselor for her, her mother, and her brothers. Things were still rocky, but at least they were talking about the hard things, and working on forgiving one another. Learning how to love each other as a family should.

Jadyn was even working on a letter telling Ian how she felt about the things he had done to her. She didn't know whether or not she would ever give Ian the letter, but that wasn't what was important. The important thing was, that it was the first step toward releasing the past so that she could enter her future. The first step toward true forgiveness.

As the music cued up for her audition, Jadyn took deep breaths to calm her nerves.

And as she leapt onto the stage, she did something she'd never done before.

She gave herself permission to be happy. Permission to be free.